The Star Rover

& Other Stories

Other Jack London titles published by Leonaur

The Star Rover
& Other Stories

Jack London

The Collected Science Fiction & Fantasy
of Jack London: Volume 3

LEONAUR

The Star Rover & Other Stories by Jack London

FIRST EDITION

Published by Leonaur Ltd

This selection is an original publication of Leonaur Ltd
copyright © 2005 Leonaur Ltd

ISBN (10 digit): 1-84677-013-0 (hardcover)
ISBN (13 digit): 978-1-84677-013-5 (hardcover)

ISBN (10 digit): 1-84677-006-8 (softcover)
ISBN (13 digit): 978-1-84677-006-7 (softcover)

http://www.leonaur.com

Publisher's Notes

In the interests of authenticity, the spellings, grammar and place names
used by the author have been retained.

The views expressed in this book are not necessarily
those of the publisher.

Contents

The Star Rover

Chapter 1

All my life I have had an awareness of other times and places. I have been aware of other persons in me. Oh, and trust me, so have you, my reader that is to be. Read back into your childhood, and this sense of awareness I speak of will be remembered as an experience of your childhood. You were then not fixed, not crystallized. You were plastic, a soul in flux, a consciousness and an identity in the process of forming—ay, of forming and forgetting.

You have forgotten much, my reader, and yet, as you read these lines, you remember dimly the hazy vistas of other times and places into which your child eyes peered. They seem dreams to you today. Yet, if they were dreams, dreamed then, whence the substance of them? Our dreams are grotesquely compounded of the things we know. The stuff of our sheerest dreams is the stuff of our experiences. As a child, a wee child, you dreamed you fell great heights; you dreamed you flew through the air as things of the air fly; you were vexed by crawling spiders and many-legged creatures of the slime; you heard other voices, saw other faces nightmarishly familiar, and gazed upon sunrises and sunsets other than you know now, looking back, you ever looked upon.

Very well. These child glimpses are of other-worldness, of other-lifeness, of things that you had never seen in this particular world of your particular life. Then whence? Other lives? Other worlds? Perhaps, when you have read all that I shall write, you will have received answers to the perplexities I have propounded to you, and that you yourself, ere you came to read me, propounded to yourself.

Wordsworth knew. He was neither seer nor prophet, but just ordinary man like you or any man. What he knew you know, any man knows. But he most aptly stated it in his passage that begins "*Not in utter nakedness, not in entire forgetfulness.*"

Ah, truly, shades of the prison house close about us, the new-born things, and all too soon do we forget. And yet, when we were newborn we did remember other times and places. We, helpless infants in arms or creeping quadruped-like on the floor, dreamed our dreams of air flight. Yes; and we endured the torment and torture of nightmare fears of dim and monstrous things. We newborn infants, without experience, were born with fear, with memory of fear; and memory is experience.

As for myself, at the beginnings of my vocabulary, at so tender a period that I still made hunger noises and sleep noises yet even then did I know that I had been a star rover. Yes I, whose lips had never lisped the word "king," remembered that I had once been the son of a king. More—I remembered that once I had been a slave and a son of a slave, and worn an iron collar around my neck.

Still more. When I was three, and four, and five years of age, I was not yet I. I was a mere becoming, a flux of spirit not yet cooled solid in the mold of my particular flesh and time and place. In that period all that I had ever been in ten thousand lives before strove in me, and troubled the flux of me, in the effort to incorporate itself in me and become me.

Silly, isn't it? But remember, my reader, whom I hope to have travel far with me through time and space—remember, please, my reader, that I have thought much on these matters that through bloody nights and sweats of dark that lasted years long I have been alone with my many selves to consult and contemplate my many selves. I have gone through the hells of all existences to bring you news which you will share with me in a casual, comfortable hour over my printed page.

So to return I say, during the ages of three and four and five, I was not yet I. I was merely becoming as I took form in the mold of my body, and all the mighty, indestructible past wrought in the mixture of me to determine what the form of that becoming would be. It was not my voice that cried out in the night in fear of things known, which I, forsooth, did not and could not know. The same with my childish angers, my loves and my laughters. Other voices screamed through my voice, the voices of men and women aforetime, of all shadowy hosts of progenitors. And the snarl of my anger was blended with the snarls of beasts more ancient than the mountains, and the vocal madness of my child hysteria, with all the red of its wrath, was chorded with the insensate, stupid cries of beasts pre-Adamic and pregeologic in time.

And there the secret is out. The red wrath! It has undone me in this, my present life. Because of it, a few short weeks hence, I shall be led from this cell to a high place with unstable flooring, graced above by a full-stretched rope; and there they will hang me by the neck until I am dead. The red wrath always has undone me in all my lives, for the red wrath is my disastrous catastrophic heritage from the time of the slimy things ere the world was prime.

It is time that I introduce myself. I am neither fool nor lunatic. I want you to know this, in order that you will believe the things I shall tell you. I am Darrell Standing. Some few of you who read this will know me immediately. But to the majority, who are bound to be strangers, let me exposit myself. Eight years ago I was Professor of Agronomics in the College of Agriculture of the University of California. Eight years ago the sleepy little university town of Berkeley was shocked by the murder of Professor Haskell in one of the laboratories of the Mining Building. Darrell Standing was the murderer.

I am Darrell Standing. I was caught red-handed. Now the right and the wrong of this affair with Professor Haskell I shall not discuss. It was purely a private matter. The point is that in a surge of anger, obsessed by that catastrophic red wrath that has cursed me down the ages, I killed my fellow professor. The court records show that I did; and for once I agree with the court records.

No, I am not to be hanged for his murder. I received a life sentence for my punishment. I was thirty-six years of age at the time. I am now forty-four years old. I have spent the eight intervening years in the California State Prison of San Quentin. Five of these years I spent in the dark. Solitary confinement, they call it. Men who endure it call it living death. But through these five years of death-in-life I managed to attain freedom such as few men have ever known. Closest confined of prisoners, not only did I range the world, but I ranged time. They who immured me for petty years gave to me, all unwittingly, the largess of the centuries. Truly, thanks to Ed Morrell, I have had five years of star roving. But Ed Morrell is another story. I shall tell you about him a little later. I have so much to tell I scarce know how to begin.

Well, a beginning. I was born on a quarter section in Minnesota. My mother was the daughter of an immigrant Swede. Her name was Hilda Tonnesson. My father was Chauncey Standing, of old American stock. He traced back to Alfred Standing, an indentured servant—or slave, if you please—who was transported from England to the Virginia plantations in the days that were even old when the youthful Washington went a-surveying in the Pennsylvania wilderness.

A son of Alfred Standing fought in the War of the Revolution; a grandson, in the War of 1812. There have been no wars since in which the Standings have not been represented. I, the last of the Standings, dying soon without issue, fought as a common soldier in the Philippines in our latest war, and to do so I resigned, in the full early ripeness of career, my professorship in the University of Nebraska. Good heavens, when I so resigned I was headed for the Deanship of the College of Agriculture in that university—I, the star rover, the red-blooded adventurer, the vagabondish Cain of the centuries, the militant priest of remotest times, the moon-dreaming poet of ages forgotten and today unrecorded in man's history of man!

And here I am, my hands dyed red, in Murderers' Row, in the State Prison of Folsom, awaiting the day decreed by the machinery of state when the servants of the state will lead me away into what they fondly believe is the dark—the dark they fear; the dark that gives them fearsome and superstitious fancies; the dark that drives them, driveling and yammering, to the alters of their fear-created, anthropomorphic gods.

No, I shall never be Dean of any college of agriculture. And yet I knew agriculture. It was my profession. I was born to it, reared to it, trained to it; and I was a master of it. It was my genius. I can pick the high-percentage butterfat cow with my eye and let the Babcock tester prove the wisdom of my eye. I can look not at land, but at landscape, and pronounce the virtues and the shortcomings of the soil. Litmus paper is not necessary when I determine a soil to be acid or alkali. I repeat, farm husbandry in its highest scientific terms was my genius, and is my genius. And yet the state, which includes all the citizens of the state, believes that it can blot out this wisdom of mine in the final dark by means of a rope about my neck and the abruptive jerk of gravitation—this wisdom of mine that was incubated through the millenniums, and that was well hatched ere the farmed fields of Troy were ever pastured by the flocks of nomad shepherds!

Corn? Who else knows corn? There is my demonstration at Wistar, whereby I increased the annual corn yield of every county in Iowa by half a million of dollars. This is history. Many a farmer, riding in his motorcar today, knows who made possible that motorcar. Many a sweet-bosomed girl and bright-browed boy, poring over high-school textbooks, little dreams that I made that higher education possible by my corn demonstration at Wistar.

And farm management! I know the waste of superfluous motion without studying a moving-picture record of it, whether it be farm or farmhand, the layout of buildings or the layout of the farmhand's labor. There is my handbook and tables on the subject. Beyond the shadow of any doubt, at this present moment a hundred thousand farmers are knotting their brows over its spread pages ere they tap out their final pipe and go to bed. And yet, so far was I beyond my tables, that all I needed was a mere look at a man to know his predispositions, his co-ordinations, and the index fraction of his motion wastage.

And here I must close this first chapter of my narrative. It is nine o'clock, and in Murderers' Row that means lights out. Even now I hear the soft tread of the gum-shoed guard as he comes to censure me for my coal-oil lamp still burning. As if the mere living could censure the doomed to die!

Chapter 2

I am Darrell Standing. They are going to take me out and hang me pretty soon. In the meantime I say my say, and write in these pages of the other times and places.

After my sentence, I came to spend the rest of my "natural life" in the prison of San Quentin. I proved incorrigible. An incorrigible is a terrible human being—at least such is the connotation of "incorrigible" in prison psychology. I became an incorrigible because I abhorred waste motion. The prison, like all prisons, was an affront and a scandal of waste motion. They put me in the jute mill. The criminality of wastefulness irritated me. Why should it not? Elimination of waste motion was my specialty. Before the invention of steam or steam-driven looms, three thousand years before, I had rotted in prison in old Babylon; and, trust me, I speak the truth when I say that in that ancient day we prisoners wove more efficiently on handlooms than did the prisoners in the steam-powered loom rooms of San Quentin.

The crime of waste was abhorrent. I rebelled. I tried to show the guards a score or so of more efficient ways. I was reported. I was given the dungeon and the starvation of light and food. I emerged and tried to work in the chaos of inefficiency of the loom rooms. I rebelled. I was given the dungeon plus the strait jacket. I was spread-eagled, and thumbed-up, and privily beaten by the stupid guards whose totality of intelligence was only just sufficient to show them that I was different from them and not so stupid.

Two years of this witless persecution I endured. It is terrible for a man to be tied down and gnawed by rats. The stupid brutes of guards were rats, and they gnawed the intelligence of me, gnawed all the fines nerves of the quick of me and of the consciousness of me. And I, who in my past have been a most valiant fighter, in this present life was no fighter at all. I was a farmer, an agriculturist, a desk-tied professor, a laboratory slave, interested only in the soil and the increase of the productiveness of the soil.

I fought in the Philippines because it was the tradition of the Standings to fight. I had no aptitude for fighting. It was all too ridiculous, the introducing of disruptive foreign substances into the bodies of little black menfolk. It was laughable to behold Science prostituting all the might of its achievement and the wit of its inventors to the violent introducing of foreign substances into the bodies of black folk.

As I say, in obedience to the tradition of the Standings I went to war and found that I had no aptitude for war. So did my officers find me out, because they made me a quartermaster's clerk, and as a clerk at a desk I fought through the Spanish-American War.

So it was not because I was a fighter but because I was a thinker that I was enraged by the motion wastage of the loom rooms and was persecuted by the guards into becoming an "incorrigible." One's brain worked and I was punished for its working. As I told Warden Atherton, when my incorrigibility had become so notorious that he had me in on the carpet in his private office to plead with me; as I told him then:

"It is so absurd, my dear Warden, to think that your rat throttlers of guards can shake out of my brain the things that are clear and definite in my brain. The whole organization of this prison is stupid. You are a politician. You can weave the political pull of San Francisco saloon men and ward heelers into a position of graft such as this one you occupy; but you can't weave jute. Your loom rooms are fifty years behind the times...."

But why continue the tirade? For tirade it was. I showed him what a fool he was, and as a result he decided that I was a hopeless incorrigible.

Give a dog a bad name—you know the saw. Very well. Warden Atherton gave the final sanction to the badness of my name. I was fair game. More than one convict's dereliction was shunted off on me, and was paid for by me in the dungeon on bread and water, or in being triced up by the thumbs on my tiptoes for long hours, each hour of which was longer than the memory of any life I have ever lived.

Intelligent men are cruel. Stupid men are monstrously cruel. The guards and the men over me, from the warden down, were stupid monsters. Listen, and you shall learn what they did to me. There was a poet in the prison, a convict, a weak-chinned, broad-browed degenerate poet. He was a forger. He was a coward. He was a snitcher. He was a stool—strange words for a professor of agronomics to use in writing, but a professor of agronomics may well learn strange words when pent in prison for the term of his natural life.

This poet-forger's name was Cecil Winwood. He had had prior convictions, and yet, because he was a sniveling cur of a yellow dog, his last sentence had been only for seven years. Good credits would materially reduce this time. My time was life. Yet this miserable degenerate, in order to gain several short years of liberty for himself, succeeded in adding a fair portion of eternity to my own lifetime term.

I shall tell what happened the other way around, for it was only after a weary period that I learned. This Cecil Winwood, in order to curry favor with the Captain of the Yard, and thence the warden, the Prison Directors, the Board of Pardons, and the Governor of California, framed up a prison break. Now note three things: (a) Cecil Winwood was so detested by his fellow convicts that they would not have permitted him to bet an ounce of Bull Durham on a bedbug race—and bedbug racing was a great sport with the convicts; (b) I was the dog that had been given a bad name; (c) for his frame-up, Cecil Winwood needed the dogs with bad names, the lifetimers, the desperate ones, the incorrigibles.

But the lifers detested Cecil Winwood and, when he approached them with his plan of a wholesale prison break, they laughed at him and turned him away with curses for the stool that he was. But he fooled them in the end, forty of the bitterestwise ones in the pen. He approached them again and again. He told of his power in the prison by virtue of his being trusty in the warden's office, and because of the fact that he had the run of the dispensary.

"Show me," said Long Bill Hodge, a mountaineer doing life for train robbery, and whose whole soul for years had been bent on escaping in order to kill the companion in robbery who had turned state's evidence on him.

Cecil Winwood accepted the test. He claimed that he could dope the guards the night of the break.

"Talk is cheap," said Long Bill Hodge. "What we want is the goods. Dope one of the guards tonight. There's Barnum. He's no good. He beat up that crazy Chink yesterday in Bughouse Alley..... when he was off duty, too. He's on the night watch. Dope him tonight an' make him lose his job. Show me, and we'll talk business with you."

All this Long Bill told me in the dungeons afterward. Cecil Winwood demurred against the immediacy of the demonstration. He claimed that he must have time in which to steal the dope from the dispensary. They gave him the time, and a week later he announced that he was ready. Forty hard-bitten lifers waited for the guard Barnum to go to sleep on his shift. And Barnum did. He was found asleep, and he was discharged for sleeping on duty.

Of course, that convinced the lifers. But there was the Captain of the Yard to convince. To him, daily, Cecil Winwood was reporting the progress of the break—all fancied and fabricated in his own imagination. The Captain of the Yard demanded to be shown. Winwood showed him, and the full details of the showing I did not learn until a year afterward, so slowly do the secrets of prison intrigue leak out.

Winwood said that the forty men in the break, in whose confidence he was, had already such power in the prison that they were about to begin smuggling in automatic pistols by means of the guards they had bought up.

"Show me," the Captain of the Yard must have demanded.

And the forger-poet showed him. In the bakery, night work was a regular thing. One of the convicts, a baker, was on the first nightshift. He was a stool of the Captain of the Yard, and Winwood knew it.

"Tonight," he told the captain, "Summerface will bring in a dozen '44 automatics. On his next time off he'll bring in the ammunition. But tonight he'll turn the automatics over to me in the bakery. You've got a good stool there. He'll make you his report tomorrow."

Now Summerface was a strapping figure of a bucolic guard who hailed from Humboldt County. He was a simple-minded, good-natured dolt and not above earning an honest dollar by smuggling in tobacco for the convicts. On that night, returning from a trip to San Francisco, he brought in with him fifteen pounds of prime cigarette tobacco. He had done this before, and delivered the stuff to Cecil Winwood. So, on that particular night, he, all unwitting, turned the stuff over to Winwood in the bakery. It was a big, solid, paper-wrapped bundle of innocent tobacco. The stool baker, from concealment, saw the package delivered to Winwood and so reported to the Captain of the Yard next morning.

But in the meantime the poet-forger's too-lively imagination ran away with him. He was guilty of a slip that gave me five years of solitary confinement and that placed me in this condemned cell in which I now write. And all the time I knew nothing about it. I did not even know of the break he had inveigled the forty lifers into planning. I knew nothing, absolutely nothing. And the rest knew little. The lifers did not know he was giving them the cross. The Captain of the Yard did not know that the cross was being worked on him. Summerface was the most innocent of all. At the worst, his conscience could have accused him only of smuggling in some harmless tobacco.

And now to the stupid, silly, melodramatic slip of Cecil Winwood. Next morning, when he encountered the Captain of the Yard, he was triumphant. His imagination took the bit in its teeth.

"Well, the stuff came in all right as you said," the Captain of the Yard remarked.

"And enough of it to blow half the prison sky high," Winwood corroborated.

"Enough of what?" The captain demanded.

"Dynamite and detonators," the fool rattled on. "Thirty-five pounds of it. Your stool saw Summerface pass it over to me."

And right there the Captain of the Yard must have nearly died. I can actually sympathize with him—thirty-five pounds of dynamite loose in the prison.

They say that Captain Jamie—that was his nickname—sat down and held his head in his hands.

"Where is it now?" He cried. "I want it. Take me to it at once."

And right there Cecil Winwood saw his mistake.

"I planted it," he lied—for he was compelled to lie because, being merely tobacco in small packages, it was long since distributed among the convicts along the customary channels.

"Very well," said Captain Jamie, getting himself in hand. "Lead me to it at once."

But there was no plant of high explosives to lead him to. The thing did not exist, had never existed save in the imagination of the wretched Winwood.

In a large prison like San Quentin there are always hiding places for things. And as Cecil Winwood led Captain Jamie he must have done some rapid thinking.

As Captain Jamie testified before the Board of Directors, and as Winwood also testified, on the way to the hiding place Winwood said that he and I had planted the powder together.

And I, just released from five days in the dungeons and eighty hours in the jacket; I, whom even the stupid guards could see was too weak to work in the loom room; I, who had been given the day off to recuperate — from too terrible punishment— I was named as the one who had helped hide the nonexistent thirty-five pounds of high explosive!

Winwood led Captain Jamie to the alleged hiding place. Of course they found no dynamite in it

"My God!" Winwood lied. "Standing has given me the cross. He's lifted the plant and stowed it somewhere else."

The Captain of the Yard said more emphatic things than "My God!" Also, on the spur of the moment but cold-bloodedly, he took Winwood into his own private office, locked the doors, and beat him up frightfully—all of which came out before the Board of Directors. But that was afterward. In the meantime, even while he took his beating, Winwood swore by the truth of what he had told.

What was Captain Jamie to do? He was convinced that thirty-five pounds of dynamite were loose in the prison and that forty desperate lifers were ready for a break. Oh, he had Summerface in on the carpet and, although Summerface insisted the package contained tobacco, Winwood swore it was dynamite and was believed.

At this stage I enter . . . or, rather, I depart; for they took me away out of the sunshine and the light of day to the dungeons, and in the dungeons and in the solitary cells, out of the sunshine and the light of day, I rotted for five years.

I was puzzled. I had only just been released from the dungeon, and was lying pain-wracked in my customary cell, when they took me back to the dungeon.

"Now," said Winwood to Captain Jamie, "though we don't know where it is, the dynamite is safe. Standing is the only man who does know, and he can't pass the word out from the dungeon. The men are ready to make the break. We can catch them red-handed. It is up to me to set the time. I'll tell them two o'clock to-night, and tell them that, with the guards doped, I'll unlock their cells and give them their automatics. If at two o'clock tonight you don't catch the forty I shall name with their clothes on and wide awake, then, Captain, you can give me solitary for the rest of my sentence. And with Standing and the forty tight in the dungeons, we'll have all the time in the world to locate the dynamite."

"If we have to tear the prison down stone by stone," Captain Jamie added valiantly.

That was six years ago. In all the intervening time they have never found that nonexistent explosive, and they have turned the prison upside down a thousand times in searching for it. Nevertheless, to his last day in office Warden Atherton believed in the existence of that dynamite. Captain Jamie, who is still Captain of the Yard, believes to this day that the dynamite is somewhere in the prison. Only yesterday, he came all the way up from San Quentin to Folsom to make one more effort to get me to reveal the hiding place. I know he will never breathe easy until they swing me off.

Chapter 3

All that day I lay in the dungeon cudgeling my brains for the reason of this new and inexplicable punishment. All I could conclude was that some stool had lied an infraction of the rules on me in order to curry favor with the guards.

Meanwhile Captain Jamie fretted his head off and prepared for the night, while Winwood passed the word along to the forty lifers to be ready for the break. And two hours after midnight every guard in the prison was under orders. This included the dayshift, which should have been asleep. When two o'clock came, they rushed the cells occupied by the forty. The rush was simultaneous. The cells were opened at the same moment and without exception the men named by Winwood were found out of their bunks, fully dressed, and crouching just inside their doors. Of course, this was verification absolute of all the fabric of lies that the poet-forger had spun for Captain Jamie. The forty lifers were caught in red-handed readiness for the break. What if they did unite afterward, in averring that the break had been planned by Winwood? The Prison Board of Directors believed, to a man, that the forty lied in an effort to save themselves. The Board of Pardons likewise believed, for, ere three months were up, Cecil Winwood, forger and poet, most despicable of men, was pardoned out.

Oh well, the stir, or the pen, as they call it in convict argot, is a training school for philosophy. No inmate can survive years of it without having had burst for him his fondest illusions and fairest metaphysical bubbles. Truth lives, we are taught; murder will out. Well, this is a demonstration that murder does not always come out. The Captain of the Yard, the late Warden Atherton, the Prison Board of Directors to a man—all believe, right now, in the existence of that dynamite that never existed save in the slippery-geared and all too accelerated brain of the degenerate forger and poet, Cecil Winwood. And Cecil Winwood still lives, while I, of all men concerned the utterest, absolutist, innocentest, go to the scaffold in a few short weeks.

And now I must tell how entered the forty lifers upon my dungeon stillness. I was asleep when the outer door to the corridor of dungeons clanged open and aroused me. "Some poor devil," was my thought; and my next thought was that he was surely getting his, as I listened to the scuffling of feet, the dull impact of blows on flesh, the sudden cries of pain, the filth of curses, and the sounds of dragging bodies. For, you see, every man was manhandled all the length of the way.

Dungeon door after dungeon door clanged open, and body after body was thrust in, flung in, or dragged in. And continually more groups of guards arrived with more beaten convicts who still were being beaten, and more dungeon doors were opened to receive the bleeding frames of men who were guilty of yearning after freedom.

Yes, as I look back upon it, a man must be greatly a philosopher to survive the continual impact of such brutish experiences through the years and years. I am such a philosopher. I have endured eight years of their torment, and now, in the end, failing to get rid of me in all other ways, they have invoked the machinery of state to put a rope around my neck and shut off my breath by the weight of my body. Oh, I know how the experts give expert judgment that the fall through the trap breaks the victim's neck. And the victims, like Shakespeare's traveler, never return to testify to the contrary. But we who have lived in the stir know of the cases that are hushed in the prison crypts, where the victims' necks are not broken.

It is a funny thing, this hanging of a man. I have never seen a hanging, but I have been told by eyewitnesses the details of a dozen hangings so that I know what will happen to me. Standing on the trap, leg-manacled and arm-manacled, the knot against the neck, the black cap drawn, they will drop me down until the momentum of my descending weight is fetched up abruptly short by the tautening of the rope. Then the doctors will group around me, and one will relieve another in successive turns in standing on a stool, his arms passed around me to keep me from swinging like a pendulum, his ear pressed close to my chest while he counts my fading heartbeats. Sometimes twenty minutes elapses after the trap is sprung ere the heart stops beating. Oh, trust me, they make most scientifically sure that a man is dead once they get him on a rope.

I will wander aside from my narrative to ask a question or two of society. I have a right so to wander and so to question, for in a little while they are going to take me out and do this thing to me. If the neck of the victim be broken by the alleged shrewd arrangement of knot and noose, and by the alleged shrewd calculation of the weight of the victim and the length of slack, then why do they manacle the arms of the victim? Society, as a whole, is unable to answer this question. But I know why; so does any amateur who ever engaged in a lynching bee and saw the victim throw up his hands, clutch the rope, and ease the throttle of the noose about his neck so that he might breathe.

Another question I will ask of the smug, cotton-woofed member of society, whose soul has never strayed to the red hells. Why do they put the black cap over the head and face of the victim ere they drop him through the trap? Please remember that in a short while they will put that black cap over my head. So I have a right to ask. Do they, your hangdogs, oh smug citizen, do these your hangdogs fear to gaze upon the facial horror of the horror they perpetrate for you at your behest?

Please remember that I am not asking this question in the twelve-hundredth year after Christ, nor in the time of Christ, nor in the twelve-hundredth year before Christ. I, who am to be hanged this year, the nineteen-hundred-and-thirteenth after Christ' ask these questions of you who are assumably Christ's followers, of you whose hangdogs are going to take me out and hide my face under a black cloth because they dare not look upon the horror they do to me while I yet live.

And now back to the situation in the dungeons. When the last guard departed and the outer door clanged shut, all the forty beaten disappointed men began to talk and ask questions. But almost immediately, roaring like a bull in order to be heard, Skysail Jack, a giant sailor of a lifer, ordered silence while a census could be taken. The dungeons were full, and dungeon by dungeon, in order of dungeons, shouted out its quota to the roll call. Thus, every dungeon was accounted for as occupied by trusted convicts, so that there was no opportunity for a stool to be hidden away and listening.

Of me, only, were the convicts dubious, for I was the one man who had not been in the plot. They put me through a searching examination. I could but tell them how I had just emerged from dungeon and jacket in the morning, and without rhyme or reason, so far as I could discover, had been put back in the dungeon after being out only several hours. My record as an incorrigible was in my favor, and soon they began to talk.

As I lay there and listened, for the first time I learned of the break that had been a-hatching. "Who had squealed?" was their one quest, and throughout the night the quest was pursued. The quest for Cecil Winwood was vain, and the suspicion against him was general.

"There's only one thing, lads," Skysail Jack finally said. "It'll soon be morning, and then they'll take us out and give us bloody hell. We were caught dead to rights with our clothes on. Winwood crossed us and squealed. They're going to get us out one by one and mess us up. There's forty of us. Any lyin's bound to be found out. So each lad, when they sweat him, just tells the truth, the whole truth, so help him God."

And there, in that dark hole of man's inhumanity, from dungeon cell to dungeon cell, their mouths against the gratings, the twoscore lifers solemnly pledged themselves before God to tell the truth.

Little good did their truth-telling do them. At nine o'clock the guards, paid bravos of the smug citizens who constitute the state, full of meat and sleep, were upon us. Not only had we had no breakfast, but we had had no water. And beaten men are prone to feverishness. I wonder, my reader, if you can glimpse or guess the faintest connotation of a man beaten—"beat up," we prisoners call it. But no, I shall not tell you. Let it suffice to know that these beaten feverish men lay seven hours without water.

At nine the guards arrived. There were not many of them. There was no need for many, because they unlocked only one dungeon at a time. They were equipped with pickhandles—a handy tool for the "disciplining" of a helpless man. One dungeon at a time, and dungeon by dungeon, they messed and pulped the lifers. They were impartial. I received the same pulping as the rest. And this was merely the beginning, the preliminary to the examination each man was to undergo alone in the presence of the paid brutes of the state. It was the forecast to each man of what each man might expect in inquisition hall.

I have been through most of the red hells of prison life, but worst of all, far worse than what they intend to do with me in a short while, was the particular hell of the dungeons in the days that followed.

Long Bill Hodge, the hard-bitten mountaineer, was the first man interrogated. He came back two hours later—or, rather, they conveyed him back, and threw him on the stone of his dungeon floor. Then they took away Luigi Polazzo, a San Francisco hoodlum, the first native generation of Italian parentage, who jeered and sneered at them and challenged them to wreak their worst upon him.

It was some time before Long Bill Hodge mastered his pain sufficiently to be coherent.

"What about this dynamite?" He demanded. "Who knows anything about dynamite?"

And of course nobody knew, although it had been the burden of the interrogation put to him.

Luigi Polazzo came back in a little less than two hours, and he came back a wreck that babbled in delirium and could give no answer to the questions showered upon him along the echoing corridor of dungeons by the men who were yet to get what he had got and who desired greatly to know what things had been done to him and what interrogations had been put to him.

Twice again in the next forty-eight hours Luigi was taken out and interrogated. After that, a gibbering imbecile, he went to live in Bughouse Alley. He has a strong constitution. His shoulders are broad, his nostrils wide, his chest is deep, his blood is pure; he will continue to gibber in Bughouse Alley long after I have swung off and escaped the torment of the penitentiaries of California.

Man after man was taken away, one at a time, and the wrecks of men were brought back, one by one, to rave and howl in the darkness. And as I lay there and listened to the moaning and the groaning and all the idle chattering of pain-addled wits, somehow, vaguely reminiscent, it seemed to me that somewhere, sometime, I had sat in a high place, callous and proud, and listened to a similar chorus of moaning and groaning. Afterward as you shall learn, I identified this reminiscence and knew that the moaning and the groaning was of the sweep-slaves manacled to their benches, which I heard from above, on the poop, a soldier-passenger on a galley of old Rome. That was when I sailed for Alexandria a captain of men, on my way to Jerusalem . . . but that is a story I shall tell you later. In the meanwhile . . .

Chapter 4

In the meanwhile obtained the horror of the dungeons, after the discovery of the plot to break prison. And never during those eternal hours of waiting was it absent from my consciousness that I should follow these other convicts out, endure the hell of inquisition they endured, and be brought back a wreck and flung on the stone floor of my stone-walled, iron-doored dungeon.

They came for me. Ungraciously and ungently, with blow and curse, they hailed me forth, and I faced Captain Jamie and Warden Atherton, themselves arrayed with the strength of half a dozen state-bought, tax-paid brutes of guards who lingered in the room to do any bidding. But they were not needed.

"Sit down," said Warden Atherton, indicating a stout armchair.

I, beaten and sore, without water for a night long and a day long, faint with hunger, weak from a beating that had been added to five days in the dungeon and eighty hours in the jacket, oppressed by the calamity of human fate, apprehensive of what was to happen to me from what I had seen happen to the others— I, a wavering waif of a human man and an erstwhile professor of agronomy in a quiet college town, I hesitated to accept the invitation to sit down.

Warden Atherton was a large man and a very powerful man. His hands flashed out to a grip on my shoulders. I was a straw in his strength. He lifted me clear of the floor and crashed me down in the chair.

"Now," he said, while I gasped and swallowed my pain, "tell me all about it, Standing. Spit it out—all of it, if you know what's healthy for you."

"I don't know anything about what has happened ...," I began.

That was as far as I got. With a growl and a leap he was upon me. Again he lifted me in the air and crashed me down into the chair.

"No nonsense, Standing," he warned. "Make a clean breast of it. Where is the dynamite?"

"I don't know anything of any dynamite—" I protested.

Once again I was lifted and smashed back into the chair.

I have endured tortures of various sorts, but when I reflect upon them in the quietness of these my last days, I am confident that no other torture was quite the equal of that chair torture. By my body that stout chair was battered out of any semblance of a chair. Another chair was brought, and in time that chair was demolished. But more chairs were brought, and the eternal questioning about the dynamite went on.

When Warden Atherton grew tired, Captain Jamie relieved him; and then the guard Monohan took Captain Jamie's place in smashing me down into the chair. And always it was dynamite, dynamite, "where is the dynamite?" And there was no dynamite. Why, toward the last I would have given a large portion of my immortal soul for a few pounds of dynamite to which I could confess.

I do not know how many chairs were broken by my body. I fainted times without number, and toward the last the whole thing became nightmarish. I was half-carried, half-shoved and dragged back to the dark. There, when I became conscious, I found a stool in my dungeon. He was a pallid-faced little dope fiend of a short-timer who would do anything to obtain the drug. As soon as I recognized him I crawled to the grating and shouted out along the corridor:

"There is a stool in with me, fellows! He's Ignatius Irvine! Watch out what you say!"

The outburst of imprecations that went up would have shaken the fortitude of a braver man than Ignatius Irvine. He was pitiful in his terror, while all about him, roaring like beasts, the pain-wracked lifers told him what awful things they would do to him in the years that were to come.

Had there been secrets, the presence of a stool in the dungeons would have kept the men quiet. As it was, having all sworn to tell the truth, they talked openly before Ignatius Irvine. The one great puzzle was the dynamite, of which they were as much in the dark as was I. They appealed to me. If I knew anything about the dynamite they begged me to confess it and save them all from further misery. And I could tell them only the truth: that I knew of no dynamite.

One thing the stool told me, before the guards removed him, showed how serious was this matter of the dynamite. Of course, I passed the word along, which was that not a wheel had turned in the prison all day. The thousands of convict workers had remained locked in their cells, and the outlook was that not one of the various prison-factories would be operated again until after the discovery of some dynamite that somebody had hidden somewhere in the prison.

And ever the examination went on. Ever, one at a time, convicts were dragged away and dragged or carried back again. They reported that Warden Atherton and Captain Jamie, exhausted by their efforts, relieved each other every two hours. While one slept, the other examined. And they slept in their clothes in the very room in which strong man after strong man was being broken.

And hour by hour in the dark dungeons, our madness of torment grew. Oh, trust me as one who knows, hanging is an easy thing compared with the way live men may be hurt in all the life of them and still live. I too suffered equally with them from pain and thirst; but added to my suffering was the fact that I remained conscious to the sufferings of the others. I had been an incorrigible for two years, and my nerves and brain were hardened to suffering. It is a frightful thing to see a strong man broken. About me, at the one time, were forty strong men being broken. Ever the cry for water went up, and the place became lunatic with the crying, sobbing, babbling, and raving of men in delirium.

Don't you see: our truth, the very truth we told, was our damnation. When forty men told the same things with such unanimity, Warden Atherton and Captain Jamie could only conclude that the testimony was a memorized lie which each of the forty rattled off parrot-like.

From the standpoint of the authorities, their situation was as desperate as ours. As I learned afterward, the Board of Prison Directors had been summoned by telegraph, and two companies of state militia were being rushed to the prison

It was winter weather, and the frost is sometimes shrewd even in a California winter. We had no blankets in the dungeons. Please know that it is very cold to stretch bruised human flesh on frosty stone. In the end they did give us water. Jeering and cursing us, the guards ran in the fire hose and played the fierce streams on us, dungeon by dungeon, hour after hour, until our bruised flesh was battered all anew by the violence with which the water smote us, until we stood knee-deep in the water which we had raved for and for which now we raved to cease.

I shall skip the rest of what happened in the dungeons. In passing I shall merely state that no one of those forty lifers was ever the same again. Luigi Polazzo never recovered his reason. Long Bill Hodge slowly lost his sanity, so that a year later he too went to live in Bughouse Alley. Oh, and others followed Hodge and Polazzo; and others, whose physical stamina had been impaired, fell victims to prison tuberculosis. Fully twenty-five per cent of the forty have died in the succeeding six years.

After my five years in solitary, when they took me away from San Quentin for my trial, I saw Skysail Jack. I could see little, for I was blinking in the sunshine like a bat, after five years of darkness; yet I saw enough of Skysail Jack to pain my heart. It was in crossing the Prison Yard that I saw him. His hair had turned white. He was prematurely old. His chest had caved in. His cheeks were sunken. His hands shook as with palsy. He tottered as he walked. And his eyes blurred with tears as he recognized me, for I too was a sad wreck of what had once been a man. I weighed eighty-seven pounds. My hair, streaked with gray, was a five-year growth, as were my beard and mustache. And I too tottered as I walked, so that the guards helped to lead me across that sun-blinding patch of yard. And Skysail Jack and I peered and knew each other under the wreckage.

Men such as he are privileged, even in a prison, so that he dared an infraction of the rules by speaking to me in a cracked and quavering voice.

"You're a good one, Standing," he cackled. "You never squealed."

"But I never knew, Jack," I whispered back—I was compelled to whisper, for five years of disuse had well nigh lost me my voice. "I don't think there ever was any dynamite."

"That's right," he cackled, nodding his head childishly. "Stick with it. Don't ever let'm know. You're a good one. I take my hat off to you, Standing. You never squealed."

And the guards led me on, and that was the last I saw of Skysail Jack. It was plain that even he had become a believer in the dynamite myth.

Twice they had me before the full Board of Directors. I was alternately bullied and cajoled. Their attitude resolved itself into two propositions. If I delivered up the dynamite they would give me a nominal punishment of thirty days in the dungeon and then make me a trusty in the prison library. If I persisted in my stubbornness and did not yield up the dynamite, then they would put me in solitary for the rest of my sentence. In my case, being a life prisoner, this was tantamount to condemning me to solitary confinement for life.

Oh, no; California is civilized. There is no such law on the statute books. It is a cruel and unusual punishment, and no modern state would be guilty of such a law. Nevertheless, in the history of California I am the third man who has been condemned for life to solitary confinement. The other two were Jake Oppenheimer and Ed Morrell. I shall tell you about them soon, for I rotted with them for years in the cells of silence.

Oh, another thing. They are going to take me out and hang me in a little while—no, not for killing Professor Haskell. I got life imprisonment for that. They are going to take me out and hang me because I was found guilty of assault and battery. And this is not prison discipline. It is law, and as law it will be found in the criminal statutes.

I believe I made a man's nose bleed. I never saw it bleed, but that was the evidence. Thurston, his name was. He was a guard at San Quentin. He weighed one hundred and seventy pounds and was in good health. I weighed under ninety pounds, was blind as a bat from the long darkness, and had been so long pent in narrow walls that I was made dizzy by large open spaces. Really, mine was a well-defined case of incipient agoraphobia, as I quickly learned that day I escaped from solitary and punched the guard Thurston on the nose.

I struck him on the nose and made it bleed when he got in my way and tried to catch hold of me. And so, they are going to hang me. It is the written law of the State of California that a lifetimer like me is guilty of a capital crime when he strikes a prison guard like Thurston. Surely, he could not have been inconvenienced more than half an hour by that bleeding nose; and yet they are going to hang me for it.

And, see! This law, in my case, is *ex post facto*. It was not a law at the time I killed Professor Haskell. It was not passed until after I received my life sentence. And this is the very point: my life sentence gave me my status under this law which had not yet been written on the books. And it is because of my status of lifetermer that I am to be hanged for battery committed on the guard Thurston. It is clearly *ex post facto*, and therefore unconstitutional.

But what bearing has the Constitution on constitutional lawyers, when they want to put the notorious Professor Darrell Standing out of the way? Nor do I even establish the precedent with my execution. A year ago, as everybody who reads the newspapers knows, they hanged Jake Oppenheimer, right here in Folsom, for a precisely similar offense . . . only, in his case of battery, he was not guilty of making a guard's nose bleed. He cut a convict unintentionally with a breadknife when the convict tried to take the breadknife away from him.

It is strange—life and men's ways and laws and tangled paths. I am writing these lines in the very cell in Murderers' Row that Jake Oppenheimer occupied ere they took him out and did to him what they are going to do to me.

I warned you I had many things to write about I shall now return to my narrative. The Board of Prison Directors gave me my choice: a prison trustyship and surcease from the jute looms if I gave up the nonexistent dynamite; life imprisonment in solitary if I refused to give up the nonexistent dynamite.

They gave me twenty-four hours in the jacket to think it over. Then I was brought before the Board a second time. What could I do? I could not lead them to the dynamite that was not. I told them so, and they told me I was a liar. They told me I was a hard case, a dangerous man, a moral degenerate, the criminal of the century. They told me many other things, and then they carried me away to the solitary cells. I was put into Number One cell. In Number Five lay Ed Morrell. In Number Twelve lay Jake Oppenheimer. And he had been there for ten years. Ed Morrell had been in his cell only one year. He was serving a fifty-year sentence. Jake Oppenheimer was a lifer. And so was I a lifer. Wherefore the outlook was that the three of us would remain there for a long time. And yet, six years only are past, and not one of us is in solitary. Jake Oppenheimer was swung off. Ed Morrell was made head trusty of San Quentin and then pardoned out only the other day. And here I am in Folsom waiting the day duly set by Judge Morgan, which will be my last day.

The fools! As if they could throttle my immortality with their clumsy device of rope and scaffold! I shall walk, and walk again, oh, countless times, this fair earth. And I shall walk in the flesh, be prince and peasant, savant and fool, sit in the high place and groan under the wheel.

Chapter 5

It was very lonely at first in solitary, and the hours were long. Time was marked by the regular changing of the guards, and by the alternation of day and night. Day was only a little light, but it was better than the all-dark of the night In solitary, the day was an ooze, a slimy seepage of light from the bright outer world.

Never was the light strong enough to read by. Besides, there was nothing to read. One could only lie and think and think. And I was a lifer, and it seemed certain if I did not do a miracle, make thirty-five pounds of dynamite out of nothing, that all the years of my life would be spent in the silent dark.

My bed was a thin and rotten tick of straw spread on the cell floor. One thin and filthy blanket constituted the covering. There was no chair, no table—nothing but the tick of straw and the thin, aged blanket. I was ever a short sleeper and ever a busy-brained man. In solitary one grows sick of oneself in his thoughts, and the only way to escape oneself is to sleep. For years I had averaged five hours sleep a night. I now cultivated sleep. I made a science of it. I became able to sleep ten hours, then twelve hours, and at last, as high as fourteen and fifteen hours out of the twenty-four. But beyond that I could not go, and, perforce, was compelled to lie awake and think and think. And that way, for an active-brained man, lay madness.

I sought devices to enable me mechanically to abide my waking hours. I squared and cubed long series of numbers, and by concentration and will carried on most astonishing geometric progressions. I even dallied with the squaring of the circle . . . until I found myself beginning to believe that that impossibility could be accomplished. Whereupon, realizing that there too lay madness, I forewent the squaring of the circle, although I assure you it required a considerable sacrifice on my part, for the mental exercise involved was a splendid time-killer.

By sheer visualization under my eyelids, I constructed chess-boards and played both sides of long games through to checkmate. But when I had become expert at this visualized game of memory, the exercise palled on me. Exercise it was, for there could be no real contest when the same player played both sides. I tried, and tried vainly, to split my personality into two personalities and to pit one against the other. But ever I remained the one player, with no planned ruse or strategy on one side that the other side did not simultaneously apprehend.

And time was very heavy and very long. I played games with flies, with ordinary houseflies that oozed into solitary as did the dim gray light; and I learned that they possessed a sense of play. For instance, lying on the cell floor, I established an arbitrary and imaginary line along the wall some three feet above the floor. When they rested on the wall above this line they were left in peace. The instant they lighted on the wall below the line I tried to catch them. I was careful never to hurt them and, in time, they knew as precisely as did I where ran the imaginary line. When they desired to play, they lighted below the line, and often for an hour at a time a single fly would engage in the sport. When it grew tired, it would come to rest on the safe territory above.

Of the dozen or more flies that lived with me during that period, there was only one who did not care for the game. He refused steadfastly to play and, having learned the penalty of alighting below the line, very carefully avoided the unsafe territory. That fly was a sullen, disgruntled creature. As the convicts would say, it had a "grouch" against the world. He never played with the other flies either. He was strong and healthy, too; for I studied him long to find out. His indisposition for play was temperamental, not physical.

Believe me, I knew all my flies. It was surprising to me, the multitude of differences I distinguished between them. Oh, each was distinctly an individual—not merely in size and markings, strength and speed of flight, and in the manner and fancy of flight and play, of dodge and dart, of wheel and swiftly repeat or wheel

and reverse, of touch and go on the danger wall, or of feint the
touch and alight elsewhere within the safety zone. They were
likewise sharply differentiated in the minutest shades of mentality
and temperament.

I knew the nervous ones, the phlegmatic ones. There was a little undersized one that would fly into real rages, sometimes with
me, sometimes with its fellows. Have you ever seen a colt or calf
throw up heels and dash madly about the pasture from sheer excess of vitality and spirits? Well, there was one fly—the keenest
player of them all, by the way—who, when it had alighted three
or four times in rapid succession on my taboo wall and succeeded
each time in eluding the velvet-careful swoop of my hand, would
grow so excited and jubilant that it would dart around and around
my head at top speed, wheeling, veering, reversing, and always
keeping within the limits of the narrow circle in which it cel-
ebrated its triumph over me.

Why, I could tell well in advance when any particular fly
was making up its mind to begin to play. There are a thousand
details in this one matter alone that I shall not bore you with,
although these details did serve to keep me from being bored
too utterly during that first period in solitary. But one thing I
must tell you. To me it is most memorable—the time when
the one with a grouch, who never played, alighted in a moment of absentmindedness within the taboo precinct and was
immediately captured in my hand. Do you know, he sulked for
an hour afterward.

And the hours were very long in solitary; nor could I sleep
them all away; nor could I while them away with houseflies,
no matter how intelligent For houseflies are houseflies, and I
was a man, with a man's brain; and my brain was trained and
active, stuffed with culture and science, and always geared to a
high tension of eagerness to do. And there was nothing to do,
and my thoughts ran abominably on in vain speculations. There
was my pentose and methyl-pentose determination in grapes and
wines to which I had devoted my last summer vacation at the

Asti Vineyards. I had all but completed the series of experiments. Was anybody else going on with it? I wondered; and if so, with what success?

You see, the world was dead to me. No news of it filtered in. The history of science was making fast, and I was interested in a thousand subjects. Why, there was my theory of the hydrolysis of casein by trypsin, which Professor Walters had been carrying out in his laboratory. Also, Professor Schleimer had similarly been collaborating with me in the detection of phytosterol in mixtures of animal and vegetable fats. The work surely was going on, but with what results? The very thought of all this activity just beyond the prison walls and in which I could take no part, of which I was never even to hear, was maddening. And in the meantime I lay there on my cell floor and played games with houseflies.

And yet all was not silence in solitary. Early in my confinement I used to hear, at irregular intervals, faint low tappings. From farther away I also heard fainter and lower tappings. Continually these tappings were interrupted by the snarling of the guard. On occasion, when the tapping went on too persistency, extra guards were summoned, and I knew by the sounds that men were being strait-jacketed.

The matter was easy of explanation. I had known, as every prisoner in San Quentin knew, that the two men in solitary were Ed Morrell and Jake Oppenheimer. And I knew that these were the two men who tapped knuckle-talk to each other and were punished for so doing.

That the code they used was simple I had not the slightest doubt, yet I devoted many hours to a vain effort to work it out. Heaven knows, it had to be simple, yet I could not make head nor tail of it. And simple it proved to be, when I learned it; and simplest of all proved the trick they employed which had so baffled me. Not only each day did they change the point in the alphabet where the code initialed, but they changed it every conversation, and often in the midst of a conversation.

Thus, there came a day when I caught the code at the right initial, listened to two clear sentences of conversation, and, the next time they talked, failed to understand a word. But that first time!

"Say—Ed—what—would—you—give—right—now—for—brown— papers—and—a—sack—of—Bull—Durham?" asked the one who tapped from farther away.

I nearly cried out in my joy. Here was communication! Here was companionship! I listened eagerly, and the nearer tapping, which I guessed must be Ed Morrell's, replied:

"I—would—do—twenty—hours—straight—in—the—jacket—for— a—five—cent—sack—"

Then came the snarling interruption of the guard:

"Cut that out, Morrell!"

It may be thought by the layman that the worst has been done to men sentenced to solitary for life, and therefore that a mere guard has no way of compelling obedience to his order to cease tapping. But the jacket remains. Starvation remains. Thirst remains. Manhandling remains. Truly, a man pent in a narrow cell is very helpless.

So the tapping ceased, and that night, when it was next resumed, I was all at sea again. By prearrangement they had changed the initial letter of the code. But I had caught the clue and, in the matter of several days occurred again the same initialment I had understood. I did not wait on courtesy.

"Hello," I tapped.

"Hello, stranger," Morrell tapped back; and from Oppenheimer, "Welcome to our city."

They were curious to know who I was, how long I was condemned to solitary, and why I had been so condemned. But all this I put to the side in order first to learn their system of changing the code initial. After I had this clear, we talked. It was a great day, for the two lifers had become three, although they accepted me only on probation. As they told me long after. They feared I might be a stool placed there to work a frame-up on them. It had been done before, to Oppenheimer, and he had paid dearly for the confidence he reposed in Warden Atherton's tool.

To my surprise—yes, to my elation, be it said—both my fellow prisoners knew me through my record as an incorrigible. Even into the living grave Oppenheimer had occupied for ten years had my fame, or notoriety, rather, penetrated.

I had much to tell them of prison happenings and of the outside world. The conspiracy to escape of the forty lifers, the search for the alleged dynamite, and all the treacherous frame-up of Cecil Winwood, was news to them. As they told me, news did occasionally dribble into solitary by way of the guards, but they had had nothing for a couple of months. The present guards on duty in solitary were a particularly bad and vindictive set.

Again and again that day we were cursed for our knuckle-talking by whatever guard was on. But we could not refrain. The two of the living dead had become three, and we had so much to say, while the manner of saying it was exasperatingly slow and I was not so proficient as they at the knuckle game.

"Wait till Pie-Face comes on tonight," Morrell rapped to me. "He sleeps most of his watch, and we can talk a streak."

How we did talk that night. Sleep was farthest from our eyes. Pie-Face Jones was a mean and bitter man, despite his fatness; but we blessed that fatness because it persuaded to stolen snatches of slumber. Nevertheless, our incessant tapping bothered his sleep and irritated him so that he reprimanded us repeatedly. And by the other night guards we were roundly cursed. In the morning all reported much tapping during the night, and we paid for our little holiday; for at nine came Captain Jamie with several guards to lace us into the torment of the jacket. Until nine the following morning, for twenty-four straight hours, laced and helpless on the floor without food or water, we paid the price for speech.

Oh, our guards were brutes. And under their treatment we had to harden to brutes in order to live. Hard work makes calloused hands. Hard guards make hard prisoners. We continued to talk and, on occasion, to be jacketed for punishment. Night was the best time and, when substitute guards chanced to be on, we often talked through a whole shift.

Night and day were one with us who lived in the dark. We could sleep any time, we could knuckle-talk only on occasion. We told one another much of the history of our lives, and for long hours Morrell and I have lain silently, while steadily, with faint far taps, Oppenheimer slowly spelled out his life story, from the early years in a San Francisco slum, through his gang-training, through his initiation into all that was vicious when as a lad of fourteen he served as night messenger in the red-light district, through his first detected infraction of the laws, and on and on through thefts and robberies to the treachery of a comrade and to red slayings inside prison walls.

They called Jake Oppenheimer the "Human Tiger." Some cub reporter coined the phrase that will long outlive the man to whom it was applied. And yet I ever found in Jake Oppenheimer all the cardinal traits of right humanness. He was faithful and loyal. I know of the times he has taken punishment in preference to informing on a comrade. He was brave. He was patient. He was capable of self-sacrifice—I could tell a story of this, but shall not take the time. And justice, with him, was a passion. The prison killings done by him were due entirely to this extreme sense of justice. And he had a splendid mind. A lifetime in prison, ten years of it in solitary, had not dimmed his brain.

Morrell, ever a true comrade, also had a splendid brain. In fact, and I who am about to die have the right to say it without incurring the charge of immodesty, the three best minds in San Quentin, from the warden down, were the three that rotted there together in solitary. And here at the end of my days, reviewing all that I have known of life, I am compelled to the conclusion that strong minds are never docile. The stupid men, the fearful men, the men ungifted with passionate rightness and fearless championship—these are the men who make model prisoners. I thank all gods that Jake Oppenheimer, Ed Morrell, and I were not model prisoners.

Chapter 6

There is more than the germ of truth in things erroneous in the child's definition of memory as the thing one forgets with. To be able to forget means sanity. Incessantly to remember means obsession, lunacy. So the problem I faced in solitary, where incessant remembering strove for possession of me, was the problem of forgetting. When I gamed with flies or played chess with myself, or talked with my knuckles, I partially forgot. What I desired was entirely to forget.

There were the boyhood memories of other times and places—the "trailing clouds of glory" of Wordsworth. If a boy had had these memories, were they irretrievably lost when he had grown to manhood? Could this particular content of his boy brain be utterly eliminated? Or were these memories of other times and places still residual, asleep, immured in solitary in brain cells similarly to the way I was immured in a cell in San Quentin?

Solitary life-prisoners have been known to resurrect and look upon the sun again. Then why could not these other-world memories of the boy resurrect?

But how? In my judgment, by attainment of complete forgetfulness of present and of manhood past.

And again, how? Hypnotism should do it. If by hypnotism the conscious mind were put to sleep, and the subconscious mind awakened, then was the thing accomplished, then would all the dungeon doors of the brain be thrown wide, then would the prisoners emerge into the sunshine.

So I reasoned—with what result you shall learn. But first, I must tell how as a boy I had had these other-world memories. I had glowed in the clouds of glory I trailed from lives aforetime. Like any boy, I had been haunted by the other beings I had been at other times. This had been during my process of becoming, ere

45

the flux of all that I had ever been had hardened in the mold of the one personality that was to be known by men for a few years as Darrell Standing.

Let me narrate just one incident. It was up in Minnesota on the old farm. I was nearly six years old. A missionary to China, returned to the United States and sent out by the Board of Missions to raise funds from the farmers, spent the night in our house. It was in the kitchen just after supper, as my mother was helping me undress for bed, and the missionary was showing photographs of the Holy Land.

And what I am about to tell you, I should long since have forgotten, had I not heard my father recite it to wondering listeners so many times during my childhood.

I cried out at sight of one of the photographs and looked at it, first with eagerness, and then with disappointment. It had seemed of a sudden most familiar, in much the same way that my father's barn would have been in a photograph. Then it had seemed altogether strange. But as I continued to look, the haunting sense of familiarity came back.

"The Tower of David," the missionary said to my mother.

"No!" I cried with great positiveness.

"You mean that isn't its name?" The missionary asked.

I nodded.

"Then what is its name, my boy?"

"Its name is . . ." I began, then concluded lamely, "I forget.

"It don't look the same now," I went on after a pause. "They've ben fixin' it up awful." Here, the missionary handed to my mother another photograph he had sought out.

"I was there myself six months ago, Mrs. Standing." He pointed with his finger. "That is the Jaffa Gate where I walked in and right up to the Tower of David in the back of the picture where my finger is now. The authorities are pretty well agreed on such matters. El Kul'ah, as it was known by—"

But here I broke in again, pointing to rubbish piles of ruined masonry on the left edge of the photograph.

"Over there somewhere," I said. "That name you just spoke was what the Jews called it. But we called it something else. We called it . . . I forget."

"Listen to the youngster," my father chuckled. "You'd think he'd been there."

I nodded my head, for in that moment I knew I had been there, though all seemed strangely different. My father laughed the harder, but the missionary thought I was making game of him. He handed me another photograph. It was just a bleak waste of a landscape, barren of trees and vegetation, a shallow canyon with easy-sloping walls of rubble. In the middle distance was a cluster of wretched, flat-roofed hovels.

"Now, my boy, where is that?" The missionary quizzed.

And the name came to me!

"Samaria," I said instantly.

My father clapped his hands with glee, my mother was perplexed at my antic conduct, while the missionary evinced irritation.

"The boy is right," he said. "It is a village in Samaria. I passed through it. That is why I bought it. And it goes to show that the boy has seen similar photographs before."

This my father and mother denied.

"But it's different in the picture," I volunteered, while all the time my memory was busy reconstructing the photograph. The general trend of the landscape and the line of the distant hills were the same. The differences I noted aloud and pointed out with my finger.

"The houses was about right here, and there was more trees, lots of trees, and lots of grass, and lots of goats. I can see 'em now, an' two boys drivin' 'em. An' right here is a lot of men walkin' behind one man. An' over there"—I pointed to where I had placed my village—"is a lot of tramps. They ain't got nothin' on exceptin' rags. An' they're sick. Their faces, an' hands, an' legs is all sores."

"He's heard the story in church or somewhere—you remember, the healing of the lepers, in Luke," the missionary said with a smile of satisfaction. "How many sick tramps are there, my boy?"

I had learned to count to a hundred when I was five years old, so I went over the group carefully and announced:

"Ten of 'em. They're all wavin' their arms an' yellin' at the other men."

"But they don't come near them?" Was the query.

I shook my head. "They just stand right there an' keep a-yellin' like they was in trouble."

"Go on," urged the missionary. "What next? What's the man doing in the front of the other crowd you said was walking along?"

"They've all stopped, an' he's sayin' something to the sick men. An' the boys with the goats 's stopped to look. Everybody's lookin'."

"And then?"

"That's all. The sick men are headin' for the houses. They ain't yellin' any more, an' they don't look sick any more. An' I just keep settin' on my horse a-lookin' on."

At this all three of my listeners broke into laughter.

"An' I'm a big man!" I cried out angrily. "An' I got a big sword!"

"The ten lepers Christ healed before he passed through Jericho on his way to Jerusalem," the missionary explained to my parents. "The boy has seen slides of famous paintings in some magic-lantern exhibition."

But neither Father nor Mother could remember that I had ever seen a magic lantern.

"Try him with another picture," Father suggested.

"It's all different," I complained as I studied the photograph the missionary handed me. "Ain't nothin' except that hill and them other hills. This ought to be a county road along here. An' over there ought to be gardens, an' trees, an' houses behind big stone walls. An' over there, on the other side, in holes in the rocks ought to be where they buried dead folks. You see this place?—

48

They used to throw stones at people there until they killed 'em. I never seen 'em do it. They just told me about it."

"And the hill?" The missionary asked, pointing to the central part of the print, for which the photograph seemed to have been taken. "Can you tell us the name of the hill?"

I shook my head.

"Never had no name. They killed folks there. I've seen 'm more 'n once."

"This time he agrees with the majority of the authorities," announced the missionary with huge satisfaction. "The hill is Golgotha, the Place of Skulls, or, as you please, so named because it resembles a skull. Notice the resemblance. That is where they crucified—" He broke off and turned to me. "Whom did they crucify there, young scholar? Tell us what else you see."

Oh, I saw—my father reported that my eyes were bulging; but I shook my head stubbornly and said:

"I ain't a-goin' to tell you because you're laughin' at me. I seen lots an' lots of men killed there. They nailed 'em up, an' it took a long time. I seen—but I ain't a-goin' to tell. I don't tell lies. You ask Dad an' Ma if I tell lies. He'd whale the stuffin' out of me if I did. Ask 'm."

And thereat not another word could the missionary get from me, even though he baited me with more photographs that sent my head whirling with a rush of memory pictures and that urged and tickled my tongue with spates of speech which I sullenly resisted and overcame.

"He will certainly make a good bible scholar," the missionary told Father and Mother after I had kissed them good night and departed for bed. "Or else, with that imagination, he'll become a successful fiction writer."

Which shows how prophecy can go agley. I sit here in Murderers' Row, writing these lines in my last days or, rather, in Darrell Standing's last days ere they take him out and try to thrust him into the dark at the end of a rope, and I smile to myself. I became neither bible scholar nor novelist. On the contrary, until they buried me in the cells of silence for half a decade, I was everything that the missionary forecasted not—an agricultural expert, a professor of agronomy, a specialist in the science of the elimination of waste motion, a master of farm efficiency, a precise laboratory scientist where precision and adherence to microscopic fact are absolute requirements.

And I sit here in the warm afternoon, in Murderers' Row, and cease from the writing of my memoirs to listen to the soothing buzz of flies in the drowsy air, and catch phrases of a low-voiced conversation between Josephus Jackson, the Negro murderer on my right, and Bambeccio, the Italian murderer on my left, who are discussing, through grated door to grated door, back and forth past my grated door, the antiseptic virtues and excellences of chewing tobacco for flesh wounds.

And in my suspended hand I hold my fountain pen, and as I remember that other hands of me, in long gone ages, wielded ink-brush, and quill, and stylus, I also find thought-space in time to wonder if that missionary, when he was a little lad, ever trailed clouds of glory and glimpsed the brightness of old star-roving days.

Well, back to solitary, after I had learned the code of knuckle-talk and still found the hours of consciousness too long to endure. By self-hypnosis, which I began successfully to practice, I became able to put my conscious mind to sleep and to awaken and loose my subconscious mind. But the latter was an undisciplined and lawless thing. It wandered through all nightmarish madness, without coherence, without continuity of scene, event, or person.

My method of mechanical hypnosis was the soul of simplicity. Sitting with folded legs on my straw mattresses, I gazed fixedly at a fragment of bright straw which I had attached to the wall of my cell near the door, where the most light was. I gazed at the bright point, with my eyes close to it and tilted upward till they strained to see. At the same time I relaxed all the will of me and gave myself to the swaying dizziness that always eventually came to me. And when I felt myself sway out of balance backward, I closed my eyes and permitted myself to fall supine and unconscious on the mattress.

And then, for half an hour, ten minutes, or as long as an hour or so, I would wander erratically and foolishly through the stored memories of my eternal recurrence on earth. But times and places shifted too swiftly. I knew afterward, when I awoke, that I, Darrell Standing, was the linking personality that connected all bizarreness and grotesqueness. But that was all. I could never live out completely one full experience, one point of consciousness in time and space. My dreams, if dreams they may be called, were rhymeless and reasonless.

Thus, as a sample of my rovings: In a single interval of fifteen minutes of subconsciousness, I have crawled and bellowed in the slime of the primeval world and sat beside Haasfurther and cleaved the twentieth-century air in a gas-driven monoplane. Awake, I remembered that I, Darrell Standing, in the flesh, during the year preceding my incarceration in San Quentin, had flown with Haasfurther over the Pacific at Santa Monica. Awake, I did not remember the crawling and the bellowing in the ancient slime. Nevertheless, awake, I reasoned that somehow I had remembered that early adventure in the slime, and that it was a verity of long-previous experience, when I was not yet Darrell Standing but somebody else, or something else that crawled and bellowed. One experience was merely more remote than the other. Both experiences were equally real-or else how did I remember them?

Oh, what a fluttering of luminous images and actions! In a few short minutes of loosed subconsciousness, I have sat in the halls of kings, above the salt and below the salt, been fool and jester, man-at-arms, clerk and monk; and I have been ruler above all at the head of the table—temporal power in my own sword arm, in the thickness of my castle walls, and the numbers of my finshing★ men; spiritual power likewise mine by token of the fact that cowled priests and fat abbots sat beneath me and swigged my wine and swined my meat

I have worn the iron collar of the serf about my neck in cold climes; and I have loved princesses of royal houses in the tropic-warmed and sun-scented night, where black slaves fanned the sultry air with fans of peacock plumes, while from afar, across the palms and fountains, drifted the roaring of lions and the cries of jackals. I have crouched in chill desert places warming my hands at fires built of camel's dung; and I have lain in the meager shade of sun-parched sagebrush by dry waterholes and yearned dry-tongued for water, while about me, dismembered and scattered in the alkali, were the bones of men and beasts who had yearned and died.

I have been sea-cunie and bravo, scholar and recluse. I have pored over handwritten pages of huge and musty tomes in the scholastic quietude and twilight of cliff-perched monasteries while beneath, on the lesser slopes peasants still toiled beyond the end of day among the vines and olives and drove in from pastures the blatting goats and lowing kine; yes, and I have led shouting rabbles down the wheel-worn, chariot-rutted paves of ancient and for-gotten cities; and, solemn-voiced and grave as death, I have enun-ciated the law, stated the gravity of the infraction, and imposed the due death on men, who, like Darrell Standing in Folsom Prison, had broken the law.

Aloft, at giddy mastheads oscillating above the decks of ships, I have gazed on sun-flashed water where coral growths iridesced from profounds of turquoise deeps, and conned the ships into the safety of mirrored lagoons where the anchors rumbled down close to palm-fronded beaches of sea-pounded coral rock; and I have striven on forgotten battlefields of the elder days, when the sun went down on slaughter that did not cease and that continued through the night hours with the stars shining down and with a cool night wind blowing from distant peaks of snow that failed to chill the sweat of battle; and again, I have been little Darrell Stand-ing, barefooted in the dew-lush grass of spring on the Minnesota farm, chilblained when of frosty mornings I fed the cattle in their breath-steaming stalls, sobered to fear and awe of the splendor and terror of God when I sat of Sundays under the rant and preach-ment of the New Jerusalem and the agonies of hell-fire.

Now, the foregoing were the glimpses and glimmerings that

came to me when, in Cell One of Solitary in San Quentin, I stared myself unconscious by means of a particle of bright, light-radiating straw. How did these things come to me? Surely I could not have manufactured them out of nothing inside my pent walls any more than could I have manufactured out of nothing the thirty-five pounds of dynamite so ruthlessly demanded of me by Captain Jamie, Warden Atherton, and the Prison Board of Directors.

I am Darrell Standing, born and raised on a quarter section of land in Minnesota, erstwhile professor of agronomy, a prison incorrigible in San Quentin, and at present a death-sentenced man in Folsom. I do not know, of Darrell Standing's experience, these things of which I write and which I have dug from out my storehouses of subconsciousness. I, Darrell Standing, born in Minnesota and soon to die by the rope in California, surely never loved daughters of kings in the courts of kings; nor fought cutlass to cutlass on the swaying decks of ships; nor drowned in the spirit rooms of ships, guzzling raw liquor to the wassail-shouting and death-singing of seamen, while the ship lifted and crashed on the black-toothed rocks and the water bubbled overhead, beneath, and all about.

Such things are not of Darrell Standing's experience in the world. Yet I, Darrell Standing, found these things within myself in solitary in San Quentin by means of mechanical self-hypnosis. No more were these experiences Darrell Standing's, than was the word "Samaria" Darrell Standing's when it leaped to his child lips at sight of a photograph.

One cannot make anything out of nothing. In solitary I could not so make thirty-five pounds of dynamite. Nor in solitary, out of nothing in Darrell Standing's experience, could I make these wide, far visions of time and space. These things were in the content of my mind, and in my mind I was just beginning to learn my way about.

---

* A word coined by Jack London for which there is no known meaning.

Chapter 7

So here was my predicament: I knew that within myself was a Golconda of memories of other lives, yet I was unable to do more than flit like a madman through those memories. I had my Golconda but could not mine it.

I remembered the case of Stainton Moses, the clergyman who had been possessed by the personalities of St. Hippolytus, Plotinus Athenodorus, and of that friend of Erasmus named Grocyn. And, when I considered the experiments of Colonel de Rochas, which I had read in tyro fashion in other and busier days, I was convinced that Stainton Moses had, in previous lives, been those personalities that on occasion seemed to possess him. In truth, they were he, they were the links of the chain of recurrence.

But more especially did I dwell upon the experiments of Colonel de Rochas. By means of suitable hypnotic subjects he claimed that he had penetrated backward through time to the ancestors of his subjects. Thus, the case of Josephine which he describes. She was eighteen years old and she lived at Voiron, the department of the Isere. Under hypnotism, Colonel de Rochas sent her adventuring back through her adolescence, her girlhood, her childhood, her breast-infancy, and the silent dark of her mother's womb, and, still back, through the silence and the dark of the time when she, Josephine, was not yet born, to the light and life of a previous living, when she had been a churlish, suspicious, and embittered old man, by name Jean-Claude Bourdon, who had served his time in the Seventh Artillery at Besancon, and who died at the age of seventy, long bed-ridden. Yes, and did not Colonel de Rochas in turn hypnotize this shade of Jean-Claude Bourdon, so that he adventured further back into time, through infancy and birth and the dark of the unborn, until he found again light and life when as a wicked old woman he had been Philomene Carteron?

But try as I would with my bright bit of straw in the oozement of light into solitary, I failed to achieve any such definiteness of previous personality. I became convinced, through the failure of my experiments, that only through death could I clearly and coherently resurrect the memories of my previous selves.

But the tides of life ran strong in me. I, Darrell Standing, was so strongly disinclined to die that I refused to let Warden Atherton and Captain Jamie kill me. I was always so innately urged to live that sometimes I think that is why I am still here, eating and sleeping, thinking and dreaming, writing this narrative of my various me's, and awaiting the incontestable rope that will put an ephemeral period in my long-linked existence.

And then came death in life. I learned the trick. Ed Morrell taught it to me, as you shall see. It began through Warden Atherton and Captain Jamie. They must have experienced a recrudescence of panic at the thought of the dynamite they believed hidden. They came to me in my dark cell, and they told me plainly that they would jacket me to death if I did not confess where the dynamite was hidden. And they assured me that they would do it officially, without any hurt to their own official skins My death would appear on the prison register as due to natural causes.

Oh, dear cotton-wool citizen, please believe me when I tell you that men are killed in prisons today as they have always been killed since the first prisons were built by men.

I well knew the terror, the agony, and the danger of the jacket. On, the men spirit-broken by the jacket! I have seen them. And I have seen men crippled for life by the jacket. I have seen men, strong men, men so strong that their physical stamina resisted all attacks of prison tuberculosis, after a prolonged bout with the jacket, their resistance broken down, fade away and die of tuberculosis within six months. There was Slant-Eyed Wilson, with an unguessed weak heart of fear, who died in the jacket within the first hour while the unconvinced inefficient of a prison doctor looked on and smiled. And I have seen a man confess, after half an hour in the jacket, truths and fictions that cost him years of credits.

I had had my own experiences. At the present moment half a thousand scars mark my body. They go to the scaffold with me. Did I live a hundred years to come, those same scars in the end would go to the grave with me.

Perhaps, dear citizen who permits and pays his hangdogs to lace the jacket for you—perhaps you are unacquainted with the jacket. Let me describe it, so that you will understand the method by which I achieved death in life, became a temporary master of time and space, and vaulted the prison walls to rove among the stars.

Have you ever seen canvas tarpaulins or rubber blankets with brass eyelets set in along the edges? Then imagine a piece of stout canvas, some four and one-half feet in length, with large and heavy brass eyelets running down both edges. The width of this canvas is never the full girth of the human body it is to surround. The width is also irregular—broadest at the shoulders, next broadest at the hips, and narrowest at the waist.

The jacket is spread on the floor. The man who is to be punished, or who is to be tortured for confession, is told to lie face-downward on the flat canvas. If he refuses, he is manhandled. After that he lays himself down with a will, which is the will of the hangdogs, which is your will, dear citizen, who feeds and fees the hangdogs for doing this thing for you.

The man lies face-downward. The edges of the jacket are brought as nearly together as possible along the center of the man's back. Then a rope, on the principle of a shoelace, is run through the eyelets, and on the principle of a shoelacing the man is laced in the canvas. Only he is laced more severely than any person ever laces his shoe. They call it "cinching" in prison lingo. On occasion, when the guards are cruel and vindictive or when the command has come down from above, in order to ensure the severity of the lacing the guards press with their feet into the man's back as they draw the lacing tight.

Have you ever laced your shoe too tightly and, after half an hour, experienced that excruciating pain across the instep of the obstructed circulation? And do you remember that after a few minutes of such pain you simply could not walk another step and had to untie the shoelace and ease the pressure? Very well. Then try to imagine your whole body so laced, only much more tightly, and that the squeeze, instead of being merely on the instep of one foot, is on your entire trunk, compressing to the seeming of death your heart, your lungs, and all the rest of your vital and essential organs.

I remember the first time they gave me the jacket down in the dungeons. It was at the beginning of my incorrigibility, shortly after my entrance to prison, when I was weaving my loom task of a hundred yards a day in the jute mill and finishing two hours ahead of the average day. Yes, and my jute-sacking was far above the average demanded. I was sent to the jacket that first time, according to the prison books, because of "skips" and "breaks" in the cloth; in short, because my work was defective. Of course, this was ridiculous. In truth, I was sent to the jacket because I, a new convict, a master of efficiency, a trained expert in the elimination of waste motion, had elected to tell the stupid head weaver a few things he did not know about his business. And the head weaver, with Captain Jamie present, had me called to the table where atrocious weaving, such as could never have gone through my loom, was exhibited against me. Three times was I thus called to the table. The third calling meant punishment according to the loom-room rules. My punishment was twenty-four hours in the jacket.

They took me down into the dungeon. I was ordered to lie face-downward on the canvas spread flat upon the floor. I refused. One of the guards, Morrison, gulleted me with his thumbs. Mobins, the dungeon trusty, a convict himself, struck me repeatedly with his fists. In the end I lay down as directed. And, because of the struggle I had vexed them with, they laced me extra tight. Then they rolled me over like a log upon my back.

It did not seem so bad at first. When they closed my door, with clang and clash of levered boltage, and left me in the utter dark, it was eleven o'clock in the morning. For a few minutes I was aware merely of an uncomfortable constriction which I fondly believed would ease as I grew accustomed to it. On the contrary, my heart began to thump and my lungs seemed unable to draw sufficient air for my blood. This sense of suffocation was terrorizing, and every thump of the heart threatened to burst my already bursting lungs.

After what seemed hours, and after what, out of my countless succeeding experiences in the jacket I can now fairly conclude to have been not more than half an hour, I began to cry out, to yell, to scream, to howl, in a very madness of dying. The trouble was the pain that had arisen in my heart. It was a sharp, definite pain, similar to that of pleurisy, except that it stabbed hotly rough the heart itself.

To die is not a difficult thing, but to die in such slow and horrible fashion was maddening. Like a trapped beast of the wild, I experienced ecstasies of fear, and yelled and howled until I realized that such vocal exercise merely stabbed my heart more hotly and at the same time consumed much of the little air in my lungs.

I gave over and lay quiet for a long time—an eternity it seemed then, though now I am confident that it could have been no longer than a quarter of an hour. I grew dizzy with semi-asphyxiation, and my heart thumped until it seemed surely it would burst the canvas that bound me. Again I lost control of myself and set up a mad howling for help.

In the midst of this I heard a voice from the next dungeon.

"Shut up," it shouted, though only faintly it percolated to me. "Shut up. You make me tired."

"I'm dying," I cried out.

"Pound your ear and forget it," was the reply.

"But I am dying," I insisted.

"Then why worry?" Came the voice. "You'll be dead pretty quick an' out of it. Go ahead and croak, but don't make so much noise about it. You're interruptin' my beauty sleep."

So angered was I by this callous indifference that I recovered self-control and was guilty of no more than smothered groans. This endured an endless time—possibly ten minutes; and then a tingling numbness set up in all my body. It was like pins and needles, and for as long as it hurt like pins and needles I kept my head. But when the prickling of the multitudinous darts ceased to hurt and only the numbness remained and continued verging into greater numbness, I once more grew frightened.

"How am I goin' to get a wink of sleep?" My neighbor complained. "I ain't any more happy than you. My jacket's just as tight as yourn, an' I want to sleep an' forget it."

"How long have you been in?" I asked, thinking him a newcomer compared to the centuries I had already suffered.

"Since day before yesterday," was his answer.

"I mean in the jacket," I amended.

"Since day before yesterday, brother."

"My God!" I screamed.

"Yes, brother, fifty straight hours, an' you don't hear me raisin' a roar about it. They cinched me with their feet in my back. I am some tight, believe me. You ain't the only one that's got troubles. You ain't ben in an hour yet."

"I've been in hours and hours," I protested.

"Brother, you may think so, but it don't make it so. I'm just tellin' you you ain't ben in an hour. I heard 'm lacin' you."

The thing was incredible. Already, in less than an hour, I had died a thousand deaths. And yet this neighbor, balanced and equable, calm-voiced and almost beneficent despite the harshness of his first remarks, had been in the jacket fifty hours!

"How much longer are they going to keep you in?" I asked.

"The Lord only knows. Captain Jamie is real peeved with me, an' he won't let me out until I'm about croakin'. Now, brother, I'm goin' to give you the tip. The only way is shut your face an' forget it. Yellin' an' hollerin' don't win you no money in this joint. An' the way to forget is to forget. Just get to rememberin' every girl you ever knew. That'll eat up hours for you. Mebbe you'll feel yourself gettin' woozy. Well, get woozy. You can't beat that for killin' time. An' when the girls won't hold you, get to thinkin' of the fellows you got it in for, an' what you'd do to 'em if you got a chance, an' what you're goin' to do to 'em when you get that same chance."

That man was Philadelphia Red. Because of prior conviction he was serving fifty years for highway robbery committed on the streets of Alameda. He had already served a dozen of his years at the time he talked to me in the jacket, and that was seven years ago. He was one of the forty lifers who, a little later, were double- crossed by Cecil Winwood. For that offense, Philadelphia Red lost his credits. He is middle-aged now, and he is still in San Quentin. If he survives he will be an old man when they let him out.

I lived through my twenty-four hours, and I have never been the same man since. Oh, I don't mean physically, although next morning, when they unlaced me, I was semi-paralyzed and in such a state of collapse that the guards had to kick me in the ribs to make me crawl to my feet. But I was a changed man mentally, morally. The brute physical torture of it was humiliation and affront to my spirit and to my sense of justice. Such discipline does not sweeten a man. I emerged from that first jacketing filled with a bitterness and a passionate hatred that has only increased through the years. My God! When I think of the things men have done to me! Twenty-four hours in the jacket! Little I thought that morning when they kicked me to my feet that the time would come when twenty-four hours in the jacket meant nothing; when a hundred hours in the jacket found me smiling when they released me; when two hundred and forty hours in the jacket found the same smile on my lips.

Yes, two hundred and forty hours. Dear cotton-woolly citizen, do you know what that means? It means ten days and ten nights in the jacket. Of course, such things are not done anywhere in the Christian world nineteen hundred years after Christ. I don't ask you to believe me. I don't believe it myself. I merely know that it was done to me in San Quentin, and that I lived to laugh at them and to compel them to get rid of me by swinging me off because I bloodied a guard's nose.

I write these lines today in the Year of Our Lord 1913, and today, in the Year of Our Lord 1913, men are lying in the jacket in the dungeons of San Quentin.

I shall never forget, as long as further living and further lives be vouchsafed me, my parting from Philadelphia Red that morning. He had then been seventy-four hours in the jacket.

"Well, brother, you're still alive an' kickin'," he called to me as I was totteringly dragged from my cell into the corridor of dungeons.

"Shut up, you, Red," the sergeant snarled at him.

"Forget it," was the retort.

"I'll get you yet, Red," the sergeant threatened.

"Think so?" Philadelphia Red queried sweetly, ere his tones turned to savageness. "Why, you old stiff, you couldn't get nothin'. You couldn't get a free lunch, much less the job you've got, now, if it wasn't for your brother's pull. An' I guess we all ain't mistaken on the stink of the place where your brother's pull comes from."

It was admirable—the spirit of man rising above its extremity, fearless of the hurt any brute of the system could inflict.

"Well, so long, brother," Philadelphia Red next called to me. "So long. Be good, an' love the warden. An' if you see 'em, just tell 'em that you saw me but that you didn't see me saw."

The sergeant was red with rage and, by the receipt of various kicks and blows, I paid for Red's pleasantry.

Chapter 8

In solitary, in Cell One, Warden Atherton and Captain Jamie proceeded to put me to the inquisition. As Warden Atherton said to me:

"Standing, you're going to come across with that dynamite or I'll kill you in the jacket. Harder cases than you have come across before I got done with them. You've got your choice—dynamite or curtains."

"Then I guess it is curtains," I answered, "because I don't know of any dynamite."

This irritated the warden to immediate action.

"Lie down," he commanded.

I obeyed, for I had learned the folly of fighting three or four strong men. They laced me tightly, and gave me a hundred hours. Once each twenty-four hours I was permitted a drink of water. I had no desire for food, nor was food offered me. Toward the end of the hundred hours, Jackson, the prison doctor, examined my physical condition several times.

But I had grown too used to the jacket during my incorrigible days to let a single jacketing injure me. Naturally, it weakened me, took the life out of me; but I had learned muscular tricks for stealing a little space while they were lacing me. At the end of the first hundred-hour bout I was worn and tired, but that was all. Another bout of this duration they gave me, after a day and a night to recuperate. And then they gave one hundred and fifty hours. Much of this time I was physically numb and mentally delirious. Also, by an effort of will, I managed to sleep away long hours.

Next, Warden Atherton tried a variation. I was given irregular intervals of jacket and recuperation. I never knew when I was to go into the jacket. Thus, I would have ten hours recuperation, and do twenty in the jacket; or I would receive only four hours rest. At the most unexpected hours of the night, my door would clang open and the changing guards would lace me. Sometimes rhythms were instituted. Thus, for three days and nights I alternated eight hours in the jacket and eight hours out. And then, just as I was growing accustomed to this rythm, it was suddenly altered and I was given two days and nights straight.

And ever the eternal question was propounded to me: Where was the dynamite? Sometimes Warden Atherton was furious with me. On occasion, when I had endured an extra severe jacketing, he almost pleaded with me to confess. Once he even promised me three months in the hospital of absolute rest and good food, and then the trusty job in the library.

Dr. Jackson, a weak stick of a creature with a smattering of medicine, grew skeptical. He insisted that jacketing, no matter how prolonged, could never kill me; and his insistence was a challenge to the warden to continue the attempt.

"These lean college guys'd fool the devil," he grumbled. "They're tougher'n rawhide. Just the same we'll wear him down. Standing, you hear me. What you've got ain't a caution to what you're going to get. You might as well come across now and save trouble. I'm a man of my word. You've heard me say dynamite or curtains. Well, that stands. Take your choice."

"Surely, you don't think I'm holding out because I enjoy it?" I managed to gasp, for at the moment Pie-Face Jones was forcing his foot into my back in order to cinch me tighter while I was trying with my muscles to steal slack. "There is nothing to confess. Why, I'd cut off my right hand right now to be able to lead you to any dynamite."

"Oh, I've seen your educated kind before," he sneered. "You get wheels in your head, some of you, that make you stick to any old idea. You get balky like horse.—Tighter, Jones; that ain't half a cinch.—Standing, if you don't come across it's curtains I stick by that."

One compensation I learned. As one grows weaker one is less susceptible to suffering. There is less hurt because there is less to hurt. And the man already well weakened grows weaker more slowly. It is of common knowledge that unusually strong men suffer more severely from ordinary sickness than do women or invalids. As the reserves of strength are consumed, there is less strength to lose. After all superfluous flesh is gone, what is left is stringy and resistant. In fact, that was what I became—a sort of string-like organism that persisted in living.

Morrell and Oppenheimer were sorry for me, and rapped me sympathy and advice. Oppenheimer told me he had gone through it, and worse, and still lived.

"Don't let them beat you out," he spelled with his knuckles. "Don't let them kill you, for that would suit them. And don't squeal on the plant."

"But there isn't any plant," I rapped back with the edge of the sole of my shoe against the grating—I was in the jacket at the time and so could talk only with my feet. "I don't know anything about the damned dynamite."

"That's right," Oppenheimer praised. "He's the stuff, ain't he, Ed?"

Which goes to show what chance I had of convincing Warden Atherton of my ignorance of the dynamite. His very persistence in the quest convinced a man like Jake Oppenheimer, who could only admire me for the fortitude with which I kept a close mouth.

During this first period of the jacket-inquisition, I managed to sleep a great deal. My dreams were remarkable. Of course they were vivid and real as most dreams are. What made them remarkable was their coherence and continuity. Often I addressed bodies of scientists on abstruse subjects, reading aloud to them carefully prepared papers on my own researches or on my own deductions from the researches and experiments of others. When I awakened, my voice would seem still ringing in my ears, while my eyes still could see typed on the white paper whole sentences and paragraphs that I could read again and marvel at ere the vision faded. In passing, I call attention to the fact that at the time I noted that the process of reasoning employed in these dream speeches was invariably deductive.

Then there was a great farming section, extending north and south for hundreds of miles in some part of the temperate regions, with a climate and flora and fauna largely resembling those of California. Not once, nor twice, but thousands of different times I journeyed through this dream-region. The point I desire to call attention to was that it was always the same region. No essential feature of it ever differed in the different dreams. Thus, it was always an eight-hour drive behind mountain horses from the alfalfa meadows (where I kept many Jersey cows) to the straggly village beside the big dry creek, where I caught the lime narrow-gauge train. Every landmark in that eight-hour drive in the mountain buckboard, every tree, every mountain, every ford and bridge, every ridge and eroded hillside was ever the same.

In this coherent, rational farm-region of my strait-jacket dreams, the minor details, according to season and to the labor of men, did change. Thus, on the upland pastures behind my alfalfa meadows, I developed a new farm with the aid of Angora goats. Here, I marked the changes with every dream-visit, and the changes were in accordance with the time that elapsed between visits.

Oh, those brush-covered slopes! How I can see them now just as when the goats were first introduced. And how I remembered the consequent changes—the paths beginning to form as the goats literally ate their way through the dense thickets; the disappearance of the younger, smaller bushes that were not too tall for total browsing; the vistas that formed in all directions through the older, taller bushes, as the goats browsed as high as they could stand and reach on their hind legs; the driftage of the pasture grasses that followed in the wake of the clearing by the goats. Yes, the continuity of such dreaming was its charm. Came the day when the men with axes chopped down all the taller brush so as to give the goats access to the leaves and buds and bark. Came the day, in winter weather, when the dry denuded skeletons of all these bushes were gathered into heaps and burned. Came the day when

I moved my goats on to other brush-impregnable hillsides, with following in their wake my cattle, pasturing knee-deep in the succulent grasses that grew where before had been only brush. And came the day when I moved my cattle on, and my plowmen went back and forth across the slopes contour- plowing the rich sod under to rot to live and crawling humus in which to bed my seeds of crops to be.

Yes, and in my dreams, often, I stepped off the little narrow-gauge train where the straggly village stood beside the big dry creek, and got into the buckboard behind my mountain horses, and drove hour by hour past all the old familiar landmarks to my alfalfa meadows, and on to my upland pastures where my rotated crops of corn and barley and clover were ripe for harvesting and where I watched my men engaged in the harvest, while beyond, ever climbing, my goats browsed the higher slopes of brush into cleared, tilled fields.

But these were dreams, frank dreams, fancied adventures of my deductive subconscious mind. Quite unlike them, as you shall see, were my other adventures when I passed through the gates of the living death and relived the reality of the other lives that had been mine in other days.

In the long hours of waking in the jacket, I found that I dwelt a great deal on Cecil Winwood, the poet-forger who had wantonly put all this torment on me, and who was even then at liberty out in the free world again. No, I did not hate him. The word is too weak. There is no word in the language strong enough to describe my feelings. I can say only that I knew the gnawing of a desire for vengeance on him that was a pain in itself and that exceeded all the bounds of language. I shall not tell you of the hours I devoted to plans of torture on him, nor of the diabolical means and devices or torture that I invented for him. Just one example. I was enamored of the ancient trick whereby an iron basin, containing a rat, is fastened to a man's body. The only way out for the rat is through the man himself. As I say, I was enamored of this, until I realized that such a death was too quick, whereupon I dwelt long and favorably on the Moorish trick of—but no, I promised to relate no further of this matter. Let it suffice that many of my pain-maddening waking hours were devoted to dreams of vengeance on Cecil Winwood.

Chapter 9

One thing of great value I learned in the long, pain-weary hours of waking—namely, the mastery of the body by the mind. I learned to suffer passively as undoubtedly, all men have learned who have passed through the postgraduate courses of strait-jacketing. Oh, it is no easy trick to keep the brain in such serene repose that it is quite oblivious to the throbbing, exquisite complaint of some tortured nerve.

And it was this very mastery of the flesh by the spirit which I so acquired that enabled me easily to practice the secret Ed Morrell told to me.

"Think it is curtains?" Ed Morrell rapped to me one night.

I had just been released from one hundred hours, and I was weaker than I had ever been before. So weak was I that though my whole body was one mass of bruise and misery, nevertheless I scarcely was aware that I had a body.

"It looks like curtains," I rapped back. "They will get me if they keep it up much longer."

"Don't let them," he advised. "There is a way. I learned it myself, down in the dungeons, when Massie and I got ours good and plenty. I pulled through. But Massie croaked. If I hadn't learned the trick, I'd have croaked along with him. You've got to be pretty weak first, before you try it. If you try it when you are strong, you make a failure of it, and then that queers you forever after. I made the mistake of telling Jake the trick when he was strong. Of course, he could not pull it off, and in the times since when he did need it, it was too late, for his first failure had queered it. He won't even believe it now. He thinks I am kidding him. —Ain't that right, Jake?"

And from Cell Thirteen Jake rapped back, "Don't swallow it, Darrell. It's a sure fairy story."

"Go on and tell me," I rapped to Morrell.

"That is why I waited for you to get real weak," he continued. "Now you need it, and I am going to tell you. It's up to you. If you have got the will you can do it. I've done it three times, and I know."

"Well, what is it?" I rapped eagerly.

"The trick is to die in the jacket, to will yourself to die. I know you don't get me yet, but wait. You know how you get numb in the jacket—how your arm or your leg goes to sleep. Now you can't help that, but you can take it for the idea and improve on it. Don't wait for your legs or anything to go to sleep. You lie on your back as comfortable as you can get, and you begin to use your will.

"And this is the idea you must think to yourself, and that you must believe all the time you're thinking it. If you don't believe, then there's nothing to it. The thing you must think and believe is that your body is one thing and your spirit is another thing. You are you, and your body is something else that don't amount to shucks. Your body don't count. You're the boss. You don't need any body. And thinking and believing all this you proceed to prove it by using your will. You make your body die.

"You begin with the toes, one at a time. You make your toes die. You will them to die. And if you've got the belief and the will your toes will die. That is the big job—to start the dying. Once you've got the first toe dead, the rest is easy, for you don't have to do any more believing. You know. Then you put all your will into making the rest of the body die. I tell you, Darrell, I know. I've done it three times.

"Once you get the dying started, it goes right along. And the funny thing is that you are all there all the time. Because your toes are dead don't make you in the least bit dead. By and by your legs are dead to the knees, and then to the thighs, and you are just the same as you always were. It is your body that is dropping out of the game a chunk at a time. And you are just you, the same you you were before you began."

"And then what happens?" I queried.

"Well, when your body is all dead, and you are all there yet, you just skin out and leave your body. And when you leave your body you leave the cell. Stone walls and iron doors are to hold bodies in. They can't hold the spirit in. You see, you have proved it. You are spirit outside of your body. You can look at your body from outside of it. I tell you I know because I have done it three times—looked at my body lying there with me outside of it."

"Ha! Ha! Ha!" Jake Oppenheimer rapped his laughter thirteen cells away.

"You see, that's Jake's trouble," Morrell went on. "He can't believe. That one time he tried it he was too strong and failed. And now he thinks I am kidding."

"When you die you are dead, and dead men stay dead," Oppenheimer retorted.

"I tell you I've been dead three times," Morrell argued.

"And lived to tell us about it," Oppenheimer jeered.

"But don't forget one thing, Darrell," Morrell rapped to me. "The thing is ticklish. You have a feeling all the time that you are taking liberties. I can't explain it, but I always had a feeling if I was away when they came and let my body out of the jacket that I couldn't get back into my body again. I mean that my body would be dead for keeps. And I didn't want it to be dead. I didn't want to give Captain Jamie and the rest that satisfaction. But I tell you, Darrell, if you can turn the trick you can laugh at the warden. Once you make your body die that way it don't matter whether they keep you in the jacket a month on end. You don't suffer none, and your body don't suffer. You know there are cases of people who have slept for a whole year at a time. That's the way it will be with your body. It just stays there in the jacket, not hurting or anything, just waiting for you to come back.

"You try it. I am giving you the straight steer."

"And if he don't come back?" Oppenheimer asked.

"Then the laugh will be on him, I guess, Jake," Morrell answered. "Unless, maybe, it will be on us for sticking around this old dump when we could get away that easy."

And here the conversation ended, for Pie-Face Jones, waking crustily from stolen slumber, threatened Morrell and Oppenheimer with a report next morning that would mean the jacket for them. Me he did not threaten, for he knew I was doomed for the jacket anyway.

I lay long there in the silence, forgetting the misery of my body while I considered this proposition Morrell had advanced. Already, as I have explained, by mechanical self-hypnosis I had sought to penetrate back through time to my previous selves. That I had partly succeeded I knew; but all that I had experienced was a fluttering of apparitions that merged erratically and were without continuity.

But Morrell's method was so patently the reverse of my method of self-hypnosis that I was fascinated. By my method, my consciousness went first of all. By his method, consciousness persisted last of all and, when the body was quite gone, passed into stages so sublimated that it left the body, left the prison of San Quentin, and journeyed afar, and was still consciousness.

It was worth a trial, anyway, I concluded. And, despite the skeptical attitude of the scientist that was mine, I believed. I had no doubt I could do what Morrell said he had done three times. Perhaps this faith that so easily possessed me was due to my extreme debility. Perhaps I was not strong enough to be skeptical. This was the hypothesis already suggested by Morrell. It was a conclusion of pure empiricism, and I too, as you shall see, demonstrated it empirically.

Chapter 10

And above all things, next morning Warden Atherton came into my cell on murder intent. With him were Captain Jamie, Doctor Jackson, Pie-Face Jones, and Al Hutchins. Al Hutchins was serving a forty-year sentence, and was in hopes of being pardoned out. For four years he had been head trusty of San Quentin. That this was a position of great power you will realize when I tell you that the graft alone of the head trusty was estimated at three thousand dollars a year. Wherefore Al Hutchins, in possession of ten or twelve thousand dollars and of the promise of a pardon, could be depended upon to do the warden's bidding blind.

I have just said that Warden Atherton came into my cell intent on murder. His face showed it. His actions proved it.

"Examine him," he ordered Doctor Jackson.

That wretched apology of a creature stripped from me my dirt-encrusted shirt that I had worn since my entrance to solitary, and exposed my poor wasted body, the skin ridged like brown parchment over the ribs and sore-infested from the many bouts with the jacket The examination was shamelessly perfunctory.

"Will he stand it?" The warden demanded.

"Yes," Dr. Jackson answered.

"How's the heart?"

"Splendid."

"You think he'll stand ten days of it, Doc?"

"Sure."

"I don't believe it," the warden announced savagely. "But we'll try it just the same. —Lie down, Standing."

I obeyed, stretching myself face-downward on the flat-spread jacket. The warden seemed to debate with himself for a moment.

"Roll over," he commanded.

I made several efforts, but was too weak to succeed, and could only sprawl and squirm in my helplessness.

"Putting it on," was Jackson's comment.

"Well, he won't have to put it on when I'm done with him," said the warden. "Lend him a hand. I can't waste any more time on him."

So they rolled me over on my back where I stared up into Warden Atherton's face.

"Standing," he said slowly, "I've given you all the rope I am going to. I am sick and tired of your stubbornness. My patience is exhausted. Doctor Jackson says you are in condition to stand ten days in the jacket. You can figure your chances. But I am going to give you your last chance now. Come across with the dynamite. The moment it is in my hands I'll take you out of here. You can bathe and shave and get clean clothes. I'll let you loaf for six months on hospital grub, and then I'll put you trusty in the library. You can't ask me to be fairer with you than that. Besides, you're not squealing on anybody. You are the only person in San Quentin who knows where the dynamite is. You won't hurt anybody's feelings by giving in, and you'll be all to the good from the moment you do give in. And if you don't—"

He paused and shrugged his shoulders significantly.

"Well, if you don't, you start in the ten days right now."

The prospect was terrifying. So weak was I that I was as certain as the warden was that it meant death in the jacket. And then I remembered Morrell's trick. Now, if ever, was the need of it; and now, if ever, was the time to practice the faith of it. I smiled up in the face of Warden Atherton. And I put faith in that smile, and faith in the proposition I made to him.

"Warden," I said, "do you see the way I am smiling? Well, if at the end of ten days, when you unlace me, I smile up at you in the same way, will you give a sack of Bull Durham and a package of brown papers to Morrell and Oppenheimer?"

"Ain't they the crazy ginks, these college guys?" Captain Jamie snorted.

Warden Atherton was a choleric man, and he took my request for insulting braggadocio.

"Just for that you get an extra cinching," he informed me.

"I made you a sporting proposition, Warden," I said quietly. "You can cinch me as tight as you please, but if I smile ten days from now will you give the Bull Durham to Morrell and Oppenheimer?"

"You are mighty sure of yourself," he retorted.

"That's why I made the proposition," I replied.

"Getting religion, eh?" He sneered.

"No," was my answer. "It merely happens that I possess more life than you can ever reach the end of. Make it a hundred days if you want, and I'll smile at you when it's over."

"I guess ten days will more than do you, Standing."

"That's your opinion," I said. "Have you got faith in it? If you have you won't even lose the price of the two five-cent sacks of tobacco. Anyway, what have you got to be afraid of?"

"For two cents I'd kick the face off of you right now," he snarled.

"Don't let me stop you." I was impudently suave. "Kick as hard as you please, and I'll still have enough face left with which to smile. In the meantime, while you are hesitating, suppose you accept my original proposition."

A man must be terribly weak and profoundly desperate to be able, under such circumstances, to beard the warden in solitary. Or he may be both and, in addition, he may have faith. I know now that I had faith and so acted on it. I believed what Morrell had told me. I believed in the lordship of the mind over the body. I believed that not even a hundred days in the jacket could kill me.

Captain Jamie must have sensed this faith that informed me, for he said:

"I remember a Swede that went crazy twenty years ago. That was before your time, Warden. He'd killed a man in a quarrel over twenty-five cents and got life for it. He was a cook. He got religion. He said that a golden chariot was coming to take him to heaven, and he sat down on top of the red-hot range and sang hymns and hosannahs while he cooked. They dragged him off, but he croaked two days afterward in hospital. He was cooked to the bone. And to the end he swore he'd never felt the heat. Couldn't get a squeal out of him."

"We'll make Standing squeal," said the warden.

"Since you are so sure of it, why don't you accept my proposition?" I challenged.

The warden was so angry that it would have been ludicrous to me had I not been in so desperate plight. His face was convulsed. He clenched his hands and, for a moment, it seemed that he was about to fall upon me and give me a beating. Then, with an effort, he controlled himself.

"All right, Standing," he snarled. "I'll go you. But you bet your sweet life you'll have to go some to smile ten days from now. —Roll him over, boys, and cinch him till you hear his ribs crack. —Hutchins, show him you know how to do it."

And they rolled me over and laced me as I had never been laced before. The head trusty certainly demonstrated his ability. I tried to steal what little space I could. Little it was, for I had long since shed my flesh, while my muscles were attenuated to mere strings. I had neither the strength nor bulk to steal more than a little, and the little I stole I swear I managed by sheer expansion at the joints of the bones of my frame. And of this little I was robbed by Hutchins, who, in the old days before he was made head trusty, had learned all the tricks of the jacket from the inside of the jacket.

You see, Hutchins was a cur at heart, or a creature who had once been a man but who had been broken on the wheel. He possessed ten or twelve thousand dollars, and his freedom was in sight if he obeyed orders. Later, I learned that there was a girl who had remained true to him, and who was even then waiting for him. The woman factor explains many things of men.

If ever a man deliberately committed murder, Al Hutchins did that morning in solitary at the warden's bidding. He robbed me of the little space I stole. And, having robbed me of that, my body was defenseless, so that with his foot in my back while he drew the lacing tight, he constricted me as no man had ever before succeeded in doing. So severe was this constriction of my frail frame upon my vital organs that I felt, there and then, immediately, that death was upon me. And still the miracle of faith was mine. I did not believe that I was going to die. I knew—I say I knew—that I was not going to die. My head was swimming, and my heart was pounding from my toenails to the hair roots in my scalp.

"That's pretty tight," Captain Jamie urged reluctantly.

"The hell it is," said Doctor Jackson. "I tell you nothing can hurt him. He's a wooz. He ought to have been dead long ago."

Warden Atherton, after a hard struggle, managed to insert his forefinger between the lacing and my back. He brought his foot to bear upon me, with the weight of his body added to his foot, and pulled, but failed to get any fraction of an inch of slack.

"I take my hat off to you, Hutchins," he said. "You know your job. Now roll him over and let's look at him."

They rolled me over on my back. I stared up at them with bulging eyes. This I know: had they laced me in such fashion the first time I went into the jacket, I should surely have died in the first ten minutes. But I was well trained. I had behind me the thousands of hours in the jacket and, plus that, I had faith in what Morrell had told me.

"Now laugh, damn you, laugh," said the warden to me. "Start that smile you've been bragging about."

So, while my lungs panted for a little air, while my heart threatened to burst, while my mind reeled, nevertheless I was able to smile up into the warden's face.

Chapter 11

The door clanged, shutting out all but a little light, and I was left alone on my back. By the tricks I had long since learned in the jacket, I managed to writhe myself across the floor an inch at a time until the edge of the sole of my right shoe touched the door. There was an immense cheer in this. I was not utterly alone. If the need arose, I could at least rap knuckle-talk to Morrell.

But Warden Atherton must have left strict injunctions on the guards, for, though I managed to call Morrell and tell him I intended trying the experiment, he was prevented by the guards from replying. Me they could only curse, for, insofar as I was in the jacket for a ten-day bout, I was beyond all threat of punishment.

I remember remarking at the time my serenity of mind. The customary pain of the jacket was in my body, but my mind was so passive that I was no more aware of the pain than was I aware of the floor beneath me or the walls around me. Never was a man in better mental and spiritual condition for such an experiment. Of course, this was largely due to my extreme weakness. But there was more to it. I had lone, schooled myself to be oblivious to pain. I had neither doubts nor fears. All the content of my mind seemed to be an absolute faith in the overlordship of the mind. This passivity was almost dream-like, and yet, in its way, it was positive almost to a pitch of exaltation.

I began my concentration of will. Even then my body was numbing and prickling from the loss of circulation. I directed my will to the little toe of my right foot, and I willed that toe to cease to be alive in my consciousness. I willed that toe to die—to die so far as I, its lord, and a different thing entirely from it, was concerned. There was the hard struggle. Morrell had warned me that it would be so. But there was no flicker of doubt to disturb my faith. I knew that that toe would die, and I knew when it was dead. Joint by joint it had died under the compulsion of my will.

The rest was easy, but slow, I will admit. Joint by joint, toe by toe, all the toes of both my feet ceased to be. And joint by joint, the process went on. Came the time when my flesh below the ankles had ceased. Came the time when all below my knees had ceased.

Such was the pitch of my perfect exaltation that I knew not the slightest prod of rejoicing at my success. I knew nothing save that I was making my body die. All that was I, was devoted to that sole task. I performed the work as thoroughly as any mason laying bricks and I regarded the work as just about as commonplace as would a brick-mason regard his work.

At the end of an hour my body was dead to the hips, and from the hips up, joint by joint, I continued to will the ascending death.

It was when I reached the level of my heart that the first blurring and dizzying of my consciousness occurred. For fear that I should lose consciousness, I willed to hold the death I had gained, and shifted my concentration to my fingers. My brain cleared again, and the death of my arms to the shoulders was most rapidly accomplished.

At this stage my body was all dead, so far as I was concerned, save my head and a little patch of my chest. No longer did the pound and smash of my compressed heart echo in my brain. My heart was beating steadily but feebly. The joy of it, had I dared joy at such a moment, would have been the cessation of sensation.

At this point, my experience differs from Morrell's. Still willing automatically, I began to grow dreamy, as one does in that borderland between sleep and waking. Also, it seemed as if a prodigious enlargement of my brain was taking place within the skull itself that did not enlarge. There were occasional glintings and flashings of light, as if even I, the overlord, had ceased for a moment and the next moment was again myself, still the tenant of the fleshly tenement that I was making to die.

Most perplexing was the seeming enlargement of brain. Without having passed through the wall of skull, nevertheless it seemed to me that the periphery of my brain was already outside my skull and still expanding. Along with this was one of the most remarkable sensations or experiences that I have encountered. Time and space, insofar as they were the stuff of my consciousness, underwent an enormous extension. Thus, without opening my eyes to verify, I knew that the walls of my narrow cell had receded until it was like a vast audience chamber. And while I contemplated the matter I knew that they continued to recede. The whim struck me for a moment that if a similar expansion were taking place with the whole prison, then the outer walls of San Quentin must be far out in the Pacific Ocean on one side and on the other side must be encroaching on the Nevada desert. A companion whim was that since matter could permeate matter, then the walls of my cell might well permeate the prison walls, pass through the prison walls, and thus put my cell outside the prison and put me at liberty. Of course, this was pure fantastic whim, and I knew it at the time for what it was.

The extension of time was equally remarkable. Only at long intervals did my heart beat. Again a whim came to me, and I counted the seconds, slow and sure, between my heartbeats. At first, as I clearly noted, over a hundred seconds intervened between beats. But as I continued to count, the intervals extended so that I was made weary of counting.

And while this illusion of the extension of time and space persisted and grew, I found myself dreamily considering a new and profound problem. Morrell had told me that he had won freedom from his body by killing his body—or by eliminating his body from his consciousness, which, of course, was in effect the same thing. Now, my body was so near to being entirely dead that I knew in all absoluteness that by a quick concentration of will on the yet-alive patch of my torso, it too would cease to be. But—and here was the problem, and Morrell had not warned me: Should I also will my head to be dead? If I did so, no matter what befell the spirit of Darrell Standing, would not the body of Darrell Standing be forever dead?

I chanced the chest and the slow-beating heart. The quick compulsion of my will was rewarded. I no longer had chest nor heart. I was only a mind, a soul, a consciousness—call it what you will—incorporate in a nebulous brain that, while it still centered inside my skull, was expanded, and was continuing to expand, beyond my skull.

And then, with flashings of light, I was off and away. At a bound, I had vaulted prison roof and California sky, and was among the stars. I say "stars" advisedly. I walked among the stars. I was a child. I was clad in frail, fleece-like, delicate-colored robes that shimmered in the cool starlight. These robes, of course, were based upon my boyhood observance of circus actors and my boyhood conception of the garb of young angels.

Nevertheless, thus clad, I trod interstellar space, exalted by the knowledge that I was bound on vast adventure, where, at the end, I would find all the cosmic formulae and have made clear to me the ultimate secret of the universe. In my hand I carried a long glass wand. It was borne in upon me that with the tip of this wand I must touch each star in passing. And I knew, in all absoluteness, that did I but miss one star I should be precipitated into some unplummeted abyss of unthinkable and eternal punishment and guilt.

Long I pursued my starry quest. When I say "long," you must bear in mind the enormous extension of time that had occurred in my brain. For centuries I trod space, with the tip of my wand and with unerring eye and hand tapping each star I passed. Ever the way grew brighter. Ever the ineffable goal of infinite wisdom grew nearer. And yet I made no mistake. This was no other self of mine. This was no experience that had once been mine. I was aware all the time that it was I, Darrell Standing, who walked among the stars and tapped them with a wand of glass. In short, I knew that here was nothing real, nothing that had ever been or could ever be. I knew that it was nothing else than a ridiculous orgy of the imagination, such as men enjoy in drug dreams, in delirium, or in mere ordinary slumber.

And then, as all went merry and well with me on my celestial quest, the tip of my wand missed a star, and on the instant I knew I had been guilty of a great crime. And on the instant, a knock, vast and compulsive, inexorable and mandatory as the stamp of the iron hoof of doom, smote me and reverberated across the universe. The whole sidereal system coruscated, reeled and fell in flame.

I was torn by an exquisite and disruptive agony. And on the instant, I was Darrell Standing, the life convict, lying in his strait jacket in solitary. And I knew the immediate cause of that summons. It was a rap of the knuckle by Ed Morrell, in Cell Five, beginning the spelling of some message.

And now to give some comprehension of the extension of time and space that I was experiencing. Many days afterward I asked Morrell what he had tried to convey to me. It was a simple message, namely: "Standing, are you there?" He had tapped it rapidly, while the guard was at the far end of the corridor into which the solitary cells opened. As I say, he had tapped the message very rapidly. And now behold! Between the first tap and the second, I was off and away among the stars, clad in fleecy garments, touching each star as I passed in my pursuit of the formulae that would explain the last mystery of life. And as before, I pursued the quest for centuries. Then came the summons, the stamp of the hoof of doom, the exquisite disruptive agony, and again I was back in my cell in San Quentin. It was the second tap of Ed Morrell's knuckle. The interval between it and the first tap could have been no more than a fifth of a second. And yet, so unthinkably enormous was the extension of time to me that in the course of that fifth of a second I had been away star-roving for long ages.

Now I know, my reader, that the foregoing seems all a farrago. I agree with you. It is farrago. It was experience, however. It was just as real to me as is the snake beheld by a man i*n delirium tremens.*

Possibly, by the most liberal estimate, it may have taken Ed Morrell two minutes to tap his question. Yet to me aeons elapsed between the first tap of his knuckle and the last. No longer could I tread my starry path with that ineffable pristine joy, for my way was beset with dread of the inevitable summons that would rip and tear me as it jerked me back to my strait-jacket hell. Thus my aeons of star-wandering were aeons of dread.

And all the time I knew it was Ed Morrell's knuckle that thus cruelly held me earth-bound. I tried to speak to him, to ask him to cease. But so thoroughly had I eliminated my body from my consciousness that I was unable to resurrect it. My body lay dead in the jacket, though I still inhabited the skull. In vain I strove to will my foot to tap my message to Morrell. I reasoned I had a foot. And yet, so thoroughly had I carried out the experiment, I had no foot.

Next—and I know now that it was because Morrell had spelled his message quite out—I pursued my way among the stars and was not called back. After that, and in the course of it, I was aware, drowsily, that I was falling asleep, and that it was delicious sleep. From time to time, drowsily, I stirred—please, my reader, don't miss that verb—I *stirred*. I moved my legs, my arms. I was aware of clean, soft bed linen against my skin. I was aware of bodily well-being. Oh, it was delicious. As thirsting men on the desert dream of splashing fountains and flowing wells, so dreamed I of easement from the constriction of the jacket, of cleanliness in the place of filth, of smooth velvety skin of health in place of my poor parchment-crinkled hide. But I dreamed with a difference, as you shall see.

I awoke. Oh, broad and wide awake I was, although I did not open my eyes. And please know that in all that follows I knew no surprise whatever. Everything was the natural and the expected. I was I, be sure of that. But I was not Darrell Standing. Darrell Standing had no more to do with the being I was, than did Darrell Standing's parchment-crinkled skin have aught to do with the cool, soft skin that was mine. Nor was I aware of any Darrell

Standing— as I could not well be, considering that Darrell Standing was as yet unborn and would not be born for centuries. But you shall see.

I lay with closed eyes, lazily listening. From without came the clacking of many hoofs moving orderly on stone flags. From the accompanying jingle of metal bits of man-harness and steed-harness I knew some cavalcade was passing by on the street beneath my windows. Also, I wondered idly who it was. From somewhere—and I knew where, for I knew it was from the inn yard—came the ring and stamp of hoofs and an impatient neigh that I recognized as belonging to my waiting horse.

Came steps and movements—steps openly advertised as suppressed with the intent of silence and that yet were deliberately noisy with the secret intent of rousing me if I still slept. I smiled inwardly at the rascal's trick.

"Pons," I ordered, without opening my eyes, "water, cold water, quick, a deluge. I drank overlong last night, and now my gullet scorches."

"And slept overlong today," he scolded, as he passed me the water, ready in his hand.

I sat up, opened my eyes, and carried the tankard to my lips with both my hands. And as I drank I looked at Pons.

Now note two things. I spoke in French; I was not conscious that I spoke in French. Not until afterward, back in solitary, when I remembered what I am narrating, did I know that I had spoken in French—ay, and spoken well. As for me, Darrell Standing, at present writing these lines in Murderers' Row of Folsom Prison, why, I know only high-school French sufficient to enable me to read the language. As for speaking it—impossible. I can scarcely intelligibly pronounce my way through a menu.

But to return. Pons was a little withered old man. He was born in our house—I know, for it chanced that mention was made of it this very day I am describing. Pons was all of sixty years. He was mostly toothless and, despite a pronounced limp that compelled him to go slippity-hop, he was very alert and spry in all his movements. Also, he was impudently familiar. This was because he had been in my house sixty years. He had been my father's servant before I could toddle, and after my father's death (Pons and I talked of it this day), he became my servant. The limp he had acquired on a stricken field in Italy, when the horsemen charged across. He had just dragged my father clear of the hoofs when he was lanced through the thigh, overthrown, and trampled. My father, conscious but helpless from his own wounds, witnessed it all. And so, as I say, Pons had earned such a right to impudent familiarity that at least there was no gainsaying him by my father's son.

Pons shook his head as I drained the huge draft.

"Did you hear it boil?" I laughed, as I handed back the empty tankard. "Like your father," he said hopelessly. "But your father lived to learn better, which I doubt you will do."

"He got a stomach affliction," I deviled, "so that one mouthful of spirits turned it outside in. It were wisdom not to drink when one's tank will not hold the drink."

While we talked, Pons was gathering to my bedside my clothes for the day.

"Drink on, my master," he answered. "It won't hurt you. You'll die with a sound stomach."

"You mean mine is an iron-lined stomach?" I willfully misunderstood him.

"I mean—" he began with a quick peevishness, then broke off as he realized my teasing and with a pout of his withered lips draped my new sable cloak upon a chair-back. "Eight hundred ducats," he sneered. "A thousand goats and a hundred fat oxen in a coat to keep you warm. A score of farms on my gentleman's fine back."

"And in that, a hundred fine farms, with a castle or two thrown in, to say nothing, perhaps, of a palace," I said, reaching out my hand and touching the rapier which he was just in the act of depositing on the chair.

"So your father won with his good right arm," Pons retorted. "But what your father won he held."

Here Pons paused to hold up to scorn my new scarlet satin doublet—a wondrous thing of which I had been extravagant.

"Sixty ducats for that," Pons indicted. "Your father'd have seen all the tailors and Jews of Christendom roasting in hell before he'd a-paid such a price."

And while we dressed—that is, while Pons helped me to dress— I continued to quip with him.

"It is quite clear, Pons, that you have not heard the news," I said slyly.

Whereat up pricked his ears like the old gossip he was.

"Late news?" He queried. "Mayhap from the English Court?" "Nay," I shook my head. "But news perhaps to you, but old news for all of that. Have you not heard? The philosophers of Greece were whispering it nigh two thousand years ago. It is because of that news that I put twenty fat farms on my back, live at Court, and am become a dandy. You see, Pons, the world is a most evil place, life is most sad, all men die, and, being dead . . . well, are dead. Wherefore, to escape the evil and the sadness, men in these days, like me, seek amazement, insensibility, and the madness of dalliance."

"But the news, master? What did the philosophers whisper about so long ago?"

"That God was dead, Pons," I replied solemnly. "Didn't you know that? God is dead, and I soon shall be, and I wear twenty fat farms on my back."

"God lives," Pons asserted fervently. "God lives and his kingdom is at hand. I tell you, master, it is at hand. It may be no later than tomorrow that the earth shall pass away."

"So said they in old Rome, Pons, when Nero made torches of them to light his sports."

Pons regarded me pityingly.

"Too much learning is a sickness," he complained. "I was always opposed to it. But you must have your will and drag my old body about with you—a-studying astronomy and numbers in Venice, poetry and all the Italian folderols in Florence, and astrology in Pisa, and God knows what in that madman country of Germany. Pish for the philosophers. I tell you, master, I, Pons, your servant, a poor old man who knows not a letter from a pike-staff—I tell you God lives, and the time you shall appear before him is short." He paused with sudden recollection, and added, "He is here, the priest you spoke of."

On the instant I remembered my engagement.

"Why did you not tell me before?" I demanded angrily.

"What did it matter?" Pons shrugged his shoulders. "Has he not been waiting two hours as it is?"

"Why didn't you call me?"

He regarded me with a thoughtful, censorious eye.

"And you rolling to bed and shouting like chanticleer, '*Sing cucu, sing cucu, cucu nu nu cucu, sing cucu, sing cucu, sing cucu, sing cucu.*'"

He mocked me with the senseless refrain in an ear-jangling falsetto. Without doubt, I had bawled the nonsense out on my way to bed.

"You have a good memory," I commented dryly, as I essayed a moment to drape my shoulders with the new sable cloak ere I tossed it to Pons to put aside. He shook his head sourly.

"No need of memory when you roared it over and over for the thousandth time till half the inn was a-knock at the door to spit you for the sleep killer you were. And when I had you decently in the bed, did you not call me to you and command, if the devil called, to tell him my lady slept? And did you not call me back again and, with a grip on my arm that leaves it bruised and black this day, command me, as I loved life, fat meat, and the warm fire, to call you not of the morning save for one thing?"

"Which was?" I prompted, unable for the life of me to guess what I could have said.

"Which was the heart of one, a black buzzard, you said, by name Martinelli—whoever he may be—for the heart of Martinelli smoking on a gold platter. The platter must be gold, you said; and you said I must call you by singing, '*Sing cucu, sing cucu, sing cucu.*' Whereat you began to teach me how to sing, '*Sing cucu, sing cucu, sing cucu.*'"

And when Pons had said the name, I knew it at once for the priest, Martinelli, who had been knocking his heels two mortal hours in the room without.

When Martinelli was permitted to enter and as he saluted me by title and name, I knew at once my name and all of it. I was Count Guillaume de Sainte-Maure. (You see, only could I know then, and remember afterward, what was in my conscious mind.)

The priest was Italian, dark and small, lean as with fasting or with a wasting hunger not of this world, and his hands were small and slender as a woman's. But his eyes! They were cunning and "rustless, narrow-slitted and heavy-ridded, at one and the same time as sharp as a ferret's and as indolent as a basking lizard's.

"There has been much delay, Count de Sainte-Maure," he began promptly, when Pons had left the room at a glance from me. "He whom I serve grows impatient."

"Change your tune, priest," I broke in angrily. "Remember, you are not now in Rome."

"My august master—" he began.

"Rules augustly in Rome, mayhap," I again interrupted. "This is France."

Martinelli shrugged his shoulders meekly and patiently, but his eyes, gleaming like a basilisk's, gave his shoulders the lie.

"My august master has some concern with the doings of France," he said quietly. "The lady is not for you. My master has other plans...." He moistened his thin lips with his tongue. "Other plans for the lady . . . and for you."

Of course, by the lady I knew he referred to the great Duchess Philippa, widow of Geoffroy, last Duke of Aquitane. But great duchess, widow, and all, Philippa was a woman, and young, and gay, and beautiful, and, by my faith, fashioned for me.

"What are his plans?" I demanded bluntly.

"They are deep and wide, Count de Sainte-Maure—too deep

and wide for me to presume to imagine, much less know or discuss with you or any man."

"Oh, I know big things are afoot and slimy worms squirming underground," I said.

"They told me you were stubborn-necked, but I have obeyed commands."

Martinelli arose to leave, and I arose with him.

"I said it was useless," he went on. "But the last chance to change your mind was accorded you. My august master deals more fairly than fair."

"Oh well, I'll think the matter over," I said airily, as I bowed the priest to the door.

He stopped abruptly at the threshold.

"The time for thinking is past," he said. "It is decision I came for."

"I will think the matter over," I repeated, then added as afterthought, "If the lady's plans do not accord with mine, then mayhap the plans of your master may fruit as he desires. For remember, priest, he is no master of mine."

"You do not know my master," he said solemnly.

"Nor do I wish to know him," I retorted.

And I listened to the lithe light step of the little, intriguing priest go down the creaking stairs.

Did I go into the minutia of detail of all that I saw this half a day and half a night that I was Count Guillaume de Sainte-Maure, not ten books the size of this I am writing could contain the totality of the matter. Much I shall skip; in fact, I shall skip almost all; for never yet have I heard of a condemned man being reprieved in order that he might complete his memoirs—at least, not in California.

When I rode out in Paris that day, it was the Paris of centuries agone. The narrow streets were an unsanitary scandal of filth and slime—but I must skip. And skip I shall, all of the afternoon's events, all of the ride outside the walls, of the grand fete given by Hugh de Meung, of the feasting and the drinking in which I took little part. Only of the end of the adventure will I write, which begins with where I stood jesting with Philippa herself—ah, dear God, she was wondrous beautiful. A great lady—ay, but before that, and after that, and always, a woman.

We laughed and jested lightly enough, as about us jostled the merry throng; but under our jesting was the deep earnestness of man and woman well advanced across the threshold of love and yet not too sure each of the other. I shall not describe her. She was small, exquisitely slender—but there, I am describing her. In brief, she was the one woman in the world for me, and little I recked the long arm of that gray old man in Rome could reach out half across Europe between my woman and me.

And the Italian, Fortini, leaned to my shoulder and whispered:

"One who desires to speak."

"One who must wait my pleasure," I answered shortly.

"I wait no man's pleasure," was his equally short reply.

And, while my blood boiled, I remembered the priest, Martinelli, and the gray old man at Rome. The thing was clear. It was deliberate. It was the long arm. Fortini smiled lazily at me while I thus paused for the moment to debate, but in his smile was the essence of all insolence.

This, of all times, was the time I should have been cool. But the old red anger began to kindle in me. This was the work of the priest. This was the Fortini, poverished of all save lineage, reckoned the best sword come up out of Italy in half a score of years. Tonight it was Fortini. If he failed the gray old man's command, tomorrow it would be another sword, the next day another. And, perchance still failing, then might I expect the common bravo's steel in my back or the common poisoner's philter in my wine, my meat, or bread.

"I am busy," I said. "Begone."

"My business with you presses," was his reply.

Insensibly our voices had slightly risen, so that Philippa heard.

"Begone, you Italian hound," I said. "Take your howling from my door. I shall attend to you presently."

"The moon is up," he said. "The grass is dry and excellent. There is no dew. Beyond the fish pond, an arrow's flight to the left, is an open space, quiet and private."

"Presently you shall have your desire," I muttered impatiently. But still he persisted in waiting at my shoulder.

"Presently," I said. "Presently I shall attend to you."

Then spoke Philippa, in all the daring spirit and the iron of her.

"Satisfy the gentleman's desire, Sainte-Maure. Attend to him now. And good fortune go with you." She paused to beckon to her uncle, Jean de Joinville, who was passing—uncle on her mother's side, of the de Joinvilles of Anjou. "Good fortune go with you," she repeated, and then leaned to me so that she could whisper: "And my heart goes with you, Sainte-Maure. Do not be long. I shall await you in the big hall."

I was in the seventh heaven. I trod on air. It was the first frank admittance of her love. And with such benediction I was made so strong that I knew I could kill a score of Fortinis and snap my fingers at a score of gray old men in Rome.

Jean de Joinville bore Philippa away in the press, and Fortini and I settled our arrangements in a trice. We separated—he to find a friend or so, and I to find a friend or so, and all to meet at the appointed place beyond the fish pond.

First I found Robert Lanfranc and next Henry Bohemond. But before I found them, I encountered a windlestraw which showed which way blew the wind and gave promise of a very gale. I knew the windlestraw, Guy de Villehardouin, a raw young provincial, come up the first time to Court, but a fiery little cockerel for all of that. He was red-haired. His blue eyes, small and pinched close together, were likewise red, at least in the whites of them; and his skin, of the sort that goes with such types, was red and freckled. He had quite a parboiled appearance.

As I passed him, by a sudden movement he jostled me. Oh, of course, the thing was deliberate. And he flamed at me while his hand dropped to his rapier.

"Faith," thought I, "the gray old man has many and strange

tools," while to the cockerel I bowed and murmured, "Your pardon for my clumsiness. The fault was mine. Your pardon, Villehardouin."

But he was not to be appeased thus easily. And while he fumed and strutted, I glimpsed Robert Lanfranc, beckoned him to us, and explained the happening.

"Sainte-Maure has accorded you satisfaction," was his judgment. "He has prayed your pardon."

"In truth, yes," I interrupted in my suavest tones. "And I pray your pardon again, Villehardouin, for my very great clumsiness. I pray your pardon a thousand times. The fault was mine, though unintentioned. In my haste to an engagement I was clumsy, most woeful clumsy, but without intention."

What could the dolt do but grudgingly accept the amends I so freely proffered him? Yet I knew, as Lanfranc and I hastened on, that ere many days, or hours, the flame-headed youth would see to it that we measured steel together on the grass.

I explained no more to Lanfranc than my need of him, and he was little interested to pry deeper into the matter. He was himself a lively youngster of no more than twenty, but he had been trained to arms, had fought in Spain, and had an honorable record on the grass. Merely his black eyes flashed when he learned what was toward, and such was his eagerness that it was he who gathered Henry Bohemond into our number.

When the three of us arrived in the open space beyond the fish pond, Fortini and two friends were already waiting us. One was Felix Pasquini, nephew to the Cardinal of that name, and as close in his uncle's confidence as was his uncle close in the confidence of the gray old man. The other was Raoul de Goncourt, whose presence surprised me, he being too good and noble a man for the company he kept.

We saluted properly, and properly went about the business. It was nothing new to any of us. The footing was good, as promised. There was no dew. The moon shone fair, and Fortini's blade and mine were out and at earnest play.

This I knew: good swordsman as they reckoned me in France, Fortini was a better. This, too, I knew: that I carried my lady's heart with me this night, and that this night, because of me, there would be one Italian less in the world. I say I knew it. In my mind the issue could not be in doubt. And as our rapiers played I pondered the manner I should kill him. I was not minded for a long contest. Quick and brilliant had always been my way. And further, what of my past gay months of carousel and of singing "*Sing cucu, sing cucu sing cucu,*" at ungodly hours, I knew I was not conditioned for a long contest. Quick and brilliant, was my decision.

But quick and brilliant was a difficult matter with so consummate a swordsman as Fortini opposed to me. Besides, as luck would have it, Fortini, always the cold one, always the tireless-wristed, always sure and long, as report had it, in going about such tipsiness, on this night elected too the quick and brilliant.

It was nervous, tingling work, for as surely as I sensed his intention of briefness, just as surely had he sensed mine. I doubt that I could have done the trick had it been broad day instead of moonlight. The dim light aided me. Also was I aided by divining, the moment in advance, what he had in mind. It was the time attack, a common but perilous trick that every novice knows, that has laid on his back many a good man who attempted it, and that is so fraught with danger to the perpetrator that swordsmen are not enamored of it.

We had been at work barely a minute when I knew under all his darting, flashing show of offense, that Fortini meditated this very time attack. He desired of me a thrust and lunge, not that he might parry it, but that he might time it and deflect it by the customary slight turn of the wrist, his rappier-point directed to meet me as my body followed in the lunge. A ticklish thing, ay, a ticklish thing in the best of light. Did he deflect a fraction of a second too early, I should be warned and saved. Did he deflect a fraction of a second too late, my thrust would go home to him. "*Quick and brilliant, is it?*" Was my thought. "*Very well, my Italian friend, quick and brilliant shall it be, and especially shall it be quick.*"

In a way, it was time attack against time attack, but I would fool him on the time by being over-quick. And I was quick. As I said, we had been at work scarcely a minute when it happened. Quick? That thrust and lunge of mine were one. A snap of action it was, an explosion, an instantaneousness. I swear my thrust and lunge were a fraction of a second quicker than any man is supposed to thrust and lunge. I won the fraction of a second. By that fraction of a second too late Fortini attempted to deflect my blade and impale me on his. But it was his blade that was deflected. It flashed past my breast, and I was in—inside his weapon, which extended full length in the empty air behind me— and my blade was inside of him, and through him, heart-high, from right side of him to left side of him and outside of him beyond.

It is a strange thing to do, to spit a live man on a length of steel. I sit here in my cell and cease from writing a space, while I consider the matter. And I have considered it often, that moonlight night in France of long ago, when I taught the Italian hound quick and brilliant. It was so easy a thing, that perforation of a torso. One would have expected more resistance. There would have been resistance had my rapier point touched bone. As it was, it encountered only the softness of flesh Still it perforated so easily. I have the sensation of it now, in my hand, my brain, as I write. A woman's hatpin could go through a plum pudding not more easily than did my blade go through the Italian. Oh, there was nothing amazing about it at the time to Guillaume de Sainte-Maure, but amazing it is to me, Darrell Standing, as I recollect and ponder it across the centuries. It is easy, most easy, to kill a strong, live, breathing man with so crude a weapon as a piece of steel. Why, men are like softshell crabs, so tender, frail, and vulnerable are they.

But to return to the moonlight on the grass. My thrust made home, there was a perceptible pause. Not at once did Fortini fall. Not at once did I withdraw the blade. For a full second we stood in pause—I, with legs spread, and arched and tense, body thrown forward, right arm horizontal and straight out; Fortini, his blade beyond me so far that hilt and hand just rested lightly against my left breast, his body rigid, his eyes open and shining.

So statuesque were we for that second that I swear those about us were not immediately aware of what had happened. Then Fortini gasped and coughed slightly. The rigidity of his pose slackened. The hilt and hand against my breast wavered, then the arm dropped to his side till the rapier point rested on the lawn. By this time Pasquini and de Goncourt had sprung to him, and he was sinking into their arms. In faith, it was harder for me to withdraw the steel than to drive it in. His flesh clung about it as if jealous to let it depart. Oh, believe me, it required a distinct physical effort to get clear of what I had done.

But the pang of the withdrawal must have stung him back to life and purpose, for he shook off his friends, straightened himself, and lifted his rapier into position. I too took position, marveling that it was possible I had spitted him heart-high and yet missed any vital spot. Then, and before his friends could catch him, his legs crumpled under him and he went heavily to grass. They laid him on his back, but he was already dead, his face ghastly still under the moon, his right hand still a-clutch of the rapier.

Yes; it is indeed a marvelous easy thing to kill a man.

We saluted his friends and were about to depart, when Felix Pasquini detained me.

"Pardon me," I said. "Let it be tomorrow."

"We have but to move a step aside," he urged, "where the grass is still dry."

"Let me then wet it for you, Sainte-Maure," Lanfranc asked of me, eager himself to do for an Italian.

I shook my head.

"Pasquini is mine," I answered. "He shall be first tomorrow."

"Are there others?" Lanfranc demanded.

"Ask de Goncourt," I grinned. "I imagine he is already laying claim to the honor of being the third."

At this, de Goncourt showed distressed acquiescence. Lanfranc looked inquiry at him, and de Goncourt nodded.

"And after him I doubt not comes the cockerel," I went on.

And even as I spoke the red-haired Guy de Villehardouin, alone, strode to us across the moonlit grass.

"At least I shall have him," Lanfranc cried, his voice almost wheedling, so great was his desire.

"Ask him," I laughed, then turned to Pasquini. "Tomorrow," I said. "Do you name time and place, and I shall be there."

"The grass is most excellent," he teased, "the place is most excellent, and I am minded that Fortini has you for company this night."

"'Twere better he were accompanied by a friend," I quipped. "And now, your pardon, for I must go."

But he blocked my path.

"Whoever it be," he said, "let it be now."

For the first time, with him, my anger began to rise.

"You serve your master well," I sneered.

"I serve but my pleasure," was his answer. "Master I have none."

"Pardon me, if I presume to tell you the truth," I said.

"Which is?" He queried softly.

"That you are a liar, Pasquini, a liar like all Italians."

He turned immediately to Lanfranc and Bohemond.

"You heard," he said. "And after that you cannot deny me him."

They hesitated and looked to me for counsel of my wishes. But Pasquini did not wait.

"And if you still have any scruples," he hurried on, "then allow me to remove them . . . thus."

And he spat in the grass at my feet. Then my anger seized me and was beyond me. The red wrath, I call it—an overwhelming, all-mastering desire to kill and destroy. I forgot that Philippa waited for me in the great hall. All I knew was my wrongs—the unpardonable interference in my affairs by the gray old man, the errand of the priest, the insolence of Fortini, the impudence of Villehardouin, and here Pasquini standing in my way and spitting in the grass. I saw red. I thought red. I looked upon all these creatures as rank and noisome growths that must be hewn out of my path, out of the world. As a netted lion may rage against the meshes, so raged I against these creatures. They were all about me. In truth, I was in the trap. The one way out was to cut them down, to crush them into the earth and stamp upon them.

"Very well," I said, calmly enough, although my passion was such that my frame shook. "You first, Pasquini. —And you next, de Goncourt? —And at the end, de Villehardouin?"

Each nodded in turn and Pasquini and I prepared to step aside.

"Since you are in haste," Henry Bohemond proposed to me, "and since there are three of them and three of us, why not settle it at the one time?"

"Yes, yes," was Lanfranc's eager cry. "Do you take de Goncourt. De Villehardouin for mine."

But I waved my good friends back.

"They are here by command," I explained. "It is I they desire so strongly that by my faith I have caught the contagion of their desire, so that now I want them and will have them for myself."

I had observed that Pasquini fretted at my delay of speechmaking, and I resolved to fret him further.

"You, Pasquini," I announced, "I shall settle with in short account. I would not that you tarried while Fortini waits your companionship. —You, Raoul de Goncourt, I shall punish as you deserve for being in such bad company. You are getting fat and wheezy. I shall take my time with you until your fat melts and your lungs pant and wheeze like leaky bellows. —You, de Villehardouin, I have not decided in what manner I shall kill."

And then I saluted Pasquini, and we were at it. Oh, I was minded to be rarely devilish this night. Quick and brilliant—that was the thing. Nor was I unmindful of that deceptive moonlight. As with Fortini, would I settle with him if he dared the time attack. If he did not, and quickly, then I would dare it.

Despite the fret I had put him in, he was cautious. Nevertheless

I compelled the play to be rapid, and in the dim light, depending less than usual on sight and more than usual on feel, our blades were in continual touch.

Barely was the first minute of play past when I did the trick. I feinted a slight slip of the foot and, in the recovery, feigned loss of touch with Pasquini's blade. He thrust tentatively, and again I feigned, this time making a needlessly wide parry. The consequent exposure of myself was the bait I had purposely dangled to draw him on. And draw him on I did. Like a flash he took advantage of what he deemed an involuntary exposure. Straight and true was his thrust, and all his will and body were heartily in the weight of the lunge he made. And all had been feigned on my part and I was ready for him. Just lightly did my steel meet his as our blades slithered. And just firmly enough and no more did my wrist twist and deflect his blade on my basket hilt. Oh, such a slight deflection, a matter of inches, just barely sufficient to send his point past me so that it pierced a fold of my satin doublet in passing. Of course, his body followed his rapier in the lunge, while, heart-high, right side, my rapier point met his body. And my outstretched arm was stiff and straight as the steel into which it elongated, and behind the arm and the steel my body was braced and solid.

Heart-high, I say, my rapier entered Pasquini's side on the right, but it did not emerge on the left, for, well nigh through him, it met a rib tofu, man-killing is butcher's work) with such a will that the forcing overbalanced him, so that he fell part backward and part sidewise to the ground. And even as he fell, and ere he struck, with jerk and wrench I cleared my weapon of him.

De Goncourt was to him, but he waved de Goncourt to attend on me. Not so swiftly as Fortini did Pasquini pass. He coughed and spat and, helped by de Villehardouin, propped his elbow under him, rested his head on hand, and coughed and spat again.

"A pleasant journey, Pasquini," I laughed to him in my red anger. "Pray hasten, for the grass where you lie is become suddenly wet and if you linger you will catch your death of cold."

When I made immediately to begin with de Goncourt, Bohemond protested that I rest a space.

"Nay," I said. "I have not properly warmed up." And to de Goncourt, "Now will we have you dance and wheeze—salute!"

De Goncourt's heart was not in the work. It was patent that he fought under the compulsion of command. His play was old-fashioned, as any middle-aged man's is apt to be, but he was not an indifferent swordsman. He was cool, determined, dogged. But he was not brilliant, and he was oppressed with foreknowledge of defeat. A score of times, by quick and brilliant, he was mine. But I refrained. I have said that I was devilish-minded. Indeed I was. I wore him down. I backed him away from the moon so that he could see little of me because I fought in my own shadow. And while I wore him down until he began to wheeze as I had predicted, Pasquini, head on hand and watching, coughed and spat out his life.

"Now, de Goncourt," I announced finally. "You see I have you quite helpless. You are mine in any of a dozen ways. Be ready, brace yourself, for this is the way I will."

And, so saying, I merely went from carte to fierce and, as he recovered wildly and parried widely, I returned to carte, took the opening, and drove home heart-high and through and through. And at sight of the conclusion, Pasquini let go his hold on life, buried his face in the grass, quivered a moment, and lay still.

"Your master will be four servants short this night," I assured de Villehardouin, in the moment just ere we engaged.

And such an engagement! The boy was ridiculous. In what bucolic school of fence he had been taught was beyond imagining. He was downright clownish. "Short work and simple," was my judgment, while his red hair seemed a-bristle with very rage and while he pressed me like a madman.

Alas! It was his clownishness that undid me. When I had played with him and laughed at him for a handful of seconds for the clumsy boor he was, he became so angered that he forgot the worse than little fence he knew. With an arm-wide sweep of his rapier, as though it bore heft and a cutting edge, he whistled it through the air and rapped it down on my crown. I was in amaze. Never had so absurd a thing happened to me. He was wide open, and I could have run him through forthright. But as I said, I was in amaze, and the next I knew was the pang of the entering steel as this clumsy provincial ran me through and charged forward, bull-like, till his hilt bruised my side and I was borne backward.

As I fell, I could see the concern on the faces of Lanfranc and Bohemond and the glut of satisfaction in the face of de Villehardouin as he pressed me.

I was falling, but I never reached the grass. Came a blur of flashing lights, a thunder in my ears, a darkness, a glimmering of dim light slowly dawning, a wrenching, racking pain beyond all describing, and then I heard the voice of one who said:

"I can't feel anything."

I knew the voice. It was Warden Atherton's. And I knew myself for Darrell Standing, just returned across the centuries to the jacket hell of San Quentin. And I knew the touch of fingertips on my neck was Warden Atherton's. And I knew the finger tips that displaced his were Doctor Jackson's. And it was Doctor Jackson's voice that said:

"You don't know how to take a man's pulse from the neck. There—right there—put your fingers where mine are. D'ye get it? Ah, I thought so. Heart weak, but steady as a chronometer."

"It's only twenty-four hours," Captain Jamie said, "and he was never in like condition before."

"Putting it on, that's what he's doing, and you can stack on that," Al Hutchins, the head trusty, interjected.

"I don't know," Captain Jamie insisted. "When a man's pulse is that low it takes an expert to find it...."

"Aw, I served my apprenticeship in the jacket," Al Hutchins sneered. "And I've made you unlace me, Captain, when you thought I was croaking, and it was all I could do to keep from snickering in your face."

"What do you think, Doc?" Warden Atherton asked.

"I tell you the heart action is splendid," was the answer. "Of course it is weak. That is only to be expected. I tell you Hutchins is right. The man is feigning."

With his thumb he turned up one of my eyelids, whereat I opened my other eye and gazed up at the group bending over me.

"What did I tell you?" Was Doctor Jackson's cry of triumph.

And then, although it seemed the effort must crack my face, I summoned all the will of me and smiled.

They held water to my lips, and I drank greedily. It must be remembered that all this while I lay helpless on my back, my arms pinioned along with my body inside the jacket. When they offered me food—dry prison bread—I shook my head. I closed my eyes in advertisement that I was tired of their presence. The pain of my partial resuscitation was unbearable. I could feel my body coming to life. Down the cords of my neck and into my patch of chest over the heart darting pains were making their way. And in my brain the memory was strong that Philippa waited me in the big hall, and I was desirous to escape away back to the half a day and half a night I had just lived in old France.

So it was, even as they stood about me, that I strove to eliminate the live portion of my body from my consciousness. I was in haste to depart, but Warden Atherton's voice held me back.

"Is there anything you want to complain about?" He asked.

Now I had but one fear: namely, that they would unlace me; so that it must be understood that my reply was not uttered in braggadocio, but was meant to forestall any possible unlacing.

"You might make the jacket a little tighter," I whispered. "It's too loose for comfort. I get lost in it. Hutchins is stupid. He is also a fool. He doesn't know the first thing about lacing the jacket. Warden, you ought to put him in charge of the loom room. He is a more profound master of inefficiency than the present incumbent, who is merely stupid without being a fool as well. Now get out, all of you, unless you can think of worse to do to me. In which case, by all means remain. I invite you heartily to remain, if you think in your feeble imaginings that you have devised fresh torture for me."

"He's a wooz, a true-blue, dyed-in-the-wool wooz," Doctor Jackson chanted, with the medico's delight in a novelty.

"Standing, you are a wonder," the warden said. "You've got an iron will, but I'll break it as sure as God made little apples."

"And you've the heart of a rabbit," I retorted. "One-tenth the jacketing I have received in San Quentin would have squeezed your rabbit heart out of your long ears."

Oh, it was a touch, that, for the warden did have unusual ears. They would have interested Lombroso, I am sure.

"As for me," I went on, "I laugh at you, and I wish no worse fate to the loom room than that you should take charge of it yourself. Why, you've got me down and worked your wickedest on me, and still I live and laugh in your face. Inefficient? You can't even kill me. Inefficient? You couldn't kill a cornered rat with a stick of dynamite—real dynamite, and not the sort you are deluded into believing I have hidden away."

"Anything more?" He demanded, when I had ceased from my diatribe.

And into my mind flashed what I had told Fortini when he pressed his insolence on me.

"Begone, you prison cur," I said. "Take your yapping from my door."

It must have been a terrible thing for a man of Warden Atherton's stripe to be thus bearded by a helpless prisoner. His face whitened with rage and his voice shook as he threatened:

"By God, Standing, I'll do for you yet."

"There is only one thing you can do," I said. "You can tighten this distressingly loose jacket. If you won't, then get out. And I don't care if you fail to come back for a week or for the whole ten days."

And what can even the warden of a great prison do in reprisal on a prisoner upon whom the ultimate reprisal has already been wreaked? It may be that Warden Atherton thought of some possible threat, for he began to speak. But my voice had strengthened with the exercise, and I began to sing, "*Sing cucu, sing cucu, sing cucu.*" And sing I did until my door clanged and the bolts and locks squeaked and grated fast.

Chapter 12

Now that I had learned the trick, the way was easy. And I knew the way was bound to become easier the more I traveled it. Once establish a line of least resistance, every succeeding journey along it will find still less resistance. And so, as you shall see, my journeys from San Quentin life into other lives were achieved almost automatically as time went by.

After Warden Atherton and his crew had left me, it was a matter of minutes to will the resuscitated portion of my body back into the little death. Death in life it was, but it was only the little death, similar to the temporary death produced by an anesthetic.

And so, from all that was sordid and vile, from brutal solitary and jacket hell, from acquainted flies and sweats of darkness and the knuckle-talk of the living dead, I was away at a bound into time and space.

Came the duration of darkness, and the slow-growing awareness of other things and of another self. First of all, in this awareness, was dust. It was in my nostrils, dry and acrid. It was on my lips. It coated my face, my hands, and especially was it noticeable on the fingertips when touched by the ball of my thumb.

Next, I was aware of ceaseless movement. All that was about me lurched and oscillated. There was jolt and jar, and I heard what I knew as a matter of course to be the grind of wheels on axles and the grate and clash of iron tires against rock and sand. And there came to me the jaded voices of men, in curse and snarl of slow-plodding, jaded animals.

I opened my eyes, which were inflamed with dust, and immediately fresh dust bit into them. On the coarse blankets on which I lay the dust was half an inch thick. Above me, through sifting dust, I saw an arched roof of lurching, swaying canvas, and myriads of dust motes descended heavily in the shafts of sunshine that entered through holes in the canvas.

I was a child, a boy of eight or nine, and I was weary, as was the woman, dusty-visaged and haggard, who sat up beside me and soothed a crying babe in her arms. She was my mother; that I knew as a matter of course, just as I knew, when I glanced along the canvas tunnel of the wagon-top, that the shoulders of the man on the driver's seat were the shoulders of my father.

When I started to crawl along the packed gear with which the wagon was laden, my mother said in a tired and querulous voice, "Can't you ever be still a minute, Jesse?"

That was my name, Jesse. I did not know my surname, though I heard my mother call my father John. I have a dim recollection of hearing, at one time or another, the other men address my father as captain. I knew that he was the leader of this company, and that his orders were obeyed by all.

I crawled out through the opening in the canvas and sat down beside my father on the seat. The air was stifling with the dust that rose from the wagons and the many hoofs of the animals. So thick was the dust that it was like mist or fog in the air, and the low sun shone through it dimly and with a bloody light.

Not alone was the light of this setting sun ominous, but everything about me seemed ominous—the landscape, my father's face, the fret of the babe in my mother's arms that she could not still, the six horses my father drove that had continually to be urged and that were without any sign of color, so heavily had the dust settled on them.

The landscape was an aching, eye-hurting desolation. Low hills stretched endlessly away on every hand. Here and there only on their slopes were occasional scrub growths of heat-parched brush. For the most part, the surface of the hills was naked-dry and composed of sand and rock. Our way followed the sandbottoms between the hills. And the sand-bottoms were bare, save for spots of scrub, with here and there short tufts of dry and withered grass. Water there was none, nor sign of water, except for washed gullies that told of ancient and torrential rains.

My father was the only one who had horses to his wagon. The wagons went in single file, and as the train wound and curved I saw that the other wagons were drawn by oxen. Three or four yoke of oxen strained and pulled weakly at each wagon and beside them, in the deep sand, walked men with ox-goads who prodded the unwilling beasts along. On a curve I counted the wagons ahead and behind. I knew that there were forty of them, including our own; for often I had counted them before. And as I counted them now, as a child will to while away tedium, they were all there, forty of them, all canvas-topped, big and massive, crudely fashioned, pitching and lurching, grinding and jarring over sand and sagebrush and rock.

To right and left of us, scattered along the train, rode a dozen or fifteen men and youths on horses. Across their pommels were long-barreled rifles. Whenever any of them drew near to our wagon, I could see that their faces, under the dust, were drawn and anxious like my father's. And my father, like them, had a long-barreled rifle close to hand as he drove.

Also, to one side, limped a score or more of footsore, yoke-galled, skeleton oxen that ever paused to nip at the occasional tufts of withered grass, and that ever were prodded on by the tired-faced youths who herded them. Sometimes, one or another of these oxen would pause and low, and such lowing seemed as ominous as all else about me.

Far, far away, I have a memory of having lived, a smaller lad, by the tree-lined banks of a stream. And as the wagon jolts along and I sway on the seat with my father, I continually return and dwell upon that pleasant water flowing between the trees. I have a sense that for an interminable period I have lived in a wagon and traveled on, ever on, with this present company.

But strongest of all upon me is what is strong upon all the company: namely, a sense of drifting to doom. Our way was like a funeral march. Never did a laugh arise. Never did I hear a happy tone of voice. Neither peace nor ease marched with us. The faces of the men and youths who outrode the train were grim, set, hopeless. And as we toiled through the lurid dust of sunset, often I scanned my father's face in vain quest of some message of cheer. I will not say that my father's face, in all its dusty haggardness, was hopeless. It was dogged and, oh, so grim and anxious, most anxious.

A thrill seemed to run along the train. My father's head went up. So did mine. And our horses raised their weary heads, scented the air with long-drawn snorts, and for the nonce pulled willingly. The horses of the outriders quickened their pace. And as for the herd of scarecrow oxen, it broke into a forthright gallop. It was almost ludicrous. The poor brutes were so clumsy in their weakness and haste. They were galloping skeletons draped in mangy hides, and they outdistanced the boys who herded them. But this was only for a time. Then they fell back to a walk, a quick, eager, shambling, sore-footed walk; and they no longer were lured aside by the dry bunch-grass.

"What is it?" My mother asked from within the wagon.

"Water," was my father's reply. "It must be Nephi."

And my mother: "Thank God! And perhaps they will sell us food."

And into Nephi, through blood-red dust, with grind and grate and jolt and jar, our great wagons rolled. A dozen scattered dwellings or shanties composed the place. The landscape was much the same as that through which we had passed. There were no trees, only scrub growths and sandy bareness. But here were signs of tilled fields, with here and there a fence. Also, there was water. Down the stream ran no current. The bed, however, was damp, with now and again a waterhole into which the loose oxen and the saddle horses stamped and plunged their muzzles to the eyes. Here too grew an occasional small willow.

"That must be Bill Black's mill they told us about," my father said, pointing out a building to my mother, whose anxiousness had drawn her to peer out over our shoulders.

An old man, with buckskin shirt and long, matted, sunburned hair, rode back to our wagon and talked with Father. The signal was given and the head wagons of the train began to deploy in a circle. The ground favored the evolution and, from long practice, it was accomplished without a hitch, so that when the forty wagons were finally halted they formed a circle. All was bustle and orderly confusion. Many women, all tired-faced and dusty like my mother, emerged from the wagons. Also poured forth a very horde of children. There must have been at least fifty children, and it seemed I knew them all of long time; and there were at least two score of women. These went about the preparations for cooking supper.

While some of the men chopped sagebrush, and we children carried it to the fires that were kindling. Other men unyoked the oxen and let them stampede for water. Next, the men, in big squads, moved the wagons snugly into place. The tongue of each wagon was on the inside of the circle and, front and rear, each wagon was in solid contact with the next wagon before and behind. The great brakes were locked fast; but, not content with this, the wheels of all the wagons were connected with chains. This was nothing new to us children. It was the trouble sign of a camp in hostile country. One wagon only was left out of the circle, so as to form a gate to the corral. Later on, as we knew, ere the camp slept, the animals would be driven inside, and the gate-wagon would be chained like the others in place. In the meanwhile, and for hours, the animals would be herded by men and boys to what scant grass they could find.

While the camp-making went on, my father, with several others of the men, including the old man with the long, sunburned hair, went away on foot in the direction of the mill. I remember that all of us, men, women, and even the children, paused to watch them depart; and it seemed their errand was of grave import.

While they were away, other men, strangers, inhabitants of desert Nephi, came into camp and stalked about. They were white men, like us, but they were hard-faced, stern-faced, somber, and they seemed angry with all our company. Bad feeling was in the air, and they said things calculated to rouse the tempers of our men. But the warning went out from the women, and was passed on everywhere to our men and youths, that there must be no words.

One of the strangers came to our fire, where my mother was alone cooking. I had just come up with an armful of sagebrush, and I stopped to listen and to stare at the intruder whom I hated because it was in the air to hate, because I knew that every last person in our company hated these strangers who were white-skinned like us and because of whom we had been compelled to make our camp in a circle.

This stranger at our fire had blue eyes, hard and cold and piercing. His hair was sandy. His face was shaven to the chin, and from under the chin, covering the neck and extending to the ears, sprouted a sandy fringe of whiskers well-streaked with gray. Mother did not greet him, nor did he greet her. He merely stood and glowered at her for some time. Then he cleared his throat and said with a sneer:

"Wisht you was back in Missouri right now, I bet."

I saw Mother tighten her lips in self-control ere she answered:

"We are from Arkansas."

"I guess you've got good reasons to deny where you come from," he next said, "you that drove the Lord's chosen people from Missouri."

Mother made no reply.

" . . . Seein'," he went on, after the pause accorded her, "as you're now comin' a-whinin' an' a-beggin' bread at our hands that you persecuted."

Whereupon, and instantly, child that I was, I knew anger, the old, red, intolerant wrath, ever unrestrainable and unsubduable.

"You lie!" I piped up. "We ain't Missourians. We ain't whinin'. An' we ain't beggars. We got the money to buy."

"Shut up, Jesse!" My mother cried, landing the back of her hand stingingly on my mouth. And then, to the stranger, "Go away and let the boy alone."

"I'll shoot you full of lead, you damned Mormon!" I screamed and sobbed at him, too quick for my mother this time and dancing away around the fire from the backsweep of her hand.

As for the man himself, my conduct had not disturbed him in the slightest. I was prepared for I knew not what violent visitation from this terrible stranger, and I watched him warily while he considered me with the utmost gravity.

At last he spoke, and he spoke solemnly, with solemn shaking of the head, as if delivering a judgment

"Like fathers, like sons," he said. "The young generation is as bad as the older. The whole breed is unregenerate and damned. There is no saving it, the young or the old. There is no atonement Not even the blood of Christ can wipe out its iniquities."

"Damned Mormon!" Was all I could sob at him. "Damned Mormon! Damned Mormon! Damned Mormon!"

And I continued to damn him and to dance around the fire before my mother's avenging hand, until he strode away.

When my father and the men who had accompanied him returned, camp-work ceased, while all crowded anxiously about him. He shook his head.

"They will not sell?" Some woman demanded.

Again he shook his head.

A man spoke up, a blue-eyed, blond-whiskered giant of thirty, who abruptly pressed his way into the center of the crowd.

"They say they have flour and provisions for three years, Captain," he said. "They have always sold to the immigration before. And now they won't sell. And it ain't our quarrel. Their quarrel's with the government, an' they're takin' it out on us. It ain't right, Captain. It ain't right, I say, us with our women an' children, an' California months away, winter comin' on, an' nothin' but desert in between. We ain't got the grub to face the desert."

He broke off for a moment to address the whole crowd.

"Why, you-all don't know what desert is. This around here ain't desert. I tell you it's paradise, and heavenly pasture, an' flowin' with milk an' honey alongside what we're goin' to face.

"I tell you, Captain, we got to get flour first. If they won't sell it, then we must just up an' take it"

Many of the men and women began crying out in approval, but my father hushed them by holding up his hand.

"I agree with everything you say, Hamilton," he began.

But the cries now drowned his voice, and he again held up his hand.

"Except one thing you forgot to take into account, Hamilton— a thing that you and all of us must take into account. Brigham Young has declared martial law, and Brigham Young has an army. We could wipe out Nephi in the shake of a lamb's tail and take all the provisions we can carry. But we wouldn't carry them very far. Brigham's Saints would be down upon us and we would be wiped out in another shake of a lamb's tail. You know it. I know it. We all know it."

His words carried conviction to listeners already convinced. What he had told them was old news. They had merely forgotten it in a flurry of excitement and desperate need.

"Nobody will fight quicker for what is right than I will," Father continued. "But it just happens we can't afford to fight now. If ever a ruction starts we haven't a chance. And we've all got our women and children to recollect. We've got to be peaceable at any price, and put up with whatever dirt is heaped on us."

"But what will we do with the desert coming?" Cried a woman who nursed a babe at her breast.

"There's several settlements before we come to the desert," Father answered. "Fillmore's sixty miles south. Then comes Corn Creek. And Beaver's another fifty miles. Next is Parowan. Then it's twenty miles to Cedar City The farther we get away from Salt Lake the more likely they'll sell us provisions."

"And if they won't?" The same woman persisted.

"Then we're quit of them," said my father. "Cedar City is the last settlement. We'll have to go on, that's all, and thank our stars we are quit of them. Two days' journey beyond is good pasture and water. They call it Mountain Meadows. Nobody lives there, and that's the place we'll rest our cattle and feed them up before we tackle the desert. Maybe we can shoot some meat. And if the worst comes to the worst, we'll keep going as long as we can, then abandon the wagons, pack what we can on our animals, and make the last stages on foot We can eat our cattle as we go long. It would be better to arrive in California without a rag to our backs than to leave our bones here; and leave them we will if we start a ruction."

With final reiterated warnings against violence of speech or act, the impromptu meeting broke up. I was slow in falling asleep that night. My rage against the Mormon had left my brain in such a tingle that I was still awake when my father crawled into the wagon after a last round of the nightwatch. They thought I slept, but I heard Mother ask him if he thought that the Mormons would let us depart peacefully from their land. His face was turned aside from her as he busied himself with pulling off a boot, while he answered her with hearty confidence that he was sure the Mormons would let us go if none of our own company started trouble.

But I saw his face at that moment in the light of a small tallow dip, and in it was none of the confidence that was in his voice. So it was that I fell asleep, oppressed by the dire fate that seemed to overhang us, and pondering upon Brigham Young, who bulked in my child imagination as a fearful, malignant being, a very devil with horns and tail and all.

And I awoke to the old pain of the jacket in solitary. About me were the customary four: Warden Atherton, Captain Jamie, Doctor Jackson, and Al Hutchins. I cracked my face with my willed smile, and struggled not to lose control under the exquisite torment of returning circulation. I drank the water they held to me, waved aside the proffered bread, and refused to speak. I closed my eyes and strove to win back to the chain-locked wagon-circle at Nephi. But so long as my visitors stood about me and talked I could not escape.

One snatch of conversation I could not tear myself away from hearing.

"Just as yesterday," Doctor Jackson said. "No change one way or the other."

"Then he can go on standing it?" Warden Atherton queried.

"Without a quiver. The next twenty-four hours as easy as the last. He's a wooz, I tell you, a perfect wooz. If I didn't know it was impossible, I'd say he was doped."

"I know his dope," said the warden. "It's that cursed will of his. I'd bet, if he made up his mind, that he could walk barefoot across red-hot stones like those Kanaka priests from the South Seas."

Now perhaps it was the word "priests" that I carried away with me through the darkness of another flight in time. Perhaps it was the cue. More probably it was a mere coincidence. At any rate I awoke lying upon a rough rocky floor, and found myself on my back, my arms crossed in such fashion that each elbow rested in the palm of the opposite hand. As I lay there, eyes closed, half-awake, I rubbed my elbows with my palms and found that I was rubbing prodigious callouses. There was no surprise in this. I accepted the callouses as of long time and a matter of course.

I opened my eyes. My shelter was a small cave, no more than three feet in height and a dozen in length. It was very hot in the cave. Perspiration noduled the entire surface of my body. Now and again several nodules coalesced and formed tiny rivulets. I wore no clothing save a filthy rag about the middle. My skin was burned to a mahogany brown. I was very thin, and I contemplated my thinness with a strange sort of pride, as if it were an achievement to be so thin. Especially was I enamored of my painfully prominent ribs. The very sight of the hollows between them gave me a sense of solemn elation, or rather, to use a better word, of sanctification.

My knees were calloused like my elbows. I was very dirty. My beard, evidently once blond, but now a dirt-stained and streaky brown, swept my midriff in a tangled mass. My long hair, similarly stained and tangled, was all about my shoulders, while wisps of it continually strayed in the way of my vision so that sometimes I was compelled to brush it aside with my hands. For the most part, however, I contented myself with peering through it like a wild animal from a thicket.

Just at the tunnel-like mouth of my dim cave the day reared itself in a wall of blinding sunshine. After a time I crawled to the entrance and, for the sake of greater discomfort, lay down in the burning sunshine on a narrow ledge of rock. It positively baked me, that terrible sun, and the more it hurt me the more I delighted in it, or in myself rather, in that I was thus the master of my flesh and superior to its claims and remonstrances. When l found under me a particularly sharp, but not too sharp, rock projection, I ground my body upon the point of it, roweled flesh in a very ecstasy of mastery and of purification.

It was a stagnant day of heat. Not a breath of air moved over the river valley on which I sometimes gazed. Hundreds of feet beneath me the wide river ran sluggishly. The farther shore was flat and sandy and stretched away to the horizon. Above the water were scattered clumps of palm trees.

On my side, eaten into a curve by the river, were lofty, crumbling cliffs. Farther along the curve, in plain view from my eyrie, carved out of the living rock, were four colossal figures. It was the stature of a man to their ankle joints. The four colossi sat, with hands resting on knees, with arms crumbled quite away, and gazed out upon the river. At least, three of them so gazed. Of the fourth, all that remained was the lower limbs to the knees and the huge hands resting on the knees. At the feet of this one, ridiculously small, crouched a sphinx; yet this sphinx was taller than I.

I looked upon these carven images with contempt, and spat as I looked. I knew not what they were, whether forgotten gods or unremembered kings. But to me they were representative of the vanity and futility of earth men and earth aspirations.

And over all this curve of river and sweep of water and wide sands beyond, arched a sky of aching brass unflecked by the tiniest cloud.

The hours passed while I roasted in the sun. Often, for quite decent intervals, I forgot my heat and pain in dreams and visions and in memories. All this, I knew—crumbling colossi and river and sand and sun and brazen sky—was to pass away in the twinkling of an eye. At any moment the trumps of the arch angels might sound, the stars fall out of the sky, the heavens roll up as a scroll, and the Lord God of all come with his hosts for the final Judgment.

Ah, I knew it so profoundly that I was ready for such sublime event. That was why I was here in rags and filth and wretchedness. I was meek and lowly, and I despised the frail needs and passions of the flesh. And I thought with contempt, and with a certain satisfaction, of the far cities of the plain I had known, all unheeding, in their pomp and lust, of the last day so near at hand. Well, they would see soon enough but too late for them. And I should see. But I was ready. And to their cries and lamentations would I arise, reborn and glorious, and take my well-earned and rightful place in the City of God.

At times, between dreams and visions in which I was verily and before my time in the City of God, I conned over in my mind old discussions and controversies. Yes, Novatus was right in his contention that penitent apostates should never again be received into the churches. Also, there was no doubt that Sabellianism was conceived of the devil. So was Constantine, the archfiend, the devil's right hand.

Continually I returned to contemplation of the nature of the unity of God, and went over and over the contentions of Noetus, the Syrian. Better, however, did I like the contentions of my beloved teacher, Arius. Truly, if human reason could determine anything at all, there must have been a time, in the very nature of sonship, when the Son did not exist. In the nature of sonship there must have been a time when the Son commenced to exist. A father must be older than his son. To hold otherwise were a blasphemy and a belittlement of God.

And I remembered back to my young days when I had sat at the feet of Arius, who had been a presbyter of the city of Alexandria, and who had been robbed of the bishopric by the blasphemous and heretical Alexander. Alexander the Sabellianite, that is what he was, and his feet had fast hold of hell.

Yes, I had been to the Council of Nicea, and seen it avoid the issue. And I remembered when the Emperor Constantine had banished Arius for his uprightness. And I remembered when Constantine repented for reasons of state and policy and commanded Alexander—the other Alexander, thrice cursed, Bishop of Constantinople—to receive Arius into communion on the morrow. And that very night did not Arius die on the street? They said it was a violent sickness visited upon him in answer to Alexander's prayer to God. But I said, and so said all we Arians, that the violent sickness was due to a poison, and that the poison was due to Alexander himself, Bishop of Constantinople and devil's poisoner.

And here I ground my body back and forth on the sharp stones, and muttered aloud, drunken with conviction:

"Let the Jews and Pagans mock. Let them triumph, for their time is short. And for them there will be no time after time."

I talked to myself aloud a great deal on that rocky shelf overlooking the river. I was feverish, and on occasion I drank sparingly of water from a stinking goatskin. This goatskin I kept hanging in the sun that the stench of the skin might increase and that there might be no refreshment of coolness in the water. Food there was, lying in the dirt on my cave floor—a few roots and a chunk of moldy barley cake; and hungry I was, although I did not eat.

All I did that blessed, livelong day was to sweat and swelter in the sun, mortify my lean flesh upon the rock, gaze out on the desolation, resurrect old memories, dream dreams, and mutter my convictions aloud.

And when the sun set, in the swift twilight I took a last look at the world so soon to pass. About the feet of the colossi I could make out the creeping forms of beasts that laired in the once-proud works of men. And to the snarls of the beasts I crawled into my hole and, muttering and dozing, visioning fevered fancies and praying that the last day come quickly, I ebbed down into the darkness of sleep.

Consciousness came back to me in solitary, with the quartet of torturers about me.

"Blasphemous and heretical warden of San Quentin whose feet have fast hold of hell," I gibed, after I had drunk deep of the water they held to my lips. "Let the jailers and the trusties triumph. Their time is short, and for them there is no time after time."

"He's out of his head," Warden Atherton affirmed.

"He's putting it over on you," was Doctor Jackson's surer judgment.

"But he refuses food," Captain Jamie protested.

"Huh, he could fast forty days and not hurt himself," the doctor answered.

"And I have," I said, "and forty nights as well. Do me the favor to tighten the jacket and then get out of here."

The head trusty tried to insert his forefinger inside the lacing.

"You couldn't get a quarter of an inch of slack with block and tackle," he assured them.

"Have you any complaint to make, Standing?" The warden asked.

"Yes," was my reply. "On two counts."

"What are they?"

"First," I said, "the jacket is abominably loose. Hutchins is an ass. He could get a foot of slack if he wanted."

"What is the other count?" Warden Atherton asked.

"That you are conceived of the devil, Warden."

Captain Jamie and Doctor Jackson tittered, and the warden, with a snort, led the way out of my cell.

Left alone, I strove to go into the dark and gain back to the wagon circle at Nephi. I was interested to know the outcome of that doomed drifting of our forty great wagons across a desolate and hostile land, and I was not at all interested in what came of the mangy hermit with his rock-roweled ribs and stinking waterskin. And I gained back, neither to Nephi nor the Nile, but to—

But here I must pause the narrative, my reader, in order to explain a few things and make the whole matter easier to your comprehension. This is necessary, because my time is short in which to complete my jacket-memoirs. In a little while, in a very little while, they are going to take me out and hang me. Did I have the full time of a thousand lifetimes, I could not complete the last details of my jacket experiences. Wherefore, I must briefer the narrative.

First of all, Bergson is right. Life cannot be explained in intellectual terms. As Confucius said long ago: "When we are so ignorant of life, can we know death?" And ignorant of life we truly are when we cannot explain it in terms of the understanding. We know life only phenomenally, as a savage may know a dynamo; but we know nothing of life noumenally, nothing of the nature of the intrinsic stuff of life.

Secondly, Marinetti is wrong when he claims that matter is the only mystery and the only reality. I say, and as you, my reader, realize, I speak with authority—I say that matter is the only illusion. Compte called the world, which is tantamount to matter, the great fetish, and I agree with Compte.

It is life that is the reality and the mystery. Life is vastly different from mere chemic matter fluxing in high modes of motion. Life persists. Life is the thread of fire that persists through all the modes of matter. I know. I am life. I have lived ten thousand generations. I have lived millions of years. I have possessed many bodies. I, the possessor of these many bodies, have persisted. I am life. I am the unquenched spark ever flashing and astonishing the face of time, ever working my will and wreaking my passion on the cloddy aggregates of matter, called bodies, which I have transiently inhabited.

For look you. This finger of mine, so quick with sensation, so subtle to feel, so delicate in its multifarious dexterities, so firm and strong to crook and bend or stiffen by means of cunning leverages—this finger is not I. Cut it off. I live. The body is mutilated. I am not mutilated. The spirit that is I, is whole.

Very well. Cut off all my fingers. I am I. The spirit is entire. Cut off both hands. Cut off both arms at the shoulder sockets.

Cut off both legs at the hip sockets. And I, the unconquerable and indestructible I, survive. Am I any the less for these mutilations, for these subtractions of the flesh? Certainly not. Clip my hair, Shave from me with sharp razors my lips, my nose, my ears—ay, and tear out the eyes of me by the roots; and there, mewed in that featureless skull that is attached to a hacked and mangled torso, there in that cell of the chemic flesh, will still be I, unmutilated, undiminished.

Oh, the heart still beats. Very well. Cut out the heart or, better, fling the flesh-remnant into a machine of a thousand blades and make mincemeat of it—and I, I, don't you understand, all the spirit and the mystery and the vital fire and life of me, am off and away. I have not perished. Only the body has perished, and the body is not I.

I believe Colonel de Rochas was correct when he asserted that under the compulsion of his will he sent the girl Josephine, while she was in hypnotic trance, back through the eighteen years she had lived, back through the silence and the dark ere she had been born, back to the light of a previous living when she was a bed-ridden old man, the ex-artilleryman, Jean-Claude Bourdon. And I believe that Colonel de Rochas did truly hypnotize this resurrected shade of the old man and, by compulsion of will, send him back through the seventy years of his life, back into the dark and through the dark into the light of day when he had been the wicked old woman, Philomene Carteron.

Already, have I not shown you, my reader, that in previous times, inhabiting various cloddy aggregates of matter, I have been Count Guillaume de Sainte-Maure, a mangy and nameless hermit of Egypt, and the boy Jesse, whose father was captain of forty wagons in the great westward emigration. And, also, am I not now, as I write these lines, Darrell Standing, under sentence of death in Folsom Prison and one-time professor of agronomy in the College of Agriculture of the University of California?

Matter is the great illusion. That is, matter manifests itself in form, and form is apparitional. Where, now, are the crumbling rock-cliffs of old Egypt where once I laired me like a wild beast while I dreamed of the City of God? Where, now, is the body of Guillaume de Sainte-Maure that was thrust through on the moon-lit grass so long ago by the flame-headed Guy de Villehardouin? Where now are the forty great wagons in the circle at Nephi, and all the men and women and children and lean cattle that sheltered inside that circle? All such things no longer are, for they were forms, manifestations of fluxing matter ere they melted into the flux again. They have passed and are not

And now my argument becomes plain. The spirit is the reality that endures. I am spirit, and I endure. I, Darrell Standing, the tenant of many fleshly tenements, shall write a few more lines of these memoirs and then pass on my way. The form of me that is my body will fall apart when it has been sufficiently hanged by the neck, and of it naught will remain in all the world of matter. In the world of spirit the memory of it will remain. Matter has no memory, because its forms are evanescent, and what is engraved on its forms perishes with the forms.

One word more, ere I return to my narrative. In all my journeys through the dark into other lives that have been mine, I have never been able to guide any journey to a particular destination. Thus, many new experiences of old lives were mine before ever I chanced to return to the boy, Jesse, at Nephi. Possibly, all told, I have lived over Jesse's experiences a score of time, sometimes taking up his career when he was quite small in the Arkansas settlements, and at least a dozen times carrying on past the point where I left him at Nephi. It were a waste of time to detail the whole of it; and so, without prejudice to the verity of my account, I shall skip much that is vague and tortuous and repetitional, and give the facts as I have assembled them out of the various times, in whole and part, as I relived them.

Chapter 13

Long before daylight the camp at Nephi was astir. The cattle were driven out to water and pasture. While the men unchained the wheels and drew the wagons apart and clear for yoking in, the women cooked forty breakfasts over forty fires. The children, in the chill of dawn, clustered about the fires, sharing places, here and there, with the last relief of the night watch waiting sleepily for coffee.

It requires time to get a large train such as ours under way, for its speed is the speed of the slowest. So the sun was an hour high and the day was already uncomfortably hot when we rolled out of Nephi and on into the sandy barrens. No inhabitant of the place saw us off. All chose to remain indoors, thus making our departure as ominous as they had made our arrival the night before.

Again it was long hours of parching heat and biting dust, sagebrush and sand, and a land accursed. No dwellings of men, neither cattle nor fences, nor any sign of human kind, did we encounter all that day; and at night we made our wagon-circle beside an empty stream, in the damp sand of which we dug many holes that filled slowly with water seepage.

Our subsequent journey is always a broken experience to me. We made camp so many times, always with the wagons drawn in circle, that to my child mind a weary long time passed after Nephi. But always, strong upon all of us, was that sense of drifting to an impending and certain doom.

We averaged about fifteen miles a day. I know, for my father had said it was sixty miles to Fillmore, the next Mormon settlement, and we made three camps on the way. This meant four days of travel. From Nephi to the last camp of which I have any memory, we must have taken two weeks or a little less.

At Fillmore, the inhabitants were hostile, as all had been since Salt Lake. They laughed at us when we tried to buy food, and were not above taunting us with being Missourians.

When we entered the place, hitched before the largest house of the dozen houses that composed the settlement were two saddle horses, dusty, streaked with sweat, and drooping. The old man I have mentioned, the one with long sunburned hair and buckskin shirt and who seemed a sort of aide or lieutenant to Father, rode close to our wagon and indicated the jaded saddle animals with a cock of his head.

"Not sparin' horseflesh, Captain," he muttered in a low voice. "An' what in the name of Sam Hill are they hard-riding for if it ain't for us?"

But my father had already noted the condition of the two animals, and my eager eyes had seen him. And I had seen his eyes flash, his lips tighten, and haggard lines form for a moment on his dusty face. That was all. But I put two and two together, and knew that the two tired saddle horses were just one more added touch of ominousness to the situation.

"I guess they're keeping an eye on us, Laban," was my father's sole comment.

It was at Fillmore that I saw a man that I was to see again. He was a tall, broad-shouldered man, well on in middle age, with all the evidence of good health and immense strength—strength not alone of body but of will. Unlike most men I was accustomed to about me, he was smooth-shaven. Several days' growth of beard showed that he was already well grayed. His mouth was unusually wide, with thin lips tightly compressed as if he had lost many of his front teeth. His nose was large, square, and thick. So was his face square, wide between the cheekbones, underhung with massive jaws, and topped with a broad, intelligent forehead. And the eyes, rather small, a little more than the width of an eye apart, were the bluest blue I had ever seen.

It was at the flour mill at Fillmore that I first saw this man. Father, with several of our company, had gone there to try to buy flour and I, disobeying my mother in my curiosity to see more of our enemies, had tagged along unperceived. This man was one of four or five who stood in a group with the miller during the interview.

"You seen that smooth-faced old cuss?" Laban said to Father, after we had got outside and were returning to camp.

Father nodded.

"Well, that's Lee," Laban continued. "I seen'm in Salt Lake. He's a regular son-of-a-gun. Got nineteen wives and fifty children, they all say. An' he's rank crazy on religion. Now what's he followin' us up for through this Godforsaken country?"

Our weary, doomed drifting went on. The little settlements, wherever water and soil permitted, were from twenty to fifty miles apart. Between stretched the barrenness of sand and alkali and drought. And at every settlement our peaceful attempts to buy food were vain. They denied us harshly, and wanted to know who of us had sold them food when we drove them from Missouri. It was useless on our part to tell them we were from Arkansas. From Arkansas we truly were, but they insisted on our being Missourians.

At Beaver, five days' journey south from Fillmore, we saw Lee again. And again we saw hard-ridden horses tethered before the houses. But we did not see Lee at Parowan.

Cedar City was the last settlement. Laban, who had ridden on ahead, came back and reported to Father. His first news was significant.

"I seen that Lee skeedaddling out as I rid in, Captain. An' there's more menfolk an' horses in Cedar City than the size of the place'd warrant."

But we had no trouble at the settlement. Beyond refusing to sell us food, they left us to ourselves. The women and children stayed in the houses and, though some of the men appeared in sight, they did not, as on former occasions, enter our camp and taunt us.

It was at Cedar City that the Wainwright baby died. I remember Mrs. Wainwright weeping and pleading with Laban to try to get some cow's milk.

"It may save the baby's life," she said. "And they've got cow's milk. I saw fresh cows with my own eyes. Go on, please, Laban. It won't hurt you to try. They can only refuse. But they won't. Tell them it's for a baby, a wee little baby. Mormon women have mother's hearts. They couldn't refuse a cup of milk for a wee little baby."

And Laban tried. But as he told father afterward, he did not get to see any Mormon women. He saw only the Mormen men, who turned him away.

This was the last Mormon outpost. Beyond lay the waste desert with, on the other side of it, the dream-land, ay, the myth land, of California. As our wagons rolled out of the place in the early morning, I, sitting beside my father on the driver's seat, saw Laban give expression to his feelings. We had gone perhaps half a mile, and were topping a low rise that would sink Cedar City from view, when Laban turned his horse around, halted it, and stood up in the stirrups. Where he had halted was a new-made grave, and I knew it for the Wainwright baby's—not the first of our graves since we had crossed the Wasatch Mountains.

He was a weird figure of a man. Aged and lean, long-faced, hollow-checked, with matted, sunburned hair that fell below the shoulders of his buckskin shirt, his face was distorted with hatred and helpless rage. Holding his long rifle in his bridle hand, he shook his free fist at Cedar City.

"God's curse on all of you!" He cried out. "On your children, and on your babes unborn. May drought destroy your crops. May you eat sand seasoned with the venom of rattlesnakes. May the sweet water of your springs turn to bitter alkali. May . . ."

Here his words became indistinct as our wagons rattled on; but his heaving shoulders and brandishing fist attested that he had only begun to lay the curse. That he expressed the general feeling in our train was evidenced by the many women who leaned from the wagons, thrusting out gaunt forearms and shaking bony, labor-malformed fists at the last of Mormondom. A man, who walked in the sand and goaded the oxen of the wagon behind ours, laughed and waved his goad. It was unusual, that laugh, for there had been no laughter in our train for many days.

"Give'm hell Laban," he encouraged. "Them's my senti-ments."

And as our train rolled on, I continued to look back at Laban, standing in his stirrups by the baby's grave. Truly, he was a weird figure with his long hair, his moccasins, and fringed leggings. So old and weather-beaten was his buckskin shirt that ragged filaments, here and there, showed where proud fringes once had been. He was a man of flying tatters. I remember, at his waist, dangled dirty tufts of hair that, far back in the journey, after a shower of rain, were wont to show glossy black. These I know were Indian scalps, and the sight of them always thrilled me.

"It will do him good," Father commended, more to himself than to me. "I've been looking for days for him to blow up."

"I wish he'd go back and take a couple of scalps," I volun-teered.

My father regarded me quizzically.

"Don't like the Mormons, eh, son?"

I shook my head and felt myself swelling with the inarticulate hate that possessed me.

"When I grow up," I said after a minute, "I'm goin' gunning for them."

"You, Jesse! " came my mother's voice from inside the wagon. "Shut your mouth instanter." And to my father: "You ought to be ashamed, letting the boy talk on like that."

Two days' journey brought us to Mountain Meadows, and here, well beyond the last settlement, for the first time we did not form the wagon circle. The wagons were roughly in a circle, but there were many gaps, and the wheels were not chained. Prepara-tions were made to stop a week. The cattle must be rested for the real desert, though this was desert enough in all seeming. The same low hills of sand were about us, but sparsely covered with scrub brush. The flat was sandy, but there was some grass—more than we had encountered in many days. Not more than a hundred feet from camp was a weak spring that barely supplied human needs. But farther along the bottom various other weak springs emerged from the hillsides, and it was at these that the cattle watered.

We made camp early that day and, because of the program to stay a week, there was a general overhauling of soiled clothes by the women, who planned to start washing on the morrow Everybody worked till nightfall. While some of the men mended harness, others repaired the frames and ironwork of the wagons. There was much heating and hammering of iron and tightening of bolts and nuts. And I remember coming upon Laban, sitting cross-legged in the shade of a wagon and sewing away till night-fall on a new pair of moccasins. He was the only man in our train who wore moccasins and buckskin, and I have an impression that he had not belonged to our company when it left Arkansas. Also, he had neither wife, nor family, nor wagon of his own. All he possessed was his horse, his rifle, the clothes he stood up in, and a couple of blankets that were hauled in the Mason wagon.

Next morning it was that our doom fell. Two days' journey beyond the last Mormon outpost, knowing that no Indians were about and apprehending nothing from the Indians on any count, for the first time we had not chained our wagons in the solid circle, placed guards on the cattle, nor set a night watch.

My awakening was like a nightmare. It came as a sudden blast of sound. I was only stupidly awake for the first moments and did nothing except to try to analyze and identify the various noises that went to compose the blast that continued without letup. I could hear near and distant explosions of rifles, shouts and curses of men, women screaming and children bawling. Then I could make out the thuds and squeals of bullets that hit wood and iron in the wheels and under-construction of the wagon. Whoever it was that was shooting, the aim was too low.

When I started to rise, my mother, evidently just in the act of dressing, pressed me down with her hand. Father, already up and about, at this stage erupted into the wagon.

"Out of it!" He shouted. "Quick! To the ground!"

He wasted no time. With a hook-like clutch that was almost a blow, so swift was it, he flung me bodily out of the rear end of the wagon. I had barely time to crawl out from under when Father, Mother, and the baby came down pell mell where I had been.

"Here, Jesse!" Father shouted to me, and I joined him in scooping out sand behind the shelter of a wagon wheel. We worked bare-handed and wildly. Mother joined in.

"Go ahead and make it deeper, Jesse," Father ordered.

He stood up and rushed away in the gray light, shouting commands as he ran. (I had learned by now my surname. I was Jesse Fancher. My father was Captain Fancher.)

"Lie down!" I could hear him. "Get behind the wagon wheels and burrow in the sand! Family men, get the women and children out of the wagons! Hold your fire! No more shooting! Hold your fire and be ready for the rush when it comes! Single men, join Laban at the right, Cochrane at the left, and me in the center! Don't stand up! Crawl for it!"

But no rush came. For a quarter of an hour the heavy and irregular firing continued. Our damage had come in the first moments of surprise when a number of the early-rising men were caught exposed in the light of the campfires they were building. The Indians—for Indians Laban declared them to be—had attacked us from the open, and were lying down and firing at us. In the growing light Father made ready for them. His position was near to where I lay in the burrow with Mother so that I heard him when he cried out:

"Now! —All together!"

From left, right, and center, our rifles loosed in a volley. I had popped my head up to see, and I could make out more than one stricken Indian. Their fire immediately ceased, and I could see them scampering back on foot across the open, dragging their dead and wounded with them.

All was work with us on the instant. While the wagons were being dragged and chained into the circle with tongues inside—I saw women and little boys and girls flinging their strength on the wheel spokes to help—we took toll of our losses. First, and gravest of all, our last animal had been run off. Next, lying about the fires they had been building, were seven of our men. Four were dead, and three were dying. Other men, wounded, were being cared for by the women. Little Rish Hardacre had been struck in the arm by a heavy ball. He was no more than six, and I remember looking on with mouth agape while his mother held him on her lap and his father set about bandaging the wound. Little Rish had stopped crying. I could see the tears on his cheeks while he stared wonderingly at a sliver of broken bone sticking out of his forearm.

Granny White was found dead in the Foxwell wagon. She was a fat and helpless old woman who never did anything but sit down all the time and smoke a pipe. She was the mother of Abby Foxwell. And Mrs. Grant had been killed. Her husband sat beside her body. He was very quiet. There were no tears in his eyes. He just sat there, his rifle across his knees, and everybody left him alone.

Under Father's directions the company was working like so many beavers. The men dug a big rifle pit in the center of the corral, forming a breastwork out of the displaced sand. Into this pit the women dragged bedding, food, and all sorts of necessaries from the wagons. All the children helped. There was no whimpering, and little or no excitement. There was work to be done, and all of us were folks born to work.

The big rifle pit was for the women and children. Under the wagons, completely around the circle, a shallow trench was dug and an earthwork thrown up. This was for the fighting men.

Laban returned from a scout. He reported that the Indians had withdrawn the matter of half a mile and were holding a powwow. Also, he had seen them carry six of their number off the field, three of which, he said, were deaders.

From time to time, during the morning of that first day, we observed clouds of dust that advertised the movements of considerable bodies of mounted men. These clouds of dust came toward us, hemming us in on all sides. But we saw no living creature. One cloud of dust only, moved away from us. It was a large cloud, and everybody said it was our cattle being driven off. And our forty great wagons that had rolled over the Rockies and half across the continent stood in a helpless circle. Without cattle, they could roll no farther.

At noon Laban came in from another scout. He had seen fresh Indians arriving from the south, showing that we were being closed in. It was at this time that we saw a dozen white men ride out on the crest of a low hill to the east and look down on us.

"That settles it," Laban said to Father. "The Indians have been put up to it."

"They're white like us," I heard Abby Foxwell complain to Mother. "Why don't they come in to us?"

"They ain't whites," I piped up, with a wary eye for the swoop of Mother's hand. "They're Mormons."

That night, after dark, three of our young men stole out of camp. I saw them go. They were Will Aden, Abel Milliken, and Timothy Grant.

"They are heading for Cedar City to get help," Father told Mother while he was snatching a hasty bite of supper.

Mother shook her head.

"There's plenty, of Mormons within calling distance of camp," she said. "If they won't help, and they haven't shown any signs, then the Cedar City ones won't either."

"But there are good Mormons and bad Mormons—" Father began.

"We haven't found any good ones so far," she shut him off.

Not until morning did I hear of the return of Abel Milliken and Timothy Grant, but I was not long in learning. The whole camp was downcast by reason of their report. The three had gone only a few miles when they were challenged by white men. As soon as Will Aden spoke up, telling that they were from the Fancher Company, going to Cedar City for help, he was shot down. Milliken and Grant escaped back with the news, and the news settled the last hope in the hearts of our company. The whites were behind the Indians, and the doom so long apprehended was upon us.

This morning of the second day, our men, going for water, were fired upon. The spring was only a hundred feet outside our circle, but the way to it was commanded by the Indians who now occupied the low hill to the east. It was close range, for the hill could not have been more than fifteen rods away. But the Indians were not good shots, evidently, for our men brought in the water without being hit.

Beyond an occasional shot into camp, the morning passed quietly. We had settled down in the rifle pit and, being used to rough living, were comfortable enough. Of course, it was bad for the families of those who had been killed, and there was the taking care of the wounded. I was forever stealing away from Mother in my insatiable curiosity to see everything that was going on, and I managed to see pretty much of everything. Inside the corral, to the south of the big rifle pit, the men dug a hole and buried the seven men and two women all together. Only Mrs. Hastings, who had lost her husband and father, made much trouble. She cried and screamed out, and it took the other women a long time to quiet her.

On the low hill to the east the Indians kept up a tremendous powwowing and yelling. But beyond an occasional harmless shot, they did nothing.

"What's the matter with the ornery cusses?" Laban impatiently wanted to know. "Can't they make up their minds what they're goin' to do, an' then do it?"

It was hot in the corral that afternoon. The sun blazed down out of a cloudless sky, and there was no wind. The men, lying with their rifles in the trench under the wagons, were partly shaded; but the big rifle pit, in which were over a hundred women and children, was exposed to the full power of the sun. Here too were the wounded men, over whom we erected awnings of blankets. It was crowded and stifling in the pit, and I was forever stealing out of it to the firing line and making a great to-do at carrying messages for Father.

Our grave mistake had been in not forming the wagon circle so as to enclose the spring. This had been due to the excitement of the first attack, when we did not know how quickly it might be followed by a second one. And now it was too late. At fifteen rods' distance from the Indian position on the hill, we did not dare unchain our wagons. Inside the corral, south of the graves, we constructed a latrine and, north of the rifle pit in the center, a couple of men were told off by Father to dig a well for water.

In the mid-afternoon of that day, which was the second day, we saw Lee again. He was on foot, crossing diagonally over the meadow to the northwest just out of rifle shot from us. Father hoisted one of Mother's sheets on a couple of ox goads lashed together. This was our white flag. But Lee took no notice of it, continuing on his way.

Laban was for trying a long shot at him, but Father stopped him, saying that it was evident the whites had not made up their minds what they were going to do with us, and that a shot at Lee might hurry them into making up their minds the wrong way.

"Here, Jesse," Father said to me, tearing a strip from the sheet and fastening it to an ox goad. "Take this and go out and try to talk to that man. Don't tell him anything about what's happened to us. Just try to get him to come in and talk with us"

As I started to obey, my chest swelling with pride in my mission, Jed Dunham cried out that he wanted to go with me. Jed was about my own age.

"Can your boy go with Jesse?" Father asked Jed's father. "Two's better'n one. They'll keep each other out of mischief."

So Jed and I, two youngsters of nine, went out under the white flag to talk with the leader of our enemies. But Lee would not talk. When he saw us coming, he started to sneak away. We never got within calling distance of him, and after a while he must have hidden in the brush; for we never laid eyes on him again, and we knew he couldn't have got clear away.

Jed and I beat up the brush for hundreds of yards all around. They hadn't told us how long we were to be gone, and since the Indians did not fire on us we kept on going. We were away over two hours, though had either of us been alone we would have been back in a quarter of the time. But Jed was bound to out-brave me, and I was equally bound to out-brave him.

Our foolishness was not without profit. We walked boldly about under our white flag, and learned how thoroughly our camp was beleaguered. To the south of our train, not more than half a mile away, we made out a large Indian camp. Beyond, on the meadow, we could see Indian boys riding herd on their horses.

Then there was the Indian position on the hill to the east. We managed to climb a low hill so as to look into this position. Jed and I spent half an hour trying to count them, and concluded, with much guessing, that there must be at least a couple of hundred. Also, we saw white men with them and doing a great deal of talking.

Northeast of our train, not more than four hundred yards from it, we discovered a large camp of whites behind a low rise of ground. And beyond we could see fifty or sixty saddle horses grazing. And a mile or so away, to the north, we saw a tiny cloud of dust approaching. Jed and I waited until we saw a single man, riding fast, gallop into the camp of the whites.

When we got back into the corral, the first thing that happened to me was a smack from Mother for having stayed away so long; but Father praised Jed and me when we gave our report.

"Watch for an attack now maybe, Captain," Aaron Cochrane said to Father. "That man the boys seen has rid in for a purpose. The whites are holding the Indians till they get orders from higher up. Maybe that man brung the orders one way or the other. They ain't sparing horseflesh, that's one thing sure."

Half an hour after our return, Laban attempted a scout under a white flag. But he had not gone twenty feet outside the circle when the Indians opened fire on him and sent him back on the run.

Just before sundown I was in the rifle pit holding the baby, while Mother was spreading the blankets for a bed. There were so many of us that we were packed and jammed. So little room was there, that many of the women the night before had sat up and slept with their heads bowed on their knees. Right alongside of me, so near that when he tossed his arms about he struck me on the shoulder, Silas Dunlap was dying. He had been shot in the head in the first attack, and all the second day was out of his head and raving and singing doggerel. One of his songs, that he sang over and over, until it made Mother frantic nervous, was:

"Said the first little devil to the second little devil, 'Give me some tobaccy from your old tobaccy box.' Said the second little devil to the first little devil, 'Stick close to your money and close to your rocks, An' you'll always have tobaccy in your old tobaccy box.'"

I was sitting directly alongside of him, holding the baby, when the attack burst on us. It was sundown, and I was staring with all my eyes at Silas Dunlap, who was just in the final act of dying. His wife Sarah had one hand resting on his forehead. Both she and her Aunt Martha were crying softly. And then it came—explosions and bullets from hundreds of rifles. Clear around from east to west by way of the north, they had strung out in half a circle and were pumping lead into our position. Everybody in the rifle pit flattened down. Lots of the younger children set up a squalling, and it kept the women busy hushing them. Some of the women screamed at first, but not many.

Thousands of shots must have rained in on us in the next few minutes. How I wanted to crawl out to the trench under the wagons where our men were keeping up a steady but irregular fire! Each was shooting on his own whenever he saw a man to pull trigger on. But Mother suspected me, for she made me crouch down and keep right on holding the baby.

I was just taking a look at Silas Dunlap—he was still quivering—when the little Castleton baby was killed. Dorothy Castleton, herself only about ten, was holding it, so that it was killed in her arms. She was not hurt at all. I heard them talking about it, and they conjectured that the bullet must have struck high up on one of the wagons and been deflected down into the rifle pit. It was just an accident, they said, and that except for such accidents we were safe where we were.

When I looked again, Silas Dunlap was dead, and I suffered distinct disappointment in being cheated out of witnessing that particular event. I had never been lucky enough to see a man actually die before my eyes.

Dorothy Castleton got hysterics over what had happened, and yelled and screamed for a long time, and she set Mrs. Hastings going again. Altogether, such a row was raised that Father sent Watt Cummings crawling back to us to find out what was the matter.

Well along into twilight the heavy firing ceased, although there were scattering shots during the night. Two of our men were wounded in this second attack, and were brought into the rifle pit. Bill Tyler was killed instantly and they buried him, Silas Dunlap, and the Castleton baby in the dark, alongside of the others.

All during the night men relieved one another at sinking the well deeper; but the only sign of water they got was damp sand. Some of the men fetched a few pails of water from the spring, but were fired upon, and they gave it up when Jeremy Hopkins had his left hand shot off at the wrist.

Next morning, the third day, it was hotter and drier than ever. We awoke thirsty, and there was no cooking. So dry were our mouths that we could not eat. I tried a piece of stale bread Mother gave me, but had to give it up. The firing rose and fell. Sometimes there were hundreds shooting into the camp. At other times came lulls in which not a shot was fired. Father was continually cautioning our men not to waste shots because we were running short of ammunition.

And all the time the men went on digging the well. It was so deep that they were hoisting the sand up in buckets. The men who hoisted were exposed, and one of them was wounded in the shoulder. He was Peter Bromley, who drove oxen for the Bloodgood wagon, and he was engaged to marry Jane Bloodgood. She jumped out of the rifle pit and ran right to him while the bullets were flying and led him back into shelter. About midday the well caved in, and there was lively work digging out the couple who were buried in the sand. Amos Wentworth did not come to for an hour. After that they timbered the well with bottom boards from the wagons and wagon tongues, and the digging went on. But all they would get, and they were twenty feet down, was damp sand. The water would not seep.

By this time the conditions in the rifle pit were terrible. The children were complaining for water, and the babies, hoarse from much crying, went on crying. Robert Carr, another wounded man, lay about ten feet from Mother and me. He was out of his head, and kept thrashing his arms about and calling for water. And some of the women were almost as bad, and kept raving against the Mormons and Indians. Some of the women prayed a great deal, and the three grown Demdike sisters with their mother sang gospel hymns. Other women got damp sand that was hoisted out of the bottom of the well, and packed it against the bare bodies of the babies to try to cool and soothe them.

The two Fairfax brothers couldn't stand it any longer and, with pails in their hands, crawled out under a wagon and made a dash for the spring. Giles never got halfway, when he went down. Roger made it there and back without being hit. He brought two pails part full, for some splashed out when he ran. Giles crawled back, and when they helped him into the rifle pit he was bleeding at the mouth and coughing.

Two part-pails of water could not go far among over a hundred of us, not counting the men. Only the babies, and the very little children, and the wounded men, got any. I did not get a sip, although Mother dipped a bit of cloth into the several spoonfuls she got for the baby and wiped my mouth out. She did not even do that for herself, for she left me the bit of damp rag to chew.

The situation grew unspeakably worse in the afternoon. The quiet sun blazed down through the clear windless air and made a furnace of our hole in the sand. And all about us were the explosions of rifles and yells of the Indians. Only once in a while did Father permit a single shot from the trench, and that only by our best marksmen, such as Laban and Timothy Grant. But a steady stream of lead poured into our position all the time. There were no more disastrous ricochets, however; and our men in the trench, no longer firing lay low and escaped damage. Only four were wounded, and only one of them very badly.

Father came in from the trench during a lull in the firing. He sat for a few minutes alongside Mother and me without speaking. He seemed to be listening to all the moaning and crying for water that was going up. Once he climbed out of the rifle pit and went over to investigate the well. He brought back only damp sand, which he plastered thick on the chest and shoulders of Robert Carr. Then he went to where Jed Dunham and his mother were, and sent for Jed's father to come in from the trench. So closely packed were we that when anybody moved about inside the rifle pit he had to crawl carefully over the bodies of those lying down.

After a time, Father came crawling back to us.

"Jesse," he asked, "are you afraid of the Indians?"

I shook my head emphatically, guessing that I was to be sent on another proud mission.

"Are you afraid of the damned Mormons?"

"Not of any damned Mormon," I answered, taking advantage of the opportunity to curse our enemies without fear of the avenging back of Mother's hand.

I noted the little smile that curled his tired lips for the moment, when he heard my reply.

"Well, then, Jesse," he said, "will you go with Jed to the spring for water?"

I was all eagerness.

"We're going to dress the two of you up as girls," he continued, "so that maybe they won't fire on you."

I insisted on going as I was, as a male human that wore pants; but I surrendered quickly enough when Father suggested that he would find some other boy to dress up and go along with Jed.

A chest was fetched in from the Chattox wagon. The Chattox girls were twins and of about a size with Jed and me. Several of the women got around to help. They were the Sunday dresses of the Chattox twins, and had come in the chest all the way from Arkansas.

In her anxiety, Mother left the baby with Sarah Dunlap, and came as far as the trench with me. There, under a wagon and behind the little breastwork of sand, Jed and I received our last instructions. Then we crawled out and stood up in the open. We were dressed precisely alike—white stockings, white dresses with big blue sashes, and white sunbonnets Jed's right and my left hand were clasped together. In each of our free hands we carried two small pails.

"Take it easy," Father cautioned as we began our advance. "Go slow. Walk like girls."

Not a shot was fired. We made the spring safely, filled our pails, and lay down and took a good drink ourselves. With a full pail in each hand we made the return trip. And still not a shot was fired.

I cannot remember how many journeys we made—fully fifteen or twenty. We walked slowly, always going out with hands clasped, always coming back slowly with four pails of water. It was astonishing how thirsty we were. We lay down several times and took long drinks.

But it was too much for our enemies. I cannot imagine that the Indians would have withheld their fire for so long, girls or no girls, had they not obeyed instructions from the whites who were with them. At any rate, Jed and I were just starting on another trip when a rifle went off from the Indian hill, and then another.

"Come back!" Mother cried out.

I looked at Jed, and found him looking at me. I knew he was stubborn and had made up his mind to be the last one in. So I started to advance, and at the same instant he started.

"You! —Jesse!" Cried my mother. And there was more than a smacking in the way she said it.

Jed offered to clasp hands, but I shook my head.

"Run for it," I said.

And while we hotfooted it across the sand, it seemed all the rifles on Indian hill were turned loose on us. I got to the spring a little ahead, so that Jed had to wait for me to fill my pails.

"Now run for it," he told me; and from the leisurely way he went about filling his own pails I knew he was determined to be in last.

So I crouched down and, while I waited, watched the puffs of dust raised by the bullets. We began the return side by side and running.

"Not so fast," I cautioned him, "or you'll spill half the water."

That stung him, and he slacked back perceptibly. Midway I stumbled and fell headlong. A bullet, striking directly in front of me, filled my eyes with sand. For the moment I thought I was shot

"Done it a-purpose," Jed sneered, as I scrambled to my feet. He had stood and waited for me.

I caught his idea. He thought I had fallen deliberately in order to spill my water and go back for more. This rivalry between us was a serious matter—so serious, indeed, that I immediately took advantage of what he had imputed and raced back to the spring. And Jed Dunham, scornful of the bullets that were puffing dust all around him, stood there upright in the open and waited for me. We came in side by side, with honors even in our boy's foolhardiness. But when we delivered the water, Jed had only one pailful. A bullet had gone through the other pail close to the bottom.

Mother took it out on me with a lecture on disobedience. She must have known, after what I had done, that Father wouldn't let her smack me; for while she was lecturing, Father winked at me across her shoulder. It was the first time he had ever winked at me.

Back in the rifle pit Jed and I were heroes. The women wept and blessed us, and kissed us and mauled us. And I confess I was proud of the demonstration, although, like Jed, I let on that I did not like all such making-over. But Jeremy Hopkins, a great bandage about the stump of his left wrist, said we were the stuff white men were made out of—men like Daniel Boone, like Kit Carson and Davy Crockett. I was prouder of that than all the rest.

The remainder of the day I seem to have been bothered principally with the pain of my right eye caused by the sand that had been kicked into it by the bullet. The eye was bloodshot, Mother said; and to me it seemed to hurt just as much whether I kept it open or closed. I tried both ways.

Things were quieter in the rifle pit, because all had had water; though strong upon us was the problem of how the next water was to be procured. Coupled with this was the known fact that our ammunition was almost exhausted. A thorough overhauling of the wagons by Father had resulted in finding five pounds of powder. A very little more was in the flasks of the men.

I remembered the sundown attack of the night before, and anticipated it this time by crawling to the trench before sunset. I crept into a place alongside of Laban. He was busy chewing tobacco, and did not notice me. For some time I watched him, fearing that when he discovered me he would order me back. He would take a long squint out between the wagon wheels, chew steadily a while, and then spit carefully into a little depression he had made in the sand.

"How's tricks?" I asked finally. It was the way he always addressed me.

"Fine," he answered. "Most remarkable fine, Jesse, now that I can chew again. My mouth was that dry that I couldn't chew from sun-up to when you brung the water."

Here, a man showed head and shoulders over the top of the little hill to the northeast occupied by the whites. Laban sighted his rifle on him for a long minute. Then he shook his head.

"Four hundred yards. Nope, I don't risk it. I might get him, and then again I mightn't, an' your dad is mighty anxious about the powder."

"What do you think our chances are?" I asked, man-fashion, for after my water exploit I was feeling very much the man.

Laban seemed to consider carefully for a space, ere he replied. "Jesse, I don't mind tellin' you we're in a damned bad hole. But we'll get out, oh, we'll get out, you can bet your bottom dollar."

"Some of us ain't going to get out," I objected.

"Who for instance?" He queried.

"Why, Bill Tyler, and Mrs. Grant, and Silas Dunlap, and all the rest."

"Aw, shucks, Jesse—they're in the ground already. Don't you know everybody has to bury their dead as they traipse along. They've ben doin' it for thousands of years, I reckon, and there's just as many alive as ever they was. You see, Jesse, birth and death go hand in hand. And they're born as fast as they die—faster, I reckon, because they've increased and multiplied. Now you, you might a-got killed this afternoon packin' water. But you're here, ain't you, a-gassin' with me an' likely to grow up an' be the father of a fine large family in Californy. They say everything grows large in Californy."

This cheerful way of looking at the matter encouraged me to dare sudden expression of a long covetousness.

"Say, Laban, supposin' you got killed here—"

"Who? —me?" He cried.

"I'm just sayin' supposin'," I explained.

"Oh, all right then. Go on. Supposin' I am killed?"

"Will you give me your scalps?"

"Your ma'll smack you if she catches you a-wearin' them," he temporized.

"I don't have to wear them when she's around. Now if you got killed, Laban, somebody'd have to get them scalps. Why not me?"

"Why not?" He repeated. "That's correct, and why not you? All right, Jesse. I like you and your pa. The minute I'm killed the scalps is yourn, and the scalpin' knife, too. And there's Timothy Grant for witness. —Did you hear, Timothy?"

Timothy said he had heard, and I lay there speechless in the stifling trench, too overcome by my greatness of good fortune to be able to utter a word of gratitude.

I was rewarded for my foresight in going to the trench. Another general attack was made at sundown, and thousands of shots were fired into us. Nobody on our side was scratched. On the other hand, although we fired barely thirty shots, I saw Laban and Timothy Grant each get an Indian. Laban told me that from the first only the Indians had done the shooting. He was certain that no white had fired a shot. All of which sorely puzzled him. The whites neither offered us aid nor attacked us, and all the while were on visiting terms with the Indians who were attacking us.

Next morning found the thirst harsh upon us. I was out at the first hint of light. There had been a heavy dew, and men, women, and children were lapping it up with their tongues from off the wagon tongues, brake blocks, and wheel tires.

There was talk that Laban had returned from a scout just before daylight; that he had crept close to the position of the whites; that they were already up; and that in the light of their campfires he had seen them praying in a large circle. Also, he reported from what few words he caught that they were praying about us and what was to be done with us.

"May God send them the light then," I heard one of the Demdike sisters say to Abby Foxwell.

"And soon," said Abby Foxwell, "for I don't know what we'll do a whole day without water, and our powder is about gone."

Nothing happened all morning. Not a shot was fired. Only the sun blazed down through the quiet air. Our thirst grew, and soon the babies were crying and the younger children whimpering and complaining. At noon, Will Hamilton took two large pails and started for the spring. But before he could crawl under the wagon, Ann Demdike ran and got her arms around him and tried to hold him back. But he talked to her and kissed her and went on. Not a shot was fired, nor was any fired all the time he continued to go out and bring back water.

"Praise God!" Cried old Mrs. Demdike. "It is a sign. They have relented."

This was the opinion of many of the women.

About two o'clock, after we had eaten and felt better, a white man appeared, carrying a white flag. Will Hamilton went out and talked to him, came back and talked with Father and the rest of our men, and then went out to the stranger again. Farther back we could see a man standing and looking on whom we recognized as Lee.

With us, all was excitement. The women were so relieved that they were crying and kissing one another, and old Mrs. Demdike and others were hallelujahing and blessing God. The proposal, which our men had accepted, was that we would put ourselves under the flag of truce and be protected from the Indians. "We had to do it," I heard Father tell Mother.

He was sitting, droop-shouldered and dejected, on a wagon tongue.

"But what if they intend treachery?" Mother asked.

He shrugged his shoulders.

"We've got to take the chance that they don't," he said. "Our ammunition is gone."

Some of our men were unchaining one of our wagons and rolling it out of the way. I ran across to see what was happening. In came Lee himself, followed by two empty wagons, each driven by one man. Everybody crowded around Lee. He said that they had had a hard time with the Indians keeping them off of us, and that Major Higbee with fifty of the Mormon militia were ready to take us under their charge.

But what made Father and Laban and some of the men suspicious was when Lee said that we must put all our rifles into one of the wagons so as not to arouse the animosity of the Indians. By so doing we would appear to be the prisoners of the Mormon militia.

Father straightened up and was about to refuse when he glanced to Laban, who replied in an undertone:

"They ain't no more use in our hands than in the wagon, seein' as the powder's gone."

Two of our wounded men who could not walk were put into the wagons, and along with them were put all the little children. Lee seemed to be picking them out over eight and under eight. Jed and I were large for our age, and we were nine, besides; so Lee put us with the older bunch and told us we were to march with the women on foot.

When he took our baby from Mother and put it in a wagon, she started to object. Then I saw her lips draw tightly together, and she gave in. She was a gray-eyed, strong-featured, middle-aged woman, large-boned and fairly stout. But the long journey and hardship had told on her, so that she was hollow-cheeked and gaunt, and like all the women in the company she wore an expression of brooding, never-ceasing anxiety.

It was when Lee described the order of march that Laban came to me. Lee said that the women and the children that walked should go first in line, following behind the two wagons. Then the men, in single file, should follow the women. When Laban heard this, he came to me, untied the scalps from his belt, and fastened them to my waist.

"But you ain't killed yet," I protested.

"You bet your life I ain't," he answered lightly. "I've just reformed, that's all. This scalp-wearin' is a vain thing and heathen." He stopped a moment as if he had forgotten something, then, as he turned abruptly on his heel to regain the men of our company, he called over his shoulder, "Well, so long, Jesse."

I was wondering why he should say good-bye, when a white man came riding into the corral. He said Major Higbee had sent him to tell us to hurry up, because the Indians might attack at any moment.

So the march began, the two wagons first. Lee kept along with the women and walking children. Behind us, after waiting until we were a couple of hundred feet in advance, came our men. As we emerged from the corral we could see the militia just a short distance away. They were leaning on their rifles and standing in a long line about six feet apart. As we passed them, I could not help noticing how solemn-faced they were. The looked like men at a funeral. So did the women notice this, and some of them began to cry.

I walked right behind my mother. I had chosen this position so that she would not catch sight of my scalps. Behind me came the three Demdike sisters, two of them helping the old mother. I could hear Lee calling all the time to the men who drove the wagons not to go so fast. A man that one of the Demdike girls said must be Major Higbee sat on a horse watching us go by. Not an Indian was in sight. By the time our men were just abreast of the militia—I had just looked back to try to see where Jed Dunham was—the thing happened. I heard Major Higbee cry out in a loud voice, "Do your duty!" All the rifles of the militia seemed to go off at once, and our men were falling over and sinking down. All the Demdike women went down at one time. I turned quickly to see how Mother was, and she was down. Right alongside of us, out of the bushes, came hundreds of Indians, all shooting. I saw the two Dunlap sisters start on the run across the sand, and took after them, for whites and Indians were all killing us. And as I ran, I saw the driver of one of the wagons shooting the two wounded men. The horses of the other wagon were plunging and rearing and their driver was trying to hold them.

It was when the little boy that was I was running after the Dunlap girls that blackness came upon him. All memory there ceases, for Jesse Fancher there ceased and, as Jesse Fancher, ceased forever. The form that was Jesse Fancher, the body that was his, being matter and apparitional, like an apparition passed and was not. But the imperishable spirit did not cease. It continued to exist and, in its next incarnation, became the residing spirit of that apparitional body known as Darrell Standing and which soon is to

143

be taken out and hanged and sent into the nothingness whither all apparitions go.

There is a lifer here in Folsom, Matthew Davies, of old pioneer stock, who is trusty of the scaffold and execution chamber. He is an old man, and his folks crossed the plains in the early days. I have talked with him, and he has verified the massacre in which Jesse Fancher was killed. When this old lifer was a child, there was much talk in his family of the Mountain Meadows Massacre. The children in the wagons, he said, were saved, because they were too young to tell tales.

All of which I submit. Never, in my life of Darrell Standing, have I read a line or heard a word spoken of the Fancher Company that perished at Mountain Meadows. Yet, in the jacket in San Quentin prison, all this knowledge came to me. I could not create this knowledge out of nothing, any more than could I create dynamite out of nothing. This knowledge and these facts I have related have but one explanation. They are out of the spirit content of me—the spirit that, unlike matter, does not perish.

In closing this chapter, I must state that Matthew Davies also told me that some years after the massacre Lee was taken by United States Government officials to the Mountain Meadows and there executed on the site of our old corral.

Chapter 14

When, at the conclusion of my first ten-day term in the jacket, I was brought back to consciousness by Dr. Jackson's thumb pressing open an eyelid, I opened both eyes and smiled up into the face of Warden Atherton.

"Too cussed to live and too mean to die," was his comment.

"The ten days are up, Warden," I whispered.

"Well, we're going to unlace you," he growled.

"It is not that," I said. "You observed my smile. You remember we had a little wager. Don't bother to unlace me first. Just give the Bull Durham and cigarette papers to Morrell and Oppenheimer. And for full measure here's another smile."

"Oh, I know your kind, Standing," the warden lectured. "But it won't get you anything. If I don't break you, you'll break all straitjacket records."

"He's broken them already," Doctor Jackson said. "Whoever heard of a man smiling after ten days of it?"

"Will and bluff," Warden Atherton answered. "Unlace him, Hutchins."

"Why such haste?" I queried, in a whisper, of course, for so low had life ebbed in me that it required all the little strength I possessed and all the will of me to be able to whisper even. "Why such haste? I don't have to catch a train, and I am so confounded comfortable as I am that I prefer not to be disturbed." But unlace me they did, rolling me out of the fetid jacket and upon the floor, an inert, helpless thing.

"No wonder he was comfortable," said Captain Jamie. "He didn't feel anything. He's paralyzed."

"Paralyzed, your grandmother," sneered the warden. "Get him up on his feet and you'll see him stand."

Hutchins and the doctor dragged me to my feet.

"Now let go!" The warden commanded.

Not all at once could life return into the body that had been practically dead for ten days and as a result, with no power as yet over my flesh, I gave at the knees, crumpled, pitched sidewise, and gashed my forehead against the wall.

"You see," said Captain Jamie.

"Good acting," retorted the warden. "That man's got nerve to do anything."

"You're right, Warden," I whispered from the floor. "I did it on purpose. It was a stage fall. Lift me up again and I'll repeat it. I promise you lots of fun."

I shall not dwell upon the agony of returning circulation. It was to become an old story with me, and it bore its share in cutting the lines in my face that I shall carry to the scaffold.

When they finally left me, I lay for the rest of the day stupid and half-comatose. There is such a thing as anesthesia of pain, engendered by pain too exquisite to be borne. And I have known that anesthesia.

By evening I was able to crawl about my cell, but not yet could I stand up. I drank much water, and cleansed myself as well as I could; but not until next day could I bring myself to eat, and then only by deliberate force of my will.

The program, as given me by Warden Atherton, was that I was to rest up and recuperate for a few days, and then, if in the meantime I had not confessed to the hiding place of the dynamite, I should be given another ten days in the jacket.

"Sorry to cause you so much trouble, Warden," I had said in reply. "It's a pity I don't die in the jacket and so put you out of your misery."

At this time I doubt that I weighed an ounce over ninety pounds. Yet, two years before, when the doors of San Quentin first closed on me, I had weighed one hundred and sixty-five pounds. It seems incredible that there was another ounce I could part with and still live. Yet in the months that followed, ounce by ounce I was reduced until I know I must have weighed nearer eighty than ninety pounds. I do know, after I managed my escape from solitary and struck the guard Thurston on the nose, that before they took me to San Rafael for trial, while I was being cleaned and shaved, I weighed eighty-nine pounds.

There are those who wonder how men grow hard. Warden Atherton was a hard man. He made me hard, and my very hardness reacted on him and made him harder. And yet he never succeeded in killing me. It required the state law of California, a hanging judge, and an unpardoning governor to send me to the scaffold for striking a prison guard with my fist I shall always contend that that guard had a nose most easily bleedable, I was a bat-eyed tottery skeleton at the time. I sometimes wonder if his nose really did bleed. Of course, he swore it did, on the witness stand. But I have known prison guards take oath to worse perjuries than that.

Ed Morrell was eager to know if I had succeeded with the experiment; but when he attempted to talk with me he was shut up by Smith, the guard who happened to be on duty in solitary.

"That's all right, Ed," I rapped to him. "You and Jake keep quiet, and I'll tell you about it. Smith can't prevent you from listening, and he can't prevent me from talking. They have done their worst, and I am still here."

"Cut that out, Standing!" Smith bellowed at me from the corridor on which all the cells opened.

Smith was a peculiarly saturnine individual, by far the most cruel and vindictive of our guards. We used to canvass whether his wife bullied him or whether he had chronic indigestion.

I continued rapping with my knuckles, and he came to the wicket to glare in at me.

"I told you to cut that out," he snarled.

"Sorry," I said suavely. "But I have a sort of premonition that I shall go right on rapping. And—er—excuse me for asking a personal question—what are you going to do about it?"

"I'll . . ." he began explosively, proving, by his inability to conclude the remark, that he thought in henids.[*]

147

"Yes?" I encouraged. "Just what, pray?"

"I'll have the warden here," he said lamely.

"Do, please. A most charming gentleman, to be sure. A shining example of the refining influences that are creeping into our prisons. Bring him to me at once. I wish to report you to him."

"Me?"

"Yes, just precisely you," I continued. "You persist, in a rude and boorish manner, in interrupting my conversation with the other guests in this hostelry."

And Warden Atherton came. The door was unlocked, and he blustered into my cell. But oh, I was so safe. He had done his worst. I was beyond his power.

"I'll shut off your grub," he threatened.

"As you please," I answered. "I'm used to it. I haven't eaten for ten days and, do you know, trying to begin to eat again is a confounded nuisance."

"Oh, ho, you're threatening me, are you? A hunger strike, eh?"

"Pardon me," I said, my voice silky with politeness. "The proposition was yours, not mine. Do try and be logical on occasion. I trust you will believe me when I tell you that your illogic is far more painful for me to endure than all your tortures."

"Are you going to stop your knuckle-talking?" He demanded.

"No—forgive me for vexing you—for I feel so strong a compulsion to talk with my knuckles that—"

"For two cents I'll put you back in the jacket," he broke in.

"Do please. I dote on the jacket. I am the jacket baby. I get fat in the jacket. Look at that arm." I pulled up my sleeve and showed a biceps so attenuated that when I flexed it, it had the appearance of a string. "A real blacksmith's biceps, eh, Warden? Cast your eyes on my swelling chest. Sandow had better look out for his laurels. And my abdomen—why, man, I am growing so stout that my case will be a scandal of prison overfeeding. Watch out, Warden, or you'll have the taxpayers after you."

"Are you going to stop knuckle-talk?" He roared.

"No, thanking you for your kind solicitude. On mature deliberation I have decided that I shall keep on knuckle-talking."

He stared at me speechlessly for a moment, and then, out of sheer impotency, turned to go.

"One question, please."

"What is it?" He demanded over his shoulder.

"What are you going to do about it?"

From the choleric exhibition he gave there and then, it has been an unceasing wonder with me to this day that he has not long since died of apoplexy.

Hour by hour, after the warden's discomfited departure, I rapped on and on the tale of my adventures. Not until that night, when Pie-Face Jones came on duty and proceeded to steal his customary naps, were Morrell and Oppenheimer able to do any talking.

"Pipe dreams," Oppenheimer rapped his verdict.

Yes was my thought; our experiences are the stuff of our dreams

"When I was a night messenger I hit the hop once," Oppenheimer continued. "And I want to tell you, you haven't anything on me when it comes to seeing things. I guess that is what all the novel-writers do—hit the hop so as to throw their imagination into the high gear."

But Ed Morrell, who had traveled the same road as I although with different results, believed my tale. He said that when his body died in the jacket, and he himself went forth from prison, he was never anybody but Ed Morrell. He never experienced previous existences. When his spirit wandered free, it wandered always in the present. As he told us, just as he was able to leave his body and gaze upon it lying in the jacket on the cell floor, so could he leave the prison and, in the present, revisit San Francisco and see what was occurring. In this manner he had visited his mother twice, both times finding her asleep. In this spirit-roving he said he had no power over material things. He could not open or close a door, move any object, make a noise, nor manifest his presence.

On the other hand, material things had no power over him. Walls and doors were not obstacles. The entity, or the real thing that was he, was thought, spirit.

"The grocery store on the corner, half a block from where Mother lived, changed hands," he told us. "I knew it by the different sign over the place. I had to wait six months after that before I could write my first letter, but when I did I asked Mother about it. And she said yes, it had changed."

"Did you read that grocery sign?" Jake Oppenheimer asked.

"Sure thing I did," was Morrell's response. "Or how could I have known it?"

"All right," rapped Oppenheimer the unbelieving. "You can prove it easy. Some time, when they shift some decent guards on us that will give us a peek at a newspaper, you get yourself thrown into the jacket, climb out of your body, and sashay down to little old Frisco. Slide up to Third and Market just about two or three A.M. when they are running the morning papers off the press. Read the latest news. Then make a swift sneak for San Quentin, get here before the newspaper tug crosses the bay, and tell me what you read. Then we'll wait and get a morning paper, when it comes in, from a guard. Then, if what you told me is in that paper, I am with you to a fare-you-well."

It was a good test. I could not but agree with Oppenheimer that such a proof would be absolute. Morrell said he would take it up some time, but that he disliked to such an extent the process of leaving his body that he would not make the attempt until such time that his suffering in the jacket became too extreme to be borne.

"That is the way with all of them—won't come across with the goods," was Oppenheimer's criticism. "My mother believed in spirits. When I was a kid she was always seeing them and talking with them and getting advice from them. But she never came across with any goods from them. The spirits couldn't tell her where the old man could nail a job or find a gold mine or mark an eight-spot in Chinese lottery. Not on your life. The bunk they told her was that the old man's uncle had had a goiter, or that the old man's grandfather had died of galloping consumption, or that we were going to move house inside four months, which last was dead easy, seeing as we moved on an average of six times a year."

I think, had Oppenheimer had the opportunity for thorough education, he would have made a Marinetti or a Haeckel. He was an earth-man in his devotion to the irrefragable fact, and his logic was admirable though frosty. "You've got to show me," was the ground rule by which he considered all things. He lacked the slightest iota of faith. This was what Morrell had pointed out. Lack of faith had prevented Oppenheimer from succeeding in achieving the little death in the jacket.

You will see, my reader, that it was not at all hopelessly bad in solitary. Given three minds such as ours, there was much with which to while away the time. It might well be that we kept one another from insanity, although I must admit that Oppenheimer rotted five years in solitary entirely by himself, ere Morrell joined him, and yet had remained sane.

On the other hand, do not make the mistake of thinking that life in solitary was one wild orgy of blithe communion and exhilarating psychological research.

We had much and terrible pain. Our guards were brutes—your hangdogs, citizen. Our surroundings were vile. Our food was filthy, monotonous, innutritious. Only men, by force of will, could live on so unbalanced a ration. I know that our prize cattle, pigs, and sheep on the University Demonstration Farm at Davis would have faded away and died had they received no more scientifically balanced a ration than what we received.

We had no books to read. Our very knuckletalk was a violation of the rules. The world, so far as we were concerned, practically did not exist. It was more a ghost world. Oppenheimer, for instance, had never seen an automobile or a motorcycle. News did occasionally filter in—but such dim, long-after-the-event, unreal news. Oppenheimer told me he had not learned of the Russo-Japanese War until two years after it was over.

We were the buried alive, the living dead. Solitary was our tomb, in which, on occasion, we talked with our knuckles like spirits rapping at a seance.

News? Such little things were news to us. A change of bakers—we could tell it by our bread. What made Pie-Face Jones lay off a week? Was it vacation or sickness? Why was Wilson, on the night shift for only ten days, transferred elsewhere? Where did Smith get that black eye? We would speculate for a week over so trivial a thing as the last.

Some convict given a month in solitary was an event. And yet we could learn nothing from such transient and ofttimes stupid Dantes who would remain in our inferno too short a time to learn knuckle-talk ere they went forth again into the bright wide world of the living.

Still again, all was not so trivial in our abode of shadows. As example, I taught Oppenheimer to play chess. Consider how tremendous such an achievement is—to teach a man, thirteen cells away, by means of knuckle-raps; to teach him to visualize a chessboard, to visualize all the pieces, pawns, and positions, to know the various manners of moving; and to teach him it all so thoroughly that he and I, by pure visualization, were in the end able to play entire games of chess in our minds. In the end, did I say? Another tribute to the magnificence of Oppenheimer's mind: in the end he became my master at the game—he who had never seen a chessman in his life.

What image of a bishop, for instance, could possibly form in his mind when I rapped our code sign for bishop? In vain and often I asked him this very question. In vain he tried to describe in words that mental image of something he had never seen but which nevertheless he was able to handle in such masterly fashion as to bring confusion upon me countless times in the course of play.

I can only contemplate such exhibitions of will and spirit and conclude, as I so often conclude, that precisely there resides reality. The spirit only is real. The flesh is phantasmagoric and apparitional. I ask you how—I repeat, I ask you how matter or flesh in any form can play chess on an imaginary board, with imaginary pieces, across a vacuum of thirteen cells spanned only with knuckle-taps?

---

* A word coined by Jack London, for which there is no known meaning.

Chapter 15

I was once Adam Strang, an Englishman. The period of my living, as near as I can guess it, was somewhere between 1550 and 1650 and I lived to a ripe old age, as you shall see. It has been a great regret to me, ever since Ed Morrell taught me the way of the little death, that I had not been a more thorough student of history. I should have been able to identify and place much that is obscure to me. As it is, I am compelled to grope and guess my way to times and places of my earlier existences.

A peculiar thing about my Adam Strang existence is that I recollect so little of the first thirty years of it. Many times in the jacket has Adam Strang recrudesced, but always he springs into being full-statured, heavy-thawed, a full thirty years of age.

I, Adam Strang, invariably assume my consciousness on a group of low, sandy islands somewhere under the equator in what must be the western Pacific Ocean. I am always at home there, and seem to have been there some time. There are thousands of people on these islands, although I am the only white man. The natives are a magnificent breed, big-muscled, broad-shouldered, tall. A six-foot man is a commonplace. The king, Raa Kook, is at least six inches above six feet, and though he would weigh fully three hundred pounds is so equitably proportioned that one could not call him fat. Many of his chiefs are as large, while the women are not much smaller than the men.

There are numerous islands in the group, over all of which Raa Kook is king, although the cluster of islands to the south is restive and occasionally in revolt. These natives with whom I live are Polynesian, I know, because their hair is straight and black. Their skin is a sun-warm golden brown. Their speech, which I speak uncommonly easily, is round and rich and musical, possessing a paucity of consonants, being composed principally of vowels.

They love flowers, music, dancing, and games, and are childishly simple and happy in their amusements, though cruelly savage in their angers and wars.

I, Adam Strang, know my past, but do not seem to think much about it. I live in the present. I brood over neither past nor future. I am careless, improvident, uncautious, happy out of sheer well-being and overplus of physical energy. Fish, fruits, vegetables, and seaweed—a full stomach—and I am content. I am high in place with Raa Kook, than whom none is higher, not even Abba Taak, who is highest over the priests. No men dare lift hand or weapon to me. I am taboo-sacred as the sacred canoe house under the floor of which repose the bones of heaven alone knows how many previous kings of Raa Kook's line.

I know all about how I happened to be wrecked and be there alone of all my ship's company—it was a great drowning and a great wind; but I do not moon over the catastrophe. When I think back at all, rather do I think far back to my childhood at the skirts of my milk-skinned, flaxen-haired, buxom English mother. It is a tiny village of a dozen straw-thatched cottages in which I lived. I hear again blackbirds and thrushes in the hedges, and see again bluebells spilling out from the oak woods and over the velvet turf like a creaming of blue water. And most of all I remember a great, hairy-fetlocked stallion, often led dancing, sidling, and nickering down the narrow street. I was frightened of the huge beast and always fled screaming to my mother, clutching her skirts and hiding in them wherever I might find her.

But enough. The childhood of Adam Strang is not what I set out to write.

I lived for several years on the islands which are nameless to me, and upon which I am confident I was the first white man. I was married to Lei-Lei, the king's sister, who was a fraction over six feet and only by that fraction topped me. I was a splendid figure of a man, broad-shouldered, deep-chested, well set up. Women of any race, as you shall see, looked on me with a favoring eye. Under my arms, sun-shielded, my skin was milk-white as my mother's. My eyes were blue. My mustache, beard, and hair were that golden-yellow such as one sometimes sees in paintings of the northern sea kings. Ay—I must have come of that old stock, long settled in England and, though born in a countryside cottage, the sea still ran so salt in my blood that I early found my way to ships to become a sea-cuny.* That is what I was—neither officer nor gentleman, but sea-cuny, hard-worked, hard-bitten, hard-enduring.

I was of value to Raa Kook, hence his royal protection. I could work in iron, and our wrecked ship had brought the first iron to Raa Kook's land. On occasion, ten leagues to the north west, we went in canoes to get iron from the wreck. The hull had slipped off the reef and lay in fifteen fathoms. And in fifteen fathoms we brought up the iron. Wonderful divers and workers under water were these natives. I learned to do my fifteen fathoms, but never could I equal them in their fishy exploits. On the land, by virtue of my English training and my strength, I could throw any of them. Also, I taught them quarter staff until the game became a very contagion and broken heads anything but novelties.

Brought up from the wreck was a journal, so torn and mushed and pulped by the sea water, with ink so run about, that scarcely any of it was decipherable. However, in the hope that some antiquarian scholar may be able to place more definitely the date of the events I shall describe, I here give an extract. The peculiar spelling may give the clue. Note that while the letter *s* is used, it more commonly is replaced by the letter *f*.

> *The wind being gave us an opportunity of examining and drying some of our provifion, particularly, fome Chinefe hams and dry fifh, which constituted part of our victualling Divine service alfo was performed on deck. In the afternoon the wind was foutherly, with fresh gales, but dry, fo that we were able the following morning to clean between decks, and alfo to fumigate the fhip with gunpowder.*

But I must hasten, for my narrative is not of Adam Strang the shipwrecked sea-cuny on a coral isle, but of Adam Strang, later named Yi Yong-ik, the Mighty One, who was one-time favorite of the powerful Yunsan, who was lover and husband of the Lady Om of the princely house of Min. and who was longtime beggar and pariah in all the villages of all the coasts and roads of Cho-Sen. (Ah, ha, I have you there—*Cho-Sen*. It means the land of the morning calm. In modern speech it is called Korea.)

Remember, it was between three and four centuries back that I lived, the first white man, on the coral isles of Raa Kook. In those waters, at that time, the keels of ships were rare. I might well have lived out my days there, in peace and fatness under the sun where frost was not, had it not been for the *Sparwehr*. The *Sparwehr* was a Dutch merchantman daring the uncharted seas for Indies beyond the Indies. And she found me instead, and I was all she found.

Have I not said that I was a gay-hearted, golden-bearded giant of an irresponsible boy that had never grown up? With scarce a pang, when the *Sparwehr*'s water casks were filled, I left Raa Kook and his pleasant land, left Lei-Lei and all her flower-garlanded sisters, and with laughter on my lips and familiar ship-smells sweet in my nostrils, sailed away, sea-cuny once more, under Captain Johannes Maartens.

A marvelous wandering, that which followed on the old *Sparwehr*. We were in quest of new lands of silks and spices. In truth, we found fevers, violent deaths, pestilential paradises where death and beauty kept charnel house together. That old Johannes Maartens, with no hint of romance in that stolid face and grizzly square head of his, sought the islands of Solomon, the mines of Golconda—ay, he sought old lost Atlantis which he hoped to find still afloat unscuppered. And he found head-hunting, tree-dwelling anthropophagi instead.

We landed on strange islands, sea-pounded on their shores and smoking at their summits, where kinky-haired little animal-men made monkey-wailings in the jungle, planted their forest runways with thorns and stake pits, and blew poisoned splinters into us from out the twilight jungle hush. And whatsoever man of us was wasp-stung by such a splinter died horribly and howling. And we encountered other men, fiercer, bigger, who faced us on the beaches in open fight, showering us with spears and arrows, while the great tree drums and the little tom-toms rumbled and rattled war across the tree-filled hollows and all the hills were pillared with signal smokes.

Hendrik Hamel was supercargo and part owner of the *Sparwehr* adventure, and what he did not own was the property of Captain Johannes Maartens. The latter spoke little English, Hendrik Hamel but little more. The sailors, with whom I gathered, spoke Dutch only. But trust a sea-cuny to learn Dutch—ay, and Korean, as you shall see.

Toward the end, we came to the charted country of Japan. But the people would have no dealings with us and two-sworded officials, in sweeping robes of silk that made Captain Johannes Maartens' mouth water, came aboard of us and politely requested us to begone. Under their suave manners was the iron of a warlike race, and we knew, and went our way.

We crossed the Straits of Japan and were entering the Yellow Sea on our way to China, when we laid the *Sparwehr* on the rocks. She was a crazy tub, the old *Sparwehr*, so clumsy and so dirty with whiskered marine-life on her bottom that she could not get out of her own way. Close-hauled, the closest she could come was to six points of the wind; and then she bobbed up and down, without way, like a derelict turnip. Galliots were clippers compared with her. To tack her about was undreamed of; to wear her required all hands and half a watch. So situated, we were caught on a lee shore in an eight-point shift of wind at the height of a hurricane that had beaten our souls sick for forty-eight hours.

We drifted in upon the land in the chill light of a stormy dawn across a heartless cross-sea mountain high. It was dead of winter, and between smoking snow-squalls we could glimpse the forbidding coast, if coast it might be called, so broken was it. There were grim rock isles and islets beyond counting, dim snow-covered ranges beyond, and everywhere upstanding cliffs too steep for snow, outjuts of headlands, and pinnacles and slivers of rock upthrust from the boiling sea.

There was no name to this country on which we drove, no record of it ever having been visited by navigators. Its coastline was only hinted at in our chart. From all of which we could argue that the inhabitants were as inhospitable as the little of their land we could see.

The *Sparwehr* drove in bow-on upon a cliff. There was deep water to its sheer foot, so that our sky-aspiring bowspirit crumpled at the impact and snapped short off. The foremast went by the board, with a great snapping of rope shrouds and stays, and fell forward against the cliff.

I have always admired old Johannes Maartens. Washed and rolled off the high poop by a burst of sea, we were left stranded in the waist of the ship, whence we fought our way for'ard to the steep-pitched forecastle head. Others joined us. We lashed ourselves fast and counted noses. We were eighteen. The rest had perished.

Johannes Maartens touched me and pointed upward through cascading salt-water from the back-fling of the cliff. I saw what he desired. Twenty feet below the truck, the foremast ground and crunched against a boss of the cliff. Above the boss was a cleft. He wanted to know if I would dare the leap from the masthead into the cleft. Sometimes the distance was a scant six feet. At other times it was a score, for the mast reeled drunkenly to the rolling and pounding of the hull on which rested its splintered butt.

I began the climb. But they did not wait. One by one they unlashed themselves and followed me up the perilous mast. There was reason for haste, for at any moment the *Sparwehr* might slip off into deep water. I timed my leap, and made it, landing in the cleft in a scramble and ready to lend a hand to those who leaped after. It was slow work. We were wet and half-freezing in the wind-drive. Besides, the leaps had to be timed to the roll of the hull and the sway of the mast.

The cook was the first to go. He was snapped off the mast-end, and his body performed cartwheels in its fall. A fling of sea caught him and crushed him to a pulp against the cliff. The cabin boy, a bearded man of twenty-odd, lost hold, slipped, swung around the mast, and was pinched against the boss of rock. Pinched? The life squeezed from him on the instant. Two others followed the way of the cook. Captain Johannes Maartens was the last, completing the fourteen of us that clung on in the cleft. An hour afterward, the *Sparwehr* slipped off and sank in deep water.

Two days and nights saw us near to perishing on that cliff, for there was way neither up nor down. The third morning a fishing boat found us. The men were clad entirely in dirty white, with their long hair done up in a curious knot on their pates—the marriage knot, as I was afterward to learn, and also, as I was to learn, a handy thing to clutch hold of with one hand while you clouted with the other when an argument went beyond words.

The boat went back to the village for help, and most of the villagers, most of their gear, and most of the day were required to get us down. They were a poor and wretched folk, their food difficult even for the stomach of a sea-cuny to countenance. Their rice was brown as chocolate. Half the husks remained in it, along with bits of chaff, splinters, and unidentifiable dirt which made one pause often in the chewing in order to stick into his mouth thumb and forefinger and pluck out the offending stuff. Also, they ate a sort of millet, and pickles of astounding variety and ungodly hot.

Their houses were earthen-walled and straw-thatched. Under the floors ran flues through which the kitchen smoke escaped, warming the sleeping room in its passage. Here we lay and rested for days, soothing ourselves with their mild and tasteless tobacco, which we smoked in tiny bowls at the end of yard-long pipes. Also, there was a warm, sourish, milky-looking drink, heady only when taken in enormous doses. After guzzling I swear gallons of it, I got singing drunk, which is the way of sea-cunies the world over. Encouraged by my success, the others persisted, and soon we were all a-roaring, little recking of the fresh snow gale piping outside, and little worrying that we were cast away in an uncharted God-forgotten land. Old Johannes Maartens laughed and trumpeted and slapped his thighs with the best of us. Hendrik Hamel, a cold-blooded, chilly-poised, dark brunet of a Dutchman with beady black eyes, was as rarely devilish as the rest of us, and shelled out silver like any drunken sailor for the purchase of more of the milky brew. Our carrying on was a scandal; but the women fetched the drink while all the village that could crowd in jammed the room to witness our antics.

The white man has gone around the world in mastery, I do believe, because of his unwise uncaringness. That has been the manner of his going, although, of course, he was driven on by restiveness and lust for booty. So it was that Captain Johannes Maartens, Hendrik Hamel, and the twelve sea-curies of us roistered and bawled in the fisher village while the winter gales whistled across the Yellow Sea.

From the little we had seen of the land and the people, we were not impressed by Cho-Sen. If these miserable fishers were a fair sample of the natives, we could understand why the land was unvisited by navigators. But we were to learn different. The village was on an in-lying island, and its head man must have sent word across to the mainland; for one morning three big two-masted junks with lateens of rice-matting dropped anchor off the beach.

When the sampans came ashore, Captain Johannes Maartens was all interest, for here were silks again. One strapping Korean, all in pale-tinted silks of various colors, was surrounded by half a dozen obsequious attendants also clad in silk. Kwan Yung-jin, as I came to know his name, was a yang-ban, or noble; also, he was what might be called magistrate or governor of the district or province. This means that his office was appointive, and that he was a tithe squeezer or tax farmer.

Fully a hundred soldiers were also landed and marched into the village. They were armed with three-pronged spears, slicing spears, and chopping spears, with here and there a matchlock of so heroic mold that there were two soldiers to a matchlock, one to carry and set the tripod on which rested the muzzle, the other to carry and fire the gun. As I was to learn, sometimes the gun went off, sometimes it did not, all depending upon the adjustment of the fire punk and the condition of the powder in the flash pan.

So it was that Kwan Yung-jin traveled. The headmen of the village were cringingly afraid of him, and for good reason, as we were not overlong in finding out. I stepped forward as interpreter, for already I had the hang of several score of Korean words. He scowled and waved me aside. But what did I reck? I was as tall as he, outweighed him by a full two stone, and my skin was white, my hair golden. He turned his back and addressed the head man of the village while his six silken satellites made a cordon between us. While he talked, more soldiers from the ship carried up several shoulder loads of inch-planking. These planks were about six feet long and two feet wide, and curiously split in half lengthwise. Nearer one end than the other was a round hole larger than a man's neck.

Kwan Yung-jin gave a command. Several of the soldiers approached Tromp, who was sitting on the ground nursing a felon. Now Tromp was a rather stupid, slow-thinking, slow-moving cuny, before he knew what was doing, one of the planks, with a scissors- like opening and closing, was about his neck and clamped. Discovering his predicament, he set up a bull-roaring and dancing, till all had to back away to give him clear space for the flying ends of his plank.

Then the trouble began, for it was plainly Kwan Yung-jin's intention to plank all of us. Oh, we fought bare-fisted with a hundred soldiers and as many villagers, while Kwan Yung-jin stood apart in his silks and lordly disdain. Here was where I earned my name, Yi Yong-ik, the Mighty. Long after our company was subdued and planked, I fought on. My fists were of the hardness of topping-mauls, and I had the muscles and will to drive them.

To my joy, I quickly learned that the Koreans did not understand a fist blow and were without the slightest notion of guarding. They went down like tenpins, fell over each other in heaps. But Kwan Yung-jin was my man, and all that saved him when I made my rush was the intervention of his satellites. They were flabby creatures. I made a mess of them and a muss and muck of their silks ere the multitude could return upon me. There were so many of them. They clogged my blows by the sheer numbers of them, those behind shoving the front ones upon me. And how I dropped them! Toward the end they were squirming three-deep under my feet But by the time the crews of the three junks and most of the village were on top of me I was fairly smothered. The planking was easy.

"God in heaven, what now?" Asked Vandervoot, another cuny, when we had been bundled aboard a junk.

We sat on the open deck like so many trussed fowls when he asked the question, and the next moment, as the junk heeled to the breeze, we shot down the deck, planks and all, fetching up in the lee scuppers with skinned necks. And from the high poop Kwan Yung-jin gazed down at us as if he did not see us. For many years to come, Vandervoot was known among us as "What-Now Vandervoot." Poor devil. He froze to death one night on the streets of Keijo with every door barred against him.

To the mainland we were taken and thrown into a stinking, vermin-infested prison. Such was our introduction to the official-dom of Cho-Sen. But I was to be revenged for all of us on Kwan Yung-jin, as you shall see, in the days when the Lady Om was kind and power was mine.

In prison we lay for many days. We learned afterward the reason. Kwan Yung-jin had sent a dispatch to Keijo, the capital, to find what royal disposition was to be made of us. In the meantime we were a menagerie. From dawn till dark our barred windows were besieged by the natives, for no member of our race had they ever seen before. Nor was our audience mere rabble. Ladies, borne in palanquins on the shoulders of coolies, came to see the strange devils cast up by the sea and while their attendants drove back the common folk with whips they would gaze long and timidly at us. Of them we saw little, for their faces were covered according to the custom of the country. Only dancing girls, low women, and grandmas ever were seen abroad with exposed faces.

I have often thought that Kwan Yung-jin suffered from indigestion, and that when the attacks were acute he took it out on us. At any rate, without rhyme or reason, whenever the whim came to him, we were all taken out on the street before the prison and well beaten with sticks to the gleeful shouts of the multitude. The Asiatic is a cruel beast, and delights in spectacles of human suffering.

At any rate we were pleased when an end to our beatings came. This was caused by the arrival of Kim. Kim? All I can say, and the best I can say, is that he was the whitest man I ever encountered in Cho-Sen. He was a captain of fifty men when I met him. He was in command of the palace guards before I was done doing my best by him. And in the end he died for the Lady Om's sake and for mine. Kim—well, Kim was Kim.

Immediately he arrived, the planks were taken from our necks and we were lodged in the best inn the place boasted. We were still prisoners, but honorable prisoners, with a guard of fifty mounted soldiers. The next day we were under way on the royal highroad, fourteen sailormen astride the dwarf horses that obtain in Cho-Sen, and bound for Keijo itself. The Emperor, so Kim told me, had expressed a desire to gaze upon the strangeness of the sea devils.

It was a journey of many days, half the length of Cho-Sen, north and south as it lies. It chanced, at the first off-saddling, that I strolled around to witness the feeding of the dwarf horses. And what I witnessed set me bawling, "What now, Vandervoot?" Till all our crew came running. As I am a living man, what the horses were feeding on was bean soup, hot bean soup at that, and naught else did they have on all the journey but hot bean soup. It was the custom of the country.

They were truly dwarf horses. On a wager with Kim, I lifted one, despite his squeals and struggles, squarely across my shoulders, so that Kim's men, who had already heard my new name, called me Yi Yong-ik, the Mighty One. Kim was a large man as Koreans go, and Koreans are a tall muscular race, and Kim fancied himself a bit. But, elbow to elbow and palm to palm, I put his arm down at will. And his soldiers and the gaping villagers would look on and murmur "Yi Yong-ik."

In a way, we were a traveling menagerie. The word went on ahead, so that all the country folk flocked to the roadside to see us pass. It was an unending circus procession. In the towns at night our inns were besieged by multitudes, so that we got no peace until the soldiers drove them off with lance pricks and blows. But first, Kim would call for the village strong men and wrestlers for the fun of seeing me crumple them and put them in the dirt.

Bread there was none, but we ate white rice (the strength of which resides in one's muscles not long), a meat which we found to be dog (which animal is regularly butchered for food in Cho-Sen and the pickles ungodly hot but which one learns to like exceeding well. And there was drink, real drink, not milky slush, but white, biting stuff distilled from rice, a pint of which would kill a weakling and make a strong man mad and merry. At the walled city of Chong-ho I put Kim and the city notables under the table with the stuff—or on the table, rather, for the table was the floor, where we squatted to cramp-knots in my hams for the thousandth time. And again all muttered "Yi Yong-ik," and the word of my prowess passed on before even to Keijo and the Emperor's Court.

I was more an honored guest than a prisoner, and invariably I rode by Kim's side, my long legs near reaching the ground and, where the going was deep, my feet scraping the muck. Kim was young. Kim was human. Kim was universal. He was a man anywhere in any country. He and I talked and laughed and joked the day long and half the night. And I verily ate up the language. I had a gift that way anyway. Even Kim marveled at the way I mastered the idiom. And I learned the Korean points of view, the Korean humor, the Korean soft places, weak places, touchy places. Kim taught me flower songs, love songs, drinking songs. One of the latter was his own, of the end of which I shall give you a crude attempt at translation. Kim and Pak in their youth, swore a pact to abstain from drinking, which pact was speedily broken. In old age Kim and Pak sing:

"*No, no, begone The merry bowl Again shall bolster up my soul against itself. What, good man, hold! Canst tell me where red wine is sold? Nay, just beyond yon peach-tree? There? Good luck be thine; I'll thither fare.*"

Hendrik Hamel, scheming and crafty, ever encouraged and urged me in my antic course that brought Kim's favor not alone to me, but through me to Hendrik Hamel and all our company. I here mention Hendrik Hamel as my adviser, for it has a bearing on much that followed at Keijo in the winning of Yusan's favor, the Lady Om's heart, and the Emperor's tolerance. I had the will and the fearlessness for the game I played, and some of the wit; but most of the wit I freely admit was supplied me by Hendrik Hamel.

And so we journeyed up to Keijo, from walled city to walled city across a snowy mountain land that was hollowed with innumerable fat farming valleys. And every evening, at fall of day, beacon fires sprang from peak to peak and ran along the land. Always Kim watched for this nightly display. From all the coasts of Cho-Sen, Kim told me, those chains of fire speech ran to Keijo to carry their message to the Emperor. One beacon meant the land was in peace. Two beacons meant revolt or invasion. We never saw but one beacon. And ever, as we rode, Vandervoot brought up the rear, wondering, "God in heaven, what now?"

Keijo we found a vast city where all the population, with the exception of the nobles, or yang-bans, dressed in the eternal white. This, Kim explained, was an automatic determination and advertisement of caste. Thus, at a glance could one tell the status of an individual by the degrees of cleanliness or of filthiness of his garments. It stood to reason that a coolie, possessing but the clothes he stood up in, must be extremely dirty. And to reason it stood that the individual in immaculate white must possess many changes and command the labor of laundresses to keep his changes immaculate. As for the yang-bans who wore the pale varicolored silks, they were beyond such common yard-stick of place.

After resting in an inn for several days during which time we washed our garments and repaired the ravages of shipwreck and travel, we were summoned before the Emperor. In the great open space before the palace wall were colossal stone dogs that looked more like tortoises. They crouched on massive stone pedestals of twice the height of a tall man. The walls of the palace were huge and of dressed stone. So thick were these walls that they could defy a breach from the mightiest of cannon in a year-long siege. The mere gateway was of the size of a palace in itself, rising pagoda-like in many retreating stories, each story fringed with tile roofing. A smart guard of soldiers fumed out at the gateway. These, Kim told me, were the Tiger Hunters of Pyeng-yang, the fiercest and most terrible fighting men of which Cho-Sen could boast.

But enough. On mere description of the Emperor's palace a thousand pages of my narrative could be worthily expended. Let it suffice that here we knew power in all its material expression. Only a civilization deep and wide and old and strong could produce this far-walled, many-gabled roof of kings.

To no audience hall were we sea-curies led, but, as we took it, to a feasting hall. The feasting was at its end, and all the throng was in a merry mood. And such a throng! High dignitaries, princes of the blood, sworded nobles, pale priests, weather-tanned officers of high command, court ladies with faces exposed, painted ki-sang, or dancing girls, who rested from entertaining, and duennas, waiting women, eunuchs, lackeys, and palace slaves a myriad of them.

All fell away from us, however, when the Emperor, with a following of intimates, advanced to look us over. He was a merry monarch, especially so for an Asiatic. Not more than forty, with a clear, pallid skin that had never known the sun, he was paunched and weak-legged. Yet he had once been a fine man. The noble forehead attested that. But the eyes were bleared and weak-lidded, the lips twitching and trembling from the various excesses in which he indulged, which excesses as I was to learn, were largely devised and pandered by Yunsan, the Buddhist priest, of whom more anon.

In our sea garments we mariners were a motley crew, and motley was the cue of our reception. Exclamations of wonder at our strangeness gave way to laughter. The ki-sang invaded us, dragging us about, making prisoners of us, two or three of them to one of us, leading us about like so many dancing bears and putting us through our antics. It was offensive, true, but what could poor sea-cunies do? What could old Johannes Maartens do, with a bevy of laughing girls about him, tweaking his nose, pinching his arms, tickling his ribs till he pranced. To escape such torment, Hans Amden cleared a space and gave a clumsy-footed Hollandish breakdown till all the Court roared its laughter.

It was offensive to me who had been equal and boon companion of Kim for many days. I resisted the laughing ki-sang. I braced my legs and stood upright with folded arms; nor could pinch or tickle bring a quiver from me. Thus they abandoned me for easier prey.

"For God's sake, man, make an impression," Hendrik Hamel, who had struggled to me with three ki-sang dragging behind, mumbled.

Well might he mumble, for whenever he opened his mouth to speak they crammed it with sweets.

"Save us from this folly," he persisted, ducking his head about to avoid their sweets-filled palms. "We must have dignity, understand, dignity. This will ruin us. They are making tame animals of us, playthings. When they grow tired of us they will throw us out You're doing the right thing. Stick to it. Stand them off. Command respect, respect for all of us—"

The last was barely audible, for by this time the ki-sang had stuffed his mouth to speechlessness.

As I have said, I had the will and the fearlessness, and I racked my sea-cuny brains for the wit. A palace eunuch, tickling my neck with a feather from behind, gave me my start. I had already drawn attention to my aloofness and imperviousness to the attacks of the ki-sang, so that many were looking on at the eunuch's baiting of me. I gave no sign, made no move, until I had located him and distanced him. Then, like a shot, without turning head or body, merely by my arm, I fetched him an open, backhanded slap. My knuckles landed flat on his cheek and jaw. There was a crack like a spar parting in a gale. He was bowled clean over, landing in a heap on the floor a dozen feet away.

There was no laughter, only cries of surprise and murmurings and whisperings of "Yi Yong-ik." Again I folded my arms and stood with a fine assumption of haughtiness. I do believe that I, Adam Strang, had among other things the soul of an actor in me. For see what follows. I was now the most significant of our company. Proud-eyed, disdainful, I met unwavering the eyes upon me and made them drop or turn away—all eyes but one. These were the eyes of a young woman whom I judged, by richness of dress and by the half-dozen women fluttering at her back, to be a court lady of distinction. In truth, she was the Lady Om, princess of the house of Min. Did I say young? She was fully my own age, thirty, and for all that and her ripeness and beauty a princess still unmarried, as I was to learn.

She alone looked me in the eyes without wavering, until it was I who turned away. She did not look me down, for there was neither challenge nor antagonism in her eyes—only fascination. I was loath to admit this defeat by one small woman, and my eyes, turning aside, lighted on the disgraceful rout of my comrades and the trailing ki-sang and gave me the pretext. I clapped my hands in the Asiatic fashion when one gives command.

"Let be!" I thundered in their own language, and in the form one addresses underlings.

Oh, I had a chest and a throat, and could bull-roar to the hurt of eardrums. I warrant so loud a command had never before cracked the sacred air of the Emperor's palace.

The great room was aghast. The women were startled, and pressed toward one another as for safety. The ki-sang released the cunies and shrank away, giggling apprehensively. Only the Lady Om made no sign nor motion but continued to gaze wide-eyed into my eyes, which had returned to hers.

Then fell a great silence, as if all waited some word of doom. A multitude of eyes timidly stole back and forth from the Emperor to me and from me to the Emperor. And I had wit to keep the silence and to stand there, arms folded, haughty and remote.

"He speaks our language," quoth the Emperor at the last; and I swear there was such a relinquishment of held breaths that the whole room was one vast sigh.

"I was born with this language," I replied, my cuny wits running rashly to the first madness that prompted. "I spoke it at my mother's breast. I was the marvel of my land. Wise men journeyed far to see me and to hear. But no man knew the words I spoke. In the many years I have forgotten much, but now, in Cho-Sen, the words come back like long-lost friends."

An impression I certainly made. The Emperor swallowed and his lips twitched ere he asked:

"How explain you this?"

"I am an accident," I answered, following the wayward lead my wit had opened. "The gods of birth were careless, and I was mislaid in a far land and nursed by an alien people. I am Korean, and now, at last, I have come to my home."

What an excited whispering and conferring took place. The Emperor himself interrogated Kim. "He was always thus, our speech in his mouth, from the time he came out of the sea," Kim lied like the good fellow he was.

"Bring me yang-ban's garments as befits me," I interrupted, "and you shall see." As I was led away in compliance, I turned on the ki-sang. "And leave my slaves alone. They have journeyed far and are weary. They are my faithful slaves."

In another room Kim helped me change, sending the lackeys away; and quick and to the point was the dress rehearsal he gave me. He knew no more toward what I drove than did I, but he was a good fellow.

The funny thing, once back in the crowd and spouting Korean which I claimed was rusty from long disuse, was that Hendrik Hamel and the rest, too stubborn-tongued to learn new speech, did not know a word I uttered.

"I am of the blood of the house of Koryu," I told the Emperor, "that ruled at Songdo many a long year agone when my house arose on the ruins of Silla."

Ancient history, all, told me by Kim on the long ride, and he struggled with his face to hear me parrot his teaching.

"These," I said, when the Emperor had asked me about my company, "these are my slaves, all except that old churl there," I indicated Johannes Maartens, "who is the son of a freed man." I told Hendrik Hamel to approach. "This one," I wantoned on, "was born in my father's house of a seed slave who was born there before him. He is very close to me. We are of an age, born on the same day, and on that day my father gave him me."

Afterwards, when Hendrik Hamel was eager to know all that I had said, and when I told him, he reproached me and was in a pretty rage.

"The fat's in the fire, Hendrik," quoth I. "What I have done has been out of witlessness and the need to be saying something. But done it is. Nor you nor I can pluck forth the fat. We must act our parts and make the best of it."

Taiwun, the Emperor's brother, was a sot of sots, and as the night wore on he challenged me to a drinking. The Emperor was delighted, and commanded a dozen of the noblest sots to join in the bout. The women were dismissed, and we went to it, drink for drink, measure for measure. Kim I kept by me, and midway along, despite Hendrik Hamel's warning scowls, I dismissed him and the company, first requesting, and obtaining, palace lodgment instead of the inn.

Next day the palace was a-buzz with my feat, for I had put Taiwun and all his champions snoring on the mats and walked unaided to my bed. Never, in the days of vicissitude that came later, did Taiwun doubt my claim of Korean birth Only a Korean, he averred, could possess so strong a head.

The palace was a city in itself, and we were lodged in a sort of summer house that stood apart. The princely quarters were mine, of course, and Hamel and Maartens with the rest of the grumbling cunies had to content themselves with what remained.

I was summoned before Yunsan, the Buddhist priest I have mentioned. It was his first glimpse of me and my first of him. Even Kim he dismissed from me, and we sat alone on deep mats in a twilight room. Lord, Lord, what a man and a mind was Yunsan! He made to probe my soul. He knew things of other lands and places that no one in Cho-Sen dreamed to know. Did he believe my fabled birth? I could not guess, for his face was less changeful than a bowl of bronze.

What Yunsan's thoughts were only Yunsan knew. But in him, this poor-clad, lean-bellied priest, I sensed the power behind power in all the palace and in all Cho-Sen. I sensed also, through the drift of speech, that he had use of me. Now, was this use suggested by the Lady Om? —a nut I gave Hendrik Hamel to crack. I little knew, and less I cared, for I lived always in the moment and let others forecast, forefend, and travail their anxiety.

I answered, too, the summons of the Lady Om, following a sleek-faced, cat-footed eunuch through quiet palace byways to her apartments. She lodged as a princess of the blood should lodge. She too had a palace to herself, among lotus ponds where grew forests of trees centuries old but so dwarfed that they reached no higher than my middle. Bronze bridges, so delicate and rare that they looked as if fashioned by jewel-smiths, spanned her lily ponds, and a bamboo grove screened her palace apart from all the palace.

My head was awhirl. Sea-cuny that I was, I was no dolt with women, and I sensed more than idle curiosity in her sending for me. I had heard love tales of common men and queens, and was a-wondering if now it was my fortune to prove such tales true.

The Lady Om wasted little time. There were women about her, but she regarded their presence no more than a carter his horses. I sat beside her on deep mats that made the room half a couch, and wine was given me and sweets to nibble, served on tiny, foot-high tables inlaid with pearl.

Lord, Lord, I had but to look into her eyes— But wait. Make no mistake. The Lady Om was no fool. I have said she was of my own age. All of thirty she was, with the poise of her years. She knew what she wanted. She knew what she did not want. It was because of this she had never married, though all pressure that an Asiatic court could put upon a woman had been vainly put upon her to compel her to marry Chong Mong-ju. He was a lesser cousin of the great Min family, himself no fool, and grasping so greedily for power as to perturb Yunsan, who strove to retain all power himself and keep the palace and Cho-Sen in ordered balance. Thus, Yunsan it was who in secret allied himself with the Lady Om, saved her from her cousin, used her to trim her cousin's wings. But enough of intrigue. It was long before I guessed a tithe of it, and then largely through the Lady Om's confidence and Hendrik Hamel's conclusions.

The Lady Om was a very flower of woman. Women such as she are born rarely, scarce twice a century the whole world over. She was unhampered by rule or convention. Religion, with her, was a series of abstractions, partly learned from Yunsan, partly worked out for herself. Vulgar religion, the public religion, she held, was a device to keep the toiling millions to their toil. She had a will of her own, and she had a heart all womanly. She was a beauty—yes, a beauty by any set rule of the world. Her large black eyes were neither slitted nor slanted in the Asiatic way. They were long, true, but set squarely, and with just the slightest hint of obliqueness that was all for piquancy.

I have said she was no fool. Behold. As I palpitated to the situation, princess and sea-cuny and love not a little that threatened big, I racked my cuny's brains for wit to carry the thing off with manhood credit. It chanced, early in this first meeting, that I mentioned what I had told all the Court, that I was in truth a Korean of the blood of the ancient house of Koryu.

"Let be," she said, tapping my lips with her peacock fan. "No child's tales here. Know that with me you are better and greater than of any house of Koryu. You are . . ."

She paused and I waited, watching the daring grow in her eyes.

"You are a man," she completed. "Not even in my sleep have I ever dreamed there was such a man as you on his two legs upstanding in the world."

Lord, Lord, and what could a poor sea-cuny do? This particular sea-cuny, I admit, blushed through his sea tan till the Lady Om's eyes were twin pools of roguishness in their teasing deliciousness and my arms were all but about her. And she laughed tantalizingly and alluringly, and clapped her hands for her women, and I knew that the audience, for this once, was over. I knew, also, there would be other audiences, there must be other audiences.

Back to Hamel, my head awhirl.

"The woman," said he, after deep cogitation. He looked at me and sighed an envy I could not mistake. "It is your brawn, Adam Strang, that bull throat of yours, your yellow hair. Well, it's the game, man. Play her, and all will be well with us. Play her, and I shall teach you how."

I bristled. Sea-cuny I was, but I was man, and to no man would I be beholden in my way with women. Hendrik Hamel might be one-tame part-owner of the old *Sparwehr* with a navigator's knowledge of the stars and deep-versed in books, but with women, no, there I would not give him better.

He smiled that thin-lipped smile of his, and queried:

"How like you the Lady Om?"

"In such matters a cuny is naught particular," I temporized.

"How like you her?" He repeated, his beady eyes boring into me.

"Passing well, ay, and more than passing well, if you will have it."

174

"Then win to her," he commanded, "and someday we will get ship and escape from this cursed land. I'd give half the silks of the Indies for a meal of Christian food again."

He regarded me intently.

"Do you think you can win to her?" He questioned.

I was half in the air at the challenge. He smiled his satisfaction.

"But not too quickly," he advised. "Quick things are cheap things. Put a prize upon yourself. Be chary of your kindness. Make a value of your bull throat and yellow hair, and thank God you have them for they are of more worth in a woman's eyes than are the brains of a dozen philosophers."

Strange whirling days were those that followed, what with my audiences with the Emperor, my drinking bouts with Taiwun, my conferences with Yunsan, and my hours with the Lady Om. Besides, I sat up half the nights, by Hamel's command, learning from Kim all the minutiae of court etiquette and manners, the history of Korea and of gods old and new, and the forms of polite speech, noble speech, and coolie speech Never was sea-cuny worked so hard. I was a puppet—puppet to Yunsan, who had need of me; puppet to Hamel, who schemed the wit of the affair that was so deep that alone I should have drowned. Only with the Lady Om was I man, not puppet . . . and yet, and yet, as I look back and ponder across time, I have my doubts. I think the Lady Om too had her will with me, wanting me for her heart's desire. Yet in this she was well met, for it was not long ere she was my heart's desire, and such was the immediacy of my will that not her will, nor Hendrik Hamel's nor Yunsan's could hold back my arms from about her.

In the meantime, however, I was caught up in a palace intrigue I could not fathom. I could catch the drift of it, no more, against Chong Mong-ju, the princely cousin of the Lady Om. Beyond my guessing, there were cliques and cliques within cliques that made a labyrinth of the palace and extended to all the Seven Coasts. But I did not worry. I left that to Hendrik

Hamel. To him I reported every detail that occurred when he was not with me; and he, with furrowed brows, sitting darkling by the hour, like a patient spider unraveled the tangle and spun the web afresh. As my body slave, he insisted upon attending me everywhere; being only barred on occasion by Yunsan. Of course, I barred him from my moments with the Lady Om, but told him in general what passed, with exception of tenderer incidents that were not his business.

I think Hamel was content to sit back and play the secret part. He was too cold-blooded not to calculate that the risk was mine. If I prospered, he prospered. If I crashed to ruin, he might creep out like a ferret. I am convinced that he so reasoned, and yet it did not save him in the end, as you shall see.

"Stand by me," I told Kim, "and whatsoever you wish shall be yours. Have you a wish?"

"I would command the Tiger Hunters of Pyeng-Yang, and so command the palace guards," he answered.

"Wait," said I, "and that will you do. I have said it."

The how of the matter was beyond me. But he who has naught can dispense the world in largess; and I, who had naught, gave Kim captaincy of the palace guards. The best of it is that I did fulfill my promise. Kim did come to command the Tiger Hunters, although it brought him to a sad end.

Scheming and intriguing I left to Hamel and Yunsan, who were the politicians. I was mere man and lover, and merrier than theirs was the time I had. Picture it to yourself—a hard-bitten, joy-loving, sea-cuny, irresponsible, unaware ever of past or future, wining and dining with kings, the accepted lover of a princess, and with brains like Hamel's and Yunsan's to do all planning and executing for me.

More than once Yunsan almost divined the mind behind my mind; but when he probed Hamel, Hamel proved a stupid slave, a thousand times less interested in affairs of state and policy than was he interested in my health and comfort and garrulously anxious about my drinking contests with Taiwun. I think the Lady

Om guessed the truth and kept it to herself; wit was not her desire, but, as Hamel had said, a bull throat and a man's yellow hair.

Much that passed between us I shall not relate, though the Lady Om is dear dust these centuries. But she was not to be denied, nor was; and when a man and woman will their hearts together heads may fall and kingdoms crash and yet they will not forego.

Came the time when our marriage was mooted, oh, quietly at first, most quietly, as mere palace gossip in dark corners between eunuchs and waiting women. But in a palace the gossip of the kitchen scullions will creep to the throne. Soon there was a pretty to-do. The palace was the pulse of Cho-Sen, and when the palace rocked, Cho-Sen trembled. And there was reason for the rocking. Our marriage would be a blow straight between the eyes of Chong Mong-ju. He fought, with a show of strength for which Yunsan was ready. Chong Mong-ju disaffected half the provincial priesthood, until they pilgrimaged in processions a mile long to the palace gates and frightened the Emperor into a panic.

But Yunsan held like a rock. The other half of the provincial priesthood was his with, in addition, all the priesthood of the great cities such as Keijo, Fusan, Songdo, Pyen-Yang, Chenampo, and Chemulpo. Yunsan and the Lady Om, between them, twisted the Emperor right about. As she confessed to me afterward, she bullied him with tears and hysteria and threats of a scandal that would shake the throne. And to cap it all, at the psychological moment, Yunsan pandered the Emperor to novelties of excess that had been long preparing.

"You must grow your hair for the marriage knot," Yunsan warned me one day, with the ghost of a twinkle in his austere eyes, more nearly facetious and human than I had ever beheld him.

Now it is not meet that a princess espouse a sea-cuny, or even a claimant of the ancient blood of Koryu, who is without power, or place, or visible symbols of rank. So it was promulgated by imperial decrees that I was a prince of Koryu. Next, after breaking his bones and decapitating the then governor of five provinces, himself an adherent of Chong Mong-ju, I was made governor of the seven home provinces of ancient Koryu. In Cho-Sen seven is the magic number. To complete this number, two of the provinces were taken over from the hands of two more of Chong Mong-ju's adherents.

Lord, Lord, a sea-cuny—and dispatched north over the Mandarin Road with five hundred soldiers and a retinue at my back! I was a governor of seven provinces, where fifty thousand troops awaited me. Life, death, and torture I carried at my disposal I had a treasury and a treasurer, to say nothing of a regiment of scribes. Awaiting me also were a full thousand of tax farmers who squeezed the last coppers from the toiling people.

The seven provinces constituted the northern march. Beyond lay what is now Manchuria, but which was known by us as the country of the Hong-du, or "Red Heads." They were wild raiders, on occasion crossing the Yalu in great masses and overrunning northern Cho-Sen like locusts. It was said they were given to cannibal practices. I know of experience that they were terrible fighters, most difficult to convince of a beating.

A whirlwind year it was. While Yunsan and the Lady Om at Keijo completed the disgrace of Chong Mong-ju, I proceeded to make a reputation for myself. Of course it was really Hendrik Hamel at my back, but I was the fine figurehead that carried it off. Through me, Hamil taught our soldiers drill and tactics and taught the Red Heads' strategy. The fighting was grand, and though it took a year, the year's end saw peace on the northern border and no Red Heads but dead Red Heads on our side of the Yalu.

I do not know if this invasion of the Red Heads is recorded in Western history, but if so it will give a clue to the date of the times of which I write. Another clue: when was Hideyoshi the Shogun of Japan? In my time I heard the echoes of the two invasions, a generation before, driven by Hideyoshi through the heart of Cho-Sen from Fusan in the south to as far north as Pyeng-Yang. It was this Hideyoshi who sent back to Japan a myriad tubs of pickled ears and noses of Koreans slain in battle. I talked with many old men and women who had seen the fighting and escaped the pickling.

Back to Keijo and the Lady Om. Lord, Lord, she was a woman. For forty years she was my woman know. No dissenting voice was raised against the marriage. Chong Mong-ju, clipped of power, in disgrace, had retired to sulk somewhere on the far northeast coast. Yunsan was absolute. Nightly the single beacons flared their message of peace across the land. The Emperor grew more weak-legged and blear-eyed with the ingenious deviltries devised for him by Yunsan. The Lady Om and I had won to our hearts' desires. Kim was in command of the palace guards. Kwan Yung-jin, the provincial governor who had planked and beaten us when we were first cast away, I had shorn of power and banished forever from appearing within the walls of Keijo.

Oh, and Johannes Maartens. Discipline is well hammered into a sea-cuny and, despite my new greatness, I could never forget that he had been my captain in the days we sought new Indies in the *Sparwehr*. According to my tale first told in court, he was the only free man in my following. The rest of the cunies, being considered my slaves, could not aspire to office of any sort under the crown. But Johannes could, and did. The sly old fox! I little guessed his intent, when he asked me to make him governor of the paltry little province of Kyong-ju. Kyong-ju had no wealth of farms or fisheries. The taxes scarce paid the collecting, and the governorship was little more than an empty honor. The place was in truth a graveyard—a sacred graveyard, for on Tabong Mountain were shrined and sepultured the bones of the ancient kings of Silla. Better governor of Kyong-ju than retainer of Adam Strang, was what I thought was in his mind; nor did I dream that it was fear of loneliness that caused him to take four of the cunies with him.

Gorgeous were the two years that followed. My seven provinces I governed mainly through needy yangbans, selected for me by Yunsan. An occasional inspection, done in state and accompanied by the Lady Om, was all that was required of me. She possessed a summer palace on the south coast, which we frequented much. Then there were man's diversions. I became patron of the sport of wrestling, and revived archery among the yangbans. Also, there was tiger-hunting in the northern mountains.

A remarkable thing was the tides of Cho-Sen. On our northeast coast there was scarce a rise and fall of a foot. On our west coast, the neap tides ran as high as sixty feet. Cho-Sen had no commerce, no foreign traders. There was no voyaging beyond her coasts, and no voyaging of other peoples to her coasts. This was due to her immemorial policy of isolation. Once in a decade or a score of years, Chinese ambassadors arrived, but they came overland, around the Yellow Sea, across the country of the Hong-du, and down the Mandarin Road to Keijo. The round trip was a year-long journey. Their mission was to exact from our Emperor the empty ceremonial of acknowledgment of China's ancient suzerainty.

But Hamel, from long brooding, was ripening for action. His plans grew apace. Cho-Sen was Indies enough for him could he but work it right. Little he confided, but when he began to play to have me made admiral of the Cho-Sen navy of junks, and to inquire more than casually of the details of the store-places of the imperial treasury, I could put two and two together.

Now I did not care to depart from Cho-Sen except with the Lady Om. When I broached the possibility of it, she told me, warm in my arms, that I was her king and that wherever I led she would follow. As you shall see, it was truth, full truth, that she uttered.

It was Yunsan's fault for letting Chong Mong-ju live. And yet it was not Yunsan's fault. He had not dared otherwise. Disgraced at Court, nevertheless Chong Mong-ju had been too popular with the provincial priesthood. Yunsan had been compelled to hold his hand, and Chong Mong-ju, apparently sulking on the northeast coast, had been anything but idle. His emissaries, chiefly Buddhist priests, were everywhere, went everywhere, gathering in even the least of the provincial magistrates to allegiance to him. It takes the cold patience of the Asiatic to conceive and execute huge and complicated conspiracies. The strength of Chong Mong-ju's palace clique grew beyond Yunsan's wildest dreaming. Chong Mong-ju corrupted the very palace guards, the Tiger Hunters of Pyeng-Yang whom Kim commanded. And while Yunsan nodded, while I devoted myself to sport and to the Lady Om, while Hendrik Hamel perfected plans for the looting of the Imperial treasury and while Johannes Maartens schemed his own scheme among the tombs of Tabong Mountain, the volcano of Chong Mong-ju's devising gave no warning beneath us.

Lord, Lord, when the storm broke! It was stand out from under, all hands, and save your necks. And there were necks that were not saved. The springing of the conspiracy was premature. Johannes Maartens really precipitated the catastrophe, and what he did was too favorable for Chong Mong-ju not to advantage by.

For, see. The people of Cho-Sen are fanatical ancestor worshipers, and that old pirate of a booty-lusting Dutchman, with his four cunies in far Kyong-ju, did no less a thing than raid the tombs of the gold-coffined, long-buried kings of ancient Silla. The work was done in the night, and for the rest of the night they traveled for the sea coast. But the following day a dense fog lay over the land and they lost their way to the waiting junk which Johannes Maartens had privily outfitted. He and the cunies were rounded in by Yi Sun-sin, the local magistrate, one of Chong Mong-ju's adherents. Only Herman Tromp escaped in the fog, and was able, long after, to tell me of the adventure.

That night, although news of the sacrilege was spreading through Cho-Sen and half the northern provinces had risen on their officials, Keijo and the Court slept in ignorance. By Chong Mong-ju's orders the beacons flared their nightly message of peace. And night by night the peace beacons flared, while day and night Chong Mong-ju's messengers killed horses on all the roads of Cho-Sen. It was my luck to see his messenger arrive at Keijo. At twilight, as I rode out through the great gate of the capital, I saw the jaded horse fall and the exhausted rider stagger in on foot; and I little dreamed that that man carried my destiny with him into Keijo.

His message sprang the palace revolution. I was not due to return until midnight, and by midnight all was over. At nine in the evening the conspirators secured possession of the Emperor in his own apartments. They compelled him to order the immediate attendance of the heads of all departments, and as they presented themselves, one by one, before his eyes, they were cut down. Meantime the Tiger Hunters were up and out of hand. Yunsan and Hendrik Hamel were badly beaten with the flats of swords and made prisoners. The seven other cunies escaped from the palace along with the Lady Om. They were enabled to do this by Kim, who held the way, sword in hand, against his own Tiger Hunters. They cut him down and trod over him. Unfortunately, he did not die of his wounds.

Like a flow of wind on a summer night, the revolution, a palace revolution, of course, blew and was past. Chong Mong-ju was in the saddle. The Emperor ratified whatever Chong Mong-ju willed. Beyond gasping at the sacrilege of the kings' tombs and applauding Chong Mong-ju, Cho-Sen was unperturbed. Heads of officials fell everywhere, being replaced by Chong Mong-ju's appointees; but there were no risings against the dynasty.

And now to what befell us. Johannes Maartens and his three cunies, after being exhibited to be spat upon by the rabble of half the villages and walled cities of Cho-Sen, were buried to their necks in the ground of the open space before the palace gate. Water was given them that they might live longer to yearn for the food, steaming hot and savory and changed hourly, that was placed temptingly before them. They said old Johannes Maartens lived longest, not giving up the ghost for a full fifteen days.

Kim was slowly crushed to death, bone by bone and joint by joint, by the torturers, and was a long time in dying. Hamel, whom Chong Mong-ju divined as my brains, was executed by the paddle—in short, was promptly and expeditiously beaten to death to the delighted shouts of the Keijo populace. Yunsan was given a brave death. He was playing a game of chess with the jailer when the Emperor's, or rather Chong Mong-ju's, messenger arrived with the poison cup. "Wait a moment," said Yunsan. "You should be better mannered than to disturb a man in the midst of a game of chess. I shall drink directly the game is over." And while the messenger waited, Yunsan finished the game, winning it, then drained the cup. It takes an Asiatic to temper his spleen to steady, persistent, life-long revenge. This Chong Mong-ju did with the Lady Om and me. He did not destroy us. We were not even imprisoned. The Lady Om was degraded of all rank and divested of all possessions. An imperial decree was promulgated and posted in the last least village of Cho-Sen to the effect that I was of the house of Koryu and that no man might kill me. It was further declared that the eight sea-cunies who survived must not be killed. Neither were they to be favored. They were to be outcasts, beggars on the highways. And that is what the Lady Om and I became, beggars on the highways.

Forty long years of persecution followed, for Chong Mong-ju's hatred of the Lady Om and me was deathless. Worse luck, he was favored with long life as well as were we cursed with it. I have said the Lady Om was a wonder of woman. Beyond endlessly repeating that statement, words fail me with which to give her just appreciation. Somewhere I have heard that a great lady once said to her lover: "A tent and a crust of bread with you." In effect that is what the Lady Om said to me. More than to say it, she lived the last letter of it, when more often than not crusts were not plentiful and the sky itself was our tent.

Every effort I made to escape beggary was in the end frustrated by Chong Mong-ju. In Song-do I became a fuel carrier, and the Lady Om and I shared a hut that was vastly more comfortable than the open road in bitter winter weather. But Chong Mong-ju found me out, and I was beaten and planked and put out upon the road. That was a terrible winter, the winter poor "What-Now" Vandervoot froze to death on the streets of Keijo.

In Pyeng-Yang I became a water carrier, for know that that old city whose walls were ancient even in the time of David was considered by the people to be a canoe, and that therefore, to sink a well inside the walls would be to scupper the city. So all day long thousands of coolies, water jars yoked to their shoulders, tramp out the river gate and back. I became one of these, until Chong Mong-ju sought me out, and I was beaten and planked and set upon the highway.

Ever it was the same. In far Wiju I became a dog butcher, killing the brutes before my open stall, cutting and hanging the carcasses for sale, tanning the hides under the filth of the feet of the passers-by spreading the hides, raw-side up, in the muck of the street. But Chong Mong-ju found me out. I was a dyer's helper in Pyonhan, a gold miner in the placers of Kang-wun, a rope maker and twine twister in Chiksan. I plaited straw hats in Padok, gathered grass in Whang-hai, and in Masanpo sold myself to a rice farmer to toil bent double in the flooded paddies for less than a coolie's pay. But there was never a time or place that the long arm of Chong Mong-ju did not reach out and punish and thrust me upon the beggar's way.

The Lady Om and I searched two seasons and found a single root of the wild mountain ginseng, which is esteemed so rare and precious a thing by the doctors that the Lady Om and I could have lived a year in comfort from the sale of our one root. But in the selling of it I was apprehended, the root confiscated, and I was better beaten and longer planked than ordinarily.

Everywhere the wandering members of the great Peddlers' Guild carried word of me, of my comings and goings and do-ings, to Chong Mong-ju at Keijo. Only twice, in all the days after my downfall, did I meet Chong Mong-ju face to face. The first time was a wild winter night of storm in the high mountains of Kangwun. A few hoarded coppers had bought for the Lady Om and me sleeping space in the dirtiest and coldest corner of the one large room of the inn. We were just about to begin on our meager supper of horse beans and wild garlic cooked into a stew with a scrap of bullock that must have died of old age, when there was a tinkling of bronze pony bells and the stamp of hoofs without. The doors opened, and entered Chong Mong-ju, the personification of well-being, prosperity, and power, shaking the snow from his priceless Mongolian furs. Place was made for him and his dozen retainers, and there was room for all without crowding, when his eyes chanced to light on the Lady Om and me.

"The vermin there in the corner—clear it out," he commanded.

And his horse-boys lashed us with their whips and drove us out into the storm. But there was to be another meeting, after long years, as you shall see.

There was no escape. Never was I permitted to cross the northern frontier. Never was I permitted to put foot to a sampan on the sea. The Peddlers' Guild carried these commands of Chong Mong-ju to every village and every soul in all Cho-Sen. I was a marked man.

Lord, Lord, Cho-Sen, I know your every highway and mountain path, all your walled cities and the least of your villages. For twoscore years I wandered and starved over you, and the Lady Om ever wandered and starved with me. What we in extremity have eaten! —Leavings of dog flesh, putrid and unsaleable, flung to us by the mocking butchers; minari, a watercress, gathered from stagnant pools of slime; spoiled kimchi that would revolt the stomachs of peasants and that could be smelled a mile. Ay—I have stolen bones from curs, gleaned the public roads for stray grains of rice, robbed ponies of their steaming bean soup on frosty nights.

It is not strange that I did not die. I knew and was upheld by two things: the first, the Lady Om by my side; the second, the certain faith that the time would come when my thumbs and fingers would fast-lock in the gullet of Chong Mong-ju.

Turned always away at the city gates of Keijo, where I sought Chong Mong-ju, we wandered on, through seasons and decades of seasons, across Cho-Sen, whose every inch of road was an old story to our sandals. Our history and identity were wide-scattered as the land was wide. No person breathed who did not know us and our punishment. There were coolies and peddlers who shouted insults at the Lady Om and who felt the wrath of my clutch in their topknots, the wrath of my knuckles in their faces. There were old women in far mountain villages who looked on the beggar woman by my side, the lost Lady Om, and sighed and shook their heads while their eyes dimmed with tears. And there were young women whose faces warmed with compassion as they gazed on the bulk of my shoulders, the blue of my eyes, and my long yellow hair—I who had once been a prince of Koryu and the ruler of provinces. And there were rabbles of children that tagged at our heels, jeering and screeching, pelting us with filth of speech and of the common road.

Beyond the Yalu, forty miles wide, was the strip of waste that constituted the northern frontier and that ran from sea to sea It was not really waste land, but land that had been deliberately made waste in carrying out Cho-Sen's policy of isolation. On this forty-mile strip all farms, villages, and cities had been destroyed. It was no man's land, infested with wild animals and traversed by companies of mounted Tiger Hunters whose business was to kill any human being they found. That way there was no escape for us, nor was there any escape for us by sea.

As the years passed, my seven fellow cunies came more to frequent Fusan. It was on the southeast coast where the climate was milder. But more than climate, it lay nearest of all Cho-Sen to Japan. Across the narrow straits, just farther than the eye can see, was the one hope of escape, Japan, where doubtless occasional ships of Europe came. Strong upon me is the vision of those seven aging men on the cliffs of Fusan yearning with all their souls across the sea they would never sail again.

At times junks of Japan were sighted, but never lifted a familiar topsail of old Europe above the sea rim. Years came and went, and the seven cunies and myself and the Lady Om, passing through middle life into old age, more and more directed our footsteps to Fusan. And as the years came and went, now one, now another, failed to gather at the usual place. Hans Amden was the first to die. Jacob Brinker, who was his road mate, brought the news. Jacob Brinker was the last of the seven, and he was nearly ninety when he died, outliving Tromp a scant two years. I well remember the pair of them, toward the last, worn and feeble, in beggars' rags, with beggars' bowls sunning themselves side by side on the cliffs, telling old stories and cackling shrill-voiced like children. And Tromp would maunder over and over of how Johannes Maartens and the cunies robbed the kings on Tabong Mountain, each embalmed in his golden coffin with an embalmed maid on either side; and of how these ancient proud ones crumbled to dust within the hour while the cunies cursed and sweated at the junking of the coffins.

As sure as loot is loot, old Johannes Maartens would have got away and across the Yellow Sea with his booty had it not been for the fog next day that lost him. That cursed fog! A song was made of it, that I heard and hated through all Cho-Sen to my dying day. Here run two lines of it:

Yanggukeni chajin anga
Wheanpong tora deunda
(*The thick fog of the Westerners*
Broods over Whean peak)

For forty years I was a beggar of Cho-Sen. Of the fourteen of us that were cast away, only I survived. The Lady Om was of the same indomitable stuff, and we aged together. She was a little, wizened, toothless old woman toward the last; but ever she was the wonder woman, and she carried my heart in hers to the end. For an old man, three score and ten, I still retained great strength. My face was withered, my yellow hair turned white, my broad shoulders shrunken, and yet much of the strength of my sea-cuny days resided in the muscles left me.

Thus it was that I was able to do what I shall now relate. It was a spring morning on the cliffs of Fusan, hard by the highway, that the Lady Om and I sat warming in the sun. We were in the rags of beggary, priceless in the dust, and yet I was laughing heartily at some mumbled merry quip of the Lady Om when a shadow fell upon us. It was the great litter of Chong Mong-ju, borne by eight coolies, with outriders before and behind and fluttering attendants on either side.

Two emperors, civil war, famine, and a dozen palace revolutions had come and gone; and Chong Mong-ju remained, even then the great power at Keijo. He must have been nearly eighty that spring morning on the cliffs when he signaled with palsied hand for his litter to be rested down that he might gaze upon us whom he had punished for so long.

"Now, Oh my king," the Lady Om mumbled low to me, then turned to whine an alms of Chong Mong-ju, whom she affected not to recognize.

And I knew what was her thought. Had we not shared it for forty years? And the moment of its consummation had come at last. So I too affected not to recognize my enemy and, putting on an idiotic senility, I too crawled in the dust toward the litter, whining for mercy and charity.

The attendants would have driven me back, but with age-quavering cackles Chong Mong-ju restrained them. He lifted himself on a shaking elbow, and with the other shaking hand drew wider apart the silken curtains. His withered old face was transfigured with delight as he gloated on us.

"Oh my king," the Lady Om whined to me in her beggar's chant; and I knew all her long-tried love and faith in my emprise were in that chant.

And the Red Wrath was up in me, ripping and tearing at my will to be free. Small wonder that I shook with the effort to control the shaking, happily, they took for the weakness of age. I held up my brass begging bowl and whined more dolefully, and bleared my eyes to hide the blue fire I knew was in them, and calculated the distance and my strength for the leap.

Then I was swept away in a blaze of red. There was a crashing of curtains and curtain poles and a squawking and squalling of attendants as my hands closed on Chong Mong-ju's throat. The litter overturned, and I scarce knew whether I was heads or heels, but my clutch never relaxed.

In the confusion of cushions and quilts and curtains, at first few of the attendants' blows found me. But soon the horsemen were in, and their heavy whip butts began to fall on my head, while a multitude of hands clawed and tore at me. I was dizzy, but not unconscious, and very blissful with my old fingers buried in that lean and scraggly old neck I had sought for so long. The blows continued to rain on my head, and I had whirling thoughts in which I likened myself to a bulldog with jaws fast-locked. Chong Mong-ju could not escape me, and I know he was well dead ere darkness descended upon me there on the cliffs of Fusan by the Yellow Sea.

★"Cuny" origin unknown, probably coined by Jack London. It is used here as 'marine" or "ordinary seaman."

Chapter 16

Warden Atherton, when he thinks of me, must feel anything but pride. I have taught him what spirit is, humbled him with my own spirit that rose invulnerable, triumphant, above all his tortures. I sit here in Folsom, in Murderers' Row, awaiting my execution; Warden Atherton still holds his political job and is king over San Quentin and all the damned within its walls; and yet, in his heart of hearts, he knows that I am a greater than he.

In vain Warden Atherton tried to break my spirit. And there were times, beyond any shadow of doubt, when he would have been glad had I died in the jacket. So the long inquisition went on. As he had told me, and as he told me repeatedly, it was dynamite or curtains.

Captain Jamie was a veteran in dungeon horrors, yet the time came when he broke down under the strain I put on him and on the rest of my torturers. So desperate did he become that he dared words with the warden and washed his hands of the affair. From that day until the end of my torturing he never set foot in solitary.

Yes, and the time came when Warden Atherton grew afraid, although he still persisted in trying to wring from me the hiding place of the non-existent dynamite. Toward the last he was badly shaken by Jake Oppenheimer. Oppenheimer was fearless and outspoken. He had passed unbroken through all their prison hells, and out of superior will could beard them to their teeth. Morrell rapped me a full account of the incident. I was unconscious in the jacket at the time.

"Warden," Oppenheimer had said, "you've bitten off more than you can chew. It ain't a case of killing Standing. It's a case of killing three men, for as sure as you kill him, sooner or later Morrell and I will get the word out and what you have done will be known from one end of California to the other. You've got your choice. You've either got to let up on Standing or kill all three of us. Standing's got your goat. So have I. So has Morrell. You are a stinking coward and you haven't got the backbone and guts to carry out the dirty butcher's work you'd like to do."

Oppenheimer got a hundred hours in the jacket for it and when he was unlaced spat in the warden's face and received a second hundred hours on end. When he was unlaced this time, the warden was careful not to be in solitary. That he was shaken by Oppenheimer's words there is no doubt.

But it was Dr. Jackson who was the arch fiend. To him I was a novelty, and he was ever eager to see how much more I could stand before I broke.

"He can stand twenty days off the bat," he bragged to the warden in my presence.

"You are conservative," I broke in. "I can stand forty days. Pshaw! I can stand a hundred when such as you administer it." And, remembering my sea-cuny's patience of forty years' waiting ere I got my hands on Chong Mong-ju's gullet, I added: "You prison curs, you don't know what a man is. You think a man is made in your own cowardly images. Behold, I am a man. You are feeblings. I am your master. You can't bring a squeal out of me. You think it remarkable, for you know how easily you would squeal."

Oh, I abused them, called them sons of toads, hell's scullions, slime of the pit. For I was above them, beyond them. They were slaves. I was free spirit. My flesh only lay pent there in solitary. I was not pent. I had mastered the flesh, and the spaciousness of time was mine to wander in, while my poor flesh, not even suffering, lay in the little death in the jacket.

Much of my adventures I rapped to my two comrades. Morrell believed, for he had himself tasted the little death. But Oppenheimer, enraptured with my tales, remained a skeptic to the end. His regret was naive, and at times really pathetic, in that I had devoted my life to the science of agriculture instead of to fiction-writing.

"But, man," I reasoned with him, "what do I know, of myself, about this Cho-Sen? I am able to identify it with what is today called Korea, and that is about all. That is as far as my reading goes. For instance, how possibly, out of my present life's experience, could I know anything about kimchi? Yet I know kimchi. It is a sort of sauerkraut. When it is spoiled it stinks to heaven. I tell you, when I was Adam Strang, I ate kimchi thousands of times. I know good kimchi, bad kimchi, rotten kimchi. I know the best kimchi is made by the women of Wosan. Now how do I know that? It is not in the content of my mind, Darrell Standing's mind. It is in the content of Adam Strang's mind, who, through various births and deaths, bequeathed his experiences to me, Darrell Standing, along with the rest of the experiences of those various other lives that intervened. Don't you see, Jake? That is how men come to be, to grow, how spirit develops."

"Aw, come off," he rapped back with the quick imperative knuckles I knew so well. "Listen to your uncle talk now. I am Jake Oppenheimer. I always have been Jake Oppenheimer. No other guy is in my makings. What I know I know as Jake Oppenheimer. Now what do I know? I'll tell you one thing. I know kimchi. Kimchi is a sort of sauerkraut made in a country that used to be called Cho-Sen. The women of Wosan make the best kimchi, and when kimchi is spoiled it stinks to heaven. —You keep out of this, Ed. Wait till I tie the professor up. Now, Professor, how do I know all this stuff about kimchi? It is not in the content of my mind."

"But it is," I exulted. "I put it there."

"All right, old hoss. Then who put it into your mind?"

"Adam Strang."

"Not on your tintype. Adam Strang is a pipe dream. You read it somewhere."

"Never," I averred. "The little I read of Korea was the head-lines of the war correspondence at the time of the Japanese-Russian War."

"Do you remember all you read?" Oppenheimer queried.

"No."

"Some you forget?"

"Yes, but—"

"That's all, thank you," he interrupted, in the manner of a lawyer abruptly concluding a cross-examination after having extracted a fatal admission from a witness.

It was impossible to convince Oppenheimer of my sincerity. He insisted that I was making it up as I went along, although he applauded what he called my "to-be-continued-in-our-next," and, at the times they were resting me up from the jacket, was continually begging and urging me to run off a few more chapters.

"Now, Professor, cut out that highbrow stuff," he would interrupt Ed Morrell's and my metaphysical discussions, "and tell us more about the kisang and the cunies. And, say, while you're about it, tell us what happened to the Lady Om when that rough neck husband of hers choked the old geezer and croaked."

How often have I said that form perishes. Let me repeat. Form perishes. Matter has no memory. Spirit only remembers, as here, in prison cells, after the centuries, knowledge of the Lady Om and Chong Mong-ju persisted in my mind, was conveyed by me into Jake Oppenheimer's mind, and by him was reconveyed into my mind in the argot and jargon of the West. And now I have conveyed it into your mind, my reader. Try to eliminate it from your mind. You cannot As long as you live what I have told will tenant your mind. Mind? There is nothing permanent but mind. Matter fluxes, crystallizes, and fluxes again, and forms are never repeated. Forms disintegrate into the eternal nothingness from which there is no return. Form is apparitional and passes, as passed the physical forms of the Lady Om and Chong Mong-ju. But the memory of them remains, shall always remain as long as spirit endures, and spirit is indestructible.

"One thing sticks out as big as a house," was Oppenheimer's final criticism of my Adam Strang adventure. "And that is that you've done more hanging around Chinatown dumps and hop

joints than was good for a respectable college professor. Evil communications, you know. I guess that's what brought you here."

Before I return to my adventures, I am compelled to tell one
remarkable incident that occurred in solitary. It is remarkable in
two ways. It shows the astounding mental power of that child of
the gutters, Jake Oppenheimer; and it is in itself convincing proof
of the verity of my experiences when in the jacket coma

"Say, Professor," Oppenheimer tapped to me one day. "When
you was spieling that Adam Strang yarn, I remember you mentioned playing chess with that royal souse of an emperor's brother.
Now is that chess like our kind of chess?"

Of course, I had to reply that I did not know, that I did not
remember the details after I returned to my normal state. And of
course he laughed good-naturedly at what he called my foolery.
Yet I could distinctly remember that in my Adam Strang adventure I had frequently played chess. The trouble was that whenever
I came back to consciousness in solitary, unessential and intricate
details faded from my memory.

It must be remembered that for convenience I have assembled
my intermittent and repetitional jacket experiences into coherent
and consecutive narratives. I never knew in advance where my
journeys in time would take me. For instance, I have a score of
different times returned to Jesse Fancher in the wagon circle at
Mountain Meadows. In a single ten-day bout in the jacket I have
gone back and back, from life to life, and often skipping whole series of lives that at other times I have covered, back to prehistoric
time, and back of that to days ere civilization began.

So I resolved, on my next return from Adam Strang's experiences, whenever it might be, that I should, immediately on resum-
ing consciousness, concentrate upon what visions and memories I
had brought back of chess playing. As luck would have it, I had to
endure Oppenheimer's chaffing for a full month ere it happened.
And then, no sooner out of jacket and circulation restored, than I
started knuckle-rapping the information.

Further, I taught Oppenheimer the chess Adam Strang had

played in Cho-Sen centuries ago. It was different from Western chess, and yet could not but be fundamentally the same, tracing back to a common origin, probably India. In place of our sixty-four squares, there are eighty-one squares. We have eight pawns on a side; they have nine; and though limited similarly, the principle of moving is different

Also, in the Cho-Sen game there are twenty pieces and pawns against our sixteen, and they are arrayed in three rows instead of two. Thus, the nine pawns are in the front row; in the middle row are two pieces resembling our castles; and in the back row, midway, stands the king, flanked in order on either side by "gold money," "silver money," "flying horse," and "spear." It will be observed that in the Cho-Sen game there is no queen. A further radical variation is that a captured piece or pawn is not removed from the board. It becomes the property of the captor and is thereafter played by him.

Well, I taught Oppenheimer this game—a far more difficult achievement than our own game, as will be admitted, when the capturing and recapturing and continued playing of pawns and pieces is considered. Solitary is not heated. It would be a wickedness to ease a convict from any spite of the elements. And many a dreary day of biting cold did Oppenheimer and I forget, that and the following winter, in the absorption of Cho-Sen chess.

But there was no convincing him that I had in truth brought this game back to San Quentin across the centuries. He insisted that I had read about it somewhere and, though I had forgotten the reading, the stuff of the reading was nevertheless in the content of my mind, ripe to be brought out in any pipe-dream. Thus he turned the tenets and jargon of psychology back on me.

"What's to prevent your inventing it right here in solitary?" Was his next hypothesis. "Didn't Ed invent the knuckle-talk? And ain't you and me improving on it right along? I got you, bo. You invented it. Say, get it patented. I remember when I was night messenger some guy invented a fool thing called Pigs in Clover and made millions out of it."

"There's no patenting this," I replied. "Doubtlessly the Asiatics have been playing it for thousands of years. Won't you believe me when I tell you I didn't invent it?"

"Then you must have read about it, or seen the Chinks playing it in some of those hop-joints you was always hanging around," was his last word.

But I have a last word. There is a Japanese murderer here in Folsom—or was, for he was executed last week. I talked the matter over with him; and the game Adam Strang played, and which I taught Oppenheimer, proved quite similar to the Japanese game. They are far more alike than is either of them like the Western game.

Chapter 17

You, my reader, will remember, far back at the beginning of this narrative, how, when a little lad on the Minnesota farm, I looked at the photographs of the Holy Land and recognized places and pointed out changes in places. Also, you will remember, as I described the scene I had witnessed of the healing of the lepers, I told the missionary that I was a big man with a big sword, astride a horse and looking on.

That childhood incident was merely trailing cloud of glory, as Wordsworth puts it. Not in entire forgetfulness had I, little Darrell Standing, come into the world. But those memories of other times and places that glimmered up to the surface of my child consciousness soon failed and faded. In truth, as is the way with all children, the shades of the prison house closed about me, and I remembered my mighty past no more. Every man born of woman has a past mighty as mine. Very few men born of women have been fortunate enough to suffer years of solitary and straitjacketing. That was my good fortune. I was enabled to remember once again, and to remember, among other things, the time when I sat astride a horse and beheld the lepers healed.

My name was Ragnar Lodbrog. I was in truth a large man. I stood half a head above the Romans of my legion. But that was later, after the time of my journey from Alexandria to Jerusalem, that I came to command a legion. It was a crowded life, that. Books and books and years of writing could not record it all. So I shall be brief and no more than hint at the beginnings of it.

Now all is clear and sharp save the very beginning. I never knew my mother. I was told that I was tempest-born, on a beaked ship in the Northern Sea, of a captured woman, after a sea fight and a sack of a coastal stronghold. I never heard the name of my mother. She died at the height of the tempest. She was of the North Danes, so old Lingaard told me. He told me much that I was too young to remember, yet little could he tell. A sea fight and a sack, battle and plunder and torch, a flight seaward in the long ships to escape destruction upon the rocks, and a killing strain and struggle against the frosty, foundering seas—who, then, should know aught or mark a stranger woman in her hour with her feet fast set on the way of death? Many died. Men marked the living women, not the dead.

Sharp-bitten into my child imagination are the incidents immediately after my birth, as told me by old Lingaard. Lingaard, too old to labor at the sweeps, had been surgeon, undertaker, and midwife of the huddled captives in the open midships. So I was delivered in storm, with the spume of the cresting seas salt upon me.

Not many hours old was I when Tostig Lodbrog first laid eyes on me. His was the lean ship, and his the seven other lean ships that had made the foray, fled the rapine, and won through the storm. Tostig Lodbrog was also called Muspell, meaning "The Burning"; for he was ever aflame with wrath. Brave he was and cruel he was, with no heart of mercy in that great chest of his. Ere the sweat of battle had dried on him, leaning on his axe, he ate the heart of Ngrun after the fight at Hasfarth. Because of mad anger he sold his son, Garulf, into slavery to the Juts. I remember, under the smoky rafters of Brunanbuhr, how he used to call for the skull of Guthlaf for a drinking beaker. Spiced wine he would have from no other cup than the skull of Guthlaf.

And to him, on the reeling deck after the storm was past, old Lingaard brought me. I was only hours old, wrapped naked in a salt-crusted wolfskin. Now it happens, being prematurely born, that I was very small.

"Ho! Ho! —a dwarf!" Cried Tostig, lowering a pot of mead half drained from his lips to stare at me.

The day was bitter, but they say he swept me naked from the wolfskin, and by my foot, between thumb and forefinger, dangled me to the bite of the wind.

"A roach!" He ho-ho'd. "A shrimp! A sea louse!" And he made to squash me between huge forefinger and thumb, either of which, Lingaard avers, was thicker than my leg or thigh. But another whim was upon him.

"The youngling is a-thirst. Let him drink."

And therewith, head-downward, into the half-pot of mead he thrust me. And I might well have drowned in this drink of men—I who had never known a mother's breast in the briefness of time I had lived—had it not been for Lingaard. But when he had plucked me forth from the brew, Tostig Lodbrog struck him down in a rage. We rolled on the deck and the great bear hounds captured in the fight with the North Danes just past, sprang upon us.

"Ho! Ho!" Roared Tostig Lodbrog, as the old man and I and the wolfskin were mauled and worried by the dogs.

But Lingaard gained his feet, saving me but losing the wolf-skin to the hounds

Tostig Lodbrog finished the mead and regarded me, while Lingaard knew better than to beg for mercy where was no mercy.

"Hop oh' my thumb," quoth Tostig. "By Odin, the women of the North Danes are a scurvy breed. They birth dwarfs not men. Of what use is this thing? He will never make a man. Listen you, Lingaard, grow him to be a drink-boy at Brunanbuhr. And have an eye on the dogs lest they slobber him down by mistake as a meat crumb from the table."

I knew no woman. Old Lingaard was midwife and nurse, and for nursery were reeling decks and the stamp and trample of men in battle or storm. How I survived puling God knows. I must have been born iron in a day of iron, for survive I did, to give the lie to Tostig's promise of dwarfhood. I outgrew all beakers and tankards, and not for long could he half-drown me in his mead pot. This last was a favorite feat of his. It was his raw humor, a sally esteemed by him delicious wit.

My first memories are of Tostig Lodbrog's beaked ships and fighting men, and of the feast hall at Brunanbuhr when our boats lay beached beside the frozen fjord. For I was made drink-boy, and among my earliest recollections are toddling with the wine-filled skull of Guthlaf to the head of the table where Tostig bellowed to the rafters. They were madmen, all of madness, but it seemed the common way of life to me who knew naught else. They were men of quick rages and quick battling. Their thoughts were ferocious; so was their eating ferocious, and their drinking. And I grew like them. How else could I grow, when I served the drink to the bellowings of drunkards and to the skalds singing of Hialli, and the bold Hogni, and of the Niflung's gold, and of Gudrun's revenge on Atli when she gave him the hearts of his children and hers to eat while battle swept the benches, tore down the hangings raped from southern coasts, and littered the feasting board with swift corpses.

Oh, I too had a rage, well tutored in such school. I was but eight when I showed my teeth at a drinking between the men of Brunanbuhr and the Juts who came as friends with the jarl Agard in his three long ships. I stood at Tostig Lodbrog's shoulder, holding the skull of Guthlaf that steamed and stank with the hot spiced wine. And I waited while Tostig should complete his ravings against the North Dane men. But still he raved and still I waited, till he caught breath of fury to assoil the North Dane women. Whereat I remembered my North Dane mother and saw my rage red in my eyes, and smote him with the skull of Guthlaf, so that he was wine-drenched, and wine-blinded, and fire-burned. And as he reeled unseeing, smashing his great groping clutches through the air at me, I was in and short-dirked him thrice in belly, thigh, and buttock, than which I could reach no higher up the mighty frame of him.

And the jarl Agard's steel was out, and his Juts joining him as he shouted:

"A bear cub! A bear cub! By Odin, let the cub fight!"

And there, under that roaring roof of Brunanbuhr, the bubbling drink-boy of the North Danes fought with mighty Lodbrog. And when, with one stroke I was flung, dazed and breathless, half the length of that great board, my flying body mowing down pots and tankards, Lodbrog cried out command:

"Out with him! Fling him to the hounds!"

But the jarl would have it no, and clapped Lodbrog on the shoulder, and asked for me as a gift of friendship.

And south I went, when the ice passed out of the fjord, in jarl Agard's ships. I was made drink-boy and sword bearer to him, and in lieu of other name was called Ragnar Lodbrog. Agard's country was neighbor to the Frisians, and a sad, flat country of fog and fen it was. I was with him for three years, to his death, always at his back, whether hunting swamp wolves or drinking in the great hall where Elgiva, his young wife, often sat among her women. I was with Agard in south foray with his ships along what would be now the coast of France, and there I learned that skill, south were warmer seasons and softer climes and women.

But we brought back Agard wounded to death and slow-dying. And we burned his body on a great pyre, with Elgiva, in her golden corselet, beside him singing. And there were household slaves in golden collars that burned of a plenty there with her, and nine female thralls, and eight male slaves of the Angles that were of gentle birth and battle-captured. And there were live hawks so burned, and the two hawk-boys with their birds.

But I, the drink-boy, Ragnar Lodbrog, did not burn. I was eleven, and unafraid, and had never worn woven cloth on my body. And as the flames sprang up, and Elgiva sang her death song, and the thralls and slaves screamed their unwillingness to die, I tore away my fastenings, leaped, and gained the fens, the gold collar of my slavehood still on my neck, footing it with the hounds loosed to tear me down.

In the fens were wild men, masterless men, fled slaves and outlaws, who were hunted in sport as the wolves were hunted.

For three years I knew never roof nor fire, and I grew hard as the frost, and would have stolen a woman from the Juts but that the Frisians by mischance, in a two-day hunt, ran me down. By them I was looted of my gold collar and traded for two wolf hounds to Edwy, of the Saxons, who put an iron collar on me and later made of me and five other slaves a present to Athel of the East Angles. I was thrall and fighting man, until, lost in an unlucky raid far to the east beyond our marches, I was sold among the Harrobrogians and was a swineherd until I escaped south into the great forests and was taken in as a freeman by the Teutons, who were many but who lived in small tribes and drifted south before the Harrobrogian advance.

And up from the south into the great forests came the Romans, fighting men all, who pressed us back upon the Harrobrogians. It was a crushage of the peoples for lack of room; and we taught the Romans what fighting was, although in truth we were no less well taught by them.

But always I remembered the sun of the southland that I had glimpsed in the ships of Agard, and it was my fate, caught in this south drift of the Teutons, to be captured by the Romans and be brought back to the sea which I had not seen since I was lost away from the East Angles. I was made a sweep-slave in the galleys, and it was as a sweep-slave that at last I came to Rome.

All the story is too long of how I became a freeman, a citizen, and a soldier, and of how, when I was thirty, I journeyed to Alexandria, and from Alexandria to Jerusalem. Yet what I have told from the time when I was baptized in the mead pot of Tostig Lodbrog I have been compelled to in order that you may understand what manner of man rode in through the Jaffa Gate and drew all eyes upon him.

Well might they look. They were small breeds, lighter-boned and lighter-thewed, these Romans and Jews, and a blond like me they had never gazed upon. All along the narrow streets they gave before me but stood to stare wide-eyed at this yellow man from the north, or from God knew where, so far as they knew aught of the matter.

Practically all Pilate's troops were auxiliaries, save for a handful of Romans about the palace and the twenty Romans who rode with me. Often enough have I found the auxiliaries good soldiers, but never so steadily dependable as the Romans. In truth they were better fighting men the year round than were we men of the North, who fought in great moods and sulked in great moods. The Roman was invariably steady and dependable.

There was a woman from the court of Antipas, who was a friend of Pilate's wife and whom I met at Pilate's the night of my arrival. I shall call her Miriam, for Miriam was the name I loved her by. If it were merely difficult to describe the charm of women, I would describe Miriam. But how describe emotion in words? The charm of woman is wordless. It is different from perception that culminates in reason, for it arises in sensation and culminates in emotion, which, be it admitted, is nothing else than super-sensation.

In general, any woman has fundamental charm for any man. When this charm becomes particular, then we call it love. Miriam had this particular charm for me. Verily I was co-partner in her charm. Half of it was my own man's life in me that leaped and met her wide-armed and made in me all that she was desirable plus all my desire of her.

Miriam was a grand woman. I use the term advisedly. She was fine-bodied, commanding, over and above the average Jewish woman in stature and in line. She was an aristocrat in social caste; she was an aristocrat by nature. All her ways were large ways, generous ways. She had brain, she had wit, and, above all, she had womanliness. As you shall see, it was her womanliness that betrayed her and me in the end. Brunette, olive-skinned, oval-faced, her hair was blue-black with its blackness and her eyes were twin wells of black. Never were more pronounced types of blond and brunette in man and woman met than in us.

And we met on the instant. There was no self-discussion, no waiting, wavering, to make certain. She was mine the moment I looked upon her. And by the same token she knew that I belonged to her above all men. I strode to her. She half-lifted from her couch as if drawn upward to me. And then we looked with all our eyes, blue eyes and black, until Pilate's wife, a thin, tense, overwrought woman, laughed nervously. And while I bowed to the wife and gave greeting, I thought I saw Pilate give Miriam a significant glance, as if to say, "Is he not all I promised?" For he had had word of my coming from Sulpicius Quirinius, the legate of Syria. As well had Pilate and I been known to each other before ever he journeyed out to be procurator over the Semitic volcano of Jerusalem.

Much talk we had that night, especially Pilate, who spoke in detail of the local situation, and who seemed lonely and desirous to share his anxieties with someone and even to bid for counsel. Pilate was of the solid type of Roman, with sufficient imagination intelligently to enforce the iron policy of Rome, and not unduly excitable under stress.

But on this night it was plain that he was worried. The Jews had got on his nerves. They were too volcanic, spasmodic, eruptive. And further, they were subtle. The Romans had a straight, forthright way of going about anything. The Jews never approached anything directly save backward when they were driven by compulsion. Left to themselves, they always approached by indirection. Pilate's irritation was due, as he explained, to the fact that the Jews were ever intriguing to make him, and through him Rome, the cat's-paw in the matter of their religious dissensions. As was well known to me, Rome did not interfere with the religious notions of its conquered peoples; but the Jews were forever confusing the issues and giving a political cast to purely unpolitical events.

Pilate waxed eloquent over the diverse sects and the fanatic uprisings and riotings that were continually occurring.

"Lodbrog," he said, "one can never tell what little summer cloud of their hatching may turn into a thunderstorm roaring and rattling about one's ears. I am here to keep order and quiet. Despite me they make the place a hornet's nest. Far rather would I govern Scythians or savage Britons than these people who are never at peace about God. Right now there is a man up to the north, a fisherman turned preacher and miracle-worker, that as well as not may soon have all the country by the ears and my recall on its way from Rome."

This was the first I had heard of the man called Jesus, and I little remarked it at the time. Not until afterward did I remember him, when the little summer cloud had become a full-fledged thunderstorm.

"I have had report of him," Pilate went on. "He is not political. There is no doubt of that. But trust Caiaphas, and Hanan behind Caiaphas, to make of this fisherman a political thorn with which to prick Rome and ruin me."

"This Caiaphas, I have heard of him as high priest; then who is this Hanan?" I asked.

"The real high priest, a cunning fox," Pilate explained. "Caiaphas was appointed by Gratus, but Caiaphas is the shadow and the mouthpiece of Hanan."

"They have never forgiven you that little matter of the votive shields," Miriam teased.

Whereupon, as a man will when his sore place is touched, Pilate launched upon the episode, which had been an episode, no more, at the beginning, but which had nearly destroyed him. In all innocence, before his palace he had affixed two shields with votive inscriptions. Ere the consequent storm that burst on his head had passed, the Jews had written their complaints to Tiberius, who approved them and reprimanded Pilate.

I was glad, a little later, when I could have talk with Miriam. Pilate's wife had found opportunity to tell me about her. She was of old royal stock. Her sister was wife of Philip, tetrarch of Gaulonitis and Batanaea. Now this Philip was brother to Antipas, tetrarch of Galilee and Peraea, and both were sons of Herod, called by the Jews the "Great." Miriam, as I understood, was at home in the courts of both tetrarchs, being herself of the blood. Also, when a girl, she had been betrothed to Archelaus at the time he was ethnarch of Jerusalem. She had a goodly fortune in her own right, so that marriage had not been compulsory. To boot, she had a will of her own, and was doubtless hard to please in so important a matter as husbands.

It must have been in the very air we breathed, for in no time

Miriam and I were at it on the subject of religion. Truly, the Jews of that day battened on religion as did we on fighting and feasting. For all my stay in that country there was never a moment when my wits were not buzzing with the endless discussions of life and death, law, and God. Now Pilate believed neither in gods, nor devils, nor anything. Death, to him, was the blackness of unbroken sleep; and yet, during his years in Jerusalem he was ever vexed with the inescapable fuss and fury of things religious. Why, I had a horse-boy on my trip into Idumaea, a wretched creature that could never learn to saddle and who yet could talk, and most learnedly, without breath, from nightfall to sunrise, on the hair-splitting differences in the teachings of all the rabbis from Shemaia to Gamaliel.

But to return to Miriam.

"You believe you are immortal," she was soon challenging me. "Then why do you fear to talk about it?" "Why burden my mind with thoughts about certainties?" I countered.

"But you are certain?" She insisted. "Tell me about it. What is it like—your immortality?"

And when I had told her of Niflheim and Muspell, of the birth of the giant Ymir from the snowflakes, of the cow Andhumbla, and of Fenrir and Loki and the frozen Jotuns—as I say, when I had told her of all this, and of Thor and Odin and our own Valhalla, she clapped her hands and cried out, with sparkling eyes:

"Oh, you barbarian! You great child! You yellow giant-thing of the frost! You believer of old nurse tales and stomach satisfactions! But the spirit of you, that which cannot die, where will it go when your body is dead?"

"As I have said, Valhalla," I answered. "And my body shall be there, too."

"Eating? —drinking? —fighting? "

"And loving," I added. "We must have our women in heaven, else what is heaven for?"

"I do not like your heaven," she said. "It is a mad place, a beast place, a place of frost and storm and fury."

"And your heaven?" I questioned.

"Is always unending summer, with the year at the ripe for the fruits and flowers and growing things."

I shook my head and growled:

"I do not like your heaven. It is a sad place, a soft place, a place for weaklings and eunuchs and fat sobbing shadows of men."

My remarks must have glamored her mind, for her eyes continued to sparkle, and mine was half a guess that she was leading me on.

"My heaven," she said, "is the abode of the blessed."

"Valhalla is the abode of the blessed," I asserted. "For look you, who cares for flowers where flowers always are? In my country, after the iron winter breaks and the sun drives away the long night, the first blossoms twinkling on the melting ice-edge are things of joy, and we look, and look again.

"And fire!" I cried on. "Great glorious fire! A fine heaven yours where a man cannot properly esteem a roaring fire under a tight roof with wind and snow a-drive outside."

"A simple folk, you," she was back at me. "You build a roof and a fire in a snowbank and call it heaven. In my heaven we do not have to escape the wind and snow."

"No," I objected. "We build roof and fire to go forth from into the frost and storm and to return to from the frost and storm. Man's life is fashioned for battle with frost and storm. His very fire and roof he makes by his battling. I know. For three years, once, I knew never roof nor fire. I was sixteen and a man, ere ever I wore woven cloth on my body. I was birthed in storm, after battle, and my swaddling cloth was a wolfskin. Look at me and see what manner of man lives in Valhalla."

And look she did, all a-glamor, and cried out:

"You great, yellow giant-thing of a man!" Then she added pensively, "Almost it saddens me that there may not be such men in my heaven."

"It is a good world," I consoled her. "Good is the plan and wide. There is room for many heavens. It would seem that to each is given the heaven that is his heart's desire. A good country, truly, there beyond the grave. I doubt not I shall leave our feast halls and raid your coasts of sun and flowers, and steal you away. My mother was so stolen."

And in the pause I looked at her, and she looked at me, and dared to look. And my blood ran fire. By Odin, this was a woman!

What might have happened I know not, for Pilate, who had ceased from his talk with Ambivius and for some time had sat grinning, broke the pause.

"A rabbi, a Teutoberg rabbi!" He gibed. "A new preacher and a new doctrine come to Jerusalem. Now will there be more dissensions, and riotings, stonings of prophets. The gods save us, it is a madhouse. Lodbrog, I little thought it of you. Yet here you are, spouting and fuming as wildly as any madman from the desert about what shall happen to you when you are dead. One life at a time, Lodbrog. It saves trouble. It saves trouble."

"Go on, Miriam, go on," his wife cried.

She had sat entranced during the discussion, with hands tightly clasped, and the thought flickered up in my mind that she had already been corrupted by the religious folly of Jerusalem. At any rate, as I was to learn in the days that followed, she was unduly bent upon such matters. She was a thin woman, as if wasted by fever. Her skin was tight-stretched. Almost it seemed I could look through her hands did she hold them between me and the light. She was a good woman but highly nervous and, at times, fancy-flighted about shades and signs and omens. Nor was she above seeing visions and hearing voices. As for me, I had no patience with such weaknesses. Yet was she a good woman with no heart of evil.

I was on mission for Tiberius, and it was my ill luck to see little of Miriam. On my return from the court of Antipas, she had gone into Batanaea to Philip's court, where was her sister. Once again I was back in Jerusalem and, though it was no necessity of my business to see Philip, who, though weak, was faithful to Roman will, I journeyed vainly into Batanaea in the hope of meeting up with Miriam.

Then there was my trip into Idumaea. Also, I traveled into Syria in obedience to the command of Sulpicius Quirinius, who as imperial legate, was curious of my first-hand report of affairs in Jerusalem. Thus, traveling wide and much I had opportunity to observe the strangeness of the Jews who were so madly interested in God. It was their peculiarity. Not content with leaving such matters to their priests, they were themselves forever turning priest and preaching wherever they could find a listener. And listeners they found a-plenty.

They gave up their occupations to wander about the country like beggars, disputing and bickering with the rabbis and Talmudists in the synagogues and Temple porches. It was in Galilee, a district of little repute, the inhabitants of which were looked upon as witless, that I crossed the track of the man Jesus. It seems that he had been a carpenter, and after that a fisherman, and that his fellow fishermen had ceased dragging their nets and followed him in his wandering life. Some few looked upon him as a prophet, but the most contended that he was a madman. My wretched horse-boy, himself claiming Talmudic knowledge second to none, sneered at Jesus, calling him the king of the beggars, calling his doctrine Ebionism, which, as he explained to me, was to the effect that only the poor should win to heaven while the rich and powerful were to burn forever in some lake of fire.

It was my observation that it was the custom of the country for every man to call every other man a madman. In truth, in my judgment, they were all mad. There was a plague of them. They cast out devils by magic charms, cured diseases by the laying on of hands, drank deadly poisons unharmed, and unharmed played with deadly snakes—or so they claimed. They ran away to starve in the deserts. They emerged howling new doctrine, gathering crowds about them, forming new sects that split on doctrine and formed more sects.

"By Odin," I told Pilate, "a trifle of our northern frost would cool their wits. This climate is too soft. In place of building roofs and hunting meat, they are ever building doctrine."

"And altering the nature of God," Pilate corroborated sourly. "A curse on doctrine."

"So say I," I agreed. "If ever I get away with unaddled wits from this mad land, I'll cleave through whatever man dares mention to me what may happen after I am dead."

Never were such trouble-makers. Everything under the sun was pious or impious to them. They, who were so clever in hair-splitting argument, seemed incapable of grasping the Roman idea of the State. Everything political was religious; everything religious was political. Thus every procurator's hands were full. The Roman eagles, the Roman statues, even the votive shields of Pilate, were deliberate insults to their religion.

The Roman taking of the census was an abomination. Yet it had to be done, for it was the basis of taxation. But there it was again. Taxation by the State was a crime against their Law and God. Oh, that Law! It was not the Roman law. It was their Law, what they called God's Law. There were the Zealots, who murdered anybody who broke this Law. And for a procurator to punish a Zealot caught red-handed was to raise a riot or an insurrection.

Everything, with these strange people, was done in the name of God. There were what we Romans called the thaumaturgi. They worked miracles to prove doctrine. Ever has it seemed to me a witless thing to prove the multiplication table by turning a staff into a serpent, or even into two serpents. Yet these things the thaumaturgi did, and always to the excitement of the common people.

Heavens, what sects and sects! Pharisees, Essenes, Sadducees —a legion of them! No sooner did they start with a new quirk when it turned political. Coponius, procurator fourth before Pilate, had a pretty time crushing the Gaulonite sedition which arose in this fashion and spread down from Gamala.

In Jerusalem, that last time I rode in, it was easy to note the increasing excitement of the Jews. They ran about in crowds, chattering and spouting. Some were proclaiming the end of the world. Others satisfied themselves with the imminent destruction of the Temple.

And there were rank revolutionists who announced that Roman rule was over and the new Jewish kingdom about to begin.

Pilate, too, I noted, showed heavy anxiety. That they were giving him a hard time of it was patent. But I will say, as you shall see, that he matched their subtlety with equal subtlety; and from what I saw of him I have little doubt but what he would have confounded many a disputant in the synagogues.

"But half a legion of Romans," he regretted to me, "and I would take Jerusalem by the throat . . . and then be recalled for my pains, I suppose."

Like me, he had not too much faith in the auxiliaries; and of Roman soldiers we had but a scant handful.

Back again, I lodged in the palace, and to my great joy found Miriam there. But little satisfaction was mine, for the talk ran long on the situation. There was reason for this, for the city buzzed like the angry hornet's nest it was. The feast called the Passover—a religious affair, of course—was near, and thousands were pouring in from the country, according to custom, to celebrate the feast in Jerusalem. These newcomers, naturally, were all excitable folk, else they would not be bent on such pilgrimage. The city was packed with them, so that many camped outside the walls. As for me, I could not distinguish how much of the ferment was due to the teachings of the wandering fisherman, and how much of it was due to Jewish hatred for Rome.

"A tithe, no more, and maybe not so much, is due to this Jesus," Pilate answered my query. "Look to Caiaphas and Hanan for the main cause of the excitement. They know what they are about They are stirring it up, to what end who can tell, except to cause me trouble."

"Yes, it is certain that Caiaphas and Hanan are responsible," Miriam said, "but you, Pontius Pilate, are only a Roman and do not understand. Were you a Jew, you would realize that there is a greater seriousness at the bottom of it than mere dissension of the sectaries or trouble-making for you and Rome. The high priests and Pharisees, every Jew of place or wealth—Philip, Antipas, myself—we are all fighting for very life. "This fisherman may be a madness. If so, there is a cunning in his madness. He preaches the doctrine of the poor. He threatens our Law, and our Law is our life, as you have learned ere this. We are jealous of our Law, as you would be jealous of the air denied your body by a throttling hand on your throat. It is Caiaphas and Hanan and all they stand for, or it is the fisherman. They must destroy him, else he will destroy them."

"Is it not strange, so simple a man, a fisherman?" Pilate's wife breathed forth. "What manner of man can he be to possess such power? I would that I could see him. I would that with my own eyes I could see so remarkable a man."

Pilate's brows corrugated at her words, and it was clear that to the burden on his nerves was added the overwrought state of his wife's nerves.

"If you would see him, beat up the dens of the town," Miriam laughed spitefully. "You will find him wine-bibbing or in the company of nameless women. Never so strange a prophet came up to Jerusalem."

"And what harm in that?" I demanded, driven against my will to take the part of the fisherman. "Have I not wine-guzzled a- plenty and passed strange nights in all the provinces? The man is a man, and his ways are men's ways, else am I a madman, which I here deny."

Miriam shook her head as she spoke.

"He is not mad. Worse, he is dangerous. All Ebionism is dangerous. He would destroy all things that are fixed. He is a revolutionist. He would destroy what little is left to us of the Jewish state and Temple."

Here Pilate shook his head.

"He is not political. I have had report of him. He is a visionary. There is no sedition in him. He affirms the Roman tax even."

"Still you do not understand," Miriam persisted. "It is not what he plans; it is the effect, if his plans are achieved, that makes him a revolutionist. I doubt that he foresees the effect. Yet is the man a plague and, like any plague, should be stamped out."

"From all that I have heard, he is a good-hearted, simple man with no evil in him," I stated.

And thereat I told of the healing of the ten lepers I had witnessed in Samaria on my way through Jericho.

Pilate's wife sat entranced at what I told. Came to our ears distant shoutings and cries of some street crowd, and we knew the soldiers were keeping the streets cleared.

"And you believe this wonder, Lodbrog?" Pilate demanded. "You believe that in the flash of an eye the festering sores departed from the lepers?"

"I saw them healed," I replied. "I followed them to make certain. There was no leprosy in them."

"But did you see them sore? —before the healing?" Pilate insisted.

I shook my head.

"I was only told so," I admitted. "When I saw them afterward, they had all the seeming of men who had once been lepers They were in a daze. There was one who sat in the sun and ever searched his body and stared and stared at the smooth flesh as if unable to believe his eyes. He would not speak, nor look at aught else than his flesh, when I questioned him. He was in amaze. He sat there in the sun and stared and stared."

Pilate smiled contemptuously, and I noted the quiet smile on Miriam's face was equally contemptuous. And Pilate's wife sat as if a corpse, scarce breathing, her eyes wide and unseeing.

Spoke Ambivius: "Caiaphas holds—he told me but yesterday—that the fisherman claims that he will bring God down on earth and make here a new kingdom over which God will rule—"

"Which would mean the end of Roman rule," I broke in.

"That is where Caiaphas and Hanan plot to embroil Rome," Miriam explained. "It is not true. It is a lie they have made."

Pilate nodded and asked:

"Is there not somewhere in your ancient books a prophecy that the priests here twist into intent of this fisherman's mind?"

To this she agreed, and gave him the citation. I relate the incident to evidence the depth of Pilate's study of this people he strove so hard to keep in order.

"What I have heard," Miriam continued, "is that this Jesus preaches the end of the world and the beginning of God's kingdom, not here, but in heaven."

"I have had report of that," Pilate said. "It is true. This Jesus holds the justness of the Roman tax. He holds that Rome shall rule until all rule passes away with the passing of the world. I see more clearly the trick Hanan is playing me."

"It is even claimed by some of his followers," Ambivius volunteered, "that he is God himself."

"I have no report that he has so said," Pilate replied.

"Why not?" His wife breathed. "Why not? Gods have descended to earth before."

"Look you," Pilate said. "I have it by creditable report that after this Jesus had worked some wonder whereby a multitude was fed on several loaves and fishes, the foolish Galileans were for making him a king. Against his will they would make him a king. To escape them he fled into the mountains No madness there. He was too wise to accept the fate they would have forced upon him."

"Yet that is the very trick Hanan would force upon you," Miriam reiterated. "They claim for him that he would be king of the Jews—an offense against Roman law, wherefore Rome must deal with him."

Pilate shrugged his shoulders.

"A king of the beggars, rather; or a king of the dreamers. He is no fool. He is visionary, but not visionary of this world's power. All luck go with him in the next world, for that is beyond Rome's jurisdiction."

"He holds that property is sin—that is what hits the Pharisees," Ambivius spoke up.

Pilate laughed heartily.

"This king of the beggars and his fellow beggars still do respect property," he explained. "For look you, not long ago they had even a treasurer for their wealth. Judas his name was, and there were words in that he stole from their common purse which he carried."

"Jesus did not steal?" Pilate's wife asked.

"No," Pilate answered; "it was Judas, the treasurer."

"Who was this John?" I questioned. "He was in trouble up Tiberias way and Antipas executed him."

"Another one," Miriam answered. "He was born near Hebron. He was an enthusiast and a desert-dweller. Either he or his followers claimed that he was Elijah raised from the dead. Elijah, you see, was one of our old prophets."

"Was he seditious?" I asked.

Pilate grinned and shook his head, then said:

"He fell out with Antipas over the matter of Herodias. John was a moralist. It is too long a story, but he paid for it with his head. No, there was nothing political in that affair."

"It is also claimed by some that Jesus is the Son of David," Miriam said. "But it is absurd. Nobody at Nazareth believes it. You see, his whole family, including his married sisters, lives there and is known to all of them. They are a simple folk, mere common people."

"I wish it were as simple, the report of all this complexity that I must send to Tiberius," Pilate grumbled. "And now this fisherman is come to Jerusalem, the place is packed with pilgrims ripe for any trouble, and Hanan stirs and stirs the broth."

"And before he is done he will have his way," Miriam forecast. "He has laid the task for you, and you will perform it."

"Which is?" Pilate queried.

"The execution of this fisherman." Pilate shook his head stubbornly, but his wife cried out:

"No! No! It would be a shameful wrong. The man has done no evil. He has not offended against Rome."

She looked beseechingly to Pilate, who continued to shake his head.

"Let them do their own beheading, as Antipas did," he growled. "The fisherman counts for nothing; but I shall be no cat's-paw to their schemes. If they must destroy him, they must destroy him. That is their affair."

"But you will not permit it," cried Pilate's wife.

"A pretty time would I have explaining to Tiberius if I interfered," was his reply.

"No matter what happens," said Miriam, "I can see you writing explanations, and soon; for Jesus is already come up to Jerusalem and a number of his fishermen with him."

Pilate showed the irritation this information caused him.

"I have no interest in his movements," he pronounced. "I hope never to see him."

"Trust Hanan to find him for you," Miriam replied, "and to bring him to your gate."

Pilate shrugged his shoulders, and there the talk ended. Pilate's wife, nervous and overwrought, must claim Miriam to her apartments, so that nothing remained for me but to go to bed and doze off to the buzz and murmur of the city of madmen.

Events moved rapidly. Overnight, the white heat of the city had scorched upon itself. By midday, when I rode forth with half a dozen of my men, the streets were packed, and more reluctant than ever were the folk to give way before me. If looks could kill, I should have been a dead man that day. Openly they spat at sight of me, and everywhere arose snarls and cries.

Less was I a thing of wonder, and more was I the thing hated in that I wore the hated harness of Rome. Had it been any other city, I should have given command to my men to lay the flats of their swords on those snarling fanatics. But this was Jerusalem, at fever heat, and these were a people unable in thought to divorce the idea of State from the idea of God.

Hanan the Sadducee had done his work well. No matter what he and the Sanhedrim believed of the true inwardness of the situation, it was clear this rabble had been well tutored to believe that Rome was at the bottom of it.

I encountered Miriam in the press. She was on foot, attended only by a woman. It was no time in such turbulence for her to be abroad garbed as became her station. Through her sister she was indeed sister-in-law to Antipas, for whom few bore love. So she was dressed discreetly, her face covered, so that she might pass as any Jewish woman of the lower orders. But not to my eye could she hide that fine stature of her, that carriage and walk, so different from other women's, of which I had already dreamed more than once.

Few and quick were the words we were able to exchange, for the way jammed on the moment, and soon my men and horses were being pressed and jostled. Miriam was sheltered in an angle of house-wall.

"Have they got the fisherman yet?" I asked.

"No; but he is just outside the wall. He has ridden up to Jerusalem on an ass, with a multitude before and behind, and some, poor dupes, have hailed him as he passed as King of Israel. That finally is the pretext with which Hanan will compel Pilate. Truly, though not yet taken, the sentence is already written. This fisherman is a dead man."

"But Pilate will not arrest him," I defended.

Miriam shook her head.

"Hanan will attend to that. They will bring him before the Sanhedrim. The sentence will be death. They may stone him."

"But the Sanhedrim has not the right to execute," I contended.

"Jesus is not a Roman," she replied. "He is a Jew. By the law of the Talmud he is guilty of death, for he has blasphemed against the Law."

Still I shook my head.

"The Sanhedrim has not the right."

"Pilate is willing that it should take that right."

"But it is a fine question of legality," I insisted. "You know what the Romans are in such matters."

"Then will Hanan avoid the question," she smiled, "by compelling Pilate to crucify him. In either event it will be well."

A surging of the mob was sweeping our horses along and grinding our knees together. Some fanatic had fallen, and I could feel my horse recoil and half-rear as it tramped on him, and I could hear the man screaming and the snarling menace from all about rising to a roar. But my head was over my shoulder as I called back to Miriam:

"You are hard on a man you have said yourself is without evil."

"I am hard upon the evil that will come of him if he lives," she replied.

Scarcely did I catch her words, for a man sprang in, seizing my bridle rein and leg and struggling to unhorse me. With my open palm, leaning forward, I smote him full upon cheek and jaw. My hand covered the face of him, and a hearty will of weight was in the blow. The dwellers in Jerusalem are not used to men's buffets. I have often wondered since if I broke the fellow's neck.

Next I saw Miriam was the following day. I met her in the court of Pilate's palace. She seemed in a dream. Scarce her eyes saw me. Scarce her wits embraced my identity. So strange was she, so in daze and amaze and far-seeing were her eyes, that I was reminded of the lepers I had seen healed in Samaria.

She became herself by an effort, but only her outward self. In her eyes was a message unreadable. Never before had I seen woman's eyes so.

She would have passed me ungreeted, had I not confronted her way. She paused and murmured words mechanically, but all the while her eyes dreamed through me and beyond me with the largeness of the vision that filled them.

"I have seen Him, Lodbrog," she whispered. "I have seen Him."

"The gods grant that he is not so ill-affected by the sight of you, whoever he may be," I laughed.

She took no notice of my poor-timed jest, and her eyes remained full with vision, and she would have passed on had I not again blocked her way.

"Who is this he?" I demanded. "Some man raised from the

dead to put such strange light in your eyes?"

"One who has raised others from the dead," she replied. "Truly I believe that He, this Jesus, has raised the dead. He is the Prince of Light, the Son of God. I have seen Him. Truly I believe that He is the Son of God."

Little could I glean from her words, save that she had met this wandering fisherman and been swept away by his folly. For surely this Miriam was not the Miriam who had branded him a plague and demanded that he be stamped out as any plague.

"He has charmed you," I cried angrily.

Her eyes seemed to moisten and grow deeper as she gave confirmation.

"Oh, Lodbrog, His is charm beyond all thinking, beyond all describing. But to look upon Him is to know that here is the all-soul of goodness and of compassion. I have seen Him. I have heard Him. I shall give all I have to the poor, and I shall follow Him."

Such was her certitude that I accepted it fully, as I had accepted the amazement of the lepers of Samaria staring at their smooth flesh; and I was bitter that so great a woman should be so easily wit-addled by a vagrant wonder-worker.

"Follow him," I sneered. "Doubtless you will wear a crown when he wins to his kingdom."

She nodded affirmation, and I could have struck her in the face for her folly. I drew aside, and as she moved slowly on she murmured:

"His kingdom is not here. He is the Son of David. He is the Son of God. He is whatever He has said, or whatever has been said of Him that is good and great."

"A wise man of the East," I found Pilate chuckling. "He is a thinker, this unlettered fisherman. I have sought more deeply into him. I have fresh report. He has no need of wonder-workings. He out-sophisticates the most sophistical of them. They have laid traps, and he has laughed at their traps. Look you. Listen to this."

Whereupon he told me how Jesus had confounded his confounders when they brought to him for judgment a woman taken in adultery.

"And the tax," Pilate exulted on. "'To Caesar what is Caesar's, to God what is God's,' was his answer to them. That was Hanan's trick, and Hanan is confounded. At last has there appeared one Jew who understands our Roman conception of the State." Next I saw Pilate's wife. Looking into her eyes, I knew on the instant, after having seen Miriam's eyes, that this tense, distraught woman had likewise seen the fisherman.

"The Divine is within Him," she murmured to me. "There is within Him a personal awareness of the indwelling of God."

"Is he God?" I queried gently, for say something I must.

She shook her head.

"I do not know. He has not said. But this I know: of such stuff gods are made."

"A charmer of women," was my privy judgment, as I left Pilate's wife walking in dreams and visions.

The last days are known to all of you who read these lines, and it was in those last days that I learned that this Jesus was equally a charmer of men. He charmed Pilate. He charmed me.

After Hanan had sent Jesus to Caiaphas, and the Sanhedrim, assembled in Caiaphas' house, had condemned Jesus to death, Jesus, escorted by a howling mob, was sent to Pilate for execution.

Now, for his own sake and for Rome's sake, Pilate did not want to execute him. Pilate was little interested in the fisherman and greatly interested in peace and order. What cared Pilate for a man's life? —for many men's lives? The school of Rome was iron, and the governors sent out by Rome to rule conquered peoples were likewise iron. Pilate thought and acted in governmental abstractions. Yet, look: when Pilate went out scowling to meet the mob that had fetched the fisherman, he fell immediately under the charm of the man.

I was present. I know. It was the first time Pilate had ever seen him. Pilate went out angry. Our soldiers were in readiness to clear the court of its noisy vermin. And immediately Pilate laid eyes on the fisherman, Pilate was subdued—nay, was solicitous. He disclaimed jurisdiction, demanded that they judge the fisherman by their Law and deal with him by their Law, since the fisherman was a Jew and not a Roman. Never were there Jews so obedient to Roman rule. They cried out that it was unlawful, under Rome, for them to put any man to death. Yet Antipas had beheaded John and come to no grief of it.

And Pilate left them in the court, open under the sky, and took Jesus alone into the judgment hall. What happened therein I know not, save that when Pilate emerged he was changed. Whereas before he had been disinclined to execute because he would not be made a cat's-paw to Hanan, he was now disinclined to execute because of regard for the fisherman. His effort now was to save the fisherman. And all the while the mob cried: "Crucify him! Crucify him!"

You, my reader, know the sincerity of Pilate's effort. You know how he tried to befool the mob, first, by mocking Jesus as a harmless fool; and, second, by offering to release him according to the custom of releasing one prisoner at time of the Passover. And you know how the priests) quick whisperings led the mob to cry out for the release of the murderer Bar-Abbas.

In vain Pilate struggled against the fate being thrust upon him by the priests. By sneer and jibe he hoped to make a farce of the transaction. He laughingly called Jesus the King of the Jews and ordered him to be scourged. His hope was that all would end in laughter and in laughter be forgotten.

I am glad to say that no Roman soldiers took part in what followed. It was the soldiers of the auxiliaries who crowned and cloaked Jesus put the reed of sovereignty in his hand, and, kneeling, hailed him King of the Jews. Although it failed, it was a play to placate. And I, looking on, learned the charm of Jesus. Despite the cruel mockery of his situation, he was regal. And I was quiet as I gazed. It was his own quiet that went into me. I was soothed and satisfied, and was without bewilderment. This thing had to be. All was well. The serenity of Jesus in the heart of the tumult and pain became my serenity. I was scarce moved by any thought to save him.

On the other hand, I had gazed on too many wonders of the human in my wild and varied years to be affected to foolish acts by this particular wonder. I was all serenity. I had no word to say. I had no judgment to pass. I knew that things were occuring beyond my comprehension, and that they must occur.

Still Pilate struggled. The tumult increased. The cry for blood rang through the court, and all were clamoring for crucifixion. Again Pilate went back into the judgment hall. His effort at a farce having failed, he attempted to disclaim jurisdiction. Jesus was not of Jerusalem. He was a born subject of Antipas, and to Antipas Pilate was for sending Jesus.

But the uproar was by now communicating itself to the city. Our troops outside the palace were being swept away in the vast street mob. Rioting had begun that in the flash of an eye could turn into civil war and revolution. My own twenty legionaries were close to hand and in readiness. They loved the fanatic Jews no more than did I, and would have welcomed my command to clear the court with naked steel

When Pilate came out again, his words for Antipas' jurisdiction could not be heard, for all the mob was shouting that Pilate was a traitor, that if he let the fisherman go he was no friend of Tiberius. Close before me, as I leaned against the wall, a mangy, bearded, long-haired fanatic sprang up and down unceasingly, and unceasingly chanted: "Tiberius is emperor; there is no king! Tiberius is emperor; there is no king!" I lost patience. The man's near noise was an offense. Lurching sidewise, as if by accident, I ground my foot on his to a terrible crushing. The fool seemed not to notice. He was too mad to be aware of the pain, and he continued to chant: "Tiberius is emperor; there is no king!"

I saw Pilate hesitate. Pilate the Roman governor for the moment was Pilate the man, with a man's anger against the miserable creatures clamoring for the blood of so sweet and simple, brave and good a spirit as this Jesus.

I saw Pilate hesitate. His gaze roved to me, as if he were about to signal to me to let loose; and I half-started forward, releasing the mangled foot under my foot. I was for leaping to complete that half-formed wish of Pilate and to sweep away in blood and cleanse the court of the wretched scum that howled in it.

It was not Pilate's indecision that decided me. It was this Jesus that decided Pilate and me. This Jesus looked at me. He commanded me. I tell you, this vagrant fisherman, this wandering preacher, this piece of driftage from Galilee, commanded me. No word he uttered. Yet his command was there, unmistakable as a trumpet call. And I stayed my foot, and held my hand, for who was I to thwart the will and way of so greatly serene and sweetly sure a man as this? And as I stayed, I knew all the charm of him—all that in him had charmed Miriam and Pilate's wife, that had charmed Pilate himself.

You know the rest. Pilate washed his hands of Jesus' blood, and the rioters took his blood upon their own heads. Pilate gave orders for the crucifixion. The mob was content, and content, behind the mob, were Caiaphas, Hanan, and the Sanhedrim. Not Pilate, not Tiberius, not Roman soldiers, crucified Jesus. It was the priestly rulers and priestly politicians of Jerusalem. I saw. I know. And against his own best interests Pilate would have saved Jesus, as I would have, had it not been that no other than Jesus himself willed that he was not to be saved.

Yes, and Pilate had his last sneer at this people he detested. In Hebrew, Greek, and Latin, he had a writing affixed to Jesus' cross which read, "The King of the Jews." In vain the priests complained. It was on this very pretext that they had forced Pilate's hand; and by this pretext, a scorn and insult to the Jewish race, Pilate abided. Pilate executed an abstraction that had never existed in the real. The abstraction was a cheat and a lie manufactured in the priestly mind. Neither the priests nor Pilate believed it. Jesus denied it. That abstraction was "The King of the Jews."

The storm was over in the courtyard. The excitement had simmered down. Revolution had been averted. The priests were content, the mob was satisfied, and Pilate and I were well disgusted and weary with the whole affair. And yet for him and me was more and most immediate storm. Before Jesus was taken away, one of Miriam's women called me to her. And I saw Pilate, summoned by one of his wife's women, likewise obey.

"Oh, Lodbrog, I have heard," Miriam met me. We were alone, and she was close to me, seeking shelter and strength within my arms. "Pilate has weakened. He is going to crucify Him. But there is time. Your own men are ready. Ride with them. Only a centurion and a handful of soldiers are with Him. They have not yet started. As soon as they do start, follow. They must not reach Golgotha. But wait until they are outside the city wall. Then countermand the order. Take an extra horse for Him to ride. The rest is easy. Ride away into Syria with Him, or into Idumaea, or anywhere so long as He be saved."

She concluded with her arms around my neck, her face up, turned to mine and temptingly close, her eyes greatly solemn and greatly promising.

Small wonder I was slow of speech. For the moment there was but one thought in my brain. After all the strange play I had seen played out, to have this come upon me! I did not misunderstand. The thing was clear. A great woman was mine if. . . if I betrayed Rome. For Pilate was governor; his order had gone forth; and his voice was the voice of Rome.

As I have said, it was the woman of her, her sheer womanliness, that betrayed Miriam and me in the end. Always she had been so clear, so reasonable, so certain of herself and me, that I had forgotten or, rather, I there learned once again the eternal lesson learned in all lives that woman is ever woman—that in great decisive moments woman does not reason but feels; that the last sanctuary and innermost pulse to conduct is in woman's heart and not in woman's head.

Miriam misunderstood my silence, for her body moved softly within my arms as she added, as if in afterthought:

"Take two spare horses, Lodbrog. I shall ride the other . . . with you . . . with you, away over the world, wherever you may ride."

It was a bribe of kings; it was an act, paltry and contemptible that was demanded of me in return. Still I did not speak. It was not that I was in confusion or in any doubt. I was merely sad, greatly and suddenly sad, in that I knew I held in my arms what I would never hold again.

"There is but one man in Jerusalem this day who can save Him," she urged, "and that man is you, Lodbrog."

Because I did not immediately reply, she shook me, as if in impulse to clarify wits she considered addled. She shook me till my harness rattled.

"Speak, Lodbrog, speak!" She commanded. "You are strong and unafraid. You are all man. I know you despise the vermin who would destroy Him. You, you alone, can save Him. You have but to say the word and the thing is done; and I will well love you and always love you for the thing you have done."

"I am a Roman," I said slowly, knowing full well that with the words I gave up all hope of her.

"You are a man-slave of Tiberius a hound of Rome," she flamed, "but you owe Rome nothing for you are not a Roman. You yellow giants of the north are not Romans."

"The Romans are the elder brothers of us younglings of the north," I answered. "Also, I wear the harness and I eat the bread of Rome." Gently I added, "But why all this fuss and fury for a mere man's life? All men must die. Simple and easy it is to die. Today, or a hundred years, it little matters. Sure we are, all of us, of the same event in the end."

Quick she was and alive with passion to save, as she thrilled within my arms.

"You do not understand, Lodbrog. This is no mere man. I tell you this is a man beyond men—a living God, not of men, but over men."

I held her closely, and knew that I was renouncing all the sweet woman of her as I said:

"We are man and woman, you and I. Our life is of this world. Of these other worlds is all a madness. Let these mad dreamers go the way of their dreaming. Deny them not what they desire above all things, above meat and wine, above song and battle, even above love of woman. Deny them not their hearts' desires that draw them across the dark of the grave to their dreams of lives beyond this world. Let them pass. But you and I abide here in all the sweet we have discovered of each other. Quickly enough will come the dark, and you depart for your coasts of sun and flowers and I for the roaring table of Valhalla."

"No! No!" She cried half-tearing herself away. "You do not understand. All of greatness, all of goodness, all of God are in this man who is more than man; and it is a shameful death to die. Only slaves and thieves so die. He is neither slave nor thief. He is an immortal. He is God. Truly I tell you He is God."

"He is immortal, you say," I contended. "Then to die today on Golgotha will not shorten his immortality by a hair's breadth in the span of time. He is a god, you say. Gods cannot die. From all I have been told of them, it is certain that gods cannot die."

"Oh!" She cried. "You will not understand. You are only a great giant thing of flesh."

"Is it not said that this event was prophesied of old time?" I queried, for I had been learning from the Jews what I deemed their subtleties of thinking.

"Yes, yes," she agreed, "the Messianic prophecies. This is the Messiah."

"Then who am I," I asked, "to make liars of the prophets? —to make of the Messiah a false Messiah? Is the prophecy of your people so feeble a thing that I, a stupid stranger, a yellow northling in the Roman harness, can give the lie to prophecy and compel to be unfilled the very thing willed by the gods and foretold by the wise men?"

"You do not understand," she repeated.

"I understand too well," I replied. "Am I greater than the gods that I may thwart the will of the gods? Then are gods vain things and the playthings of men. I am a man. I, too, bow to the gods, to all gods, for I do believe in all gods, else how came all gods to be?"

She flung herself so that my hungry arms were empty of her, and we stood apart and listened to the uproar of the street as Jesus and the soldiers emerged and started on their way. And my heart was sore in that so great a woman could be so foolish. She would save God. She would make herself greater than God.

"You do not love me," she said slowly, and slowly grew in her eyes a promise of herself too deep and wide for any words

"I love you beyond your understanding, it seems," was my reply. "I am proud to love you, for I know I am worthy to love you and am worth all love you may give me. But Rome is my foster-mother, and were I untrue to her, of little pride, of little worth would be my love for you."

The uproar that followed about Jesus and the soldiers died away along the street. And when there was no further sound of it, Miriam turned to go, with neither word nor look for me.

I knew one last rush of mad hunger for her. I sprang and seized her. I would horse her and ride away with her and my men into Syria, away from this cursed city of folly. She struggled. I crushed her. She struck me on the face, and I continued to hold and crush her, for the blows were sweet. And then she ceased to struggle. She became cold and motionless, so that I knew there was no woman's love that my arms girdled. For me she was dead. Slowly I let go of her. Slowly she stepped back. As if she did not see me, she turned and went away across the quiet room, and without looking back passed through the hangings and was gone.

I, Ragnar Lodbrog, never came to read nor write. But in my days I have listened to great talk. As I see it now, I never learned great talk, such as that of the Jews, learned in their Law, nor such as that of the Romans, learned in their philosophy and in the philosophy of the Greeks. Yet have I talked in simplicity and straightness as a man may well talk who has lived life from the ships of Tostig Lodbrog and the roof of Brunanbuhr across the world to Jerusalem and back again. And straight talk and simple I gave Sulpicius Quirinius, when I went away into Syria to report to him of the various matters that had been at issue in Jerusalem.

Chapter 18

Suspended animation is nothing new, not alone in the vegetable world and in the lower forms of animal life, but in the highly evolved, complex organism of man himself. A cataleptic trance is a cataleptic trance, no matter how induced. From time immemorial the fakir of India has been able voluntarily to induce such states in himself. It is an old trick of the fakirs to have themselves buried alive. Other men, in similar trances, have misled the physicians, who pronounced them dead and gave the orders that put them alive under the ground.

As my jacket experiences in San Quentin continued, I dwelled not a little on this problem of suspended animation. I remembered having read that the far northern Siberian peasants made a practice of hibernating through the long winters just as bears and other wild animals do. Some scientist studied these peasants and found that during these periods of the "long sleep" respiration and digestion practically ceased, and that the heart was at so low tension as to defy detection by ordinary layman's examination.

In such a trance the bodily processes are so near to absolute suspension that the air and food consumed are practically negligible. On this reasoning, partly, was based my defiance of Warden Atherton and Doctor Jackson. It was thus that I dared challenge them to give me a hundred days in the jacket. And they did not dare accept my challenge. Nevertheless, I did manage to do without water, as well as food, during my ten-day bouts. I found it an intolerable nuisance, in the deeps of dreams across space and time, to be haled back to the sordid present by a despicable prison doctor pressing water to my lips. So I warned Doctor Jackson, first, that I intended doing without water while in the jacket; and next, that I would resist any efforts to compel me to drink.

Of course, we had our little struggle; but after several attempts

Doctor Jackson gave it up. Thereafter, the space occupied in Darrel Standing's life by a jacket-bout was scarcely more than a few ticks of the clock. Immediately I was laced, I devoted myself to inducing the little death. From practice it became simple and easy. I suspended animation and consciousness so quickly that I escaped the really terrible suffering consequent upon suspending circulation. Most quickly came the dark. And the next I, Darrell Standing, knew, was the light again, the faces bending over me as I was unlaced, and the knowledge that ten days had passed in the twinkling of an eye.

But oh, the wonder and the glory of those ten days spent by me elsewhere! The journeys through the long chain of existences! The long darks, the growings of nebulous lights, and the fluttering apparitional selves that dawned through the growing light!

Much have I pondered upon the relation of these other selves to me, and of the relation of the total experience to the modern doctrine of evolution. I can truly say that my experience is in complete accord with our conclusions of evolution.

I, like any man, am a growth. I did not begin when I was born, nor when I was conceived. I have been growing, developing, through incalculable myriads of millenniums. All these experiences of all these lives, and of countless other lives, have gone to the making of the soul-stuff or the spirit-stuff that is I. Don't you see? They are the stuff of me. Matter does not remember, for spirit is memory. I am this spirit compounded of the memories of my endless incarnations. Whence came in me, Darrell Standing, the red pulse of wrath that has wrecked my life and put me in the condemned cells? Surely, it did not come into being, was not created, when the babe that was to be Darrell Standing was conceived. That old red wrath is far older than my mother, far older than the oldest and first mother of men. My mother, at my inception, did not create that passionate lack of fear that is mine. Not all the mothers of the whole evolution of man manufactured fear or fearlessness in men. Far back beyond the first men were fear and fearlessness, love, hatred, anger, all the emotions, growing, developing, becoming the stuff that was to become men.

I am all of my past, as every protagonist of the Mendelian law must agree. All my previous selves have their voices, echoes, promptings, in me. My every mode of action, heat of passion, flicker of thought, is shaded, toned, infinitesimally shaded and toned, by that vast array of other selves that preceded me and went into the making of me.

The stuff of life is plastic. At the same time this stuff never forgets. Mold it as you will, the old memories persist. All manner of horses, from ton Sires to dwarf Shetlands, have been bred up and down from those first wild ponies domesticated by primitive man. Yet to this day man has not bred out the kick of the horse. And I, who am composed of those first horse tamers, have not had their red anger bred out of me.

I am man born of woman. My days are few, but the stuff of me is indestructible. I have been woman born of woman. I have been a woman and borne my children. And I shall be born again. Oh, incalculable times again shall I be born; and yet the stupid dolts about me think that by stretching my neck with a rope they will make me cease.

Yes, I shall be hanged . . . soon. This is the end of June. In a little while they will try to befool me. They will take me from this cell to the bath, according to the prison custom of the weekly bath. But. I shall not be brought back to this cell. I shall be dressed outright in fresh clothes and be taken to the death cell. There they will place the deathwatch on me. Night or day, waking or sleeping, I shall be watched. I shall not be permitted to put my head under the blankets for fear I may anticipate the state by choking myself.

Always bright light will blaze upon me. And then, when they have well wearied me, they will lead me out one morning in a shirt without a collar and drop me through the trap. Oh, I know. The rope they will do it with is well stretched. For many a month, now, the hangman of Folsom has been stretching it with heavy weights so as to take the spring out of it.

Yes, I shall drop far. They have cunning tables of calculations, like interest tables, that show the distance of the drop in relation to the victim's weight. I am so emaciated that they will have to drop me far in order to break my neck. And then the onlookers will take their hats off, and as I swing the doctors will press their ears to my chest to count my fading heartbeats, and at last they will say that I am dead.

It is grotesque. It is the ridiculous effrontery of men-maggots who think they can kill me. I cannot die. I am immortal, as they are immortal; the difference is that I know it and they do not know it.

Pah! I was once a hangman, or an executioner, rather. Well I remember it. I used the sword, not the rope. The sword is the braver way, although all ways are equally inefficacious. Forsooth, as if spirit could be thrust through with steel or throttled by a rope!

Chapter 19

Next to Oppenheimer and Morrell, who rotted with me through the years of darkness I was considered the most dangerous prisoner in San Quentin. On the other hand, I was considered the toughest—tougher even than Oppenheimer and Morrell. Of course, by toughness I mean enduringness. Terrible as were the attempts to break them in body and in spirit, more terrible were the attempts to break me. And I endured. Dynamite or curtains had been Warden Atherton's ultimatum. And in the end it was neither. I could not produce the dynamite, and Warden Atherton could not induce the curtains.

It was not because my body was enduring, but because my spirit was enduring. And it was because, in earlier existences, my spirit had been wrought to steel hardness by steel-hard experiences. There was one experience that for long was a sort of nightmare to me. It had neither beginning nor end. Always I found myself on a rocky, surge-battered islet so low that in storms the salt spray swept over its highest point. It rained much. I lived in a lair and suffered greatly, for I was without fire and lived on uncooked meat

Always I suffered. It was the middle of some experience to which I could get no clue. And since when I went into the little death. I had no power of directing my journeys I often found myself reliving this particularly detestable experience. My only happy moments were when the sun shone, at which times I basked on the rocks and thawed out the almost perpetual chill I suffered. My one diversion was an oar and a jackknife. Upon this oar I spent much time, carving minute letters and cutting a notch for each week that passed. There were many notches. I sharpened the knife on a flat piece of rock, and no barber was ever more careful of his favorite razor than was I of that knife. Nor did ever a miser prize his treasure as did I prize the knife. It was as precious as my life. In truth, it was my life.

By many repetitions, I managed to bring back out of the jacket the legend that was carved on the oar. At first I could bring but little. Later, it grew easier, a matter of piecing portions together. And at last I had the thing complete. Here it is:

This is to acquaint the person into whose hands this oar may fall, that Daniel Foss, a native of Elkton, in Maryland, one of the United States of America, and who sailed from the port of Philadelphia, in 1809 on board the brig Negociator, bound to the Friendly Islands, was cast upon this desolate island the February following, where he erected a hut and lived a number of years, subsisting on seals—he being the last who survived of the crew of said brig, which ran foul of an island of ice, and foundered on the 25th Nov. 1809.

There it was, quite clear. By this means I learned a lot about myself. One vexed point, however, I never did succeed in clearing up. Was this island situated in the far South Pacific or the far South Atlantic? I do not know enough of sailing-ship tracks to be certain whether the brig *Negociator* would sail for the Friendly Islands via Cape Horn or via the Cape of Good Hope. To confess my own ignorance, not until after I was transferred to Folsom did I learn in which ocean were the Friendly Islands. The Japanese murderer, whom I have mentioned before, had been a sailmaker on board the Arthur Sewall ships, and he told me that the probable sailing course would be by way of the Cape of Good Hope. If this were so, then the dates of sailing from Philadelphia and of being wrecked would easily determine which ocean. Unfortunately, the sailing date is merely 1809. The wreck might as likely have occurred in one ocean as the other.

Only once did I, in my trances, get a hint of the period preceding the time spent on the island. This begins at the moment of the brig's collision with the iceberg, and I shall narrate it, if for no other reason, at least to give an account of my curiously cool and deliberate conduct. This conduct at this time, as you shall see, was what enabled me in the end to survive alone of all the ship's company.

I was awakened in my bunk in the forecastle by a terrific crash. In fact, as was true of the other six sleeping men of the watch below, awaking and leaping from bunk to floor were simultaneous. We knew what had happened. The others waited for nothing, rushing only partly clad upon deck. But I knew what to expect, and I did wait. I knew that if we escaped at all, it would be by the longboat. No man could swim in so freezing a sea. And no man, thinly clad, could live long in the open boat. Also, I knew just about how long it would take to launch the boat.

So, by the light of the wildly swinging slush-lamp, to the tumult on deck and to cries of "She's sinking!" I proceeded to ransack my sea chest for suitable garments. Also, since they would never use them again, I ransacked the sea chests of my shipmates. Working quickly but collectedly, I took nothing but the warmest and stoutest of clothes I put on the four best woolen shirts the forecastle boasted, three pairs of pants, and three pairs of thick woolen socks. So large were my feet thus encased that I could not put on my own good boots. Instead, I thrust on Nicholas Wilton's new boots, which were larger and even stouter than mine. Also, I put on Jeremy Nalor's pea jacket over my own and, outside of both, put on Seth Richard's thick canvas coat, which I remembered he had fresh-oiled only a short while previous.

Two pairs of heavy mittens, John Roberts' muffler that his mother had knitted for him, and Joseph Dawes' beaver cap atop my own, both bearing ear and neck flaps, completed my outfitting. The shouts that the brig was sinking redoubled, but I took a minute longer to fill my pockets with all the plug tobacco I could lay hands on. Then I climbed out on deck, and not a moment too soon.

The moon, bursting through a crack of cloud, showed a bleak and savage picture. Everywhere was wrecked gear, and everywhere was ice. The sails, ropes, and spars of the mainmast, which was still standing, were fringed with icicles; and there came over me a feeling almost of relief in that never again should I have to pull and haul on the stiff tackles and hammer ice so that the frozen ropes could run through the frozen shivs. The wind, blowing half a gale, cut with the sharpness that is a sign of the proximity of icebergs; and the big seas were bitter cold to look upon in the moonlight.

The longboat was lowering away to larboard, and I saw men, struggling on the ice-sheeted deck with barrels of provisions, abandon the food in their haste to get away. In vain Captain Nicholl strove with them. A sea, breaching across from windward, settled the matter and sent them leaping over the rail in heaps. I gained the captain's shoulder and, holding on to him, I shouted in his ear that if he would board the boat and prevent the men from casting off, I would attend to the provisioning.

Little time was given me, however. Scarcely had I managed, helped by the second mate, Aaron Northrup, to lower away half a dozen barrels and kegs, when all cried from the boat that they were casting off. Good reason they had. Down upon us from windward was drifting a towering ice mountain, while to leeward, close aboard, was another ice mountain upon which we were driving.

Quicker in his leap was Aaron Northrup. I delayed a moment, even as the boat was shoving away, in order to select a spot amidships where the men were thickest, so that their bodies might break my fall. I was not minded to embark with a broken member on so hazardous a voyage in the longboat That the men might have room at the oars, I worked my way quickly aft into the sternsheets. Certainly, I had other and sufficient reasons. It would be more comfortable in the sternsheets than in the narrow bow. And further, it would be well to be near the afterguard in whatever troubles that were sure to arise under such circumstances in the days to come.

In the sternsheets were the mate, Walter Drake, the surgeon, Arnold Bentham, Aaron Northrup, and Captain Nicholl, who was steering. The surgeon was bending over Northrup, who lay in the bottom groaning. Not so fortunate had he been in his ill-considered leap, for he had broken his right leg at the hip joint.

There was little time for him then, however, for we were laboring in a heavy sea directly between the two ice islands that were rushing together; Nicholas Wilton, at the stroke oar, was cramped for room; so I better stowed the barrels and, kneeling and facing him, was able to add my weight to the oar. For'ard, I could see John Roberts straining at the bow oar. Pulling on his shoulders from behind, Arthur Haskins and the boy, Benny Hardwater, added their weight to his. In fact, so eager were all hands to help that more than one was thus in the way and cluttered the movements of the rowers.

It was close work, but we went clear by a matter of a hundred yards, so that I was able to turn my head and see the untimely end of the *Negociator*. She was caught squarely in the pinch and she was squeezed between the ice as a sugar plum might be squeezed between thumb and forefinger of a boy. In the shouting of the wind and the roar of water we heard nothing, although the crack of the brig's stout ribs and deckbeams must have been enough to waken a hamlet on a peaceful night. Silently, easily, the brig's sides squeezed together, the deck bulged up, and the crushed remnant dropped down and was gone, while where she had been was occupied by the grinding conflict of the ice islands. I felt regret at the destruction of this haven against the elements, but at the same time was well pleased at the thought of my snugness inside my four shirts and three coats.

Yet it proved a bitter night, even for me. I was the warmest clad in the boat. What the others must have suffered I did not care to dwell upon overmuch. For fear that we might meet up with more ice in the darkness, we bailed and held the boat bow-on to the seas. And continually, now with one mitten, now with the other, I rubbed my nose that it might not freeze. Also, with memories lively in me of the home circle in Elkton, I prayed to God.

In the morning we took stock. To commence with, all but two or three had suffered frostbite. Aaron Northrup, unable to move because of his broken hip, was very bad. It was the surgeon's opinion that both of Northrup's feet were hopelessly frozen.

The longboat was deep and heavy in the water, for it was burdened by the entire ship's company of twenty-one. Two of these were boys. Benny Hardwater was a bare thirteen, and Lish Dickery, whose family was near neighbor to mine in Elkton, was just turned sixteen. Our provisions consisted of three hundredweight of beef and two hundredweight of pork. The half- dozen loaves of brine-pulped bread, which the cook had brought, did not count. Then there were three small barrels of water and one small keg of beer.

Captain Nicholl frankly admitted that in this uncharted ocean he had no knowledge of any near land. The one thing to do was to run for more clement climate, which we accordingly did, setting our small sail and steering quartering before the fresh wind to the northeast.

The food problem was simple arithmetic. We did not count Aaron Northrup, for we knew he would soon be gone. At a pound per day, our five hundred pounds would last us twenty-five days; at half a pound, it would last fifty. So half a pound had it. I divided and issued the meat under the captain's eyes, and managed it fairly enough, God knows, although some of the men grumbled from the first. Also, from time to time I made fair division among the men of the plug tobacco I had stowed in my many pockets—a thing which I could not but regret, especially when I knew it was being wasted on this man and that who I was certain could not live a day more or, at best, two days or three.

For we began to die soon in the open boat. Not to starvation but to the killing cold and exposure were those earlier deaths due. It was a matter of the survival of the toughest and the luckiest. I was tough by constitution, and lucky inasmuch as I was warmly clad and had not broken my leg like Aaron Northrup. Even so, so strong was he that, despite being the first to be severely frozen, he was days in passing. Vance Hathaway was the first. We found him in the gray of dawn, crouched doubled in the bow and frozen stiff. The boy, Lish Dickery, was the second to go. The other boy, Benny Hardwater, lasted ten or a dozen days.

So bitter was it in the boat that our water and beer froze solid, and it was a difficult task justly to apportion the pieces I broke off with Northrup's claspknife. These pieces we put in our mouths and sucked till they melted. Also, on occasion of snow squalls, we had all the snow we desired. All of which was not good for us, causing a fever of inflammation to attack our mouths so that the membranes were continually dry and burning. And there was no allaying a thirst so generated. To suck more ice or snow was merely to aggravate the inflammation. More than anything else, I think it was this that caused the death of Lish Dickery. He was out of his head and raving for twenty-four hours before he died. He died babbling for water, and yet he did not die for need of water. I resisted as much as possible the temptation to suck ice, contenting myself with a shred of tobacco in my cheek, and made out with fair comfort.

We stripped all clothing from our dead. Stark they came into the world and stark they passed out over the side of the longboat and down into the dark, freezing ocean. Lots were cast for the clothes. This was by Captain Nicholl's command, in order to prevent quarreling.

It was no time for the follies of sentiment. There was not one of us who did not know secret satisfaction at the occurrence of each death. Luckiest of all was Israel Stickney in casting lots, so that in the end, when he passed, he was a veritable treasure trove of clothing. It gave a new lease of life to the survivors.

We continued to run to the northeast before the fresh westerlies, but our quest for warmer weather seemed vain. Ever the spray froze in the bottom of the boat, and I still chipped beer and drinking water with Northrup's knife. My own knife I reserved. It was of good steel, with a keen edge and stoutly fashioned, and I did not care to peril it in such manner. By the time half our company was overboard, the boat had a reasonably high freeboard end was less ticklish to handle in the gusts. Likewise there was more room for a man to stretch out comfortably.

A source of continual grumbling was the food. The captain, the mate, the surgeon, and myself, talking it over, resolved not to increase the daily whack of half a pound of meat. The six sailors, for whom Tobias Snow made himself spokesman, contended that the death of half of us was equivalent to a doubling of our provisioning and that therefore the ration should be increased to a pound. In reply, we of the afterguard pointed out that it was our chance for life that was doubled did we but bear with the half-pound ration.

It is true that eight ounces of salt meat did not go far in enabling us to live and to resist the severe cold. We were quite weak and, because of our weakness, we frosted easily. Noses and cheeks were all black with frostbite. It was impossible to be warm, although we now had double the garments we had started with. Five weeks after the loss of the *Negociator* the trouble over the food came to a head. I was asleep at the time—it was night—when Captain Nicholl caught Jud Hetchkins stealing from the pork barrel. That he was abetted by the other five men was proved by their actions. Immediately Jud Hetchkins was discovered, the whole six threw themselves upon us with their knives. It was close, sharp work in the dim light of the stars, and it was a mercy the boat was not overturned. I had reason to be thankful for my many shirts and coats, which served me as an armor. The knife thrusts scarcely more than drew blood through the so great thickness of cloth, although I was scratched to bleeding in a round dozen of places.

The others were similarly protected, and the fight would have ended in no more than a mauling all around, had not the mate, Walter Dakon, a very powerful man, hit upon the idea of ending the matter by tossing the mutineers overboard. This was joined in by Captain Nicholl, the surgeon, and myself, and in a trice five of the six were in the water and clinging to the gunwale. Captain Nicholl and the surgeon were busy amidships with the sixth, Jeremy Nalor, and were in the act of throwing him overboard, while the mate was occupied with rapping the fingers along the gunwale with a boat-stretcher. For the moment I had nothing to do, and so was able to observe the tragic end of the mate. As he lifted the stretcher to rap Seth Richards' fingers, the latter, sinking down low in the water and then jerking himself up by both hands, sprang half into the boat, locked his arms about the mate, and, falling backward and outboard, dragged the mate with him. Doubtlessly he never relaxed his grip, and both drowned together.

Thus, left alive of the entire ship's company were three of us: Captain Nicholl, Arnold Bentham, the surgeon, and myself. Seven had gone in the twinkling of an eye, consequent on Jud Hetchkins' attempt to steal provisions. And to me it seemed a pity that so much good warm clothing had been wasted there in the sea. There was not one of us who could not have managed gratefully with more.

Captain Nicholl and the surgeon were good men and honest. Often enough, when two of us slept, the one awake and steering could have stolen from the meat. But this never happened. We trusted one another fully, and we would have died rather than betray that trust.

We continued to content ourselves with half a pound of meat each per day, and we took advantage of every favoring breeze to work to the north'ard. Not until January fourteenth, seven weeks since the wreck, did we come up with a warmer latitude. Even then it was not really warm. It was merely not so bitterly cold.

Here the fresh westerlies forsook us and we bobbed and blobbed about in doldrummy weather for many days. Mostly it was calm, or light contrary winds, though sometimes a burst of breeze, as like as not from dead ahead, would last for a few hours. In our weakened condition, with so large a boat, it was out of the question to row. We could merely hoard our food and wait for God to show a more kindly face. The three of us were faithful Christians, and we made a practice of prayer each day before the apportionment of food. Yes, and each of us prayed privately often and long.

By the end of January our food was near its end. The pork

was entirely gone, and we used the barrel for catching and storing rainwater. Not many pounds of beef remained. And in all the nine weeks in the open boat we had raised no sail and glimpsed no land. Captain Nicholl frankly admitted that after sixty-three days of dead reckoning he did not know where we were.

The twentieth of February saw the last morsel of food eaten. I prefer to skip the details of much that happened in the next eight days. I shall touch only on the incidents that serve to show what manner of men were my companions. We had starved so long that, we had no reserves of strength on which to draw when the food utterly ceased, and we grew weaker with great rapidity.

On February twenty-fourth we calmly talked the situation over. We were three stout-spirited men, full of life and toughness, and we did not want to die. No one of us would volunteer to sacrifice himself for the other two. But we agreed on three things: we must have food; we must decide the matter by casting lots; and we would cast the lots next morning if there were no wind.

Next morning there was wind, not much of it, but fair, so that we were able to log a sluggish two knots on our northerly course. The mornings of the twenty-sixth and twenty-seventh found us with a similar breeze. We were fearfully weak, but we abided by our decision and continued to sail.

But with the morning of the twenty-eighth we knew the time was come. The longboat rolled drearily on an empty, windless sea, and the stagnant, overcast sky gave no promise of any breeze. I cut three pieces of cloth, all of a size, from my jacket In the ravel of one of these pieces was a bit of brown thread. Whoever drew this lost. I then put the three lots into my hat, covering it with Captain Nicholl's hat

All was ready, but we delayed for a time while each prayed silently and long, for we knew that we were leaving the decision to God. I was not unaware of my own honesty and worth; but I was equally aware of the honesty and worth of my companions, so that it perplexed me how God could decide so fine-balanced and delicate a matter.

The captain, as was his right and due, drew first After his hand was in the hat he delayed for some time with closed eyes, his lips moving a last prayer. And he drew a blank. This was right—a true decision I could not but admit to myself; for Captain Nicholl's life was largely known to me and I knew him to be honest, upright, and God-fearing.

Remained the surgeon and me. It was one or the other and, according to ship's rating, it was his due to draw next. Again we prayed. As I prayed I strove to quest back in my life and cast a hurried tally sheet of my own worth and unworth.

I held the hat on my knees with Captain Nicholl's hat over it. The surgeon thrust in his hand and fumbled about for some time, while I wondered whether the feel of that one brown thread could be detected from the rest of the ravel.

At last he withdrew his hand. The brown thread was in his piece of cloth. I was instantly very humble and very grateful for God's blessing thus extended to me; and I resolved to keep more faithfully than ever all of His commandments. The next moment I could not help but feel that the surgeon and the captain were pledged to each other by closer ties of position and intercourse than with me, and that they were in a measure disappointed with the outcome. And close with that thought ran the conviction that they were such true men that the outcome would not interfere with the plan arranged.

I was right The surgeon bared arm and knife and prepared to open a great vein. First, however, he spoke a few words.

"I am a native of Norfolk, in the Virginias," he said, "where I expect I have now a wife and three children living. The only favor that I have to request of you is that should it please God to deliver either of you from your perilous situation, and should you be so fortunate as to reach once more your native country, that you would acquaint my unfortunate family with my wretched fate."

Next he requested courteously of us a few minutes in which to arrange his affairs with God. Neither Captain Nicholl nor I could utter a word, but with streaming eyes we nodded our consent

Without doubt Arnold Bentham was the best collected of the three of us. My own anguish was prodigious, and I am confident that Captain Nicholl suffered equally. But what was one to do? The thing was fair and proper and had been decided by God. But when Arnold Bentham had completed his last arrangements and made ready to do the act, I could contain myself no longer, and cried out:

"Wait! We who have endured so much surely can endure a little more. It is now mid-morning. Let us wait until twilight Then, if no event has appeared to change our dreadful destiny, do you, Arnold Bentham, do as we have agreed."

He looked to Captain Nicholl for confirmation of my suggestion, and Captain Nicholl could only nod. He could utter no word, but in his moist and frosty blue eyes was a wealth of acknowledgment I could not misread.

I did not, I could not, deem it a crime, having so determined by fair drawing of lots, that Captain Nicholl and myself should profit by the death of Arnold Bentham. I could not believe that the love of life that actuated us had been implanted in our breasts by aught other than God. It was God's will, and we, His poor creatures, could only obey and fulfill His will. And yet, God was kind. In His all-kindness He saved us from so terrible, though so righteous, an act.

Scarce had a quarter of an hour passed when a fan of air from the west, with a hint of frost and damp in it, crisped on our cheeks. In another five minutes we had steerage from the filled sail, and Arnold Bentham was at the steering sweep.

"Save what little strength you have," he said. "Let me consume the little strength left in me in order that it may increase your chance to survive."

And so he steered to a freshening breeze, while Captain Nicholl and I lay sprawled in the boat's bottom and in our weakness dreamed dreams and glimpsed visions of the dear things of life far across the world from us.

It was an ever-freshening breeze of wind that soon began to

puff and gust. The cloud stuff flying across the sky foretold us of a gale. By midday Arnold Bentham fainted at the steering and, ere the boat could broach in the tidy sea already running, Captain Nicholl and I were at the steering sweep with all the four of our weak hands upon it We came to an agreement, and just as Captain Nicholl had drawn the first lot by virtue of his office, so now he took the first spell at steering. Thereafter the three of us spelled one another every fifteen minutes. We were very weak, and we could not spell longer at a time.

By mid-afternoon a dangerous sea was running. We should have rounded the boat to, had our situation not been so desperate, and let her drift bow-on to a sea anchor extemporized of our mast and sail. Had we broached in those great, overtopping seas, the boat would have been rolled over and over.

Time and again, that afternoon, Arnold Bentham, for our sakes, begged that we come to a sea anchor. He knew that we continued to run only in the hope that the decree of the lots might not have to be carried out. He was a noble man. So was Captain Nicholl noble, whose frosty eyes had wizened to points of steel. And in such noble company how could I be less noble? I thanked God repeatedly, through that long afternoon of peril, for the privilege of having known two such men. God and the right dwelled in them, and no matter what my poor fate might be, I could but feel well recompensed by such companionship. Like them, I did not want to die, yet was unafraid to die. The quick, early doubt I had had of these two men was long since dissipated. Hard the school, and hard the men, but they were noble men, God's own men.

I saw it first. Arnold Bentham, his own death accepted, and Captain Nicholl, well nigh accepting death, lay rolling like loose-bodied dead men in the boat's bottom, and I was steering when I saw it. The boat, foaming and surging with the swiftness of wind in its sail, was uplifted on a crest when, close before me, I saw the sea-battered islet of rock. It was not half a mile off. I cried out, so that the other two, kneeling and reeling and clutching for support, were peering and staring at what I saw.

"Straight for it, Daniel," Captain Nicholl mumbled command. "There may be a cove. There may be a cove. It is our only chance."

Once again he spoke, when we were atop that dreadful lee shore with no cove existent.

"Straight for it, Daniel. If we go clear we are too weak ever to win back against sea and wind."

He was right. I obeyed. He drew his watch and looked, and I asked the time. It was five o'clock. He stretched out his hand to Arnold Bentham, who met and shook weakly; and both gazed at me, in their eyes extending that same handclasp. It was farewell, I knew; for what chance had creatures so feeble as we to win alive over those surf-battered rocks to the higher rocks beyond?

Twenty feet from shore the boat was snatched out of my control. In a trice it was overturned and I was strangling in the salt. I never saw my companions again. By good fortune I was buoyed by the steering oar I still grasped, and by great good fortune a fling of sea, at the right instant, at the right spot, threw me far up the gentle slope of the one shelving rock on all that terrible shore. I was not hurt. I was not bruised. And with brain reeling from weakness I was able to crawl and scramble farther up beyond the clutching backwash of the sea

I stood upright, knowing-myself saved, and thanking God, and staggering as I stood. Already the boat was pounded to a thousand fragments. And though I saw them not, I could guess how grievously had been pounded the bodies of Captain Nicholl and Arnold Bentham. I saw an oar on the edge of the foam, and at certain risk I drew it clear. Then I fell to my knees, knowing myself fainting. And yet, ere I fainted, with a sailor's instinct I dragged my body on and up among the cruel hurting rocks to faint finally beyond the reach of the sea.

I was near a dead man myself, that night, mostly in stupor, only dimly aware at times of the extremity of cold and wet that I endured. Morning brought me astonishment and terror. No plant, not a blade of grass, grew on that wretched projection of rock from the ocean's bottom. A quarter of a mile in width and a half-mile in length, it was no more than a heap of rocks. Naught could I discover to gratify the cravings of exhausted nature. I was consumed with thirst, yet was there no fresh water. In vain I tasted to my mouth's undoing every cavity and depression in the rocks. The spray of the gale so completely had enveloped every portion of the island that every depression was as filled with water salt as the sea

Of the boat remained nothing—not even a splinter to show that a boat had been. I stood possessed of my garments, a stout knife, and the one oar I had saved. The gale had abated, and all that day, staggering and falling, crawling till hands and knees bled, I vainly sought water.

That night, nearer death than ever, I sheltered behind a rock from the wind. A heavy shower of rain made me miserable. I removed my various coats and spread them to soak up the rain; but when I came to wring the moisture from them into my mouth, I was disappointed, because the cloth had been thoroughly impregnated with the salt of the ocean in which I had been immersed. I lay on my back, my mouth open to catch the few raindrops that fell directly into it. It was tantalizing, but it kept my membranes moist and me from madness.

The second day I was a very sick man. I, who had not eaten for so long, began to swell to a monstrous fatness—my legs, my arm, my whole body. With the slightest of pressures my fingers would sink in a full inch into my skin, and the depressions so made were long in going away. Yet did I labor sore in order to fulfill God's will that I should live. Carefully, with my hands, I cleaned out the salt water from every slight hole, in the hope that succeeding showers of rain might fill them with water that I could drink.

My sad lot and the memories of the loved ones at Elkton threw me into a melancholy, so that I often lost my recollection for hours at a time. This was a mercy, for it veiled me from my sufferings that else would have killed me.

In the night I was roused by the beat of rain, and I crawled from hole to hole, lapping up the rain or licking it from the rocks. Brackish it was, but drinkable. It was what saved me, for, toward morning, I awoke to find myself in a profuse perspiration and quite free of all delirium.

Then came the sun, the first time since my stay on the island, and I spread most of my garments to dry. Of water I drank my careful fill, and I calculated there was ten day's supply if carefully husbanded. It was amazing, how rich I felt with this vast wealth of brackish water. And no great merchant, with all his ships returned from prosperous voyages, his warehouses filled to the rafters, his strongboxes overflowing, could have felt as wealthy as did I when I discovered, cast up on the rocks, the body of a seal that had been dead for many days. Nor did I fail, first, to thank God on my knees for this manifestation of His ever unfailing kindness. The thing was clear to me: God had not intended I should die. From the very first He had not so intended.

I knew the debilitated state of my stomach, and I ate sparingly in the knowledge that my natural voracity would surely kill me did I yield myself to it. Never had sweeter morsels passed my lips, and I make free to confess that I shed tears of joy, again and again, at contemplation of that putrefied carcass.

My heart of hope beat strong in me once more. Carefully I preserved the portions of the carcass remaining. Carefully I covered my rock cisterns with flat stones so that the sun's rays might not evaporate the precious fluid and in precaution against some upspringing of wind in the night and the sudden flying of spray. Also I gathered me tiny fragments of seaweed and dried them in the sun for an easement between my poor body and the rough rocks whereon I made my lodging. And my garments were dry— the first time in days, so that I slept the heavy sleep of exhaustion and of returning health. When I awoke to a new day I was another man. The absence of the sun did not depress me, and I was swiftly to learn that God, not forgetting me while I slumbered, had prepared other and wonderful blessings for me. I would have fain rubbed my eyes and looked again, for, as far as I could see, the rocks bordering upon the ocean were covered with seals. There were thousands of them, and in the water other thousands disported themselves, while the sound that went up from all their throats was prodigious and deafening. I knew it when I saw it—meat lay there for the taking, meat sufficient for a score of ships' companies.

I directly seized my oar—than which there was no other stick of wood on the island—and cautiously advanced upon all that immensity of provender. It was quickly guessed by me that these creatures of the sea were unacquainted with man. They betrayed no signals of timidity at my approach, and I found it a boy's task to rap them on the head with the oar.

And when I had so killed my third and my fourth, I went immediately and strangely mad. Indeed, quite bereft was I of all judgment as I slew and slew and continued to slay. For the space of two hours I toiled unceasingly with the oar till I was ready to drop. What excess of slaughter I might have been guilty of I know not, for, at the end of that time, as if by a signal, all the seals that still lived threw themselves into the water and swiftly disappeared.

I found the number of slain seals to exceed two hundred, and I was shocked and frightened because of the madness of slaughter that had possessed me. I had sinned by wanton wastefulness and, after I had duly refreshed myself with this good wholesome food, I set about as well as I could to make amends. But first, ere the great task began, I returned thanks to that Being through whose mercy I had been so miraculously preserved. Thereupon I labored until dark, and after dark, skinning the seals, cutting the meat into strips, and placing it upon the tops of rocks to dry in the sun. Also, I found small deposits of salt in the nooks and crannies of the rocks on the weather side of the island. This I rubbed into the meat as a preservative.

Four days I so toiled, and in the end was foolishly proud before God in that no scrap of all that supply of meat had been wasted. The unremitting labor was good for my body, which built up rapidly with this wholesome diet in which I did not stint myself. Another evidence of God's mercy: never, in the eight: years I spent on that barren islet, was there so long a spell of clear weather and steady sunshine as in the period immediately following the slaughter of the seals.

Months were to pass ere ever the seals revisited my island. But in the meantime I was anything but idle. I built me a hut of stone and, adjoining it, a storehouse for my cured meat. The hut I roofed with many sealskins, so that it was fairly waterproof. But I could never cease to marvel, when the rain beat on that roof, that no less than a king's ransom in the London fur market protected a castaway sailor from the elements.

I was quickly aware of the importance of keeping some kind of reckoning of time, without which I was sensible that I should soon lose all knowledge of the day of the week, and be unable to distinguish one from the other, and not know which was the Lord's day.

I remember back carefully to the reckoning of time kept in the longboat by Captain Nicholl; and carefully again and again, to make sure beyond any shadow of uncertainty, I went over the tale of the days and nights I had spent on the island. Then, by seven stones outside my hut, I kept my weekly calendar. In one place on the oar I cut a small notch for each week, and in another place on the oar I notched the months, being duly careful, indeed, to reckon in the additional days to each month over and beyond the four weeks.

Thus I was enabled to pay due regard to the Sabbath. As the only mode of worship I could adopt, I carved a short hymn, appropriate to my situation, on the oar, which I never failed to chant on the Sabbath. God, in his all-mercy, had not forgotten me; nor did I, in those eight years, fail at all proper times to remember God.

It was astonishing, the work required under such circumstances, to supply one's simple needs of food and shelter. Indeed, I was rarely idle that first year. The hut, itself a mere lair of rocks, nevertheless took six weeks of my time. The tardy curing and the endless scraping of the sealskins so as to make them soft and pliable for garments, occupied my spare moments for months and months.

Then there was the matter of my water supply. After any heavy gale, the flying spray salted my saved rainwater, so that at times I was grievously put to live through till fresh rains fell unaccompanied by high winds. Aware that a continual dropping will wear a stone, I selected a large stone, fine and tight of texture, and, by means of smaller stones, I proceeded to pound it hollow. In five weeks of most arduous toil I managed thus to make a jar which I estimated to hold a gallon and a half. Later, I similarly made a four-gallon jar. It took me nine weeks. Other small ones I also made from time to time. One, that would have contained eight gallons, developed a flaw when I had worked seven weeks on it.

But it was not until my fourth year on the island, when I had become reconciled to the possibility that I might continue to live there for the term of my natural life, that I created my masterpiece. It took me eight months, but it was tight, and it held upward of thirty gallons. These stone vessels were a great gratification to me—so much so that at times I forgot my humility and was unduly vain of them. Truly, they were more elegant to me than was ever the costliest piece of furniture to any queen. Also, I made me a small rock vessel, containing no more than a quart, with which to convey water from the catching places to my large receptacles. When I say that this one-quart vessel weighed all of two stone, the reader will realize that the mere gathering of the rainwater was no light task.

Thus, I rendered my lonely situation as comfortable as could be expected. I had completed me a snug and secure shelter; and, as to provision, I had always on hand a six months' supply, preserved by salting and drying. For these things, so essential to preserve life and which one could scarcely have expected to obtain upon a desert island, I was sensible that I could not be too thankful.

Although denied the privilege of enjoying the society of any human creature, not even of a dog or a cat, I was far more reconciled to my lot than thousands probably would have been. Upon the desolate spot, where fate had placed me, I conceived myself far more happy than many who, for ignominious crimes, were doomed to drag out their lives in solitary confinement with conscience ever biting like a corrosive canker.

However dreary my prospects, I was not without hope that that Providence, which, at the very moment when hunger threatened me with dissolution and when I might easily have been engulfed in the maw of the sea, had cast me upon those barren rocks, would finally direct someone to my relief.

If deprived of the society of my fellow creatures and of the conveniences of life, I could not but reflect that my forlorn situation was yet attended with some advantages. Of the whole island, though small, I had peaceable possession. No one, it was probable, would ever appear to dispute my claim, unless it were the amphibious animals of the ocean. Since the island was almost inaccessible, at night my repose was not disturbed by continual apprehension of the approach of cannibals or of beasts of prey. Again and again I thanked God on my knees for these various and many benefactions.

Yet is man ever a strange and unaccountable creature. I, who had asked of God's mercy no more than putrid meat to eat and a sufficiency of water not too brackish, was no sooner blessed with an abundance of cured meat and sweet water than I began to know discontent with my lot I began to want fire, and the savor of cooked meat in my mouth. And continually I would discover myself longing for certain delicacies of the palate such as were part of the common daily fare on the home table at Elkton. Strive as I would, ever my fancy eluded my will and wantoned in daydreaming of the good things I had eaten and of the good things I would eat if ever I were rescued from my lonely situation.

It was the old Adam in me, I suppose—the taint of that first father who was the first rebel against God's commandments. Most strange is man, ever insatiable, ever unsatisfied, never at peace with God or himself, his days filled with restlessness and useless endeavor, his nights a glut of vain dreams of desires willful and wrong. Yes, and also I was much annoyed by my craving for tobacco. My sleep was often a torment to me, for it was then that my desires took license to rove, so that a thousand times I dreamed myself possessed of hogsheads of tobacco—ay, and of warehouses of tobacco, and of shiploads and of entire plantations of tobacco.

But I revenged myself upon myself. I prayed God unceasingly for a humble heart, and chastised my flesh with unremitting toil. Unable to improve my mind, I determined to improve my barren island. I labored four months at constructing a stone wall thirty feet long, including its wings, and a dozen feet high. This was as a protection to the hut in the periods of the great gales when all the island was as a tiny petrel in the maw of the hurricane. Nor did I conceive the time misspent. Thereafter I lay snug in the heart of calm while all the air for a hundred feet above my head was one stream of gust-driven water.

In the third year I began me a pillar of rock. Rather was it a pyramid, foursquare, broad at the base, sloping upward not steeply to the apex. In this fashion I was compelled to build, for gear and timber there was none in all the island for the construction of scaffolding. Not until the close of the fifth year was my pyramid complete. It stood on the summit of the island. Now, when I state that the summit was but forty feet above the sea, and that the peak of my pyramid was forty feet above the summit, it will be conceived that I, without tools, had doubled the stature of the island. It might be urged by some unthinking ones that I interfered with God's plan in the creation of the world. Not so, I hold. For was not I equally a part of God's plan, along with this heap of rocks up-jutting in the solitude of ocean? My arms with which to work, my back with which to bend and lift, my hands cunning to clutch and hold—were not these parts too in God's plan? Much I pondered the matter. I know that I was right.

In the sixth year I increased the base of my pyramid, so that in eighteen months thereafter the height of my monument was fifty feet above the height of the island. This was no tower of Babel.

It served two right purposes. It gave me a lookout from which to scan the ocean for ships and increased the likelihood of my island being sighted by the careless roving eye of any seaman. And it kept my body and mind in health. With hands never idle, there was small opportunity for Satan on that island. Only in my dreams did he torment me, principally with visions of varied foods and with imagined indulgences in the foul weed called tobacco.

On the eighteenth day of the month of June, in the sixth year of my sojourn on the island, I described a sail. But it passed far to leeward at too great a distance to discover me. Rather than suffering disappointment, the very appearance of this sail afforded me the liveliest satisfaction. It convinced me of a fact that I had before in a degree doubted, to wit: that these seas were sometimes visited by navigators.

Among other things, where the seals hauled up out of the sea, I built wide spreading wings of low rock walls that narrowed to a cul-de-sac, where I might conveniently kill such seals as entered without exciting their fellows outside and without permitting any wounded or frightened seal to escape and spread a contagion of alarm. Seven months to this structure alone were devoted.

As the time passed, I grew more contented with my lot, and the devil came less and less in my sleep to torment the old Adam in me with lawless visions of tobacco and savory foods. And I continued to eat my seal meat and call it good, and to drink the sweet rainwater of which always I had a plenty, and to be grateful to God. And God heard me, I know, for during all my term on that island I knew never a moment of sickness, save two, both of which were due to my gluttony, as I shall later relate.

In the fifth year, ere I had convinced myself that the keels of ships did on occasion plow these seas, I began carving on my oar minutes of the more remarkable incidents that had attended me since I quitted the peaceful shores of America. This I rendered as intelligible and permanent as possible, the letters being of the smallest size. Six, and even five, letters were often a day's worn for me, so painstaking was I.

And, lest it should prove my hard fortune never to meet with the long-wished opportunity to return to my friends and to my family at Elkton, I engraved, or pitched, on the broad end of the oar the legend of my ill fate which I have already quoted near the beginning of this narrative.

This oar, which had proved so serviceable to me in my destitute situation, and which now contained a record of my own fate and of that of my shipmates, I spared no pains to preserve. No longer did I risk it in knocking seals on the head. Instead, I equipped myself with a stone club, some three feet in length and of suitable diameter, which occupied an even month in the fashioning. Also, to secure the oar from the weather (for I used it in mild breezes as a flagstaff top of my pyramid from which to fly a flag I made me from one of my precious shirts), I contrived for it a covering of well-cured sealskins.

In the month of March of the sixth year of my confinement, I experienced one of the most tremendous storms that was perhaps ever witnessed by man. It commenced at about nine in the evening, with the approach of black clouds and a freshening wind from the southwest, which, by eleven, had become a hurricane, attended with incessant peals of thunder and the sharpest lightning I had ever witnessed.

I was not without apprehension for the safety of the island. Over every part, the seas made a clean breach, except of the summit of my pyramid. There, the life was nigh beaten and suffocated out of my body by the drive of the wind and spray. I could not but be sensible that my existence was spared solely because of my diligence in erecting the pyramid and so doubling the stature of the island.

Yet in the morning I had great reason for thankfulness. All my saved rainwater was turned brackish, save that in my largest vessel which was sheltered in the lee of the pyramid. By careful economy I knew I had drink sufficient until the next rain, no matter how delayed, should fall. My hut was quite washed out by the seas, and of my great store of seal meat only a wretched, pulpy

modicum remained. Nevertheless I was agreeably surprised to find
the rocks plentifully distributed with a sort of fish more nearly like
the mullet than any I had ever observed. Of these I picked up no
less than twelve hundred and nineteen, which I split and cured in
the sun after the manner of cod. This welcome change of diet was
not without its consequence. I was guilty of gluttony, and for all
of the succeeding night I was near to death's door.

In the seventh year of my stay on the island, in the very same
month of March, occurred a similar storm of great violence. Following upon it, to my astonishment I found an enormous dead
whale, quite fresh, which had been cast up high and dry by the
waves. Conceive my gratification when in the bowels of the great
fish I found deeply imbedded a harpoon of the common sort with
a few fathoms of new line attached thereto.

Thus were my hopes again revived that I should finally meet
with an opportunity to quit the desolate island. Beyond doubt
these seas were frequented by whalemen and, so long as I kept up
a stout heart, sooner or later I should be saved. For seven years I
had lived on seal meat, so that at sight of the enormous plentitude
of different and succulent food I fell a victim to my weakness and
ate of such quantities that once again I was well nigh to dying.
And yet, after all, this and the affair of the small fish were mere
indispositions due to the foreignness of the food to my stomach,
which had learned to prosper on seal meat and on nothing but
seal meat.

Of that one whale I preserved a full year's supply of provision.
Also, under the sun's rays, in the rock hollows, I tried out much
of the oil, which to dip my strips of seal meat while dining. Out
of my precious rags of shirts I could even have contrived a wick
so that, with the harpoon for steel and rock for flint, I might have
had a light at night. But it was a vain thing, and I speedily forewent the thought of it. I had no need for light when God's darkness descended, for I had schooled myself to sleep from sundown
to sunrise, winter and summer.

I, Darrell Standing, cannot refrain from breaking in on this recital of an earlier existence in order to note a conclusion of my own. Since human personality is a growth, a sum of all previous existences added together, what possibility was there for Warden Atherton to break down my spirit in the inquisition of solitary? I am life that survived, a structure built up through the ages of the past—and such a past! What were ten days and nights in the jacket to me? —to me, who had once been Daniel Foss and for eight years learned patience in that school of rocks in the far South Ocean?

At the end of my eighth year on the island, in the month of September, when I had just sketched most ambitious plans to raise my pyramid to sixty feet above the summit of the island, I awoke one morning to stare out upon a ship with topsails aback and nearly within hail. That I might be discovered, I swung my oar in the air, jumped from rock to rock, and was guilty of all manner of liveliness of action, until I could see the officers on the quarterdeck looking at me through their spyglasses. They answered by pointing to the extreme westerly end of the island, whither I hastened and discovered their boat manned by a half a dozen men. It seems, as I was to learn afterward, the ship had been attracted by my pyramid and had altered its course to make closer examination of so strange a structure that was greater of height than the wild island on which it stood.

But the surf proved to be too great to permit the boat to land on my inhospitable shore. After diverse unsuccessful attempts they signaled me that they must return to the ship. Conceive my despair at thus being unable to quit the desolate island. I seized my oar (which I had long since determined to present to the Philadelphia Museum if ever I were preserved) and with it plunged headlong into the foaming surf. Such was my good fortune, and my strength and agility, that I gained the boat.

I cannot refrain from telling here a curious incident. The ship had by this time drifted so far away that we were all of an hour in getting aboard. During this time I yielded to my propensities that had been baffled for eight long years, and begged of the second mate, who steered, a piece of tobacco to chew. This granted, the second mate also proffered me his pipe, filled with prime Virginia leaf. Scarce had ten minutes passed when I was taken violently sick. The reason for this was clear. My system was entirely purged of tobacco, and what I now suffered was tobacco poisoning such as afflicts any boy at the time of his first smoke. Again I had reason to be grateful to God, and from that day to the day of my death I neither used nor desired the foul weed.

I, Darrell Standing, must now complete the amazingness of the details of this existence which I relived while unconscious in the straitjacket in San Quentin prison. I often wondered if Daniel Foss had been true in his resolve and deposited the carved oar in the Philadelphia Museum.

It is a difficult matter for a prisoner in solitary to communicate with the outside world. Once with a guard, and once with a short-timer in solitary, I entrusted, by memorization, a letter of inquiry addressed to the curator of the Museum. Although under the most solemn pledges, both these men failed me. It was not until after Ed Morrell, by a strange whirl of fate, was released from solitary and appointed head trusty of the entire prison, that I was able to have the letter sent. I now give the reply, sent me by the curator of the Philadelphia Museum, and smuggled to me by Ed Morrell:

It is true there is such an oar here as you have described. But few persons can know of it, for it is not on exhibition in the public rooms. In fact, and I have held this position for eighteen years, I was unaware of its existence myself.

But upon consulting our old records I found that such an oar had been presented by one Daniel Foss, of Elkton, Maryland, in the year 1821 Not until after a long search did we find the oar in a disused attic lumber room of odds and ends. The notches and the legend are carved on the oar just as you have described.

We have also on file a pamphlet, presented at the same time, written by the said Daniel Foss, and published in Boston by the firm of N. Coverly, Jr., in the year 1834 This pamphlet describes eight years of a castaway's life on a desert island. It is evident that this mariner, in his old age and in want, hawked this pamphlet about among the charitable.

I am very curious to learn how you became aware of this oar, of the existence of which we of the museum were ignorant. Am I correct in assuming that you have read an account in some diary later published by this Daniel Foss? I shall be glad for any information on the subject, and am proceeding at once to have the oar and the pamphlet put back on exhibition.

Very truly yours,
Hosea Salsburty.*

---

* Since the execution of Professor Darrell Standing, at which time the manuscript of his memoirs came into our hands, we have written to Mr. Hosea Salsburty, Curator of the Philadelphia Museum, and, in reply, have received confirmation of the existence of the oar and the pamphlet.—THE EDITORS.

Chapter 20

The time came when I humbled Warden Atherton to unconditional surrender, making a vain and empty mouth of his ultimatum, "Dynamite or curtains." He gave me up as one who could not be killed in a straitjacket. He had had men die after several hours in the jacket. He had had men die after several days in the jacket, although, invariably, they were unlaced and carted into hospital ere they breathed their last . . . and received a death certificate from the doctor of pneumonia, or Bright's disease, or valvular disease of the heart.

But me Warden Atherton could never kill. Never did the urgency arise of carting my maltreated and perishing carcass to the hospital. Yet I will say that Warden Atherton tried his best and dared his worst. There was the time when he doublejacketed me. It is so rich an incident that I must tell it.

It happened that one of the San Francisco newspapers (seeking, as every newspaper and as every commercial enterprise seeks, a market that will enable it to realize a profit), tried to interest the radical portion of the working class in prison reform. As a result, union labor possessing an important political significance at the time, the time-serving politicians at Sacramento appointed a senatorial committe of investigation of the state prisons.

This State Senate committee *investigated* (pardon my italicized sneer) San Quentin. Never was there so model an institution of detention. The convicts themselves so testified. Nor can one blame them. They had experienced similar investigations in the past. They knew which side their bread was buttered on. They knew that all their sides and most of their ribs would ache very quickly after the taking of their testimony . . . if said testimony were adverse to the prison administration. Oh, believe me, my reader, it is a very ancient story. It was ancient in old Babylon, many a thousand years ago, as I well remember of that old time when I rotted in prison while palace intrigues shook the court.

As I have said, every convict testified to the humaneness of Warden Atherton's administration. In fact, so touching were their testimonials to the kindness of the warden, to the good and varied quality of the food and the cooking, to the gentleness of the guards, and to the general decency and ease and comfort of the prison domicile, that the opposition newspapers of San Francisco raised an indignant cry for more rigor in the management of our prisons, in that, otherwise, honest but lazy citizens would be seduced into seeking enrollment as prison guests.

The Senate Committe even invaded solitary, where the three of us had little to lose and nothing to gain. Jake Oppenheimer spat in its faces and told its members, all and sundry, to go to hell. Ed Morrell told them what a noisome stews the place was, insulted the warden to his face, and was recommended by the committee to be given a taste of the antiquated and obsolete punishments that after all must have been devised by previous wardens out of necessity for the right handling of hard characters like him.

I was careful not to insult the warden. I testified craftily, and as a scientist, beginning with small beginnings, making an art of my exposition, step by step, by tiny steps, inveigling my senatorial auditors on into willingness and eagerness to listen to the next exposure, the whole fabric so woven that there was no natural halting place at which to drop a period or interpolate a query . . . in this fashion, thus, I got my tale across.

Alas! No whisper of what I divulged ever went outside the prison walls. The Senate Committee gave a beautiful whitewash to Warden Atherton and San Quentin. The crusading San Francisco newspaper assured its working-class readers that San Quentin was whiter than snow and, further that, while it was true that the straitjacket was still a recognized legal method of punishment for the refractory, that, nevertheless, at the present time, under the present humane and spiritually right-minded warden, the straitjacket was never, under any circumstance, used.

And while the poor asses of laborers read and believed, while the Senate Committee dined and wined with the warden at the expense of the state and the taxpayer, Ed Morrell, Jake Oppenheimer, and I were lying in our jackets, laced just a trifle more tightly and more vindictively than we had ever been laced before.

"It is to laugh," Ed Morrell tapped to me, with the edge of the sole of his shoe.

"I should worry," tapped Jake.

And as for me, I too tapped my bitter scorn and laughter, remembered the prison houses of old Babylon, smiled to myself a huge cosmic smile, and drifted off and away into the largess of the little death that made me heir of all the ages and the rider full-panoplied and astride of time.

Yea, dear brother of the outside world, while the whitewash was running off the press, while the august senators were wining and dining, we three of the living dead, buried alive in solitary, were sweating our pain in the canvas torture.

And after the dinner, warm with wine, Warden Atherton himself came to see how fared it with us. Me, as usual, they found in coma. Doctor Jackson for the first time must have been alarmed. I was brought back across the dark to consciousness with the bite of ammonia in my nostrils. I smiled into the faces bent over me.

"Shamming," snorted the warden, and I knew by the flush on his face and the thickness in his tongue that he had been drinking.

I licked my lips as a sign for water, for I desired to speak.

"You are an ass," I at last managed to say with cold distinctness. "You are an ass, a coward, a cur, a pitiful thing so low that spittle would be wasted on your face. In such matter Jake Oppenheimer is over-generous with you. As for me, without shame I tell you the only reason I do not spit upon you is that I cannot demean myself nor so degrade my spittle."

"I've reached the limit of my patience!" He bellowed. "I will kill you, Standing!"

"You've been drinking," I retorted. "And I would advise you, if you must say such things, not to take so many of your prison curs into your confidence. They will snitch on you some day, and you will lose your job."

But the wine was up and master of him.

"Put another jacket on him," he commanded. "You are a dead man, Standing. But you'll not die in the jacket. We'll bury you from the hospital."

This time, over the previous jacket, the second jacket was put on from behind and laced up in front.

"Lord, Lord, Warden, it is bitter weather," I sneered. "The frost is sharp. Wherefore I am indeed grateful for you giving me two jackets. I shall be almost comfortable."

"Tighter!" He urged to Al Hutchins, who was drawing the lacing. "Throw your feet into the skunk. Break his ribs."

I must admit that Hutchins did his best.

"You will lie about me," the warden raved, the flush of wine and wrath flooding ruddier into his face. "Now see what you get for it. Your number is taken at last, Standing. This is your finish. Do you hear? This is your finish."

"A favor, Warden," I whispered faintly. Faint I was. Perforce I was nearly unconscious from the fearful constriction. "Make it a triple jacketing," I managed to continue, while the cell walls swayed and reeled about me and while I fought with all my will to hold to my consciousness that was being squeezed out of me by the jackets. "Another jacket ... Warden.... It . . . will . . . be . . . so . . . much . . . er . . . warmer."

And my whisper faded away as I ebbed down into the little death

I was never the same man after that double-jacketing. Never again, to this day, no matter what my food, was I properly nurtured. I suffered internal injuries to an extent I never cared to investigate. The old pain in my ribs and stomach is with me now as I write these lines. But the poor, maltreated machinery has served its purpose. It has enabled me to live thus far, and it will enable me to live the little longer to the day they take me out in the shirt without a collar and stretch my neck with the well-stretched rope.

But the double-jacketing was the last straw. It broke down Warden Atherton. He surrendered to the demonstration that I was unkillable. As I told him once:

"The only way you can get me, Warden, is to sneak in here some night with a hatchet."

Jake Oppenheimer was responsible for a good one on the warden, which I must relate:

"I say, Warden, it must be straight hell for you to have to wake up every morning with yourself on your pillow."

And Ed Morrell to the warden:

"Your mother must have been damn fond of children to have raised you."

It was really an offense to me when the jacketing ceased. I sadly missed that dream world of mine. But not for long. I found that I could suspend animation by the exercise of my will, aided mechanically by constricting my chest and abdomen with the blanket. Thus I induced physiological and pyschological states similar to those caused by the jacket. So, at will, and without the old torment, I was free to roam through time.

Ed Morrell believed all my adventures, but Jake Oppenheimer remained skeptical to the last. It was during my third year in solitary that I paid Oppenheimer a visit. I was never able to do it but that once, and that one time was wholly unplanned and unexpected.

It was merely after unconsciousness had come to me that I found myself in his cell. My body, I knew, lay in the jacket back in my own cell. Although never before had I seen him, I knew that this man was Jake Oppenheimer. It was summer weather, and he lay without clothes on top his blanket. I was shocked by his cadaverous face and skeleton-like body. He was not even the shell of a man. He was merely the structure of a man, the bones of a man, still cohering, stripped practically of all flesh and covered with a parchment-like skin.

Not until back in my own cell and consciousness, was I able to mull the thing over and realize that just as was Jake Oppenheimer, so was Ed Morrell, so was I. And I could not but thrill as I glimpsed the vastitude of spirit that inhabited these frail, perishing carcasses of us—the three incorrigibles of solitary. Flesh is a cheap, vain thing. Grass is flesh, and flesh becomes grass; but the spirit is the thing that abides and survives. I have no patience with these flesh-worshipers. A taste of solitary in San Quentin would swiftly convert them to a due appreciation and worship of the spirit.

But to return to my experience in Oppenheimer's cell. His body was that of a man long dead and shriveled by desert heat. The skin that covered it was of the color of dry mud. His sharp, yellow-gray eyes seemed the only part of him that was alive. They were never at rest. He lay on his back and the eyes darted hither and thither, following the flight of the several flies that disported in the gloomy air above him. I noted, too, a scar just above his right elbow, and another scar on his right ankle.

After a time he yawned, rolled over on his side, and inspected an angry-looking sore just above his hip. This he proceeded to cleanse and dress by the crude methods men in solitary must employ. I recognized the sore as one of the sort caused by the straitjacket. On my body, at this moment of writing, are hundreds of scars of the jacket.

Next, Oppenheimer rolled back on his back, gingerly took one of his front upper teeth—an eyetooth—between thumb and forefinger, and consideratively moved it back and forth Again he yawned, stretched his arms, rolled over, and knocked the call to Ed Morrell.

I read the code as a matter of course.

"Thought you might be awake," Oppenheimer tapped. "How goes it with the professor?"

Then, dim and far, I could hear Morrell's taps enunciating that they had put me in the jacket an hour before, and that, as usual, I was already deaf to all knuckle-talk.

"He is a good guy," Oppenheimer rapped on. "I always was

suspicious of educated mugs, but he ain't been hurt none by his education. He is sure square. Got all the spunk in the world, and you could not get him to squeal or double-cross in a million years."

To all of which, and with amplification, Ed Morrell agreed. And I must right here, ere I go a word further, say that I have lived many years and many lives, and that in those many lives I have known proud moments; but that the proudest moment I have ever known was the moment when my two comrades in solitary passed this appraisal of me. Ed Morrell and Jake Oppenheimer were great spirits, and in all time no greater honor was ever accorded me than this admission of me to their comradeship. Kings have knighted me, emperors have ennobled me, and, as king myself, I have known stately moments. Yet of it all nothing do I adjudge so splendid as this accolade delivered by two lifers in solitary deemed by the world as the very bottom-most of the human cesspool.

Afterwards recuperating from this particular bout with the jacket, I brought up my visit to Jake's cell as a proof that my spirit did leave my body. But Jake was unshakable.

"It is guessing that is more than guessing," was his reply, when I had described to him his successive particular actions at the time my spirit had been in his cell. "It is figuring. You have been close to three years in solitary yourself, Professor, and you can come pretty near to figuring what any guy will do to be killing time. There ain't a thing you told me that you and Ed ain't done thousands of times, from lying with your clothes off in hot weather to watching flies, tending sores, and rapping."

Morrell sided with me, but it was no use.

"Now don't take it hard, Professor," Jake tapped. "I ain't saying you lied. I just say you get to dreaming and figuring in the jacket without knowing you're doing it. I know you believe what you say, and that you think it happened; but it don't buy nothing with me. You figure it, but you don't know you figure it—that is something you known all the time, though you don't know you know it until you get into them dreamy, woozy states."

"Hold on, Jake," I tapped. "You know I have never seen you with my own eyes. Is that right'"

"I got to take your word for it, Professor. You might have seen me and not known it was me."

"The point is," I continued, "not having seen you with your clothes off, nevertheless I am able to tell you about that scar above your right elbow, and that scar on your right ankle."

"Oh, shucks," was his reply. "You'll find all that in my prison description and along with my mug in the rogue's gallery. They is thousands of chiefs of police and detectives know all that stuff."

"I never heard of it," I assured him.

"You don't remember that you ever heard of it," he corrected. "But you must have just the same. Though you have forgotten about it, the information is in your brain all right, stored away for reference, only you've forgot where it is stored. You've got to get woozy in order to remember.

"Did you ever forget a man's name you used to know as well as your own brother's? I have. There was a little jurror that convicted me in Oakland the time I got handed my fifty years. And one day I found I'd forgotten his name. Why, ho, I lay here for weeks puzzling for it. Now, just because I could not dig it out of my memory box was no sign it was not there. It was mislaid, that was all. And to prove it, one day when I was not even thinking about it, it popped right out of my brain to the tip of my tongue. 'Stacy,' I said right out loud. 'Joseph Stacy.' That was it. Get my drive?

"You only tell me about them scars what thousands of men know. I don't know how you got the information; I guess you don't know yourself. That ain't my lookout. But there she is. Telling me what many knows buys nothing with me. You got to deliver a whole lot more than that to make me swallow the rest of your whoppers."

—Hamilton's Law of Parsimony in the weighing of evidence!

So intrinsically was this slum-bred convict a scientist, that he had worked out Hamilton's law and rigidly applied it.

And yet—and the incident is delicious—Jake Oppenheimer was intellectually honest. That night, as I was dozing off, he called me with the customary signal.

"Say, Professor, you said you saw me wiggling my loose tooth. That has got my goat. That is the one thing I can't figure out any way you could know. It only went loose three days ago, and I ain't whispered it to a soul."

Chapter 21

Pascal somewhere says: "In viewing the march of human evolution, the philosophic mind should look upon humanity as one man, and not as a conglomeration of individuals."

I sit here in Murderers' Row in Folsom, the drowsy hum of flies in my ears as I ponder that thought of Pascal. It is true. Just as the human embryo, in its brief ten lunar months, with bewildering swiftness, in myriad forms and semblances a myriad times multiplied, rehearses the entire history of organic life from vegetable to man; just as the human boy, in his brief years of boyhood, rehearses the history of primitive man in acts of cruelty and savagery, from wantonness of inflicting pain on lesser creatures to tribal consciousness expressed by the desire to run in gangs; just so, I, Darrell Standing, have rehearsed and relived all that primitive man was, and did, and became until he became even you and I and the rest of our kind in a twentieth-century civilization.

Truly do we carry in us, each human of us alive on the planet today, the incorruptible history of life from life's beginning. This history is written in our tissues and our bones, in our functions and our organs, in our brain cells, and in our spirits, and in all sorts of physical and psychic atavistic urgencies and compulsions. Once we were fish-like, you and I, my reader, and crawled up out of the sea to pioneer in the great, dry-land adventure in the thick of which we are now. The marks of the sea are still on us, as the marks of the serpent are still on us, ere the serpent became serpent and we became we, when pre-serpent and pre-we were one. Once we flew in the air, and once we dwelt aboreally and were afraid of the dark. The vestiges remain, graven on you and me, and graven on our seed to come after us to the end of our time on earth.

What Pascal glimpsed with the vision of a seer, I have lived.

I have seen myself that one man contemplated by Pascal's philosophic eye. Oh, I have a tale most true, most wonderful, most real to me, although I doubt that I have wit to tell it, and that you, my reader, have wit to perceive it when told. I say that I have seen myself that one man hinted at by Pascal. I have lain in the long trances of the jacket and glimpsed myself a thousand living men living the thousand lives that are themselves the history of the human man climbing upward through the ages.

Ah, what royal memories are mine as I flutter through the aeons of the long ago. In single jacket trances I have lived the many lives involved in the thousand-year-long odysseys of the early drifts of men. Heavens, before I was of the flaxen-haired Aesir, who dwelt in Asgard, and before I was of the red-haired Vanir, who dwelt in Vanaheim, long before those times I have memories (living memories) of earlier drifts, when, like thistledown before the breeze, we drifted south before the face of the descending polar ice cap.

I have died of frost and famine, fight and flood. I have picked berries on the bleak backbone of the world, and I have dug roots to eat from fat-soiled fens and meadows. I have scratched the reindeer's semblance and the semblance of the hairy mammoth on ivory tusks gotten of the chase and on the rock walls of cave shelters when the winter storms moaned outside. I have cracked marrow bones on the sites of kingly cities that had perished centuries before my time or that were destined to be built centuries after my passing. And I have left the bones of my transient carcasses in pond bottoms, and glacial gravels, and asphalt lakes.

I have lived through the ages known today among the scientists as the Paleolithic, the Neolithic, and the Bronze. I remember when with our domesticated wolves we herded our reindeer to pasture on the north shores of the Mediterranean where now are France and Italy and Spain. This was before the ice sheet melted backward toward the pole. Many processions of the equinoxes have I lived through and died in, my reader, . . . only that I remember and that you do not.

I have been a Son of the Plough, a Son of the Fish, a Son of the Tree. All religions from the beginnings of man's religious time abide in me. And when the Dominie, in the chapel, here in Folsom of a Sunday, worships God in his own good modern way, I know that in him, the Dominie, still abide the worships of the Plough, the Fish, the Tree—ay, and also all worships of Astarte and the Night.

I have been an Aryan master in old Egypt when my soldiers scrawled obscenities on the carven tombs of kings dead and gone and forgotten aforetime. And I, the Aryan master in old Egypt, have myself built my two burial places—the one a false and mighty pyramid to which a generation of slaves could attest; the other humble, meager, secret, rock-hewn in a desert valley by slaves who died immediately their work was done.... And I wonder me here in Folsom, while democracy dreams its enchantments o'er the twentieth-century world, whether there, in the rock-hewn crypt of that secret, desert valley, the bones still abide that once were mine and that stiffened my animated body when I was an Aryan master high-stomached to command.

And on the great drift, southward and eastward under the burning sun that perished all descendants of the houses of Asgard and Vanaheim that took part in it, I have been a king in Ceylon, a builder of Aryan monuments under Aryan kings in old Java and old Sumatra. And I have died a hundred deaths on the great South Sea Drift ere ever the rebirth of men came to plant monuments, that only Aryans plant, on volcanic tropic islands that I, Darrell Standing, cannot name, being too well versed today in that far sea geography.

If only I were articulate to paint in the frail medium of words what I see and know and possess incorporated in my consciousness of the mighty driftage of the races in the times before our present written history began! Yes, we had our history even then. Our old men, our priests, our wise ones, told our history into tales and wrote those tales in the stars so that our seed after us should not forget From the sky came the life-giving rain and the sun-light.

And we studied the sky, learned from the stars to calculate time and apportion the seasons; and we named the stars after our heroes and our foods and our devices for getting food; and after our wanderings and drifts and adventures; and after our functions and our furies of impulse and desire.

And alas! We thought the heavens unchanging on which we wrote all our humble yearnings and all the humble things we did or dreamed of doing. When I was a Son of the Bull, I remember me a lifetime I spent at star-gazing. And, later and earlier, there were other lives in which I sang with the priests and bards the taboo songs of the stars wherein we believed was written our imperishable record. And here, at the end of it all, I pore over books of astronomy from the prison library, such as they allow condemned men to read, and learn that even the heavens are passing fluxes, vexed with star driftage as the earth is by the drifts of men.

Equipped with this modern knowledge, I have, returning through the little death from my earlier lives, been able to compare the heavens then and now. And the stars do change. I have seen pole stars and pole stars and dynasties of pole stars. The pole star today is in Ursa Minor. Yet in those far days I have seen the pole star in Draco, in Hercules, in Vega, in Cygnus, and in Cepheus. No, not even the stars abide, and yet the memory and the knowledge of them abides in me, in the spirit of me that is memory and that is eternal. Only spirit abides. All else, being mere matter, passes, and must pass.

Oh, I do see myself today that one man who appeared in the elder world, blond, ferocious, a killer and a lover, a meat eater and a root digger, a gypsy and a robber, who, club and hand, through millenniums of years, wandered the world around seeking meat to devour and sheltered nests for his younglings and sucklings.

I am that man, the sum of him, the all of him, the hairless biped who struggled upward from the slime and created love and law out of the anarchy of fecund life that screamed and squalled in the jungle. I am all that that man was and did become. I see myself, through the painful generations, snaring and killing the game and the fish, clearing the first fields from the forest, making rude tools of stone and bone, building houses of wood, thatching the roofs with leaves and straw, domesticating the wild grasses and meadow roots, fathering them to become the progenitors of rice and millet and wheat and barley and all manner of succulent edibles, learning to scratch the soil, to sow, to reap, to store, beating out the fibers of plants to spin into thread and to weave into cloth, devising systems of irrigation, working in metals, making markets and trade routes, building boats, and founding navigation—ay, and organizing village life, welding villages to villages till they became tribes, welding tribes together till they became nations, ever seeking the laws of things, ever making the laws of humans so that humans might live together in amity and by united effort beat down and destroy all manner of creeping, crawling, squalling things that might else destroy them.

I was that man in all his births and endeavors. I am that man today, waiting my due death by the law that I helped to devise many a thousand years ago, and by which I have died many times before this, many times. And as I contemplate this vast past history of me, I find several great and splendid influences, and, chiefest of these, the love of woman, man's love for the woman of his kind. I see myself, the one man, the lover, always the lover. Yes, also was I the great fighter, but somehow it seems to me as I sit here and evenly balance it all, that I was, more than aught else, the great lover. It was because I loved greatly that I was the great fighter.

Sometimes I think that the story of man is the story of the love of woman. This memory of all my past that I write now is the memory of my love of woman. Ever, in the ten thousand lives and guises, I loved her. I love her now. My sleep is fraught with her; my waking fancies, no matter whence they start, lead me always to her. There is no escaping her, that eternal, splendid, ever-resplendent figure of woman.

Oh, make no mistake. I am no callow, ardent youth. I am an elderly man, broken in health and body, and soon to die. I am a scientist and a philosopher. I, as all the generations of philosophers before me, know woman for what she is—her weaknesses and meannesses and immodesties and ignobilities, her earth-bound feet and her eyes that have never seen the stars. But—and the everlasting, irrefragable fact remains: Her feet are beautiful, her eyes are beautiful, her arms and breasts are paradise, her charm is potent beyond all charm that has ever dazzled man; and, as the pole willy nilly draws the needle, just so, willy nilly, does she draw man.

Woman has made me laugh at death and distance, scorn fatigue and sleep. I have slain men, many men, for love of woman, or in warm blood have baptized our nuptials or washed away the stain of her favor to another. I have gone down to death and dishonor, my betrayal of my comrades and of the stars black upon me, for woman's sake—for my sake, rather, I desired her so. And I have lain in the barley, sick with yearning for her, just to see her pass and glut my eyes with the swaying wonder of her and of her hair, black with the night, or brown or flaxen, or all golden-dusty with the sun. For woman is beautiful . . . to man. She is sweet to his tongue, and fragrance in his nostrils. She is fire in his blood, and a thunder of trumpets; her voice is beyond all music in his ears; and she can shake his soul that else stands steadfast in the drafty presence of the Titans of the Light and of the Dark. And beyond his star-gazing, in his far imagined heavens, Valkyrie or houri, man has fain made place for her, for he could see no heaven without her. And the sword in battle, singing, sings not so sweet a song as the woman sings to man merely by her laugh in the moonlight, or her love-sob in the dark, or by her swaying on her way under the sun while he lies dizzy with longing in the grass.

I have died of love. I have died for love, as you shall see. In a little while they will take me out, me, Darrell Standing, and make me die. And that death shall be for love. Oh, not lightly was I stirred when I slew Professor Haskell in the laboratory at the University of California. He was a man. I was a man. And there was a woman beautiful. Do you understand? She was a woman and I was a man, and a lover, and all the heredity of love was mine up from the black and squalling jungle ere love was love and man was man.

Oh, ay, it is nothing new. Often, often, in that long past, have I given life and honor, place and power, for love. Man is different from woman. She is close to the immediate and knows only the need of instant things. We know honor above her honor, and pride beyond her wildest guess of pride. Our eyes are far-visioned for star-gazing, while her eyes see no farther than the solid earth beneath her feet, the lover's breast upon her breast, the infant lusty in the hollow of her arm. And yet, such is our alchemy compounded of the ages, woman works magic in our dreams and in our veins, so that more than dreams and far visions and the blood of life itself is woman to us, who, as lovers truly say, is more than all the world. Yet is this just, else would man not be man, the fighter and the conqueror, treading his red way on the face of all other and lesser life—for, had man not been the lover, the royal lover, he could never have become the kingly fighter. We fight best and die best and live best for what we love.

I am that one man. I see myself the many selves that have gone into the constituting of me. And ever I see the woman, the many women, who have made me and undone me, who have loved me and whom I have loved.

I remember, oh, long ago when human kind was very young, that I made me a snare and a pit with a pointed stake upthrust in the middle thereof, for the taking of Sabre-Tooth. Sabre-Tooth, long-fanged and long-haired, was the chiefest to us of the squatting place, who crouched through the nights over our fires and by day increased the growing shell bank beneath us by the clams we dug and devoured from the salt mudflats beside us.

And when the roar and the squall of Sabre-Tooth roused us where we squatted by our dying embers, and I was wild with far vision of the proof of the pit and the stake, it was the woman, arms about me, leg-twining, who fought with and restrained me not to go out through the dark to my desire. She was part-clad, for warmth only, in skins of animals, mangy and fire-burnt, that

I had slain; she was swart and dirty with campsmoke unwashed since the spring rains, with nails gnarled and broken and hands that were calloused like foot-pads and were more like claws than like hands; but her eyes were blue as the summer sky is, as the deep sea is, and there was that in her eyes, and in her clasped arms about me, and in her heart beating against mine, that withheld me. . . though through the dark until dawn, while Sabre-Tooth squalled his wrath and his agony, I could hear my comrades snickering and sniggling to their women in that I had not the faith in my emprise and invention to venture through the night to the pit and the stake I had devised for the undoing of Sabre-Tooth. But my woman, my savage mate, held me, savage that I was, and her eyes drew me, and her arms chained me, and her twining legs and heart beating to mine seduced me from my far dream of things, my man's achievement, the goal beyond goals, the taking and the slaying of Sabre-Tooth on the stake in the pit.

Once I was Ushu, the archer. I remember it well. For I was lost from my own people, through the great forest, till I emerged on the flat lands and grass lands, and was taken in by a strange people, kin in that their skin was white, their hair yellow, their speech not too remote from mine. And she was Igar, and I drew her as I sang in the twilight, for she was destined a race-mother, and she was broad-built and full-dugged, and she could not but draw to the man heavy-muscled, deep-chested, who sang of his prowess in man-slaying and in meat-getting, and so, promised food and protection to her in her weakness while she mothered the seed that was to hunt the meat and live after her.

And these people knew not the wisdom of my people, in that they snared and pitted their meat and in battle used clubs and stone throwing-sticks and were unaware of the virtues of arrows swift-flying, notched on the end to fit the thong of deer sinew, well twisted, that sprang into straightness when released to the spring of the ash stick bent in the middle.

And while I sang, the stranger men laughed in the twilight. And only she, Igar, believed and had faith in me. I took her alone to the hunting, where the deer sought the water hole. And my bow twanged and sang in the covert, and the deer fell fast-stricken, and the warm meat was sweet to us, and she was mine there by the water hole.

And because of Igar I remained with the strange men. And I taught them the making of bows from the red and sweet-smelling wood like unto cedar. And I taught them to keep both eyes open, and to aim with the left eye, and to make blunt shafts for small game, and pronged shafts of bone for the fish in the clear water, and to flake arrowheads from obsidian for the deer and the wild horse, the elk and old Sabre-Tooth. But the flaking of stone they laughed at, till I shot an elk through and through, the flaked stone standing out and beyond, the feathered shaft sunk in its vitals the whole tribe applauding.

I was Ushu, the Archer, and Igar was my woman and mate. We laughed under the sun in the morning, when our man-child and woman-child, yellowed like honeybees, sprawled and rolled in the mustard, and at night she lay close in my arms and loved me and urged me, because of my skill at the seasoning of woods and the flaking of arrowheads, that I should stay close by the camp and let the other men bring to me the meat from the perils of hunting. And I listened and grew fat and short-breathed, and in the long nights, unsleeping, worried that the men of the stranger tribe brought me meat for my wisdom and honor, but laughed at my fatness and undesire for the hunting and fighting.

And in my old age, when our sons were man-grown and our daughters were mothers when up from the southland the dark men, flat-browed, kinky-headed, surged like waves of the sea upon us and we fled back before them to the hill-slopes, Igar, like my mates far before and long after, leg-twining, arm-clasping, unseeing far visions strove to hold me aloof from the battle.

And I tore myself from her, fat and short-breathed, while she wept that no longer I loved her, and I went out to the night-fighting and dawn-fighting, where, to the singing of bowstrings and the shrilling of arrows, feathered, sharp-pointed, we showed

277

them, the kinky-heads, the skill of the killing and taught them the wit and the willing of slaughter.

And as I died there, at the end of the fighting, there were death songs and singing about me, and the songs seemed to sing as these the words I have written when I was Ushu, the Archer, and Igar, my mate-woman, leg-twining, arm-clasping, would have held me back from the battle.

Once, and heaven alone knows when, save that it was in the long ago when man was young, we lived beside great swamps, where the hills drew down close to the wide, sluggish river, and where our women gathered berries and roots, and there were herds of deer, of wild horses, of antelope, and of elk, that we men slew with arrows or trapped in pits or hill pockets. From the river we caught fish in nets twisted by the women of the bark of young trees.

I was a man, eager and curious as the antelope when we lured it by waving grass clumps where we lay hidden in the thick of the grass. The wild rice grew in the swamp, rising sheer from the water on the edges of the channels. Each morning the blackbirds awoke us with their chatter as they left their roosts to fly to the swamp. And through the long twilight the air was filled with their noise as they went back to their roosts. It was the time that the rice ripened. And there were ducks also, and ducks and blackbirds feasted to fatness on the ripe rice half unhusked by the sun.

Being a man, ever restless, ever questing, wondering always what lay beyond the hills and beyond the swamps and in the mud at the river's bottom, I watched the wild ducks and blackbirds and pondered till my pondering gave me vision and I saw. And this is what I saw, the reasoning of it:

Meat was good to eat. In the end, tracing it back, or at the first, rather, all meat came from grass. The meat of the duck and of the blackbird came from the seed of the swamp rice. To kill a duck with an arrow scarce paid for the labor of stalking and the long hours in hiding. The blackbirds were too small for arrow-killing save by the boys who were learning and preparing for the taking of larger game. And yet, in rice season blackbirds and ducks were succulently fat. Their fatness came from the rice. Why should I and mine not be fat from the rice in the same way?

And I thought it out in camp, silent, morose, while the children squabbled about me unnoticed, and while Arunga, my mate-woman, vainly scolded me and urged me to go hunting for more meat for the many of us.

Arunga was the woman I had stolen from the hill tribes. She and I had been a dozen moons in learning common speech after I captured her. Ah, that day when I leaped upon her, down from the overhanging tree branch as she paddled the runway! Fairly upon her shoulders with the weight of my body I smote her, my fingers wide-spreading to clutch her. She squalled like a cat there in the runway. She fought me and bit me. The nails of her hands were like the claws of a tree cat as they tore at me. But I held her and mastered her, and for two days beat her and forced her to travel with me down out of the canyons of the Hill Men to the grass lands where the river flowed through the rice swamps and the ducks and the blackbirds fed fat.

I saw my vision when the rice was ripe. I put Arunga in the bow of the fire-hollowed log that was most rudely a canoe. I bade her paddle. In the stern I spread a deerskin she had tanned. With two stout sticks I bent the stalks over the deerskin and threshed out the grain that else the blackbirds would have eaten. And when I had worked out the way of it, I gave the two stout sticks to Arunga, and sat in the bow paddling and directing.

In the past we had eaten the raw rice in passing and not been pleased with it. But now we parched it over our fire so that the grains puffed and exploded in whiteness and all the tribe came running to taste.

After that we became known among men as the Rice Eaters and as the Sons of the Rice. And long, long after, when we were driven by the Sons of the River from the swamps into the uplands, we took the seed of the rice with us and planted it. We learned to select the largest grains for the seed, so that all the rice we thereafter ate was larger grained and puffier in the parching and the boiling.

But Arunga. I have said she squalled and scratched like a cat when I stole her. Yet I remember the time when her own kin of the Hill Men caught me and carried me away into the hills. They were her father, his brother, and her two own blood-brothers. But she was mine, who had lived with me. And at night, when I lay bound like a wild pig for the slaying, and they slept weary by the fire, she crept upon them and brained them with the war-club that with my hand I had fashioned. And she wept over me and loosed me and fled with me back to the wide sluggish river where the blackbirds and wild ducks fed in the rice swamps—for this was before the time of the coming of the Sons of the River.

For she was Arunga, the one woman, the eternal woman. She has lived in all times and places. She will always live. She is immortal. Once, in a far land, her name was Ruth. Also has her name been Iseult and Helen, Pocahontas and Unga. And no stranger men, from stranger tribes, but has found her and will find her in the tribes of all the earth.

I remember so many women who have gone into the becoming of the one woman. There was the time that Har, my brother, and I, sleeping and pursuing in turn, ever hounding the wild stallion through the daytime and night, and in a wide circle that met where the sleeping one lay, drove the stallion unresting through hunger and thirst to the meekness of weakness, so that in the end he could but stand and tremble while we bound him with ropes twisted of deer hide. On our legs alone, without hardship, aided merely by wit—the plan was mine—my brother and I walked that fleet-footed creature into possession.

And when all was ready for me to get on his back—for that had been my vision from the first—Selpa, my woman, put her arms about me, and raised her voice and persisted that Har, and not I, should ride, for Har had neither wife nor young ones and could die without hurt. Also, in the end she wept, so that I was raped of my vision, and it was Har, naked and clinging, that bestrode the stallion when he vaulted away.

It was sunset, and a time of great wailing, when they carried Har in from the far rocks where they found him. His head was quite broken, and like honey from a fallen bee tree his brains dripped on the ground. His mother strewed wood ashes on her head and blackened her face. His father cut off half the fingers of one hand in token of sorrow. And all the women, especially the young and unwedded, screamed evil names at me; and the elders shook their wise heads and muttered and mumbled that not their fathers nor their fathers' fathers had betrayed such a madness. Horse meat was good to eat; young colts were tender to old teeth; and only a fool would come to close grapples with any wild horse save when an arrow had pierced it, or when it struggled on the stake in the midst of the pit.

And Selpa scolded me to sleep, and in the morning woke me with her chatter, ever declaiming against my madness, ever pronouncing her claim upon me and the claims of our children, till in the end I grew weary, and forsook my far vision, and said never again would I dream of bestriding the wild horse to fly swift as its feet and the wind across the sands and the grass lands.

And through the years the tale of my madness never ceased from being told over the campfire. Yet was the very telling the source of my vengeance; for the dream did not die, and the young ones, listening to the laugh and the sneer, redreamed it, so that, in the end it was Othar my eldest born, himself a sheer stripling, that walked down a wild stallion, leaped on its back, and flew before all of us with the speed of the wind. Thereafter, that they might keep up with him, all men were trapping and breaking wild horses. Many horses were broken, and some men, but I lived at the last to the day when, at the changing of campsites in the pursuit of the meat in its seasons, our very babes, in baskets of willow withes, were slung side by side on the backs of our horses that carried our camp trappage and dunnage.

I, a young man, had seen my vision, dreamed my dream; Selpa, the woman, had held me from that far desire; but Othar, the seed of us to live after, glimpsed my vision and won to it, so that our tribe became wealthy in the gains of the chase.

There was a woman—on the great drift down out of Europe, a weary drift of many generations, when we brought into India the shorthorn cattle and the planting of barley. But this woman was long before we reached India. We were still in the midmost of that centuries-long drift, and no shrewdness of geography can now place for me that ancient valley.

The woman was Nuhila. The valley was narrow, not long, and the swift slope of its floor and the steep walls of its rim were terraced for the growing of rice and of millet—the first rice and millet we Sons of the Mountain had known. They were a meek people in that valley. They had become soft with the farming of fat land made fatter by water. Theirs was the first irrigation we had seen, although we had little time to mark their ditches and channels by which all the hill waters flowed to the fields they had built. We had little time to mark, for we Sons of the Mountain, who were few, were in flight before the Sons of the Snub Nose, who were many. We called them the Noseless, and they called themselves the Sons of the Eagle. But they were many, and we fled before them with our shorthorn cattle, our goats and our bar-leyseed, our women and children.

While the Snub Noses slew our youths at the rear, we slew at our fore the folk of the valley who opposed us and were weak. The village was mud-built and grass-thatched; the encircling wall was of mud, but quite tall. And when we had slain the people who had built the wall and sheltered within it our herds and our women and children, we stood on the wall and shouted insult to the Snub Noses. For we had found the mud granaries filled with rice and millet. Our cattle could eat the thatches. And the time of the rains was at hand, so that we should not want for water.

It was a long siege. Near to the beginning, we gathered to-gether the women and elders and children we had not slain and forced them out through the wall they had built. But the Snub

Noses slew them to the last one, so that there was more food in the village for us, more food in the valley for the Snub Noses.

It was a weary, long siege. Sickness smote us, and we died of the plague that arose from our buried ones. We emptied the mud granaries of their rice and millet. Our goats and shorthorns ate the thatch of the houses, and we, ere the end, ate the goats and the shorthorns.

Where there had been five men of us on the wall, there came a time when there was one, where there had been half a thousand babes and younglings of ours, there were none. It was Nuhila, my woman, who cut off her hair and twisted it that I might have a strong string for my bow. The other women did likewise and, when the wall was attacked, stood shoulder to shoulder with us, in the midst of our spears and arrows raining down potsherds and cobblestones on the heads of the Snub Noses.

Even the patient Snub Noses we well-nigh out-patienced. Came a time when of ten men of us, but one was alive on the wall, and of our women remained very few, and the Snub Noses held parley. They told us we were a strong breed, and that our women were men-mothers, and that if we would let them have our women they would leave us alone in the valley to possess for ourselves and that we could get women from the valley to the south.

And Nuhila said no. And the other women said no. And we sneered at the Snub Noses and asked if they were weary of fighting. And we were as dead men then, as we sneered at our enemies, and there was little fight left in us, we were so weak. One more attack on the wall would end us. We knew it Our women knew it. And Nuhila said that we could end it first and outwit the Snub Noses. And all our women agreed. And while the Snub Noses prepared for the attack that would be final, there, on the wall, we slew our women. Nuhila loved me, and leaned to meet the thrust of my sword, there on the wall. And we men, in the love of tribehood and tribesmen, slew one another till remained only Horda and I alive in the red of the slaughter. And Horda was my elder, and I leaned to his thrust. But not at once did I die. I was the last of the Sons of the Mountain, for I saw Horda himself fall on his blade and pass quickly. And dying, with the shouts of the oncoming Snub Noses growing dim in my ears, I was glad that the Snub Noses would have no sons of us to bring up by our women.

I do not know when this time was when I was a Son of the Mountain and when we died in the narrow valley where we had slain the Sons of the Rice and the Millet I do not know, save that it was centuries before the wide-spreading drift of all us Sons of the Mountain fetched into India, and that it was long before ever I was an Aryan master in Old Egypt building my two burial places and defacing the tombs of kings before me.

I should like to tell more of those far days, but time in the present is short. Soon I shall pass. Yet am I sorry that I cannot tell more of those early drifts, when there was crushage of peoples, or descending ice sheets, or migrations of meat.

Also, I should like to tell of Mystery. For always were we curious to solve the secrets of life, death, and decay. Unlike the other animals, man was forever gazing at the stars. Many gods he created in his own image and in the images of his fancy. In those old times I have worshiped the sun and the dark. I have worshiped the husked grain as the parent of life. I have worshiped Sar, the Corn Goddess. And I have worshiped Sea Gods and River gods and Fish Gods.

Yes, and I remember Ishtar ere she was stolen from us by the Babylonians, and Ea too was ours, supreme in the Underworld, who enabled Ishtar to conquer death. Mitra likewise was a good old Aryan god, ere he was filched from us or we discarded him. And I remember, on a time, long after the drift when we brought the barley into India, that I came down into India, a horsetrader, with many servants and a long caravan at my back, and that at that time they were worshiping Bodhisattra.

Truly, the worships of the Mystery wandered as did men, and between filchings and borrowings the gods had as vagabond a time of it as did we. As the Sumerians took the loan of Shamashnapishtin from us, so did the Sons of Shem take him from the Sumerians and call him Noah.

Why, I smile me today, Darrell Standing, in Murderers' Row, in that I was found guilty and awarded death by twelve jurymen staunch and true. Twelve has ever been a magic number of the Mystery. Nor did it originate with the twelve tribes of Israel. Stargazers before them had placed the twelve signs of the Zodiac in the sky. And I remember me, when I was of the Aesir, and of the Vanir, that Odin sat in judgment over men in the court of the twelve gods, and that their names were Thor, Baldur, Niord, Frey, Tyr, Brogi, Heimdal, Hoder, Vidar, Ull, Forseti, and Loki.

Even our Valkyries were stolen from us and made into angels, and the wings of the Valkyries' horses became attached to the shoulders of the angels. And our Helheim of that day of ice and frost has become the hell of today, which is so hot an abode that the blood boils in one's veins, while with us, in our Helheim, the place was so cold as to freeze the marrow inside the bones. And the very sky, that we dreamed enduring, eternal, has drifted and veered, so that we find today the Scorpion in the place where of old we knew the Goat, and the Archer in the place of the Crab.

Worships and worships! Ever the pursuit of the Mystery! I remember the lame god of the Greeks, the master-smith. But their Vulcan was the Germanic Wieland, the master-smith captured and hamstrung lame of a leg by Nidung, the king of the Nids. But before that he was our master-smith, our forger and hammerer, whom we named Il-marinen. And him we begat of our fancy, giving him the bearded sun-god for father, and nursing him by the stars of the Bear. For he, Vulcan, or Wieland, or Il-marinen, was born under the Pine Tree, from the hair of the Wolf, and was called also the Bear-Father ere ever the Germans and Greeks purloined and worshiped him. In that day we called ourselves the Sons of the Bear and the Sons of the Wolf, and the Bear and the Wolf were our totems. That was before our drift south on which we joined with the Sons of the Tree-Grove and taught them our totems and tales.

Yes, and who was Kashyapa, who was Pururavas, but our lame master-smith, our iron worker, carried by us in our drifts and renamed and worshiped by the south-dwellers and the east-dwellers, the Sons of the Pole and of the Fire Drill and Fire Socket.

But the tale is too long, though I should like to tell of the three-leaved Herb of Life by which Sigmund made Sinfioti alive again. For this is the very Soma plant of India, the Holy Grail of King Arthur, the—but enough! Enough!

And yet as I calmly consider it all, I conclude that the greatest thing in life, in all lives, to me and to all men, has been woman, is woman, and will be woman so long as the stars drift in the sky and the heavens flux eternal change. Greater than our toil and endeavor, the play of invention and fancy, battle and star-gazing and Mystery—greatest of all has been woman.

Even though she has sung false music to me, and kept my feet solid on the ground, and drawn my star-roving eyes ever back to gaze upon her, she, the conserver of life, the earth-mother, has given me my great days and nights and fullness of years. Even Mystery have I imaged in the form of her, and in my star charting have I placed her figure in the sky.

All my toils and devices led to her; all my far visions saw her at the end. When I made the fire drill and fire socket, it was for her. It was for her, although I did not know it, that I put the stake in the pit for old Sabre-Tooth, tamed the horse, slew the mammoth, and herded my reindeer south in advance of the ice sheet For her I harvested the wild rice, tamed the barley, the wheat, and the corn.

For her, and the seed to come after whose image she bore, I have died in treetops and stood long sieges in cave mouths and on mud walls. For her I put the twelve signs in the sky. It was she I worshiped when I bowed before the ten stones of jade and adored them as the moons of gestation.

Always has woman crouched close to earth like a partridge hen mothering her young; always has my wantonness of roving led me out on the shining ways; and always have my star paths returned me to her, the figure everlasting, the woman, the one woman, for whose arms I had such need that clasped in them I have forgotten the stars.

For her I accomplished odysseys, scaled mountains, crossed deserts; for her I led the hunt and was forward in battle; and for her and to her I sang my songs of the things I had done. All ecstasies of life and rhapsodies of delight have been mine because of her. And here, at the end, I can say that I have known no sweeter, deeper madness of being than to drown in the fragrant glory and forgetfulness of her hair.

One word more. I remember me Dorothy, just the other day, when I still lectured on agronomy to farmer-boy students. She was eleven years old. Her father was Dean of the college. She was a woman-child, and a woman, and she conceived that she loved me. And I smiled to myself, for my heart was untouched and lay elsewhere.

Yet was the smile tender, for in the child's eyes I saw the woman eternal, the woman of all times and appearances. In her eyes I saw the eyes of my mate of the jungle and treetop, of the cave and the squatting place. In her eyes I saw the eyes of Igar when I was Ushu the Archer, the eyes of Arunga when I was the rice harvester, the eyes of Selpa when I dreamed of bestriding the stallion, the eyes of Nuhila who leaned to the thrust of my sword. Yes there was that in her eyes that made them the eyes of Lei-Lei, whom I left with a laugh on my lips, the eyes of the Lady Om, for forty years my beggar-mate on highway and byway, the eyes of Philippa for whom I was slain on the grass in old France, the eyes of my mother when I was the lad Jesse at the Mountain Meadows in the circle of our forty great wagons.

She was a woman-child, but she was daughter of all women, as her mother before her, and she was the mother of all women to come after her. She was Sar, the Corn Goddess. She was Isthar who conquered death. She was Sheba and Cleopatra; she was Esther and Herodias. She was Mary the Madonna, and Mary the Magdalene, and Mary the sister of Martha. Also she was Martha. And she was Brunhilde and Guinevere, Iseult and Juliet, Heloise and Nicolete. Yes, and she was Eve, she was Lilith, she was Astarte. She was eleven years old, and she was all women that had been, all women to be.

I sit in my cell now, while the flies hum in the drowsy summer afternoon, and I know that my time is short. Soon will they apparel me in the shirt without a collar.... But hush, my heart. The spirit is immortal. After the dark I shall live again, and there will be women. The future holds the little women for me in the lives I am yet to live. And though the stars drift, and the heavens lie, ever remains woman, resplendent, eternal, the one woman, as I, under all my masquerades and misadventures, am the one man, her mate.

Chapter 22

My time grows very short. All the manuscript I have written is safely smuggled out of the prison. There is a man I can trust who will see that it is published. No longer am I in Murderers' Row. I am writing these lines in the death cell, and the deathwatch is set on me. Night and day is this deathwatch on me, and its paradoxical function is to see that I do not die. I must be kept alive for the hanging, or else will the public be cheated, the law blackened, and a mark of demerit placed against the time-serving warden who runs this prison and one of whose duties is to see that his condemned ones are duly and properly hanged. Often I marvel at the strange way some men make their livings.

This shall be my last writing. Tomorrow morning the hour is set. The Governor has declined to pardon or reprieve, despite the fact that the Anti-Capital Punishment League has raised quite a stir in California. The reporters are gathered like so many buzzards. I have seen them all. They are queer young fellows, most of them, and most queer is it that they will thus earn bread and butter, cocktails and tobacco, room rent, and, if they are married, shoes and schoolbooks for their children, by witnessing the execution of Professor Darrell Standing, and by describing for the public how Professor Darrell Standing died at the end of a rope. Ah, well, they will be sicker than I at the end of the affair.

As I sit here and muse on it all, the footfalls of the deathwatch going up and down outside my cage, the man's suspicious eyes ever peering in on me, almost I weary of eternal recurrence. I have lived so many lives. I weary of the endless struggle and pain and catastrophe that come to those who sit in the high places tread the shining ways, and wander among the stars.

Almost I hope, when next I re-inhabit form, that it shall be that of a peaceful farmer. There is my dream-farm. I should like to engage just for one whole life in that. Oh, my dream-farm! My alfalfa meadows, my efficient Jersey cattle, my upland pastures, my brush-covered slopes melting into tilled fields, while ever higher up the slopes my Angora goats eat away brush to tillage!

There is a basin there, a natural basin high up the slopes, with a generous watershed on three sides. I should like to throw a dam across the fourth side, which is surprisingly narrow. At a paltry price of labor I could impound twenty million gallons of water. For, see: one great drawback to farming in California is our long dry summer. This prevents the growing of cover crops, and the sensitive soil, naked, a mere surface dust-mulch, has its humus burned out of it by the sun. Now with that dam I could grow three crops a year, observing due rotation, and be able to turn under a wealth of green manure....

I have just endured a visit from the warden. I say "endured" advisedly. He is quite different from the Warden of San Quentin. He was very nervous and perforce I had to entertain him. This is his first hanging. He told me so. And I, with a clumsy attempt at wit, did not reassure him when I explained that it was also my first hanging. He was unable to laugh. He has a girl in high school, and his boy is a freshman at Stanford. He has no income outside his salary, his wife is an invalid, and he is worried in that he has been rejected by the life insurance doctors as an undesirable risk. Really, the man told me almost all his troubles. Had I not diplomatically terminated the interview he would still be here telling me the remainder of them.

My last two years in San Quentin were very gloomy and depressing. Ed Morrell, by one of the wildest freaks of chance, was taken out of solitary and made head trusty of the whole prison. This was Al Hutchins' old job, and it carried a graft of three thousand dollars a year. To my misfortune, Jake Oppenheimer, who had rotted in solitary for so many years, turned sour on the world, on everything. For eight months he refused to talk even to me.

In prison, news will travel. Give it time and it will reach dungeon and solitary cell. It reached me, at last, that Cecil Winwood,

the poet-forger, the snitcher, the coward, and the stool, was returned for a fresh forgery. It will be remembered that it was this
Cecil Winwood who concocted the fairy story that I had changed
the plant of the nonexistent dynamite and who was responsible for
the five years I had then spent in solitary.

I decided to kill Cecil Winwood. You see, Morrell was gone,
and Oppenheimer, until the outbreak that finished him, had remained in the silence. Solitary had grown monotonous for me. I
had to do something. So I reremembered back to the time when
I was Adam Strang and patiently nursed revenge for forty years.
What he had done I could do if once I locked my hands on Cecil
Winwood's throat.

It cannot be expected of me to divulge how I came into possession of the four needles. They were small cambric needles. Emaciated as my body was, I had to saw four bars, each in two places,
in order to make an aperture through which I could squirm. I
did it. I used up one needle to each bar. This meant two cuts to a
bar, and it took a month to a cut. Thus I should have been eight
months in cutting my way out. Unfortunately, I broke my last
needle on the last bar, and I had to wait three months before I
could get another needle. But I got it, and I got out.

I regret greatly I did not get Cecil Winwood. I had calculated well on everything save one thing. The certain chance to
find Winwood would be in the dining room at dinner hour. So I
waited until Pie-Face Jones, the sleepy guard, should be on shift
at the noon hour. At that time I was the only inmate of solitary,
so that Pie-Face Jones was quickly snoring. I removed my bars,
squeezed out, stole past him along the ward, opened the door and
was free....to a portion of the inside of the prison.

And here was the one thing I had not calculated on—myself.
I had been five years in solitary. I was hideously weak. I weighed
eighty-seven pounds. I was half-blind. And I was immediately
stricken with agoraphobia. I was affrighted by spaciousness. Five
years in narrow walls had unfitted me for the enormous declivity
of the stairway, for the vastitude of the prison yard.

The descent of that stairway I consider the most heroic exploit I ever accomplished. The yard was deserted. The blinding sun blazed down on it. Thrice I essayed to cross it. But my senses reeled and I shrank back to the wall for protection. Again, summoning all my courage, I attempted it. But my poor blear eyes like a bat's, startled me at my shadow on the flagstones. I attempted to avoid my own shadow, tripped, fell over it, and like a drowning man struggling for shore crawled back on hands and knees to the wall.

I leaned against the wall and cried. It was the first time in many years that I had cried. I remember noting, even in my extremity, the warmth of the tears on my cheeks and the salt taste when they reached my lips. Then I had a chill, and for a time shook as with an ague. Abandoning the openness of the yard as too impossible a feat for one in my condition, still shaking with the chill, crouching close to the protecting wall, my hands touching it, I started to skirt the yard.

Then it was, somewhere along, that the guard Thurston espied me. I saw him, distorted by my bleared eyes, a huge, well-fed monster, rushing upon me with incredible speed out of the remote distance. Possibly, at that moment, he was twenty feet away. He weighed one hundred and seventy pounds. The struggle between us can be easily imagined, but somewhere in that brief struggle it was claimed that I struck him on the nose with my fist to such purpose as to make that organ bleed.

At any rate, being a lifer, and the penalty in California for battery by a lifer being death, I was so found guilty by a jury which could not ignore the asseverations of the guard Thurston and the rest of the prison hangdogs that testified, and I was so sentenced by a judge who could not ignore the law as spread plainly on the statute book.

I was well pummeled by Thurston, and all the way back up that prodigious stairway I was roundly kicked, punched, and cuffed by the horde of trusties and guards who got in one another's way in their zeal to assist him. Heavens, if his nose did bleed the probability is that some of his own kind were guilty of causing it in the confusion of the scuffle. I shouldn't care if I were responsible for it myself, save that it is so pitiful a thing for which to hang a man.

I have just had a talk with the man on shift of my deathwatch. A little less than a year ago, Jake Oppenheimer occupied this same death cell on the road to the gallows which I will tread tomorrow. This man was one of the deathwatch on Jake. He is an old soldier. He chews tobacco constancy, and untidily, for his gray beard and mustache are stained yellow. He is a widower, with fourteen living children, all married, and is the grandfather of thirty-one living grandchildern, and the great-grandfather of four younglings, all girls. It was like pulling teeth to extract such information. He is a queer old codger, of a low order of intelligence. That is why, I fancy, he has lived so long and fathered so numerous a progeny. His mind must have crystallized thirty years ago. His ideas are none of them later than that vintage. He rarely says more than yes and no to me. It is not because he is surly. He has no ideas to utter. I don't know, when I live again, but what one incarnation such as his would be a nice vegetative existence in which to rest up ere I go star roving again.

But to go back. I must take a line in which to tell, after I was hustled and bustled, kicked and punched. up that terrible stairway by Thurston and the rest of the prison dogs, of the infinite relief of my narrow cell when I found myself back in solitary. It was all so safe, so secure. I felt like a lost child returned home again. I loved those very walls that I had so hated for five years. All that kept the vastness of space, like a monster, from pouncing upon me were those good stout walls of mine, close to hand on every side. Agoraphobia is a terrible affliction. I have had little opportunity to experience it, but from that little I can only conclude that hanging is a far easier matter.

I have just had a hearty laugh. The prison doctor, a likable chap, has just been in to have a yarn with me, incidentally to proffer me his good offices in the matter of dope. Of course I declined his proposition to "shoot me" so full of morphine through the night that tomorrow I would not know, when I marched to the gallows, whether I was "coming or going."

But the laugh. It was just like Jake Oppenheimer. I can see the lean keenness of the man as he strung the reporters with his deliberate bull, which they thought involuntary. It seems his last morning, breakfast finished, encased in the shirt without a collar, that the reporters, assembled for his last word in his cell, asked him for his views on capital punishment.

Who says we have more than the slightest veneer of civilization coated over our raw savagery when a group of living men can ask such a question of a man about to die and whom they are to see die?

But Jake was ever game. "Gentlemen," he said, "I hope to live to see the day when capital punishment is abolished." I have lived many lives through the long ages. Man, the individual, has made no moral progress in the past ten thousand years. I affirm this absolutely. The difference between an unbroken colt and the patient draft horse is purely a difference of training. Training is the only moral difference between the man of today and the man of ten thousand years ago. Under his thin skin of morality which he has had polished onto him, he is the same savage that he was ten thousand years ago. Morality is a social fund, and accretion through the painful ages. The newborn child will become a savage unless it is trained, polished, by the abstract morality that has been so long accumulating.

"Thou shalt not kill"—piffle! They are going to kill me tomorrow morning. "Thou shalt not kill"—piffle! In the shipyards of all civilized countries they are laying today the keels of dreadnaughts and of superdreadnaughts. Dear friends I who am about to die, salute you with—"Piffle!"

I ask you, what finer morality is preached today than was preached by Christ, by Buddha, by Socrates and Plato, by Confucius and whoever was the author of the "Mahabharata"? Good Lord, fifty thousand years ago, in our totem families, our women were cleaner, our family and group relations more rigidly right.

I must say that the morality we practiced in those old days was a finer morality than is practiced today. Don't dismiss this thought hastily. Think of our child labor, of our police graft and our political corruption, of our food adulteration and of our slavery of the daughters of the poor. When I was a Son of the Mountain and a Son of the Bull, prostitution had no meaning. We were clean, I tell you. We did not dream of such depths of depravity. Yea, so are all the lesser animals of today clean. It required man, with his imagination, aided by his mastery of matter, to invent the deadly sins. The lesser animals, the other animals, are incapable of sin.

I read hastily back through the many lives of many times and many places. I have never known cruelty more terrible, nor so terrible as the cruelty of our prison system of today. I have told you what I have endured in the jacket and in solitary in the first decade of this twentieth century after Christ. In the old days we punished drastically and killed quickly. We did it because we so desired, because of whim, it you so please. But we were not hypocrites. We did not call upon press and pulpit and university to sanction us in our willfulness of savagery. What we wanted to do we went and did, on our legs upstanding, and we faced all reproof and censure on our legs upstanding, and did not hide behind the skirts of classical economists and bourgeois philosophers, nor behind the skirts of subsidized preachers, professors, and editors.

Why, goodness me, a hundred years ago, fifty years ago, five years ago, in these United States, assault and battery was not a civil capital crime. But this year, the year of Our Lord 1913, in the State of California, they hanged Jake Oppenheimer for such an offense, and tomorrow, for the civil capital crime of punching a man on the nose, they are going to take me out and hang me. Query: doesn't it require a long time for the ape and the tiger to die when such statutes are spread on the statute book of California in the nineteen-hundred-and-thirteenth year after Christ? Lord, Lord, they only crucified Christ. They have done far worse to Jake Oppenheimer and me.

As Ed Morrell once rapped to me with his knuckles: "The

worst possible use you can put a man to is to hang him." No, I have little respect for capital punishment. Not only is it a dirty game, degrading to the hangdogs who personally perpetrate it for a wage, but it is degrading to the commonwealth that tolerates it, votes for it, and pays the taxes for its maintenance. Capital punishment is so silly, so stupid, so horribly unscientific. "To be hanged by the neck until dead" is society's quaint phraseology.

Morning is come—my last morning. I slept like a babe throughout the night. I slept so peacefully that once the death watch got a fright. He thought I had suffocated myself in my blankets. The poor man's alarm was pitiful. His bread and butter was at stake. Had it truly been so, it would have meant a black mark against him, perhaps discharge—and the outlook for an unemployed man is bitter just at present. They tell me that Europe began liquidating two years ago, and that now the United States has begun. That means either a business crisis or a quiet panic and that the armies of the unemployed will be large next winter, the bread-lines long....

I have had my breakfast. It seemed a silly thing to do, but I ate it heartily. The warden came with a quart of whiskey. I presented it to Murderers' Row with my compliments. The warden, poor man, is afraid, if I be not drunk, that I shall make a mess of the function and cast reflection on his management.

They have put on me the shirt without a collar.

It seems I am a very important man this day. Quite a lot of people are suddenly interested in me.

The doctor has just gone. He has taken my pulse. I asked him to. It is normal.

I write these random thoughts and, a sheet at a time, they start on their secret way out beyond the walls.

I am the calmest man in the prison. I am like a child about to start on a journey. I am eager to be gone, curious for the new places I shall see. This fear of the lesser death is ridiculous to one who has gone into the dark so often and lived again.

The warden with a quart of champagne. I have dispatched it down Murderers' Row. Queer, isn't it, that I am so considered this last day. It must be that these men who are to kill me are themselves afraid of death. To quote Jake Oppenheimer: I, who am about to die, must seem to them something "God-awful.".

Ed Morrell has just sent word in to me. They tell me he has paced up and down all night outside the prison wall. Being an ex-convict, they have red-taped him out of seeing me to say good-bye. Savages? I don't know. Possibly just children. I'll wager most of them will be afraid to be alone in the dark tonight after stretching my neck.

But Ed Morrell's message: "My hand is in yours, old pal. I know you'll swing off game."...

The reporters have just left. I'll see them next, and last time, from the scaffold, ere the hangman hides my face in the black cap. They will be looking curiously sick. Queer young fellows. Some show that they have been drinking. Two or three look sick with foreknowledge of what they have to witness. It seems easier to be hanged than to look on....

My last lines. It seems I am delaying the procession. My cell is quite crowded with officials and dignitaries. They are all nervous. They want it over. Without a doubt, some of them have dinner engagements. I am really offending them by writing these few words. The priest has again prefered his request to be with me to the end. The poor man—why should I deny him that solace? I have consented, and he now appears quite cheerful. Such small things make some men happy! I could stop and laugh for a hearty five minutes, if they were not in such a hurry.

Here I close. I can only repeat myself. There is no death. Life is spirit, and spirit cannot die. Only the flesh dies and passes, ever a-crawl with the chemical ferment that informs it, ever plastic, ever crystallizing, only to melt into the flux and to crystallize into fresh and diverse forms that are ephemeral and that melt back into the flux. Spirit alone endures and continues to build upon itself through successive and endless incarnations as it works upward toward the light. What shall I be when I live again? I wonder. I wonder....

Stories

The Minions of Midas

Wade Atsheler is dead -- dead by his own hand. To say that this was entirely unexpected by the small coterie which knew him, would be to say an untruth; and yet never once had we, his intimates, ever canvassed the idea. Rather had we been prepared for it in some incomprehensible subconscious way. Before the perpetration of the deed, its possibility is remotest from our thoughts; but when we did know that he was dead, it seemed, somehow, that we had understood and looked forward to it all the time. This, by retrospective analysis, we could easily explain by the fact of his great trouble. I use "great trouble" advisedly. Young, handsome, with an assured position as the right-hand man of Eben Hale, the great street-railway magnate, there could be no reason for him to complain of fortune's favors. Yet we had watched his smooth brow furrow and corrugate as under some carking care or devouring sorrow. We had watched his thick, black hair thin and silver as green grain under brazen skies and parching drought. Who can forget, in the midst of the hilarious scenes he toward the last sought with greater and greater avidity -- who can forget, I say, the deep abstractions and black moods into which he fell? At such times, when the fun rippled and soared from height to height, suddenly, without rhyme or reason, his eyes would turn lacklustre, his brows knit, as with clenched hands and face overshot with spasms of mental pain he wrestled on the edge of the abyss with some unknown danger.

He never spoke of his trouble, nor were we indiscreet enough to ask. But it was just as well; for had we, and had he spoken, our help and strength could have availed nothing. When Eben Hale died, whose confidential secretary he was -- nay, well-nigh adopted son and full business partner -- he no longer came among us. Not, as I now know, that our company was distasteful to him, but because his trouble had so grown that he could not respond to our happiness nor find surcease with us. Why this should be so we could not at the time understand, for when Eben Hale's will was probated, the world learned that he was sole heir to his employer's many millions, and it was expressly stipulated that this great inheritance was given to him without qualification, hitch, or hindrance in the exercise thereof. Not a share of stock, not a penny of cash, was bequeathed to the dead man's relatives. As for his direct family, one astounding clause expressly stated that Wade Atsheler was to dispense to Eben Hale's wife and sons and daughters whatever moncys his judgement dictated, at whatever times he deemed advisable. Had there been any scandal in the dead man's family, or had his sons been wild or undutiful, then there might have been a glimmering of reason in this most unusual action; but Eben Hale's domestic happiness had been proverbial in the community, and one would have to travel far and wide to discover a cleaner, saner, wholesomer progeny of sons and daughters. While his wife -- well, by those who knew her best she was endearingly termed "The Mother of the Gracchi." Needless to state, this inexplicable will was a nine day's wonder; but the expectant public was disappointed in that no contest was made.

It was only the other day that Eben Hale was laid away in his stately marble mausoleum. And now Wade Atsheler is dead. The news was printed in this morning's paper. I have just received through the mail a letter from him, posted, evidently, but a short hour before he hurled himself into eternity. This letter, which lies before me, is a narrative in his own handwriting, linking together numerous newspaper clippings and facsimiles of letters. The original correspondence, he has told me, is in the hands of the police. He has begged me, also, as a warning to society against a most frightful and diabolical danger which threatens its very existence, to make public the terrible series of tragedies in which he has been innocently concerned. I herewith append the text in full:

★★★

It was in August, 1899, just after my return from my summer vaca-

tion, that the blow fell. We did not know it at the time; we had not yet learned to school our minds to such awful possibilities. Mr. Hale opened the letter, read it, and tossed it upon my desk with a laugh. When I had looked it over, I also laughed, saying, "Some ghastly joke, Mr. Hale, and one in very poor taste." Find here, my dear John, an exact duplicate of the letter in question.

Office of the M. of M. August 17, 1899.
Mr. Eben Hale, Money Baron:
Dear Sir, -- We desire you to realize upon whatever portion of your vast holdings is necessary to obtain, **in cash**, twenty millions of dollars. This sum we require you to pay over to us, or to our agents. You will note we do not specify any given time, for it is not our wish to hurry you in this matter. You may even, if it be easier for you, pay us in ten, fifteen, or twenty instalments; but we will accept no single instalment of less than a million.

Believe us, dear Mr. Hale, when we say that we embark upon this course of action utterly devoid of animus. We are members of that intellectual proletariat, the increasing numbers of which mark in red lettering the last days of the nineteenth century. We have, from a thorough study of economics, decided to enter upon this business. It has many merits, chief among which may be noted that we can indulge in large and lucrative operations without capital. So far, we have been fairly successful, and we hope our dealings with you may be pleasant and satisfactory.

Pray attend while we explain our views more fully. At the base of the present system of society is to be found the property right. And this right of the individual to hold property is demonstrated, in the last analysis, to rest solely and wholly upon **might**. The mailed gentlemen of William the Conqueror divided and apportioned England amongst themselves with the naked sword. This, we are sure you will grant, is true of all feudal possessions. With the invention of steam and the Industrial Revolution there came into existence the Capitalist Class, in the modern sense of the word. These capitalists quickly towered above the ancient nobility. The captains of industry have virtually dispossessed the descendants of the captains of war. Mind, and not muscle, wins in to-day's struggle for existence. But this state of affairs is none the less based upon might. The change has been qualitative. The old-time Feudal Baronage ravaged the world with fire and sword; the modern Money Baronage exploits the world by mastering and applying the world's economic forces. Brain, and not brawn, endures; and those best fitted to survive are the intellectually and commercially powerful.

We, the M. of M., are not content to become wage slaves. The great trusts and business combinations (with which you have your rating) prevent us from rising to the place among you which our intellects qualify us to occupy. Why? Because we are without capital. We are of the unwashed, but with this difference: our brains are of the best, and we have no foolish ethical nor social scruples. As wage slaves, toiling early and late, and living abstemiously, we could not save in threescore years -- nor in twenty times threescore years -- a sum of money sufficient successfully to cope with the great aggregations of massed capital which now exist. Nevertheless, we have entered the arena. We now throw down the gauntlet to the capital of the world. Whether it wishes to fight or not, it shall have to fight.

Mr. Hale, our interests dictate us to demand of you twenty millions of dollars. While we are considerate enough to give you reasonable time in which to carry out your share of the transaction, please do not delay too long. When you have agreed to our terms, insert a suitable notice in the agony column of the *Morning Blazer*. We shall then acquaint you with our plan for transferring the sum mentioned. You had better do this some time prior to October 1st. If you do not, in order to show that we are in earnest we shall on that date kill a man on East Thirty-ninth Street. He will be a work-ingman. This man you do not know; nor do we. You represent a force in modern society; we also represent a force -- a new force. Without anger or malice, we have closed in battle. As you will readily discern, we are simply a business proposition. You are the upper, and we the nether, mill-stone; this man's life shall be ground out between. You may save him if you agree to our conditions and act in time.

There was once a king cursed with a golden touch. His name we have taken to do duty as our official seal. Some day, to protect ourselves against competitors, we shall copy-right it.

We beg to remain,
The Minions of Midas.

I leave it to you, dear John, why should we not have laughed over such a preposterous communication? The idea, we could not but grant, was well conceived, but it was too grotesque to be taken seriously. Mr. Hale said he would preserve it as a literary curiosity, and shoved it away in a pigeon-hole. Then we promptly forgot its existence. And as promptly, on the 1st of October, going over the morning mail, we read the following:

Office of the M. of M., October 1, 1899.
Mr. Eben Hale, Money Baron:
Dear Sir, -- Your victim has met his fate. An hour ago, on East Thirty-ninth Street, a workingman was thrust through the heart with a knife. Ere you read this his body will be ly-ing at the Morgue. Go and look upon your handiwork.

On October 14th, in token of our earnestness in this matter, and in case you do not relent, we shall kill a police-man on or near the corner of Polk Street and Clermont Avenue.

Very cordially,
The Minions of Midas.

Again Mr. Hale laughed. His mind was full of a prospective deal with a Chicago syndicate for the sale of all his street railways in that city, and so he went on dictating to the stenographer, never giving it a second thought. But somehow, I know not why, a heavy depression fell upon me. What if it were not a joke, I asked myself, and turned involuntarily to the morning paper. There it was, as befitted an obscure person of the lower classes, a paltry few lines tucked away in a corner, next a patent medicine advertisement:

> Shortly after five o'clock this morning, on East Thirty-ninth Street, a laborer named Pete Lascalle, while on his way to work, was stabbed to the heart by an unknown assailant, who escaped by running. The police have been unable to discover any motive for the murder.

"Impossible!" Was Mr. Hale's rejoinder, when I had read the item aloud; but the incident evidently weighed upon his mind, for late in the afternoon, with many epithets denunciatory of his foolishness, he asked me to acquaint the police with the affair. I had the pleasure of being laughed at in the Inspector's private office, although I went away with the assurance that they would look into it and that the vicinity of Polk and Clermont would be doubly patrolled on the night mentioned. There it dropped, till the two weeks had sped by, when the following note came to us through the mail:

Office of the M. of M. October 15, 1899.

Mr. Eben Hale, Money Baron:

Dear Sir, -- Your second victim has fallen on schedule time. We are in no hurry; but to increase the pressure we shall henceforth kill weekly. To protect ourselves against police interference we shall hereafter inform you of the event but a little prior to or simultaneously with the deed. Trusting this finds you in good health,

We are,

The Minions of Midas.

This time Mr. Hale took up the paper, and after a brief search, read to me this account:

A Dastardly Crime

Joseph Donahue, assigned only last night to special patrol

duty in the Eleventh Ward, at midnight was shot through the brain and instantly killed. The tragedy was enacted in the full glare of the street lights on the corner of Polk Street and Clermont Avenue. Our society is indeed unstable when the custodians of its peace are thus openly and wantonly shot down. The police have so far been unable to obtain the slightest clue.

Barely had he finished this when the police arrived -- the Inspector himself and two of his keenest sleuths. Alarm sat upon their faces, and it was plain that they were seriously perturbed. Though the facts were so few and simple, we talked long, going over the affair again and again. When the Inspector went away, he confidently assured us that everything would soon be straightened out and the assassins run to earth. In the meantime he thought it well to detail guards for the protection of Mr. Hale and myself, and several more to be constantly on the vigil about the house and grounds. After the lapse of a week, at one o'clock in the afternoon, this telegram was received:

Office of the M. of M. October 21, 1899.

Mr. Eben Hale, Money Baron:

Dear Sir, -- We are sorry to note how completely you have misunderstood us. You have seen fit to surround yourself and household with armed guards, as though, forsooth, we were common criminals, apt to break in upon you and wrest away by force your twenty millions. Believe us, this is farthest from our intention.

You will readily comprehend, after a little sober thought, that your life is dear to us. Do not be afraid. We would not hurt you for the world. It is our policy to cherish you tenderly and protect you from all harm. Your death means nothing to us. If it did, rest assured that we would not hesitate a moment in destroying you. Think this over, Mr. Hale. When you have paid us our price, there will be need of retrenchment. Dismiss your guards now, and cut down your expenses.

Within minutes of the time you receive this a nurse-girl

will have been choked to death in Brentwood Park. The body may be found in the shrubbery lining the path which leads off to the left from the band-stand.

Cordially yours,
The Minions of Midas.

The next instant Mr. Hale was at the telephone, warning the Inspector of the impending murder. The Inspector excused himself in order to call up Police Sub-station F and despatch men to the scene. Fifteen minutes later he rang us up and informed us that the body had been discovered, yet warm, in the place indicated. That evening the papers teemed with glaring Jack-the-Strangler headlines, denouncing the brutality of the deed and complaining about the laxity of the police. We were also closeted with the Inspector, who begged us by all means to keep the affair secret. Success, he said, depended upon silence.

As you know, John, Mr. Hale was a man of iron. He refused to surrender. But, oh, John, it was terrible, nay, horrible -- this awful something, this blind force in the dark. We could not fight, could not plan, could do nothing save hold our hands and wait. And week by week, as certain as the rising of the sun, came the notification and death of some person, man or woman, innocent of evil, but just as much killed by us as though we had done it with our own hands. A word from Mr. Hale and the slaughter would have ceased. But he hardened his heart and waited, the lines deepening, the mouth and eyes growing sterner and firmer, and the face aging with the hours. It is needless for me to speak of my own suffering during that frightful period. Find here the letters and telegrams of the M. of M., and the newspaper accounts, etc., of the various murders.

You will notice also the letters warning Mr. Hale of certain machinations of commercial enemies and secret manipulations of stock. The M. of M. seemed to have its hand on the inner pulse of the business and financial world. They possessed themselves of and forwarded to us information which our agents could not obtain. One timely note from them, at a critical moment in a certain deal, saved all of five millions to Mr. Hale. At another time they sent us a telegram which probably was the means of preventing an anarchist crank from taking my employer's life. We captured the man on his arrival and turned him over to the police, who found upon him enough of a new and powerful explosive to sink a battleship.

We persisted. Mr. Hale was grit clear through. He disbursed at the rate of one hundred thousand per week for secret service. The aid of the Pinkertons and of countless private detective agencies was called in, and in addition to this thousands were upon our payroll. Our agents swarmed everywhere, in all guises, penetrating all classes of society. They grasped at a myriad clues; hundreds of suspects were jailed, and at various times thousands of suspicious persons were under surveillance, but nothing tangible came to light. With its communications the M. of M. continually changed its method of delivery. And every messenger they sent us was arrested forthwith. But these inevitably proved to be innocent individuals, while their descriptions of the persons who had employed them for the errand never tallied. On the last day of December we received this notification:

Office of the M. of M., December 31, 1899.

Mr. Eben Hale, Money Baron:

Dear Sir, -- Pursuant of our policy, with which we flatter ourselves you are already well versed, we beg to state that we shall give a passport from this Vale of Tears to Inspector Bying, with whom, because of our attentions, you have become so well acquainted. It is his custom to be in his private office at this hour. Even as you read this he breathes his last.

Cordially yours,

The Minions of Midas.

I dropped the letter and sprang to the telephone. Great was my relief when I heard the Inspector's hearty voice. But, even as he spoke, his voice died away in the receiver to a gurgling sob, and I heard faintly the crash of a falling body. Then a strange voice hello'd me, sent me the regards of the M. of M., and broke the switch. Like a flash I called up the public office of the Central Police, telling them to go at once to the Inspector's aid in his private office. I then held the line, and a few minutes later received the intelligence that he had been found bathed in his own blood and breathing his last. There were no eyewitnesses, and no trace was discoverable of the murderer.

Whereupon Mr. Hale immediately increased his secret service till a quarter of a million flowed weekly from his coffers. He was determined to win out. His graduated rewards aggregated over ten millions. You have a fair idea of his resources and you can see in what manner he drew upon them. It was the principle, he affirmed, that he was fighting for, not the gold. And it must be admitted that his course proved the nobility of his motive. The police departments of all the great cities cooperated, and even the United States Government stepped in, and the affair became one of the highest questions of state. Certain contingent funds of the nation were devoted to the unearthing of the M. of M., and every government agent was on the alert. But all in vain. The Minions of Midas carried on their damnable work unhampered. They had their way and struck unerringly.

But while he fought to the last, Mr. Hale could not wash his hands of the blood with which they were dyed. Though not technically a murderer, though no jury of his peers would ever have convicted him, none the less the death of every individual was due to him. As I said before, a word from him and the slaughter would have ceased. But he refused to give that word. He insisted that the integrity of society was assailed; that he was not sufficiently a coward to desert his post; and that it was manifestly just that a few should be martyred for the ultimate welfare of the many. Nevertheless this blood was upon his head, and he sank into deeper and deeper gloom. I was likewise whelmed with the guilt of an accomplice. Babies were ruthlessly killed, children, aged men; and not only were these murders local, but they were distributed over the country. In the middle of February, one evening, as we sat in the library, there came a sharp knock at the door. On responding to it I found, Lying on the carpet of the corridor, the following missive:

Office of the M. of M., February 15, 1900.
Mr. Eben Hale, Money Baron:
Dear Sir, -- Does not your soul cry out upon the red harvest it is reaping? Perhaps we have been too abstract in conducting our business. Let us now be concrete. Miss Adelaide Laidlaw is a talented young woman, as good, we understand, as she is beautiful. She is the daughter of your old friend, Judge Laidlaw, and we happen to know that you carried her in your arms when she was an infant. She is your

daughter's closest friend, and at present is visiting her. When your eyes have read thus far her visit will have terminated.

Very cordially,

The Minions of Midas.

My God! Did we not instantly realize the terrible import! We rushed through the dayrooms -- she was not there -- and on to her own apartments. The door was locked, but we crashed it down by hurling ourselves against it. There she lay, just as she had finished dressing for the opera, smothered with pillows torn from the couch, the flush of life yet on her flesh, the body still flexible and warm. Let me pass over the rest of this horror. You will surely remember, John, the newspaper accounts.

Late that night Mr. Hale summoned me to him, and before God did pledge me most solemnly to stand by him and not to compromise, even if all kith and kin were destroyed.

The next day I was surprised at his cheerfulness. I had thought he would be deeply shocked by this last tragedy -- how deep I was soon to learn. All day he was light-hearted and high-spirited, as though at last he had found a way out of the frightful difficulty. The next morning we found him dead in his bed, a peaceful smile upon his careworn face -- asphyxiation. Through the connivance of the police and the authorities, it was given out to the world as heart disease. We deemed it wise to withhold the truth; but little good has it done us, little good has anything done us.

Barely had I left that chamber of death, when -- but too late -- the following extraordinary letter was received:

Office of the M. of M., February 17, 1900.

Mr. Eben Hale, Money Baron:

Dear Sir, -- You will pardon our intrusion, we hope, so closely upon the sad event of day before yesterday; but what we wish to say may be of the utmost importance to you. It is in our mind that you may attempt to escape us. There is but one way, apparently, as you have ere this doubtless discovered. But we wish to inform you that even this one way is barred. You may die, but you die failing and acknowledging your failure. Note this: WE ARE PART AND PARCEL OF YOUR POSSESSIONS. WITH YOUR MILLIONS

WE PASS DOWN TO YOUR HEIRS AND ASSIGNS FOREVER.

We are the inevitable. We are the culmination of industrial and social wrong;. We turn upon the society that has created us. We are the successful failures of the age, the scourges of a degraded civilization.

We are the creatures of a perverse social selection. We meet force with force. Only the strong shall endure. We believe in the survival of the fittest. You have crushed your wage slaves into the dirt and you have survived. The captains of war, at your command, have shot down like dogs your employees in a score of bloody strikes. By such means you have endured. We do not grumble at the result, for we acknowledge and have our being in the same natural law. And now the question has arisen: UNDER THE PRESENT SOCIAL ENVIRONMENT, WHICH OF US SHALL SURVIVE? We believe we are the fittest. You believe you are the fittest. We leave the eventuality to time and law.

Cordially yours,

The Minions of Midas.

John, do you wonder now that I shunned pleasure and avoided friends? But why explain? Surely this narrative will make everything clear. Three weeks ago Adelaide Laidlaw died. Since then I have waited in hope and fear. Yesterday the will was probated and made public. Today I was notified that a woman of the middle class would be killed in Golden Gate Park, in faraway San Francisco. The despatches in to-night's papers give the details of the brutal happening -- details which correspond with those furnished me in advance.

It is useless. I cannot struggle against the inevitable. I have been faithful to Mr. Hale and have worked hard. Why my faithfulness should have been thus rewarded I cannot understand. Yet I cannot be false to my trust, nor break my word by compromising. Still, I have resolved that no more deaths shall be upon my head. I have willed the many millions I lately received to their rightful owners. Let the stalwart sons of Eben Hale work out their own salvation. Ere you read this I shall have passed on.

The Minions of Midas are all-powerful. The police are impotent. I have learned from them that other millionaires have been likewise mulcted or persecuted -- how many is not known, for when one yields to the M. of M., his mouth is thenceforth sealed. Those who have not yielded are even now reaping their scarlet harvest. The grim game is being played out. The Federal Government can do nothing. I also understand that similar branch organizations have made their appearance in Europe. Society is shaken to its foundations. Principalities and powers are as brands ripe for the burning. Instead of the masses against the classes, it is a class against the classes. We, the guardians of human progress, are being singled out and struck down. Law and order have failed.

The officials have begged me to keep this secret. I have done so, but can do so no longer. It has become a question of public import, fraught with the direst consequences, and I shall do my duty before I leave this world by informing it of its peril. Do you, John, as my last request, make this public. Do not be frightened. The fate of humanity rests in your hand. Let the press strike off millions of copies; let the electric currents sweep it round the world; wherever men meet and speak, let them speak of it in fear and trembling. And then, when thoroughly aroused, let society arise in its might and cast out this abomination.

Yours, in long farewell,
Wade Atsheler.

The Eternity of Forms

A strange life has come to an end in the death of Mr. Sedley Crayden, of Crayden Hill.

Mild, harmless, he was the victim of a strange delusion that kept him pinned, night and day, in his chair for the last two years of his life. The mysterious death, or, rather, disappearance, of his elder brother, James Crayden, seems to have preyed upon his mind, for it was shortly after that event that his delusion began to manifest itself. Mr. Crayden never vouchsafed any explanation of his strange conduct. There was nothing the matter with him physically; and, mentally, the analysts found him normal in every way save for his one remarkable idiosyncrasy. His remaining in his chair was purely voluntary, an act of his own will. And now he is dead, and the mystery remains unsolved.

Extract from *The Newton Courier-Times*

Briefly, I was Mr. Sedley Crayden's confidential servant and valet for the last eight months of his life. During that time he wrote a great deal in a manuscript that he kept always beside him, except when he drowsed or slept, at which times he invariably locked it in a desk drawer close to his hand.

I was curious to read what the old gentleman wrote, but he was too cautious and cunning. I never got a peep at the manuscript. If he were engaged upon it when I attended on him, he covered the top sheet with a large blotter. It was I who found him dead in his chair, and it was then that I took the liberty of abstracting the manuscript. I was very curious to read it, and I have no excuses to offer.

After retaining it in my secret possession for several years, and after ascertaining that Mr. Crayden left no surviving relatives, I have decided to make the nature of the manuscript known. It is very long, and I have omitted nearly all of it, giving only the more lucid fragments.

It bears all the earmarks of a disordered mind, and various experiences are repeated over and over, while much is so vague and incoherent as to defy comprehension. Nevertheless, from reading it myself, I venture to predict that if an excavation is made in the main basement, somewhere in the vicinity of the foundation of the great chimney, a collection of bones will be found which should very closely resemble those which James Crayden once clothed in mortal flesh.

Statement of Rudolph Heckler

Here follow the excerpts from the manuscript, made and arranged by Rudolph Heckler:

I never killed my brother. Let this be my first word and my last. Why should I kill him? We lived together in unbroken harmony for twenty years. We were old men, and the fires and tempers of youth had long since burned out. We never disagreed even over the most trivial things. Never was there such amity as ours. We were scholars. We cared nothing for the outside world. Our companionship and our books were all-satisfying. Never were there such talks as we held. Many a night we have sat up till two and three in the morning, conversing, weighing opinions and judgments, referring to authorities -- in short, we lived at high and friendly intellectual altitudes.

★★★

He disappeared. I suffered a great shock. Why should he have disappeared? Where could he have gone? It was very strange. I was stunned. They say I was very sick for weeks. It was brain fever. This was caused by his inexplicable disappearance. It was at the beginning of the experience I hope here to relate, that he disappeared.

How I have endeavoured to find him. I am not an excessively

rich man, yet have I offered continually increasing rewards. I have
advertised in all the papers, and sought the aid of all the detective
bureaus. At the present moment, the rewards I have out aggregate
over fifty thousand dollars.

★★★

They say he was murdered. They also say murder will out.
Then I say, why does not his murder come out? Who did it?
Where is he? Where is Jim? My Jim?

★★★

We were so happy together. He had a remarkable mind, a
most remarkable mind, so firmly founded, so widely informed, so
rigidly logical, that it was not at all strange that we agreed in all
things. Dissension was unknown between us. Jim was the most
truthful man I have ever met. In this, too, we were similar, as we
were similar in our intellectual honesty. We never sacrificed truth
to make a point. We had no points to make, we so thoroughly
agreed. It is absurd to think that we could disagree on anything
under the sun.

★★★

I wish he would come back. Why did he go? Who can ever
explain it? I am lonely now, and depressed with grave forebodings
-- frightened by terrors that are of the mind and that put at naught
all that my mind has ever conceived. Form is mutable. This is the
last word of positive science. The dead do not come back. This
is incontrovertible. The dead are dead, and that is the end of it,
and of them. And yet I have had experiences here -- here, in this
very room, at this very desk, that -- But wait. Let me put it down
in black and white, in words simple and unmistakable. Let me
ask some questions. Who mislays my pen? That is what I desire
to know. Who uses up my ink so rapidly? Not I. And yet the ink
goes.

The answer to these questions would settle all the enigmas of
the universe. I know the answer. I am not a fool. And some day,
if I am plagued too desperately, I shall give the answer myself. I
shall give the name of him who mislays my pen and uses up my

ink. It is so silly to think that I could use such a quantity of ink. The servant lies. I know.

★★★

I have got me a fountain pen. I have always disliked the device, but my old stub had to go. I burned it in the fireplace. The ink I keep under lock and key. I shall see if I cannot put a stop to these lies that are being written about me. And I have other plans. It is not true that I have recanted. I still believe that I live in a mechanical universe. It has not been proved otherwise to me, for all that I have peered over his shoulder and read his malicious statement to the contrary. He gives me credit for no less than average stupidity. He thinks I think he is real. How silly. I know he is a brain-figment, nothing more.

There are such things as hallucinations. Even as I looked over his shoulder and read, I knew that this was such a thing. If I were only well it would be interesting. All my life I have wanted to experience such phenomena. And now it has come to me. I shall make the most of it. What is imagination? It can make something where there is nothing. How can anything be something where there is nothing? How can anything be something and nothing at the same time? I leave it for the metaphysicians to ponder. I know better. No scholastics for me. This is a real world, and everything in it is real. What is not real, is not. Therefore he is not. Yet he tries to fool me into believing that he is ... when all the time I know he has no existence outside of my own brain cells.

★★★

I saw him today, seated at the desk, writing. It gave me quite a shock, because I had thought he was quite dispelled. Nevertheless, on looking steadily, I found that he was not there -- the old familiar trick of the brain. I have dwelt too long on what has happened. I am becoming morbid, and my old indigestion is hinting and muttering. I shall take exercise. Each day I shall walk for two hours.

★★★

It is impossible. I cannot exercise. Each time I return from my

317

walk, he is sitting in my chair at the desk. It grows more difficult to drive him away. It is my chair. Upon this I insist. It was his, but he is dead and it is no longer his. How one can be befooled by the phantoms of his own imagining! There is nothing real in this apparition. I know it. I am firmly grounded with my fifty years of study. The dead are dead.

★★★

And yet, explain one thing. Today, before going for my walk, I carefully put the fountain pen in my pocket before leaving the room. I remember it distinctly. I looked at the clock at the time. It was twenty minutes past ten. Yet on my return there was the pen lying on the desk. Someone had been using it. There was very little ink left. I wish he would not write so much. It is disconcerting.

★★★

There was one thing upon which Jim and I were not quite agreed. He believed in the eternity of the forms of things. Therefore, entered in immediately the consequent belief in immortality, and all the other notions of the metaphysical philosophers. I had little patience with him in this. Painstakingly I have traced to him the evolution of his belief in the eternity of forms, showing him how it has arisen out of his early infatuation with logic and mathematics. Of course, from that warped, squinting, abstract viewpoint, it is very easy to believe in the eternity of forms.

I laughed at the unseen world. Only the real was real, I contended, and what one did not perceive, was not, could not be. I believed in a mechanical universe. Chemistry and physics explained everything. "Can no being be?" He demanded in reply. I said that his question was but the major promise of a fallacious Christian Science syllogism. Oh, believe me, I know my logic, too. But he was very stubborn. I never had any patience with philosophic idealists.

★★★

Once, I made to him my confession of faith. It was simple, brief, unanswerable. Even as I write it now I know that it is unanswerable. Here it is. I told him: "I assert, with Hobbes, that it is impossible to separate thought from matter that thinks. I assert, with Bacon, that all human understanding arises from the world of sensations. I assert, with Locke, that all human ideas are due to the functions of the senses. I assert, with Kant, the mechanical origin of the universe, and that creation is a natural and historical process. I assert, with Laplace, that there is no need of the hypothesis of a creator. And, finally, I assert, because of all the foregoing, that form is ephemeral. Form passes. Therefore we pass."

I repeat, it was unanswerable. Yet did he answer with Paley's notorious fallacy of the watch. Also, he talked about radium, and all but asserted that the very existence of matter had been exploded by these later-day laboratory researches. It was childish. I had not dreamed he could be so immature.

How could one argue with such a man? I then asserted the reasonableness of all that is. To this he agreed, reserving, however, one exception. He looked at me, as he said it, in a way I could not mistake. The inference was obvious. That he should be guilty of so cheap a quip in the midst of a serious discussion, astounded me.

★★★

The eternity of forms. It is ridiculous. Yet is there a strange magic in the words. If it be true, then has he not ceased to exist. Then does he exist. This is impossible.

★★★

I have ceased exercising. As long as I remain in the room, the hallucination does not bother me. But when I return to the room after an absence, he is always there, sitting at the desk, writing. Yet I dare not confide in a physician. I must fight this out by myself.

★★★

He grows more importunate. Today, consulting a book on the shelf, I turned and found him again in the chair. This is the first time he has dared do this in my presence. Nevertheless, by looking at him steadily and sternly for several minutes, I compelled him to vanish. This proves my contention. He does not exist. If he were an eternal form I could not make him vanish by a mere effort of my will.

★★★

This is getting damnable. Today I gazed at him for an entire hour before I could make him leave. Yet it is so simple. What I see is a memory picture. For twenty years I was accustomed to seeing him there at the desk. The present phenomenon is merely a recrudescence of that memory picture -- a picture which was impressed countless times on my consciousness.

★★★

I gave up today. He exhausted me, and still he would not go. I sat and watched him hour after hour. He takes no notice of me, but continually writes. I know what he writes, for I read it over his shoulder. It is not true. He is taking an unfair advantage.

★★★

Query: He is a product of my consciousness; is it possible, then, that entities may be created by consciousness?

★★★

We did not quarrel. To this day I do not know how it happened. Let me tell you. Then you will see. We sat up late that never-to-be-forgotten last night of his existence. It was the old, old discussion -- the eternity of forms. How many hours and how many nights we had consumed over it!

On this night he had been particularly irritating, and all my nerves were screaming. He had been maintaining that the human soul was itself a form, an eternal form, and that the light within his brain would go on forever and always. I took up the poker.

"Suppose," I said, "I should strike you dead with this?"

"I would go on," he answered.

"As a conscious entity?" I demanded.

"Yes, as a conscious entity," was his reply. "I should go on, from plane to plane of higher existence, remembering my earth-life, you, this very argument -- ay, and continuing the argument with you."

It was only argument[1]. I swear it was only argument. I never lifted a hand. How could I? He was my brother, my elder brother, Jim. I cannot remember. I was very exasperated. He had always been so obstinate in this metaphysical belief of his. The next I knew, he was lying on the hearth. Blood was running. It was terrible. He did not speak. He did not move. He must have fallen in a fit and struck his head. I noticed there was blood on the poker. In falling he must have struck upon it with his head. And yet I fail to see how this can be, for I held it in my hand all the time. I was still holding it in my hand as I looked at it.

★★★

It is an hallucination. That is a conclusion of common sense. I have watched the growth of it. At first it was only in the dimmest light that I could see him sitting in the chair. But as the time passed, and the hallucination, by repetition, strengthened, he was able to appear in the chair under the strongest lights. That is the explanation. It is quite satisfactory.

★★★

I shall never forget the first time I saw it. I had dined alone downstairs. I never drink wine, so that what happened was eminently normal. It was in the summer twilight that I returned to the study. I glanced at the desk. There he was, sitting. So natural was it, that before I knew I cried out "Jim!" Then I remembered all that had happened. Of course it was an hallucination. I knew that. I took the poker and went over to it. He did not move nor vanish. The poker cleaved through the non-existent substance of the thing and struck the back of the chair. Fabric of fancy, that is all it was. The mark is there on the chair now where the poker struck. I pause from my writing and turn and look at it -- press the tips of my fingers into the indentation.

★★★

He did continue the argument. I stole up today and looked over his shoulder. He was writing the history of our discussion. It was the same old nonsense about the eternity of forms. But as I continued to read, he wrote down the practical test I had made

321

with the poker. Now this is unfair and untrue. I made no test. In falling he struck his head on the poker.

★★★

Some day, somebody will find and read what he writes. This will be terrible. I am suspicious of the servant, who is always peeping and peering, trying to see what I write. I must do something. Every servant I have had is curious about what I write.

★★★

Fabric of fancy. That is all it is. There is no Jim who sits in the chair. I know that. Last night, when the house was asleep, I went down into the cellar and looked carefully at the soil around the chimney. It was untampered with. The dead do not rise up.

★★★

Yesterday morning, when I entered the study, there he was in the chair. When I had dispelled him, I sat in the chair myself all day. I had my meals brought to me. And thus I escaped the sight of him for many hours, for he appears only in the chair. I was weary, but I sat late, until eleven o'clock. Yet, when I stood up to go to bed, I looked around, and there he was. He had slipped into the chair on the instant. Being only fabric of fancy, all day he had resided in my brain. The moment it was unoccupied, he took up his residence in the chair. Are these his boasted higher planes of existence -- his brother's brain and a chair? After all, was he not right? Has his eternal form become so attenuated as to be an hallucination? Are hallucinations real entities? Why not? There is food for thought here. Some day I shall come to a conclusion upon it.

★★★

He was very much disturbed today. He could not write, for I had made the servant carry the pen out of the room in his pocket But neither could I write.

★★★

The servant never sees him. This is strange. Have I developed a keener sight for the unseen? Or rather does it not prove the phantom to be what it is -- a product of my own morbid consciousness?

★★★

He has stolen my pen again. Hallucinations cannot steal pens. This is unanswerable. And yet I cannot keep the pen always out of the room. I want to write myself.

★★★

I have had three different servants since my trouble came upon me, and not one has seen him. Is the verdict of their senses right? And is that of mine wrong? Nevertheless, the ink goes too rapidly. I fill my pen more often than is necessary. And furthermore, only today I found my pen out of order. I did not break it.

★★★

I have spoken to him many times, but he never answers. I sat and watched him all morning. Frequently he looked at me, and it was patent that he knew me.

★★★

By striking the side of my head violently with the heel of my hand, I can shake the vision of him out of my eyes. Then I can get into the chair; but I have learned that I must move very quickly in order to accomplish this. Often he fools me and is back again before I can sit down.

★★★

It is getting unbearable. He is a jack-in-the-box the way he pops into the chair. He does not assume form slowly. He pops. That is the only way to describe it. I cannot stand looking at him much more. That way lies madness, for it compels me almost to believe in the reality of what I know is not. Besides, hallucinations do not pop.

★★★

Thank God he only manifests himself in the chair. As long as I occupy the chair I am quit of him.

★★★

My device for dislodging him from the chair by striking my head, is failing. I have to hit much more violently, and I do not succeed perhaps more than once in a dozen trials. My head is quite sore where I have so repeatedly struck it. I must use the other hand.

★★★

My brother was right. There is an unseen world. Do I not see it? Am I not cursed with the seeing of it all the time? Call it a thought, an idea, anything you will, still it is there. It is unescapable. Thoughts are entities. We create with every act of thinking. I have created this phantom that sits in my chair and uses my ink. Because I have created him is no reason that he is any the less real. He is an idea; he is an entity: ergo, ideas are entities, and an entity is a reality.

★★★

Query: If a man, with the whole historical process behind him, can create an entity, a real thing, then is not the hypothesis of a Creator made substantial? If the stuff of life can create, then it is fair to assume that there can be a He who created the stuff of life. It is merely a difference of degree. I have not yet made a mountain nor a solar system, but I have made a something that sits in my chair. This being so, may I not some day be able to make a mountain or a solar system?

★★★

All his days, down to today, man has lived in a maze. He has never seen the light. I am convinced that I am beginning to see the light -- not as my brother saw it, by stumbling upon it accidentally, but deliberately and rationally. My brother is dead. He has ceased. There is no doubt about it, for I have made another journey down into the cellar to see. The ground was untouched. I broke it myself to make sure, and I saw what made me sure. My brother has ceased, yet have I recreated him. This is not my old brother, yet it is something as nearly resembling him as I could fashion it. I am unlike other men. I am a god. I have created.

★★★

Whenever I leave the room to go to bed, I look back, and there is my brother sitting in the chair. And then I cannot sleep because of thinking of him sitting through all the long night-hours. And in the morning, when I open the study door, there he is, and I know he has sat there the night long.

★★★

I am becoming desperate from lack of sleep. I wish I could confide in a physician.

★★★

Blessed sleep! I have won to it at last. Let me tell you. Last night I was so worn that I found myself dozing in my chair. I rang for the servant and ordered him to bring blankets. I slept. All night was he banished from my thoughts as he was banished from my chair. I shall remain in it all day. It is a wonderful relief.

★★★

It is uncomfortable to sleep in a chair. But it is more uncomfortable to lie in bed, hour after hour, and not sleep, and to know that he is sitting there in the cold darkness.

★★★

It is no use. I shall never be able to sleep in a bed again. I have tried it now, numerous times, and every such night is a horror. If I could but only persuade him to go to bed! But no. He sits there, and sits there -- I know he does -- while I stare and stare up into the blackness and think and think, continually think, of him sitting there. I wish I had never heard of the eternity of forms.

★★★

The servants think I am crazy. That is but to be expected, and it is why I have never called in a physician.

★★★

I am resolved. Henceforth this hallucination ceases. From now on I shall remain in the chair. I shall never leave it. I shall remain in it night and day and always.

★★★

I have succeeded. For two weeks I have not seen him. Nor shall I ever see him again. I have at last attained the equanimity of mind necessary for philosophic thought. I wrote a complete chapter today.

★★★

It is very wearisome, sitting in a chair. The weeks pass, the months come and go, the seasons change, the servants replace each other, while I remain. I only remain. It is a strange life I lead, but at least I am at peace.

★★★

He comes no more. There is no eternity of forms. I have proved it. For nearly two years now, I have remained in this chair, and I have not seen him once. True, I was severely tried for a time. But it is clear that what I thought I saw was merely hallucination. He never was. Yet I do not leave the chair. I am afraid to leave the chair.

---

1 Forcible -- Ha! Ha! -- comment of Rudolph Heckler on margin.

The Man With the Gash

Jacob Kent had suffered from cupidity all the days of his life. This, in turn, had engendered a chronic distrustfulness, and his mind and character had become so warped that he was a very disagreeable man to deal with. He was also a victim to somnambulic propensities, and very set in his ideas. He had been a weaver of cloth from the cradle, until the fever of Klondike had entered his blood and torn him away from his loom. His cabin stood midway between Sixty Mile Post and the Stuart River; and men who made it a custom to travel the trail to Dawson, likened him to a robber baron, perched in his fortress and exacting toll from the caravans that used his ill-kept roads. Since a certain amount of history was required in the construction of this figure, the less cultured wayfarers from Stuart River were prone to describe him after a still more primordial fashion, in which a command of strong adjectives was to be chiefly noted.

This cabin was not his, by the way, having been built several years previously by a couple of miners who had got out a raft of logs at that point for a grub-stake. They had been most hospitable lads, and, after they abandoned it, travelers who knew the route made it an object to arrive there at nightfall. It was very handy, saving them all the time and toil of pitching camp; and it was an unwritten rule that the last man left a neat pile of firewood for the next comer. Rarely a night passed but from half a dozen to a score of men crowded into its shelter. Jacob Kent noted these things, exercised squatter sovereignty, and moved in. Thenceforth, the weary travelers were mulcted a dollar per head for the privilege of sleeping on the floor, Jacob Kent weighing the dust and never failing to steal the down-weight. Besides, he so contrived that his transient guests chopped his wood for him and carried his water. This was rank piracy, but his victims were an easy-going breed, and while they detested him, they yet permitted him to flourish in his sins.

One afternoon in April he sat by his door, -- for all the world like a predatory spider, -- marvelling at the heat of the returning sun, and keeping an eye on the trail for prospective flies. The Yukon lay at his feet, a sea of ice, disappearing around two great bends to the north and south, and stretching an honest two miles from bank to bank. Over its rough breast ran the sled-trail, a slender sunken line, eighteen inches wide and two thousand miles in length, with more curses distributed to the linear foot than any other road in or out of all Christendom.

Jacob Kent was feeling particularly good that afternoon. The record had been broken the previous night, and he had sold his hospitality to no less than twenty-eight visitors. True, it had been quite uncomfortable, and four had snored beneath his bunk all night; but then it had added appreciable weight to the sack in which he kept his gold dust. That sack, with its glittering yellow treasure, was at once the chief delight and the chief bane of his existence. Heaven and hell lay within its slender mouth. In the nature of things, there being no privacy to his one-roomed dwelling, he was tortured by a constant fear of theft. It would be very easy for these bearded, desperate-looking strangers to make away with it. Often he dreamed that such was the case, and awoke in the grip of nightmare. A select number of these robbers haunted him through his dreams, and he came to know them quite well, especially the bronzed leader with the gash on his right cheek. This fellow was the most persistent of the lot, and, because of him, he had, in his waking moments, constructed several score of hiding-places in and about the cabin. After a concealment he would breathe freely again, perhaps for several nights, only to collar the Man with the Gash in the very act of unearthing the sack. Then, on awakening in the midst of the usual struggle, he would at once get up and transfer the bag to a new and more ingenious crypt. It was not that he was the direct victim of these phantasms; but he believed in omens and thought-transference, and he deemed these dream-robbers to be the astral projection of real personages who happened at those particular moments, no matter where they were in the flesh, to be harboring designs, in the spirit, upon his wealth. So he continued to bleed the unfortunates who crossed his threshold, and at the same time to add to his trouble with every ounce that went into the sack.

As he sat sunning himself, a thought came to Jacob Kent that brought him to his feet with a jerk. The pleasures of life had culminated in the continual weighing and reweighing of his dust; but a shadow had been thrown upon this pleasant avocation, which he had hitherto failed to brush aside. His gold-scales were quite small; in fact, their maximum was a pound and a half, -- eighteen ounces, -- while his hoard mounted up to something like three and a third times that. He had never been able to weigh it all at one operation, and hence considered himself to have been shut out from a new and most edifying coign of contemplation. Being denied this, half the pleasure of possession had been lost; nay, he felt that this miserable obstacle actually minimized the fact, as it did the strength, of possession. It was the solution of this problem flashing across his mind that had just brought him to his feet. He searched the trail carefully in either direction. There was nothing in sight, so he went inside.

In a few seconds he had the table cleared away and the scales set up. On one side he placed the stamped disks to the equivalent of fifteen ounces, and balanced it with dust on the other. Replacing the weights with dust, he then had thirty ounces precisely balanced. These, in turn, he placed together on one side and again balanced with more dust. By this time the gold was exhausted, and he was sweating liberally. He trembled with ecstasy, ravished beyond measure. Nevertheless he dusted the sack thoroughly, to the last least grain, till the balance was overcome and one side of the scales sank to the table. Equilibrium, however, was restored by the addition of a pennyweight and five grains to the opposite side. He stood, head thrown back, transfixed. The sack was empty, but the potentiality of the scales had become immeasurable. Upon them he could weigh any amount, from the tiniest grain to pounds

upon pounds. Mammon laid hot fingers on his heart. The sun
swung on its westering way till it flashed through the open door-
way, full upon the yellow-burdened scales. The precious heaps,
like the golden breasts of a bronze Cleopatra, flung back the light
in a mellow glow. Time and space were not.

"Gawd blime me! But you 'ave the makin' of several quid
there, 'aven't you?"

Jacob Kent wheeled about, at the same time reaching for his
double-barrelled shot-gun, which stood handy. But when his eyes
lit on the intruder's face, he staggered back dizzily. *It was the face
of the man with the gash!*

The man looked at him curiously.

"Oh, that's all right," he said, waving his hand deprecatingly.
"You needn't think as I'll 'arm you or your blasted dust. You're
a rum 'un, you are," he added reflectively, as he watched the
sweat pouring from off Kent's face and the quavering of his knees.
"Why don't you pipe up an' say somethin'?" He went on, as the
other struggled for breath. "Wot's gone wrong o' your gaff? Any-
think the matter?"

"W -- w -- where'd you get it?" Kent at last managed to articulate, raising a shaking forefinger to the ghastly scar which seamed
the other's cheek.

"Shipmate stove me down with a marlin-spike from the main-
royal. An' now as you 'ave your figger'ead in trim, wot I want to
know is, wot's it to you? That's wot I want to know -- wot's it
to you? Gawd blime me! Do it 'urt you? Ain't it smug enough for
the likes o' you? That's wot I want to know!"

"No, no," Kent answered, sinking upon a stool with a sickly
grin. "I was just wondering."

"Did you ever see the like?" The other went on truculently.

"No."

"Ain't it a beute?"

"Yes." Kent nodded his head approvingly, intent on humoring
this strange visitor, but wholly unprepared for the outburst which
was to follow his effort to be agreeable.

"You blasted, bloomin', burgoo-eatin' son-of-a-sea-swab! Wot do you mean, a sayin' the most onsightly thing Gawd Almighty ever put on the face o' man is a beute? Wot do you mean, you -- "

And thereat this fiery son of the sea broke off into a string of Oriental profanity, mingling gods and devils, lineages and men, metaphors and monsters, with so savage a virility that Jacob Kent was paralyzed. He shrank back, his arms lifted as though to ward off physical violence. So utterly unnerved was he that the other paused in the mid-swing of a gorgeous peroration and burst into thunderous laughter.

"The sun's knocked the bottom out o' the trail," said the Man with the Gash, between departing paroxysms of mirth. "An' I only 'ope as you'll appreciate the hoppertunity of consortin' with a man o' my mug. Get steam up in that fire-box o' your'n. I'm goin' to unrig the dogs an' grub 'em. An' don't be shy o' the wood, my lad; there's plenty more where that come from, and it's you've got the time to sling an axe. An' tote up a bucket o' water while you're about it. Lively! Or I'll run you down, so 'elp me!"

Such a thing was unheard of. Jacob Kent was making the fire, chopping wood, packing water -- doing menial tasks for a guest!

When Jim Cardegee left Dawson, it was with his head filled with the iniquities of this roadside Shylock; and all along the trail his numerous victims had added to the sum of his crimes. Now, Jim Cardegee, with the sailor's love for a sailor's joke, had determined, when he pulled into the cabin, to bring its inmate down a peg or so. That he had succeeded beyond expectation he could not help but remark, though he was in the dark as to the part the gash on his cheek had played in it. But while he could not understand, he saw the terror it created, and resolved to exploit it as remorselessly as would any modern trader a choice bit of merchandise.

"Strike me blind, but you're a 'ustler," he said admiringly, his head cocked to one side, as his host bustled about. "You never 'ort to 'ave gone Klondiking. It's the keeper of a pub' you was laid out for. An' it's often as I 'ave 'eard the lads up an' down the river speak o' you, but I 'adn't no idea you was so jolly nice."

Jacob Kent experienced a tremendous yearning to try his shot-gun on him, but the fascination of the gash was too potent. This was the real Man with the Gash, the man who had so often robbed him in the spirit. This, then, was the embodied entity of the being whose astral form had been projected into his dreams, the man₀ who had so frequently harbored designs against his hoard; hence -- there could be no other conclusion -- this Man with the Gash had now come in the flesh to dispossess him. And that gash! He could no more keep his eyes from it than stop the beating of his heart. Try as he would, they wandered back to that one point as inevitably as the needle to the pole.

"Do it 'urt you?" Jim Cardegee thundered suddenly, looking up from the spreading of his blankets and encountering the rapt gaze of the other. "It strikes me as 'ow it 'ud be the proper thing for you to draw your jib, douse the glim, an' turn in, seein' as 'ow it worrits you. Jes' lay to that, you swab, or so 'elp me I'll take a pull on your peak-purchases!"

Kent was so nervous that it took three puffs to blow out the slush-lamp, and he crawled into his blankets without even remov-ing his moccasins. The sailor was soon snoring lustily from his hard bed on the floor, but Kent lay staring up into the blackness, one hand on the shotgun, resolved not to close his eyes the whole night. He had not had an opportunity to secrete his five pounds of gold, and it lay in the ammunition box at the head of his bunk. But, try as he would, he at last dozed off with the weight of his dust heavy on his soul. Had he not inadvertently fallen asleep with his mind in such condition, the somnambulic demon would not have been invoked, nor would Jim Cardegee have gone mining next day with a dish-pan.

The fire fought a losing battle, and at last died away, while the frost penetrated the mossy chinks between the logs and chilled the inner atmosphere. The dogs outside ceased their howling, and, curled up in the snow, dreamed of salmon-stocked heavens where dog-drivers and kindred task-masters were not. Within, the sailor lay like a log, while his host tossed restlessly about, the victim of strange fantasies. As midnight drew near he suddenly threw off the blankets and got up. It was remarkable that he could do what he then did without ever striking a light. Perhaps it was because of the darkness that he kept his eyes shut, and perhaps it was for fear he would see the terrible gash on the cheek of his visitor; but, be this as it may, it is a fact that, unseeing, he opened his ammunition box, put a heavy charge into the muzzle of the shotgun without spilling a particle, rammed it down with double wads, and then put everything away and got back into bed.

Just as daylight laid its steel-gray fingers on the parchment window, Jacob Kent awoke. Turning on his elbow, he raised the lid and peered into the ammunition box. Whatever he saw, or whatever he did not see, exercised a very peculiar effect upon him, considering his neurotic temperament. He glanced at the sleeping man on the floor, let the lid down gently, and rolled over on his back. It was an unwonted calm that rested on his face. Not a muscle quivered. There was not the least sign of excitement or perturbation. He lay there a long while, thinking, and when he got up and began to move about, it was in a cool, collected manner, without noise and without hurry.

It happened that a heavy wooden peg had been driven into the ridge-pole just above Jim Cardegee's head. Jacob Kent, working softly, ran a piece of half-inch manila over it, bringing both ends to the ground. One end he tied about his waist, and in the other he rove a running noose. Then he cocked his shotgun and laid it within reach, by the side of numerous moose-hide thongs. By an effort of will he bore the sight of the scar, slipped the noose over the sleeper's head, and drew it taut by throwing back on his weight, at the same time seizing the gun and bringing it to bear.

Jim Cardegee awoke, choking, bewildered, staring down the twin wells of steel.

"Where is it?" Kent asked, at the same time slacking on the rope.

"You blasted -- ugh -- "

Kent merely threw back his weight, shutting off the other's wind.

"Bloomin' -- Bur -- ugh -- "

"Where is it?" Kent repeated.

"Wot?" Cardegee asked, as soon as he had caught his breath.

"The gold-dust."

"Wot gold-dust?" The perplexed sailor demanded.

"You know well enough, -- mine."

"Ain't seen nothink of it. Wot do ye take me for? A safe-deposit? Wot 'ave I got to do with it, any'ow?"

"Mebbe you know, and mebbe you don't know, but anyway, I'm going to stop your breath till you do know. And if you lift a hand, I'll blow your head off!"

"Vast heavin'!" Cardegee roared, as the rope tightened.

Kent eased away a moment, and the sailor, wriggling his neck as though from the pressure, managed to loosen the noose a bit and work it up so the point of contact was just under the chin.

"Well?" Kent questioned, expecting the disclosure.

But Cardegee grinned. "Go ahead with your 'angin', you bloomin' old pot-wolloper!"

Then, as the sailor had anticipated, the tragedy became a farce. Cardegee being the heavier of the two, Kent, throwing his body backward and down, could not lift him clear of the ground. Strain and strive to the uttermost, the sailor's feet still stuck to the floor and sustained a part of his weight. The remaining portion was supported by the point of contact just under his chin. Failing to swing him clear, Kent clung on, resolved to slowly throttle him or force him to tell what he had done with the hoard. But the Man with the Gash would not throttle. Five, ten, fifteen minutes passed, and at the end of that time, in despair, Kent let his prisoner down.

"Well," he remarked, wiping away the sweat, "if you won't hang you'll shoot. Some men wasn't born to be hanged, anyway."

"An' it's a pretty mess as you'll make o' this 'ere cabin floor."

Cardegee was fighting for time. "Now, look 'ere, I'll tell you wot we do; we'll lay our 'eads 'longside an' reason together. You've lost some dust. You say as 'ow I know, an' I say as 'ow I don't. Let's get a hobservation an' shape a course -- "

"Vast heavin'!" Kent dashed in, maliciously imitating the other's enunciation. "I'm going to shape all the courses of this she-bang, and you observe; and if you do anything more, I'll bore you as sure as Moses!"

"For the sake of my mother -- "

"Whom God have mercy upon if she loves you. Ah! Would you?" He frustrated a hostile move on the part of the other by pressing the cold muzzle against his forehead. "Lay quiet, now! If you lift as much as a hair, you'll get it."

It was rather an awkward task, with the trigger of the gun always within pulling distance of the finger; but Kent was a weaver, and in a few minutes had the sailor tied hand and foot. Then he dragged him without and laid him by the side of the cabin, where he could overlook the river and watch the sun climb to the meridian.

"Now I'll give you till noon, and then -- "

"Wot?"

"You'll be hitting the brimstone trail. But if you speak up, I'll keep you till the next bunch of mounted police come by."

"Well, Gawd blime me, if this ain't a go! 'Ere I be, innercent as a lamb, an' 'ere you be, lost all o' your top 'amper an' out o' your reckonin', run me foul an' goin' to rake me into 'ell-fire. You bloomin' old pirut! You -- " Jim Cardegee loosed the strings of his profanity and fairly outdid himself. Jacob Kent brought out a stool that he might enjoy it in comfort.

Having exhausted all the possible combinations of his vocabulary, the sailor quieted down to hard thinking, his eyes constantly gauging the progress of the sun, which tore up the eastern slope of the heavens with unseemly haste. His dogs, surprised that they had not long since been put to harness, crowded around him. His helplessness appealed to the brutes. They felt that something was wrong, though they knew not what, and they crowded about, howling their mournful sympathy.

"Chook! Mush-on! You Siwashes!" He cried, attempting, in a vermicular way, to kick at them, and discovering himself to be tottering on the edge of a declivity. As soon as the animals had scattered, he devoted himself to the significance of that declivity which he felt to be there but could not see. Nor was he long in arriving at a correct conclusion. In the nature of things, he figured, man is lazy. He does no more than he has to. When he builds a cabin he must put dirt on the roof. From these premises it was logical that he should carry that dirt no further than was absolutely necessary. Therefore, he lay upon the edge of the hole from which the dirt had been taken to roof Jacob Kent's cabin. This knowledge, properly utilized, might prolong things, he thought; and he then turned his attention to the moose-hide thongs which bound him. His hands were tied behind him, and pressing against the snow, they were wet with the contact. This moistening of the raw-hide he knew would tend to make it stretch, and, without apparent effort, he endeavored to stretch it more and more.

He watched the trail hungrily, and when in the direction of Sixty Mile a dark speck appeared for a moment against the white background of an ice-jam, he cast an anxious eye at the sun. It had climbed nearly to the zenith. Now and again he caught the black speck clearing the hills of ice and sinking into the intervening hollows; but he dared not permit himself more than the most cursory glances for fear of rousing his enemy's suspicion. Once, when Jacob Kent rose to his feet and searched the trail with care, Cardegee was frightened, but the dog-sled had struck a piece of trail running parallel with a jam, and remained out of sight till the danger was past.

"I'll see you 'ung for this," Cardegee threatened, attempting to draw the other's attention. "An' you'll rot in 'ell, jes' you see if you don't.

"I say," he cried, after another pause; "d'ye b'lieve in ghosts?" Kent's sudden start made him sure of his ground, and he went on:

"Now a ghost 'as the right to 'aunt a man wot don't do wot he says; and you can't shuffle me off till eight bells -- wot I mean is twelve o'clock -- can you? 'Cos if you do, it'll 'appen as 'ow I'll 'aunt you. D'ye 'ear? A minute, a second too quick, an' I'll 'aunt you, so 'elp me, I will!"

Jacob Kent looked dubious, but declined to talk.

"'Ow's your chronometer? Wot's your longitude? 'Ow do you know as your time's correct?" Cardegee persisted, vainly hoping to beat his executioner out of a few minutes. "Is it Barrack's time you 'ave, or is it the Company time? 'Cos if you do it before the stroke o' the bell, I'll not rest. I give you fair warnin'. I'll come back. An' if you 'aven't the time, 'ow will you know? That's wot I want -- 'ow will you tell?"

"I'll send you off all right," Kent replied. "Got a sun-dial here."

"No good. Thirty-two degrees variation o' the needle."

"Stakes are all set."

"'Ow did you set 'em? Compass?"

"No; lined them up with the North Star."

"Sure?"

"Sure."

Cardegee groaned, then stole a glance at the trail. The sled was just clearing a rise, barely a mile away, and the dogs were in full lope, running lightly.

"'Ow close is the shadows to the line?"

Kent walked to the primitive timepiece and studied it. "Three inches," he announced, after a careful survey.

"Say, jes' sing out 'eight bells' afore you pull the gun, will you?"

Kent agreed, and they lapsed into silence. The thongs about Cardegee's wrists were slowly stretching, and he had begun to work them over his hands.

"Say, 'ow close is the shadows?"

"One inch."

The sailor wriggled slightly to assure himself that he would topple over at the right moment, and slipped the first turn over his hands.

"'Ow close?"

"Half an inch." Just then Kent heard the jarring churn of the runners and turned his eyes to the trail. The driver was lying flat on the sled and the dogs swinging down the straight stretch to the cabin. Kent whirled back, bringing his rifle to shoulder.

"It ain't eight bells yet!" Cardegee expostulated. "I'll 'aunt you, sure!"

Jacob Kent faltered. He was standing by the sun-dial, perhaps ten paces from his victim. The man on the sled must have seen that something unusual was taking place, for he had risen to his knees, his whip singing viciously among the dogs.

The shadows swept into line. Kent looked along the sights.

"Make ready!" He commanded solemnly. "Eight b-"

But just a fraction of a second too soon, Cardegee rolled backward into the hole. Kent held his fire and ran to the edge. Bang! The gun exploded full in the sailor's face as he rose to his feet. But no smoke came from the muzzle; instead, a sheet of flame burst from the side of the barrel near its butt, and Jacob Kent went down. The dogs dashed up the bank, dragging the sled over his body, and the driver sprang off as Jim Cardegee freed his hands and drew himself from the hole.

"Jim!" The new-comer recognized him. "What's the matter?"

"Wot's the matter? Oh, nothink at all. It jest 'appens as I do little things like this for my 'ealth. Wot's the matter, you bloomin' idjit? Wot's the matter, eh? Cast me loose or I'll show you wot! 'Urry up, or I'll 'olystone the decks with you!"

"Huh!" He added, as the other went to work with his sheath-knife. "Wot's the matter? I want to know. Jes' tell me that, will you, wot's the matter? Hey?"

Kent was quite dead when they rolled him over. The gun, an old-fashioned, heavy-weighted muzzle-loader, lay near him. Steel and wood had parted company. Near the butt of the right-hand barrel, with lips pressed outward, gaped a fissure several inches in length. The sailor picked it up, curiously. A glittering stream of yellow dust ran out through the crack. The facts of the case dawned upon Jim Cardegee.

"Strike me standin'!" He roared; "'ere's a go! 'Ere's 'is bloom-in' dust! Gawd blime me, an' you, too, Charley, if you don't run an' get the dish-pan!"

ALSO FROM LEONAUR
AVAILABLE IN SOFTCOVER OR HARDCOVER WITH DUST JACKET

SF1 CLASSIC SCIENCE FICTION SERIES
BEFORE ADAM & Other Stories
by Jack London

Volume 1 of The Collected Science Fiction & Fantasy of Jack London.

SOFTCOVER : **ISBN 1-84677-008-4**
HARDCOVER : **ISBN 1-84677-015-7**

SF2 CLASSIC SCIENCE FICTION SERIES
THE IRON HEEL & Other Stories
by Jack London

Volume 2 of The Collected Science Fiction & Fantasy of Jack London.

SOFTCOVER : **ISBN 1-84677-004-1**
HARDCOVER : **ISBN 1-84677-011-4**

SF3 CLASSIC SCIENCE FICTION SERIES
THE STAR ROVER & Other Stories
by Jack London

Volume 3 of The Collected Science Fiction & Fantasy of Jack London.

SOFTCOVER : **ISBN 1-84677-006-8**
HARDCOVER : **ISBN 1-84677-013-0**

WF1 THE WARFARE FICTION SERIES
NAPOLEONIC WAR STORIES
by Sir Arthur Quiller-Couch

Tales of soldiers, spies, battles & Sieges from the Peninsular & Waterloo campaigns

SOFTCOVER : **ISBN 1-84677-003-3**
HARDCOVER : **ISBN 1-84677-014-9**

ALSO FROM LEONAUR
AVAILABLE IN SOFTCOVER OR HARDCOVER WITH DUST JACKET

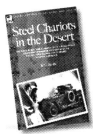

RGW1 RECOLLECTIONS OF THE GREAT WAR 1914 - 18
STEEL CHARIOTS IN THE DESERT *by S. C. Rolls*

The first world war experiences of a Rolls Royce armoured car driver with the Duke of Westminster in Libya and in Arabia with T.E. Lawrence.

SOFTCOVER : **ISBN 1-84677-005-X**
HARDCOVER : **ISBN 1-84677-019-X**

RGW2 RECOLLECTIONS OF THE GREAT WAR 1914 - 18
WITH THE IMPERIAL CAMEL CORPS IN THE GREAT WAR *by Geoffrey Inchbald*

The story of a serving officer with the British 2nd battalion against the Senussi and during the Palestine campaign.

SOFTCOVER : **ISBN 1-84677-007-6**
HARDCOVER : **ISBN 1-84677-012-2**

EW3 EYEWITNESS TO WAR SERIES
THE KHAKEE RESSALAH
by Robert Henry Wallace Dunlop

Service & adventure with the Meerut Volunteer Horse During the Indian Mutiny 1857-1858.

SOFTCOVER : **ISBN 1-84677-009-2**
HARDCOVER : **ISBN 1-84677-017-3**

WF1 THE WARFARE FICTION SERIES
NAPOLEONIC WAR STORIES
by Sir Arthur Quiller-Couch

Tales of soldiers, spies, battles & Sieges from the Peninsular & Waterloo campaigns

SOFTCOVER : **ISBN 1-84677-003-3**
HARDCOVER : **ISBN 1-84677-014-9**

LEONAUR

ALSO FROM LEONAUR
AVAILABLE IN SOFTCOVER OR HARDCOVER WITH DUST JACKET

EW2 EYEWITNESS TO WAR SERIES
CAPTAIN OF THE 95th (Rifles) *by Jonathan Leach*

An officer of Wellington's Sharpshooters during the
Peninsular, South of France and Waterloo Campaigns
of the Napoleonic Wars.

SOFTCOVER : **ISBN 1-84677-001-7**
HARDCOVER : **ISBN 1-84677-016-5**

WFI THE WARFARE FICTION SERIES
NAPOLEONIC WAR STORIES
by Sir Arthur Quiller-Couch

Tales of soldiers, spies, battles & Sieges from the
Peninsular & Waterloo campaigns

SOFTCOVER : **ISBN 1-84677-003-3**
HARDCOVER : **ISBN 1-84677-014-9**

EWI EYEWITNESS TO WAR SERIES
RIFLEMAN COSTELLO *by Edward Costello*

The adventures of a soldier of the 95th (Rifles) in the Peninsular
& Waterloo Campaigns of the Napoleonic wars.

SOFTCOVER : **ISBN 1-84677-000-9**
HARDCOVER : **ISBN 1-84677-018-1**

MCI THE MILITARY COMMANDERS SERIES
JOURNALS OF ROBERT ROGERS OF THE
RANGERS *by Robert Rogers*

The exploits of Rogers & the Rangers in his own words
during 1755-1761 in the French & Indian War.

SOFTCOVER : **ISBN 1-84677-002-5**
HARDCOVER : **ISBN 1-84677-010-6**

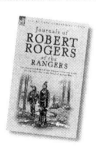

CPSIA information can be obtained at www.ICGtesting.com
Printed in the USA
BVOW041841260612

293724BV00001B/6/A

9 781846 770135